DASHIELL HAMMETT
DETECTIVE STORIES

In these stories and novellas he wrote for *Black Mask* and other pulp magazines of the 1920s and 1930s, Dashiell Hammett transformed the American detective story into something original—a medium to explore the jarring textures and revved-up cadences of American life. As a chronicler of this underworld of criminality, he created the Continental Op, the nameless, stoic detective, jaded and fearless, who's cast in the role of protagonist of most of the stories in this volume.

Hammett's experience as a Pinkerton detective gave his heavily plotted mysteries a gritty reality. His first-hand knowledge of San Francisco made him a natural chronicler of its seedy waterfronts, police stations, back alleys, and luxury hotels. By connecting the reality of American street life with American speech, Hammett pioneered a method of storytelling that came to be known as *noir fiction*, which would have a huge impact on fiction and movies for decades to come.

DETECTIVE STORIES

DASHIELL HAMMETT

DETECTIVE STORIES

COYOTE CANYON PRESS
CLAREMONT, CALIFORNIA

First Coyote Canyon Press Edition, March 2009
Selection Copyright © 2009 by Coyote Canyon Press

Library of Congress Cataloging-in-Publication Data

Hammett, Dashiell, 1894-1961.
 [Selections. 2009]
 Detective stories / Dashiell Hammett. — 1st Coyote Canyon Press ed.
    p. cm.
 Stories and novellas.
 ISBN 978-0-9821298-0-7
 1. Detective and mystery stories, American. I. Title.

PS3515.A4347A6 2009
813'.52—dc22

2009003631

ORIGINAL PUBLICATION HISTORY:

"From the Memoirs of a Private Detective": *The Smart Set* 30.1, March 1923: 88–90
"Arson Plus": *The Black Mask* 6.13, October 1923: 25–36
"The Tenth Clew": *The Black Mask* 6.19, January 1924: 3–23
"Zigzags of Treachery": *The Black Mask* 6.23, March 1924: 80–102
"The Assistant Murderer": *The Black Mask* 8.12, February 1926: 57–59
"The Man Who Killed Dan Odams": *The Black Mask* 6.20, January 1924: 35–41
"Women, Politics and Murder": *The Black Mask* 7.7, September 1924: 67–83
"Who Killed Bob Teal?": *True Detective* 2.2, November 1924: 60–64
"Mike, Alec, or Rufus": *The Black Mask*, January 1925
"Nightmare Town": *Argosy All-Story Weekly* 165.4, December 1924: 502–26
"Night Shots": *The Black Mask* 6.21, February 1924: 33–34
"One Hour": *The Black Mask* 7.7, April 1924: 44–52
"The Bodies Piled Up": *The Black Mask* 6.17, December 1923: 39–45
"The Road Home": *The Black Mask*, December 1922 (pseud. Peter Collinson)
"Ruffian's Wife": *Sunset Magazine*, October 1925
"The Second-Story Angel": *The Black Mask* 6.16, Nobember 1923: 110–18
"Afraid of a Gun": *The Black Mask* 6.23, March 1924: 39–45

CONTENTS

From The Memoirs of a Private Detective 3
Arson Plus 10
The Tenth Clew 30
Zigzags of Treachery 65
The Assistant Murderer 109
The Man Who Killed Dan Odams 152
Women, Politics and Murder 164
Who Killed Bob Teal? 196
Mike, Alec, or Rufus 215
Nightmare Town 232
Night Shots 283
One Hour 302
The Bodies Piled Up 317
The Road Home 334
Ruffian's Wife 338
The Second-Story Angel 355
Afraid of a Gun 371

FROM THE MEMOIRS OF A PRIVATE DETECTIVE

1

Wishing to get some information from members of the W. C. T. U. in an Oregon city, I introduced myself as the secretary of the Butte Civic Purity League. One of them read me a long discourse on the erotic effects of cigarettes upon young girls. Subsequent experiments proved this trip worthless.

2

A man whom I was shadowing went out into the country for a walk one Sunday afternoon and lost his bearings completely. I had to direct him back to the city.

3

House burglary is probably the poorest paid trade in the world; I have never known anyone to make a living at it. But for that matter few criminals of any class are self-supporting unless they toil at something legitimate between times. Most of them, however, live on their women.

DETECTIVE STORIES

4

I know an operative who while looking for pickpockets at the Havre de Grace race track had his wallet stolen. He later became an official in an Eastern detective agency.

5

Three times I have been mistaken for a Prohibition agent, but never had any trouble clearing myself.

6

Taking a prisoner from a ranch near Gilt Edge, Mont., to Lewistown one night, my machine broke down and we had to sit there until daylight. The prisoner, who stoutly affirmed his innocence, was clothed only in overalls and shirt. After shivering all night on the front seat his morale was low, and I had no difficulty in getting a complete confession from him while walking to the nearest ranch early the following morning.

7

Of all the men embezzling from their employers with whom I have had contact, I can't remember a dozen who smoked, drank, or had any of the vices in which bonding companies are so interested.

8

I was once falsely accused of perjury and had to perjure myself to escape arrest.

THE MEMOIRS OF A PRIVATE DETECTIVE

9

A detective agency official in San Francisco once substituted "truthful" for "voracious" in one of my reports on the grounds that the client might not understand the latter. A few days later in another report "simulate" became "quicken" for the same reason.

10

Of all the nationalities haled into the criminal courts, the Greek is the most difficult to convict. He simply denies everything, no matter how conclusive the proof may be; and nothing so impresses a jury as a bare statement of fact, regardless of the fact's inherent improbability or obvious absurdity in the face of overwhelming contrary evidence.

11

I know a man who will forge the impressions of any set of fingers in the world for $50.

12

I have never known a man capable of turning out first-rate work in a trade, a profession or an art, who was a professional criminal.

13

I know a detective who once attempted to disguise himself thoroughly. The first policeman he met took him into custody.

DETECTIVE STORIES

14

I know a deputy sheriff in Montana who, approaching the cabin of a homesteader for whose arrest he had a warrant, was confronted by the homesteader with a rifle in his hands. The deputy sheriff drew his revolver and tried to shoot over the homesteader's head to frighten him. The range was long and a strong wind was blowing. The bullet knocked the rifle from the homesteader's hands. As time went by the deputy sheriff came to accept as the truth the reputation for expertness that this incident gave him, and he not only let his friends enter him in a shooting contest, but wagered everything he owned upon his skill. When the contest was held he missed the target completely with all six shots.

15

Once in Seattle the wife of a fugitive swindler offered to sell me a photograph of her husband for $15. I knew where I could get one free, so I didn't buy it.

16

I was once engaged to discharge a woman's housekeeper.

17

The slang in use among criminals is for the most part a conscious, artificial growth, designed more to confuse outsiders than for any other purpose, but sometimes it is singularly expressive; for instance, *two-time loser*—one who has been convicted twice; and the older *gone to read and write*—found it advisable to go away for a while.

THE MEMOIRS OF A PRIVATE DETECTIVE

18

Pocket-picking is the easiest to master of all the criminal trades. Anyone who is not crippled can become an adept in a day.

19

In 1917, in Washington, D. C, I met a young woman who did not remark that my work must be very interesting.

20

Even where the criminal makes no attempt to efface the prints of his fingers, but leaves them all over the scene of the crime, the chances are about one in ten of finding a print that is sufficiently clear to be of any value.

21

The chief of police of a Southern city once gave me a description of a man, complete even to a mole on his neck, but neglected to mention that he had only one arm.

22

I know a forger who left his wife because she had learned to smoke cigarettes while he was serving a term in prison.

23

Second only to "Dr. Jekyll and Mr. Hyde" is "Raffles" in the affections of the daily press. The phrase "gentleman crook" is used on the slightest provocation. A composite portrait of the gentry upon whom the newspapers have bestowed this title would show a laudanum-drinker, with a large rhinestone horseshoe aglow in

DETECTIVE STORIES

the soiled bosom of his shirt below a bow tie, leering at his victim, and saying: "Now don't get scared, lady, I ain't gonna crack you on the bean. I ain't a rough-neck!"

24

The cleverest and most uniformly successful detective I have ever known is extremely myopic.

25

Going from the larger cities out into the remote rural communities, one finds a steadily decreasing percentage of crimes that have to do with money and a proportionate increase in the frequency of sex as a criminal motive.

26

While trying to peer into the upper story of a roadhouse in northern California one night—and the man I was looking for was in Seattle at the time —part of the porch roof crumbled under me and I fell, spraining an ankle. The proprietor of the roadhouse gave me water to bathe it in.

27

The chief difference between the exceptionally knotty problem confronting the detective of fiction and that facing the real detective is that in the former there is usually a paucity of clues, and in the latter altogether too many.

28

I know a man who once stole a Ferris-wheel.

THE MEMOIRS OF A PRIVATE DETECTIVE

29

That the law-breaker is invariably soon or late apprehended is probably the least challenged of extant myths. And yet the files of every detective bureau bulge with the records of unsolved mysteries and uncaught criminals.

ARSON PLUS

Jim Tarr picked up the cigar I rolled across his desk, looked at the band, bit off an end, and reached for a match.

"Three for a buck," he said. "You must want me to break a *couple* of laws for you this time."

I had been doing business with this fat sheriff of Sacramento County for four or five years—ever since I came to the Continental Detective Agency's San Francisco office—and I had never known him to miss an opening for a sour crack; but it didn't mean anything.

"Wrong both times," I told him. "I get them for two bits each, and I'm here to do you a favor instead of asking for one. The company that insured Thornburgh's house thinks somebody touched it off."

"That's right enough, according to the fire department. They tell me the lower part of the house was soaked with gasoline, but the Lord knows how they could tell—there wasn't a stick left standing. I've got McClump working on it, but he hasn't found anything to get excited about yet."

"What's the layout? All I know is that there was a fire."

Tarr leaned back in his chair and bellowed:

"Hey, Mac!"

The pearl push buttons on his desk are ornaments so far as he

ARSON PLUS

is concerned. Deputy sheriffs McHale, McClump, and Macklin came to the door together—MacNab apparently wasn't within hearing.

"What's the idea?" the sheriff demanded of McClump. "Are you carrying a bodyguard around with you?"

The two other deputies, thus informed as to whom "Mac" referred this time, went back to their cribbage game.

"We got a city slicker here to catch our firebug for us," Tarr told his deputy. "But we got to tell him what it's all about first."

McClump and I had worked together on an express robbery several months before. He's a rangy, towheaded youngster of twenty-five or six, with all the nerve in the world—and most of the laziness.

"Ain't the Lord good to us?"

He had himself draped across a chair by now—always his first objective when he comes into a room.

"Well, here's how she stands: This fellow Thornburgh's house was a couple miles out of town, on the old county road—an old frame house. About midnight, night before last, Jeff Pringle—the nearest neighbor, a half-mile or so to the east—saw a glare in the sky from over that way, and phoned in the alarm; but by the time the fire wagons got there, there wasn't enough of the house left to bother about. Pringle was the first of the neighbors to get to the house, and the roof had already fallen in then.

"Nobody saw anything suspicious—no strangers hanging around or nothing. Thornburgh's help just managed to save themselves, and that was all. They don't know much about what happened—too scared, I reckon. But they did see Thornburgh at his window just before the fire got him. A fellow here in town—name of Handerson—saw that part of it too. He was driving home from Wayton, and got to the house just before the roof caved in.

"The fire department people say they found signs of gasoline. The Coonses, Thornburgh's help, say they didn't have no gas on the place. So there you are."

"Thornburgh have any relatives?"

"Yeah. A niece in San Francisco—a Mrs. Evelyn Trowbridge. She was up yesterday, but there wasn't nothing she could do, and she couldn't tell us nothing much, so she went back home."

"Where are the servants now?"

"Here in town. Staying at a hotel on I Street. I told 'em to stick around for a few days."

"Thornburgh own the house?"

"Uh-huh. Bought it from Newning & Weed a couple months ago."

"You got anything to do this morning?"

"Nothing but this."

"Good. Let's get out and dig around."

We found the Coonses in their room at the hotel on I Street. Mr. Coons was a small-boned, plump man with the smooth, meaningless face and the suavity of the typical male house-servant.

His wife was a tall, stringy woman, perhaps five years older than her husband—say, forty—with a mouth and chin that seemed shaped for gossiping. But he did all the talking, while she nodded her agreement to every second or third word.

"We went to work for Mr. Thornburgh on the fifteenth of June I think," he said, in reply to my first question. "We came to Sacramento, around the first of the month, and put in applications at the Allis Employment Bureau. A couple of weeks later they sent us out to see Mr. Thornburgh, and he took us on."

"Where were you before you came here?"

"In Seattle, sir, with a Mrs. Comerford; but the climate there didn't agree with my wife—she has bronchial trouble—so we decided to come to California. We most likely would have stayed in Seattle, though, if Mrs. Comerford hadn't given up her house."

"What do you know about Thornburgh?"

"Very little, sir. He wasn't a talkative gentleman. He hadn't any business that I know of. I think he was a retired seafaring man. He never said he was, but he had that manner and look. He never went out or had anybody in to see him, except his niece once, and he didn't write or get any mail. He had a room next to his bedroom fixed up as a sort of workshop. He spent most of his time in there. I always thought he was working on some kind of invention, but he kept the door locked, and wouldn't let us go near it."

"Haven't you any idea at all what it was?"

"No, sir. We never heard any hammering or noises from it, and never smelled anything either. And none of his clothes were ever the least bit soiled, even when they were ready to go out to the laundry. They would have been if he had been working on anything like machinery."

"Was he an old man?"

"He couldn't have been over fifty, sir. He was very erect, and his hair and beard were thick, with no gray hairs."

"Ever have any trouble with him?"

"Oh, no, sir! He was, if I may say it, a very peculiar gentleman in a way; and he didn't care about anything except having his meals fixed right, having his clothes taken care of—he was very particular about them—and not being disturbed. Except early in the morning and at night, we'd hardly see him all day."

"Now about the fire. Tell us everything you remember."

"Well, sir, my wife and I had gone to bed about ten o'clock, our regular time, and had gone to sleep. Our room was on the second floor, in the rear. Some time later—I never did exactly know what time it was—I woke up, coughing. The room was all full of smoke, and my wife was sort of strangling. I jumped up, and dragged her down the back stairs and out the back door.

"When I had her safe in the yard, I thought of Mr. Thornburgh, and tried to get back in the house; but the whole first floor was just flames. I ran around front then, to see if he had got out, but didn't see anything of him. The whole yard was as light as day by then. Then I heard him scream—a horrible scream, sir—I can hear it yet! And I looked up at his window—that was the front second-story room—and saw him there, trying to get out the window! But all the woodwork was burning, and he screamed again and fell back, and right after that the roof over his room fell in.

"There wasn't a ladder or anything that I could have put up to the window—there wasn't anything I could have done.

"In the meantime, a gentleman had left his automobile in the road, and come up to where I was standing; but there wasn't anything we could do—the house was burning everywhere and falling in here and there. So we went back to where I had left my wife, and carried her farther away from the fire, and brought her to—she had fainted. And that's all I know about it, sir."

"Hear any noises earlier that night? Or see anybody hanging around?"

"No, sir."

"Have any gasoline around the place?"

"No, sir. Mr. Thornburgh didn't have a car."

"No gasoline for cleaning?"

"No, sir, none at all, unless Mr. Thornburgh had it in his workshop. When his clothes needed cleaning, I took them to town, and all his laundry was taken by the grocer's man, when he brought our provisions."

"Don't know anything that might have some bearing on the fire?"

"No, sir. I was surprised when I heard that somebody had set the house afire. I could hardly believe it. I don't know why anybody should want to do that...."

"What do you think of them?" I asked McClump, as we left the hotel.

"They might pad the bills, or even go South with some of the silver, but they don't figure as killers in my mind."

That was my opinion, too; but they were the only persons known to have been there when the fire started except the man who had died. We went around to the Allis Employment Bureau and talked to the manager.

He told us that the Coonses had come into his office on June second, looking for work; and had given Mrs. Edward Comerford, 45 Woodmansee Terrace, Seattle, Washington, as reference. In reply to a letter—he always checked up the references of servants—Mrs. Comerford had written that the Coonses had been in her employ for a number of years, and had been "extremely satisfactory in every respect." On June thirteenth, Thornburgh had telephoned the bureau, asking that a man and his wife be sent out to keep house for him, and Allis sent out two couples he had listed. Neither couple had been employed by Thornburgh, though Allis considered them more desirable than the Coonses, who were finally hired by Thornburgh.

All that would certainly seem to indicate that the Coonses hadn't deliberately maneuvered themselves into the place, unless they were the luckiest people in the world—and a detective can't afford to believe in luck or coincidence, unless he has unquestionable proof of it.

At the office of the real-estate agents, through whom Thornburgh had bought the house—Newning & Weed—we were told that Thornburgh had come in on the eleventh of June, and had said that he had been told that the house was for sale, had looked it over, and wanted to know the price. The deal had been closed the next morning, and he had paid for the house with a check for $14,500 on the Seamen's Bank of San Francisco. The house was already furnished.

After luncheon, McClump and I called on Howard Handerson—the man who had seen the fire while driving home from Wayton. He had an office in the Empire Building, with his name and the title Northern California Agent for Krispy Korn Krumbs on the door. He was a big, careless-looking man of forty-five or so, with the professionally jovial smile that belongs to the traveling salesman.

He had been in Wayton on business the day of the fire, he said, and had stayed there until rather late, going to dinner and afterward playing pool with a grocer named Hammersmith—one of his customers. He had left Wayton in his machine, at about ten thirty, and set out for Sacramento. At lavender he had stopped at the garage for oil and gas, and to have one of his tires blown up.

Just as he was about to leave the garage, the garage man had called his attention to a red glare in the sky, and had told him that it was probably from a fire somewhere along the old county road that paralleled the state road into Sacramento; so Handerson had taken the county road, and had arrived at the burning house just in time to see Thornburgh try to fight his way through the flames that enveloped him.

It was too late to make any attempt to put out the fire, and the man upstairs was beyond saving by then—undoubtedly dead even before the roof collapsed; so Handerson had helped Coons revive his wife, and stayed there watching the fire until it had burned itself out. He had seen no one on that county road while driving to the fire. . . .

"What do you know about Handerson?" I asked McClump, when we were on the street.

"Came here, from somewhere in the East, I think, early in the summer to open that breakfast-cereal agency. Lives at the Garden Hotel. Where do we go next?"

"We get a car, and take a look at what's left of the Thornburgh house."

An enterprising incendiary couldn't have found a lovelier spot in which to turn himself loose, if he looked the whole county over. Tree-topped hills hid it from the rest of the world, on three sides; while away from the fourth, an uninhabited plain rolled down to the river. The county road that passed the front gate was shunned by automobiles, so McClump said, in favor of the state highway to the north.

Where the house had been was now a mound of blackened ruins. We poked around in the ashes for a few minutes—not that we expected to find anything, but because it's the nature of man

ARSON PLUS

to poke around in ruins.

A garage in the rear, whose interior gave no evidence of recent occupation, had a badly scorched roof and front, but was otherwise undamaged. A shed behind it, sheltering an ax, a shovel, and various odds and ends of gardening tools, had escaped the fire altogether. The lawn in front of the house, and the garden behind the shed—about an acre in all—had been pretty thoroughly cut and trampled by wagon wheels, and the feet of the firemen and the spectators.

Having ruined our shoeshines, McClump and I got back in our car and swung off in a circle around the place, calling at all the houses within a mile radius, and getting little besides jolts for our trouble.

The nearest house was that of Pringle, the man who had turned in the alarm; but he not only knew nothing about the dead man, he said he had never even seen him. In fact, only one of the neighbors had ever seen him: a Mrs. Jabine, who lived about a mile to the south.

She had taken care of the key to the house while it was vacant; and a day or two before he bought it, Thornburgh had come to her house, inquiring about the vacant one. She had gone over there with him and showed him through it, and he had told her that he intended buying it, if the price wasn't too high.

He had been alone, except for the chauffeur of the hired car in which he had come from Sacramento, and, save that he had no family, he had told her nothing about himself.

Hearing that he had moved in, she went over to call on him several days later—"just a neighborly visit"—but had been told by Mrs. Coons that he was not at home. Most of the neighbors had talked to the Coonses, and had got the impression that Thornburgh did not care for visitors, so they had let him alone. The Coonses were described as "pleasant enough to talk to when you meet them," but reflecting their employer's desire not to make friends.

McClump summarized what the afternoon had taught us as we pointed our car toward Tavender: "Any of these folks could have touched off the place, but we got nothing to show that any of 'em even knew Thornburgh, let alone had a bone to pick with him."

Tavender turned out to be a crossroads settlement of a general store and post office, a garage, a church, and six dwellings, about two miles from Thornburgh's place. McClump knew the storekeeper and postmaster, a scrawny little man named Philo, who stuttered moistly.

"I n-n-never s-saw Th-thornburgh," he said, "and I n-n-never had any m-mail for him. C-coons"—it sounded like one of these things butterflies come out of—"used to c-come in once a week to-to order groceries—they d-didn't have a phone. He used to walk in, and I'd s-send the stuff over in my c-c-car. Th-then I'd s-see him once in a while, waiting f-for the stage to S-s-sacramento."

"Who drove the stuff out to Thornburgh's?"

"M-m-my b-boy. Want to t-talk to him?"

The boy was a juvenile edition of the old man, but without the stutter. He had never seen Thornburgh on any of his visits, but his business had taken him only as far as the kitchen. He hadn't noticed anything peculiar about the place.

"Who's the night man at the garage?" I asked him.

"Billy Luce. I think you can catch him there now. I saw him go in a few minutes ago."

We crossed the road and found Luce.

"Night before last—the night of the fire down the road—was there a man here talking to you when you first saw it?"

He turned his eyes upward in that vacant stare which people use to aid their memory.

"Yes, I remember now! He was going to town, and I told him that if he took the county road instead of the state road he'd see the fire on his way in."

"What kind of looking man was he?"

"Middle-aged—a big man, but sort of slouchy. I think he had on a brown suit, baggy and wrinkled."

"Medium complexion?"

"Yes."

"Smile when he talked?"

"Yes, a pleasant sort of fellow."

"Brown hair?"

"Yeah, but have a heart!" Luce laughed. "I didn't put him under a magnifying glass."

From Tavender we drove over to Wayton. Luce's description had fit Henderson all right, but while we were at it, we thought we might as well check up to make sure that he had been coming from Wayton.

We spent exactly twenty-five minutes in Wayton; ten of them finding Hammersmith, the grocer with whom Henderson had said he dined and played pool; five minutes finding the proprietor of the pool room; and ten verifying Henderson's story. . . .

"What do you think of it now, Mac?" I asked, as we rolled back toward Sacramento.

Mac's too lazy to express an opinion, or even form one, unless he's driven to it; but that doesn't mean they aren't worth listening to, if you can get them.

"There ain't a hell of a lot to think," he said cheerfully. "Henderson is out of it, if he ever was in it. There's nothing to show that anybody but the Coonses and Thornburgh were there when the fire started—but there may have been a regiment there. Them Coonses ain't too honest-looking, maybe, but they ain't killers, or I miss my guess. But the fact remains that they're the only bet we got so far. Maybe we ought to try to get a line on them."

"All right," I agreed. "Soon as we get back to town, I'll get a wire off to our Seattle office asking them to interview Mrs. Comerford, and see what she can tell about them. Then I'm going to catch a train for San Francisco and see Thornburgh's niece in the morning."

* * * * *

Next morning, at the address McClump had given me—a rather elaborate apartment building on California Street—I had to wait three-quarters of an hour for Mrs. Evelyn Trowbridge to dress. If I had been younger, or a social caller, I suppose I'd have felt amply rewarded when she finally came in—a tall, slender woman of less than thirty; in some sort of clinging black affair; with a lot of black hair over a very white face, strikingly set off by a small red mouth and big hazel eyes.

But I was a busy, middle-aged detective, who was fuming over having his time wasted; and I was a lot more interested in finding the bird who struck the match than I was in feminine beauty. However, I smothered my grouch, apologized for disturbing her at such an early hour, and got down to business.

"I want you to tell me all you know about your uncle—his family, friends, enemies, business connections—everything."

I had scribbled on the back of the card I had sent into her what my business was.

"He hadn't any family," she said; "unless I might be it. He was my mother's brother, and I am the only one of that family now living."

"Where was he born?"

"Here in San Francisco. I don't know the date, but he was about fifty years old, I think—three years older than my mother."

"What was his business?"

"He went to sea when he was a boy, and, so far as I know, always followed it until a few months ago."

"Captain?"

"I don't know. Sometimes I wouldn't see or hear from him for several years, and he never talked about what he was doing; though he would mention some of the places he had visited—Rio de Janeiro, Madagascar, Tobago, Christiania. Then, about three months ago—some time in May—he came here and told me that he was through with wandering; that he was going to take a house in some quiet place where he could work undisturbed on an invention in which he was interested.

"He lived at the Francisco Hotel while he was in San Francisco. After a couple of weeks he suddenly disappeared. And then, about a month ago, I received a telegram from him, asking me to come to see him at his house near Sacramento. I went up the very next day, and I thought that he was acting queerly—he seemed very excited over something. He gave me a will that he had just drawn up and some life-insurance policies in which I was beneficiary.

"Immediately after that he insisted that I return home, and hinted rather plainly that he did not wish me to either visit him again or write until I heard from him. I thought all that rather peculiar, as he had always seemed fond of me. I never saw him again."

"What was this invention he was working on?"

"I really don't know. I asked him once, but he became so excited—even suspicious—that I changed the subject, and never mentioned it again."

"Are you sure that he really did follow the sea all those years?"

"No, I am not. I just took it for granted; but he may have been doing something altogether different."

"Was he ever married?"

"Not that I know of."

"Know any of his friends or enemies?"

"No, none."

"Remember anybody's name that he ever mentioned?"

"No."

"I don't want you to think this next question insulting, though I admit it is. Where were you the night of the fire?"

"At home; I had some friends here to dinner, and they stayed until about midnight. Mr. and Mrs. Walker Kellogg, Mrs. John Dupree, and a Mr. Killmer, who is a lawyer. I can give you their addresses, if you want to question them."

From Mrs. Trowbridge's apartment I went to the Francisco Hotel. Thornburgh had been registered there from May tenth to June thirteenth, and hadn't attracted much attention. He had been a tall, broad-shouldered, erect man of about fifty, with rather long brown hair brushed straight back; a short, pointed brown beard, and a healthy, ruddy complexion—grave, quiet, punctilious in dress and manner; his hours had been regular and he had had no visitors that any of the hotel employees remembered.

At the Seamen's Bank—upon which Thornburgh's check, in payment of the house, had been drawn—I was told that he had opened an account there on May fifteenth, having been introduced by W. W. Jeffers & Sons, local stockbrokers. A balance of a little more than four hundred dollars remained to his credit. The cancelled checks on hand were all to the order of various life-insurance companies; and for amounts that, if they represented premiums, testified to rather large policies. I jotted down the names of the life-insurance companies, and then went to the offices of W. W. Jeffers & Sons.

Thornburgh had come in, I was told, on the tenth of May with $15,000 worth of bonds that he had wanted sold. During one of his conversations with Jeffers he had asked the broker to recommend a bank, and Jeffers had given him a letter of introduction to the Seamen's Bank.

That was all Jeffers knew about him. He gave me the numbers of the bonds, but tracing bonds isn't always the easiest thing in the world.

The reply to my Seattle telegram was waiting for me at the Continental Detective Agency when I arrived.

MRS EDWARD COMERFORD RENTED APARTMENT AT ADDRESS YOU GAVE ON MAY TWENTY-FIVE. GAVE IT UP JUNE 6. TRUNKS TO SAN FRANCISCO SAME DAY CHECK NUMBERS ON FOUR FIVE TWO FIVE EIGHT SEVEN AND EIGHT AND NINE.

Tracing baggage is no trick at all, if you have the dates and check numbers to start with—as many a bird who is wearing somewhat similar numbers on his chest and back, because he overlooked that detail when making his getaway, can tell you—and twenty-five minutes in a baggage-room at the Ferry and half an hour in the

ARSON PLUS

office of a transfer company gave me my answer.

The trunks had been delivered to Mrs. Evelyn Trowbridge's apartment!

I got Jim Tarr on the phone and told him about it.

"Good shooting!" he said, forgetting for once to indulge his wit. "We'll grab the Coonses here and Mrs. Trowbridge there, and that's the end of another mystery."

"Wait a minute!" I cautioned him. "It's not all straightened out yet—there're still a few kinks in the plot."

"It's straight enough for me. I'm satisfied."

"You're the boss, but I think you're being a little hasty. I'm going up and talk with the niece again. Give me a little time before you phone the police here to make the pinch. I'll hold her until they get there."

Evelyn Trowbridge let me in this time, instead of the maid who had opened the door for me in the morning, and she led me to the same room in which we had had our first talk. I let her pick out a seat, and then I selected one that was closer to either door than hers was.

On the way up I had planned a lot of innocent-sounding questions that would get her all snarled up; but after taking a good look at this woman sitting in front of me, leaning comfortably back in her chair, coolly waiting for me to speak my piece, I discarded the trick stuff and came out cold-turkey.

"Ever use the name Mrs. Edward Comerford?"

"Oh, yes." As casual as a nod on the street.

"When?"

"Often. You see, I happen to have been married not so long ago to Mr. Edward Comerford. So it's not really strange that I should have used the name."

"Use it in Seattle recently?"

"I would suggest," she said sweetly, "that if you are leading up to the references I gave Coons and his wife, you might save time by coming right to it."

"That's fair enough," I said. "Let's do that."

There wasn't a tone or shading, in voice, manner, or expression, to indicate that she was talking about anything half so serious or important to her as a possibility of being charged with murder. She might have been talking about the weather.

"During the time that Mr. Comerford and I were married, we lived in Seattle, where he still lives. After the divorce, I left Seattle and resumed my maiden name. And the Coonses *were* in our employ, as you might learn if you care to look it up. You'll find my husband—or former husband—at the Chelsea Apartments, I think.

"Last summer, or late spring, I decided to return to Seattle. The truth of it is—I suppose all my personal affairs will be aired anyhow—that I thought perhaps Edward and I might patch up our differences; so I went back and took an apartment on Woodmansee Terrace. As I was known in Seattle as Mrs. Edward Comerford, and as I thought my using his name might influence him a little, I used it while I was there.

"Also I telephoned the Coonses to make tentative arrangements in case Edward and I should open our house again; but Coons told me that they were going to California, and so I gladly gave them an excellent recommendation when, some days later, I received a letter of inquiry from an employment bureau in Sacramento. After I had been in Seattle for about two weeks, I changed my mind about the reconciliation—Edward's interest, I learned, was all centered elsewhere; so I returned to San Francisco—"

"Very nice! But—"

"If you will permit me to finish," she interrupted. "When I went to see my uncle in response to his telegram, I was surprised to find the Coonses in his house. Knowing my uncle's peculiarities, and finding them now increased, and remembering his extreme secretiveness about his mysterious invention, I cautioned the Coonses not to tell him that they had been in my employ.

"He certainly would have discharged them, and just as certainly

ARSON PLUS

would have quarreled with me—he would have thought that I was having him spied on. Then, when Coons telephoned me after the fire, I knew that to admit that the Coonses had been formerly in my employ, would, in view of the fact that I was my uncle's only heir, cast suspicion on all three of us. So we foolishly agreed to say nothing and carry on the deception."

That didn't sound all wrong—but it didn't sound all right. I wished Tarr had taken it easier and let us get a better line on these people, before having them thrown in the coop.

"The coincidence of the Coonses stumbling into my uncle's house is, I fancy, too much for your detecting instincts," she went on. "Am I to consider myself under arrest?"

I'm beginning to like this girl; she's a nice, cool piece of work.

"Not yet," I told her. "But I'm afraid it's going to happen pretty soon."

She smiled a little mocking smile at that, and another when the doorbell rang.

It was O'Hara from police headquarters. We turned the apartment upside down and inside out, but didn't find anything of importance except the will she had told me about, dated July eighth, and her uncle's life-insurance policies. They were all dated between May fifteenth and June tenth, and added up to a little more than $200,000.

I spent an hour grilling the maid after O'Hara had taken Evelyn Trowbridge away, but she didn't know any more than I did. However, between her, the janitor, the manager of the apartments, and the names Mrs. Trowbridge had given me, I learned that she had really been entertaining friends on the night of the fire—until after eleven o'clock, anyway—and that was late enough.

Half an hour later I was riding the Short Line back to Sacramento. I was getting to be one of the line's best customers, and my anatomy was on bouncing terms with every bump in the road.

Between bumps I tried to fit the pieces of this Thornburgh puzzle together. The niece and the Coonses fit in somewhere, but not just where we had them. We had been working on the job sort of lopsided, but it was the best we could do with it. In the beginning we had turned to the Coonses and Evelyn Trowbridge because there was no other direction to go; and now we had something on them—but a good lawyer could make hash out of it.

The Coonses were in the county jail when I got to Sacramento. After some questioning they had admitted their connection with the niece, and had come through with stories that matched hers.

Tarr, McClump and I sat around the sheriff's desk and argued.

"Those yarns are pipe dreams," the sheriff said. "We got all three of 'em cold, and they're as good as convicted."

McClump grinned derisively at his superior, and then turned to me.

"Go on, you tell him about the holes in his little case. He ain't your boss, and can't take it out on you later for being smarter than he is!"

Tarr glared from one of us to the other.

"Spill it, you wise guys!" he ordered.

"Our dope is," I told him, figuring that McClump's view of it was the same as mine, "that there's nothing to show that even Thornburgh knew he was going to buy that house before the tenth of June, and that the Coonses were in town looking for work on the second. And besides, it was only by luck that they got the jobs. The employment office sent two couples out there ahead of them."

"We'll take a chance on letting the jury figure that out."

"Yes? You'll also take a chance on them figuring out that Thornburgh, who seems to have been a nut, might have touched off the place himself! We've got something on these people, Jim, but not enough to go into court with them. How are you going to prove that when the Coonses were planted in Thornburgh's house—if you can even prove that they were planted—they and the Trowbridge woman knew he was going to load up with insurance policies?"

The sheriff spat disgustedly.

ARSON PLUS

"You guys are the limit! You run around in circles, digging up the dope on these people until you get enough to hang 'em, and then you run around hunting for outs! What's the matter with you now?"

I answered him from halfway to the door—the pieces were beginning to fit together under my skull.

"Going to run some more circles—come on, Mac!"

McClump and I held a conference on the fly, and then I got a car from the nearest garage and headed for Tavender. We made time going out, and got there before the general store had closed for the night. The stuttering Philo separated himself from the two men with whom he had been talking Hiram Johnson,[1] and followed me to the rear of the store.

"Do you keep an itemized list of the laundry you handle?"

"N-n-no; just the amounts."

"Let's look at Thornburgh's."

He produced a begrimed and rumpled account book, and we picked out the weekly items I wanted: $2.60, $3.10, $2.25, and so on.

"Got the last batch of laundry here?"

"Y-yes," he said. "It j-just c-c-came out from the city t-today."

I tore open the bundle—some sheets, pillowcases, tablecloths, towels, napkins; some feminine clothing; some shirts, collars, underwear, and socks that were unmistakably Coons's. I thanked Philo while running back to the car.

Back in Sacramento again, McClump was waiting for me at the garage where I had hired the car.

"Registered at the hotel on June fifteenth; rented the office on the sixteenth. I think he's in the hotel now," he greeted me.

We hurried around the block to the Garden Hotel.

"Mr. Handerson went out a minute or two ago," the night clerk told us. "He seemed to be in a hurry."

---

1 Governor of California (1911-17) and Theodore Roosevelt's running mate on the Progressive ticket in 1912.

"Know where he keeps his car?"

"In the hotel garage around the corner."

We were within ten feet of the garage, when Handerson's automobile shot out and turned up the street.

"Oh, Mr. Handerson!" I cried, trying to keep my voice level.

He stepped on the gas and streaked away from us.

"Want him?" McClump asked; and at my nod he stopped a passing roadster by the simple expedient of stepping in front of it.

We climbed in, McClump flashed his star at the bewildered driver, and pointed out Handerson's dwindling tail-light. After he had persuaded himself that he wasn't being boarded by a couple of bandits, the commandeered driver did his best, and we picked up Handerson's tail-light after two or three turnings, and closed in on him—though his car was going at a good clip.

By the time we reached the outskirts of the city, we had crawled up to within safe shooting distance, and I sent a bullet over the fleeing man's head. Thus encouraged, he managed to get a little more speed out of his car; but we were overhauling him now.

Just at the wrong minute Handerson decided to look over his shoulder at us—an unevenness in the road twisted his wheels—his machine swayed—skidded—went over on its side. Almost immediately, from the heart of the tangle, came a flash and a bullet moaned past my ear. Another. And then, while I was still hunting for something to shoot at in the pile of junk we were drawing down upon, McClump's ancient and battered revolver roared in my other ear.

Handerson was dead when we got to him—McClump's bullet had taken him over one eye.

McClump spoke to me over the body.

"I ain't an inquisitive sort of fellow, but I hope you don't mind telling me why I shot this lad."

"Because he was—Thornburgh."

He didn't say anything for about five minutes. Then: "I reckon that's right. How'd you know it?"

ARSON PLUS

We were sitting beside the wreckage now, waiting for the police that we had sent our commandeered chauffeur to phone for.

"He had to be," I said, "when you think it all over. Funny we didn't hit on it before! All that stuff we were told about Thornburgh had a fishy sound. Whiskers and an unknown profession, immaculate and working on a mysterious invention, very secretive and born in San Francisco—where the fire wiped out all the old records—just the sort of fake that could be cooked up easily.

"Now, consider Handerson. You had told me he came to Sacramento sometime early this summer—and the dates you got tonight show that he didn't come until after Thornburgh had bought his house. All right! Now compare Handerson with the descriptions we got of Thornburgh.

"Both are about the same size and age, and with the same color hair. The differences are all things that can be manufactured—clothes, a little sunburn, and a month's growth of beard, along with a little acting, would do the trick. Tonight I went out to Taven-der and took a look at the last batch of laundry—and there wasn't any that didn't fit the Coonses! And none of the bills all the way back were large enough for Thornburgh to have been as careful about his clothes as we were told he was."

"It must be great to be a detective!" McClump grinned as the police ambulance came up and began disgorging policemen. "I reckon somebody must have tipped Handerson off that I was asking about him this evening." And then, regretfully: "So we ain't going to hang them folks for murder after all."

"No, but we oughtn't have any trouble convicting them of arson plus conspiracy to defraud, and anything else that the Prosecuting Attorney can think up."

THE TENTH CLEW

CHAPTER I

"Do you know ... Emil Bonfils?"

r. Leopold Gantvoort is not at home," the servant who opened the door said, "but his son, Mr. Charles, is—if you wish to see him."

"No, I had an appointment with Mr. Leopold Gantvoort for nine or a little after. It's just nine now. No doubt he'll be back soon. I'll wait."

"Very well, sir."

He stepped aside for me to enter the house, took my overcoat and hat, guided me to a room on the second floor—Gantvoort's library—and left me. I picked up a magazine from the stack on the table, pulled an ash tray over beside me, and made myself comfortable.

An hour passed. I stopped reading and began to grow impatient. Another hour passed—and I was fidgeting.

A clock somewhere below had begun to strike eleven when a young man of twenty-five or—six, tall and slender, with remarkably white skin and very dark hair and eyes, came into the room.

"My father hasn't returned yet," he said. "It's too bad that you should have been kept waiting all this time. Isn't there anything I could do for you? I am Charles Gantvoort."

"No, thank you." I got up from my chair, accepting the courteous dismissal. "I'll get in touch with him tomorrow."

"I'm sorry," he murmured, and we moved toward the door together.

As we reached the hall an extension telephone in one corner of the room we were leaving buzzed softly, and I halted in the doorway while Charles Gantvoort went over to answer it.

His back was toward me as he spoke into the instrument.

"Yes. Yes, Yes!"—sharply—"*What?* Yes"—very weakly—"Yes."

He turned slowly around and faced me with a face that was gray and tortured, with wide shocked eyes and gaping mouth—the telephone still in his hand.

"Father," he gasped, "is dead—killed!"

"Where? How?"

"I don't know. That was the police. They want me to come down at once."

He straightened his shoulders with an effort, pulling himself together, put down the telephone, and his face fell into less strained lines.

"You will pardon my—"

"Mr. Gantvoort," I interrupted his apology, "I am connected with the Continental Detective Agency. Your father called up this afternoon and asked that a detective be sent to see him tonight. He said his life had been threatened. He hadn't definitely engaged us, however, so unless you—"

"Certainly! You are employed! If the police haven't already caught the murderer I want you to do everything possible to catch him."

"All right! Let's get down to headquarters."

Neither of us spoke during the ride to the Hall of Justice. Gantvoort bent over the wheel of his car, sending it through the streets at a terrific speed. There were several questions that needed answers, but all his attention was required for his driving if he was to maintain the pace at which he was driving without piling us into something. So I didn't disturb him, but hung on and kept quiet.

Half a dozen police detectives were waiting for us when we reached the detective bureau. O'Gar—a bullet-headed detective sergeant who dresses like the village constable in a movie, wide-brimmed black hat and all, but who isn't to be put out of the reckoning on that account—was in charge of the investigation. He and I had worked on two or three jobs together before, and hit it off excellently.

He led us into one of the small offices below the assembly room. Spread out on the flat top of a desk there were a dozen or more objects.

"I want you to look these things over carefully," the detective-sergeant told Gantvoort, "and pick out the ones that belonged to your father."

"But where is he?"

"Do this first," O'Gar insisted, "and then you can see him."

I looked at the things on the table while Charles Gantvoort made his selections. An empty jewel case; a memorandum book; three letters in slit envelopes that were addressed to the dead man; some other papers; a bunch or keys; a fountain pen; two white linen handkerchiefs; two pistol cartridges; a gold watch, with a gold knife and a gold pencil attached to it by a gold-and-platinum chain; two black leather wallets, one of them very new and the other worn; some money, both paper and silver; and a small portable typewriter, bent and twisted, and matted with hair and blood. Some of the other things were smeared with blood and some were clean.

Gantvoort picked out the watch and its attachments, the keys, the fountain pen, the memoranda book, the handkerchiefs, the letters and other papers, and the older wallet.

"These were Father's," he told us. "I've never seen any of the others before. I don't know, of course, how much money he had with him tonight, so I can't say how much of this is his."

"You're sure none of the rest of this stuff was his?" O'Gar asked.

"I don't think so, but I'm not sure. Whipple could tell you." He turned to me. "He's the man who let you in tonight. He looked after Father, and he'd know positively whether any of these other things belonged to him or not."

One of the police detectives went to the telephone to tell Whipple to come down immediately.

I resumed the questioning.

"Is anything that your father usually carried with him missing? Anything of value?"

"Not that I know of. All the things that he might have been expected to have with him seem to be here."

"At what time tonight did he leave the house?"

"Before seven-thirty. Possibly as early as seven."

"Know where he was going?"

"He didn't tell me, but I supposed he was going to call on Miss Dexter."

The faces of the police detectives brightened, and their eyes grew sharp. I suppose mine did, too. There are many, many murders with never a woman in them anywhere; but seldom a very conspicuous killing.

"Who's this Miss Dexter?" O'Gar took up the inquiry.

"She's, well—" Charles Gantvoort hesitated. "Well, Father was on very friendly terms with her and her brother. He usually called on them—on her several evenings a week. In fact, I suspected that he intended marrying her."

"Who and what is she?"

"Father became acquainted with them six or seven months ago. I've met them several times, but don't know them very well. Miss Dexter—Creda is her given name—is about twenty-three years old, I should judge, and her brother Madden is four or five years older. He is in New York now, or on his way there, to transact some business for Father."

"Did your father tell you he was going to marry her?" O'Gar hammered away at the woman angle.

"No; but it was pretty obvious that he was very much—ah—infatuated. We had some words over it a few days ago—last week.

Not a quarrel, you understand, but words. From the way he talked I feared that he meant to marry her."

"What do you mean 'feared'?" O'Gar snapped at that word.

Charles Gantvoort's pale face flushed a little, and he cleared his throat embarrassedly.

"I don't want to put the Dexters in a bad light to you. I don't think—I'm sure they had nothing to do with father's—with this. But I didn't care especially for them—didn't like them. I thought they were—well—fortune hunters, perhaps. Father wasn't fabulously wealthy, but he had considerable means. And, while he wasn't feeble, still he was past fifty-seven, old enough for me to feel that Creda Dexter was more interested in his money than in him."

"How about your father's will?"

"The last one of which I have any knowledge—drawn up two or three years ago—left everything to my wife and me, jointly. Father's attorney, Mr. Murray Abernathy, could tell you if there was a later will, but I hardly think there was."

"Your father had retired from business, hadn't he?"

"Yes; he turned his import and export business over to me about a year ago. He had quite a few investments scattered around, but he wasn't actively engaged in the management of any concern."

O'Gar tilted his village constable hat back and scratched his bullet head reflectively for a moment. Then he looked at me.

"Anything else you want to ask?"

"Yes. Mr. Gantvoort, do you know or did you ever hear your father or anyone else speak of an Emil Bonfils?"

"No."

"Did your father ever tell you that he had received a threatening letter? Or that he had been shot at on the street?"

"No."

"Was your father in Paris in 1902?"

"Very likely. He used to go abroad every year up until the time of his retirement from business."

THE TENTH CLEW

CHAPTER II

"That's Something!"

O'Gar and I took Gantvoort around to the morgue to see his father, then. The dead man wasn't pleasant to look at, even to O'Gar and me, who hadn't known him except by sight. I remembered him as a small wiry man, always smartly tailored, and with a brisk springiness that was far younger than his years.

He lay now with the top of his head beaten into a red and pulpy mess.

We left Gantvoort at the morgue and set out afoot for the Hall of Justice.

"What's this deep stuff you're pulling about Emil Bonfils and Paris in 1902?" the detective-sergeant asked as soon as we were out in the street.

"This: the dead man phoned the Agency this afternoon and said he had received a threatening letter from an Emil Bonfils with whom he had had trouble in Paris in 1902. He also said that Bonfils had shot at him the previous evening, in the street. He wanted somebody to come around and see him about it tonight. And he said that under no circumstances were the police to be let in on it—that he'd rather have Bonfils get him than have the trouble made public. That's all he would say over the phone; and that's how I happened to be on hand when Charles Gantvoort was notified of his father's death."

O'Gar stopped in the middle of the sidewalk and whistled softly.

"That's something!" he exclaimed. "Wait till we get back to headquarters—I'll show you something."

Whipple was waiting in the assembly room when we arrived at headquarters. His face at first glance was as smooth and mask-like as when he had admitted me to the house on Russian Hill earlier in the evening. But beneath his perfect servant's manner he was twitching and trembling.

We took him into the little office where we had questioned Charles Gantvoort.

Whipple verified all that the dead man's son had told us. He was positive that neither the typewriter, the jewel case, the two cartridges, or the newer wallet had belonged to Gantvoort.

We couldn't get him to put his opinion of the Dexters in words, but that he disapproved of them was easily seen. Miss Dexter, he said, had called up on the telephone three times this night at about eight o'clock, at nine, and at nine-thirty. She had asked for Mr. Leopold Gantvoort each time, but she had left no message. Whipple was of the opinion that she was expecting Gantvoort, and he had not arrived.

He knew nothing, he said, of Emil Bonfils or of any threatening letters. Gantvoort had been out the previous night from eight until midnight. Whipple had not seen him closely enough when he came home to say whether he seemed excited or not. Gantvoort usually carried about a hundred dollars in his pockets.

"Is there anything that you know of that Gantvoort had on his person tonight which isn't among these things on the desk?" O'Gar asked.

"No, sir. Everything seems to be here—watch and chain, money, memorandum book, wallet, keys, handkerchiefs, fountain pen—everything that I know of."

"Did Charles Gantvoort go out tonight?"

"No, sir. He and Mrs. Gantvoort were at home all evening."

"Positive?"

Whipple thought a moment.

"Yes, sir, I'm fairly certain. But I know Mrs. Gantvoort wasn't out. To tell the truth, I didn't see Mr. Charles from about eight o'clock until he came downstairs with this gentleman"—pointing to me—"at eleven. But I'm fairly certain he was home all evening. I think Mrs. Gantvoort said he was."

Then O'Gar put another question—one that puzzled me at the time.

THE TENTH CLEW

"What kind of collar buttons did Mr. Gantvoort wear?"
"You mean Mr. Leopold?"
"Yes."
"Plain gold ones, made all in one piece. They had a London jeweler's mark on them."
"Would you know them if you saw them?"
"Yes, sir."

We let Whipple go home then.

"Don't you think," I suggested when O'Gar and I were alone with this desk-load of evidence that didn't mean anything at all to me yet, "it's time you were loosening up and telling me what's what?"

"I guess so—listen! A man named Lagerquist, a grocer, was driving through Golden Gate Park tonight, and passed a machine standing on a dark road, with its lights out. He thought there was something funny about the way the man in it was sitting at the wheel, so he told the first patrolman he met about it.

"The patrolman investigated and found Gantvoort sitting at the wheel—dead—with his head smashed in and this dingus"—putting one hand on the bloody typewriter—"on the seat beside him. That was at a quarter of ten. The doc says Gantvoort was killed—his skull crushed—with this typewriter.

"The dead man's pockets, we found, had all been turned inside out; and all this stuff on the desk, except this new wallet, was scattered about in the car—some of it on the floor and some on the seats. This money was there too—nearly a hundred dollars of it. Among the papers was this."

He handed me a sheet of white paper upon which the following had been typewritten:

L.F.G.—

I WANT WHAT IS MINE. 6,000 MILES AND 21 YEARS ARE NOT ENOUGH TO HIDE YOU FROM THE VICTIM OF YOUR TREACHERY. I MEAN TO HAVE WHAT YOU STOLE.

E.B.

"L. F. G. could be Leopold F. Gantvoort," I said. "And E. B. could be Emil Bonfils. Twenty-one years is the time from 1902 to 1923, and 6,000 miles is, roughly, the distance between Paris and San Francisco."

I laid the letter down and picked up the jewel case. It was a black imitation leather one, lined with white satin, and unmarked in any way.

Then I examined the cartridges. There were two of them, S. W. 45-caliber, and deep crosses had been cut in their soft noses—an old trick that makes the bullet spread out like a saucer when it hits.

"These in the car, too?"

"Yep—and this."

From a vest pocket O'Gar produced a short tuft of blond hair—hairs between an inch and two inches in length. They had been cut off, not pulled out by the roots.

"Any more?"

There seemed to be an endless stream of things.

He picked up the new wallet from the desk—the one that both Whipple and Charles Gantvoort had said did not belong to the dead man—and slid it over to me.

"That was found in the road, three or four feet from the car."

It was of a cheap quality, and had neither manufacturer's name nor owner's initials on it. In it were two ten-dollar bills, three small newspaper clippings, and a typewritten list of six names and addresses, headed by Gantvoort's.

The three clippings were apparently from the Personal columns of three different newspapers—the type wasn't the same—and they read:

GEORGE—
EVERYTHING IS FIXED. DON'T WAIT TOO LONG.
D. D. D.

THE TENTH CLEW

R. H. T.—
  THEY DO NOT ANSWER.
      —FLO

CAPPY—
  TWELVE ON THE DOT AND LOOK SHARP.
      —BINGO

The names and addresses on the typewritten list, under Gantvoort's, were:

Quincy Heathcote, 1223 S. Jason Street, Denver; B. D. Thornton, 96 Hughes Circle, Dallas; Luther G. Randall, 615 Columbia Street, Portsmouth; J. H. Boyd Willis, 4544 Harvard Street, Boston; Hannah Hindmarsh, 218 E. 79th Street, Cleveland.

"What else?" I asked when I had studied these. The detective-sergeant's supply hadn't been exhausted yet.

"The dead man's collar buttons—both front and back—had been taken out, though his collar and tie were still in place. And his left shoe was gone. We hunted high and low all around, but didn't find either shoe or collar buttons."

"Is that all?"

I was prepared for anything now.

"What the hell do you want?" he growled. "Ain't that enough?"

"How about fingerprints?"

"Nothing stirring! All we found belonged to the dead man."

"How about the machine he was found in?"

"A coupé belonging to a Dr. Wallace Girargo. He phoned in at six this evening that it had been stolen from near the corner of McAllister and Polk streets. We're checking up on him—but I think he's all right."

The things that Whipple and Charles Gantvoort had identified as belonging to the dead man told us nothing. We went over them carefully, but to no advantage. The memorandum book contained many entries, but they all seemed totally foreign to the murder. The letters were quite as irrelevant.

The serial number of the typewriter with which the murder had been committed had been removed, we found—apparently filed out of the frame.

"Well, what do you think?" O'Gar asked when we had given up our examination of our clews and sat back burning tobacco.

"I think we want to find Monsieur Emil Bonfils."

"It wouldn't hurt to do that," he grunted. "I guess our best bet is to get in touch with these five people on the list with Gantvoort's name. Suppose that's a murder list? That this Bonfils is out to get all of them?"

"Maybe. We'll get hold of them anyway. Maybe we'll find that some of them have already been killed. But whether they have been killed or are to be killed or not, it's a cinch they have some connection with this affair. I'll get off a batch of telegrams to the Agency's branches, having the names on the list taken care of. I'll try to have the three clippings traced, too."

O'Gar looked at his watch and yawned.

"It's after four. What say we knock off and get some sleep? I'll leave word for the department's expert to compare the typewriter with that letter signed E. B. and with that list to see if they were written on it. I guess they were, but we'll make sure. I'll have the park searched all around where we found Gantvoort as soon as it gets light enough to see, and maybe the missing shoe and the collar buttons will be found. And I'll have a couple of the boys out calling on all the typewriter shops in the city to see if they can get a line on this one."

I stopped at the nearest telegraph office and got off a wad of messages. Then I went home to dream of nothing even remotely connected with crime or the detecting business.

THE TENTH CLEW

CHAPTER III

"A sleek kitten that dame!"

At eleven o'clock that same morning, when, brisk and fresh with five hours' sleep under my belt, I arrived at the police detective bureau, I found O'Gar slumped down at his desk, staring dazedly at a black shoe, half a dozen collar buttons, a rusty flat key, and a rumpled newspaper—all lined up before him.

"What's all this? Souvenir of your wedding?"

"Might as well be." His voice was heavy with disgust. "Listen to this: one of the porters of the Seamen's National Bank found a package in the vestibule when he started cleaning up this morning. It was this shoe—Gantvoort's missing one—wrapped in this sheet of a five-day-old *Philadelphia Record*, and with these collar buttons and this old key in it. The heel of the shoe, you'll notice, has been pried off, and is still missing. Whipple identifies it all right, as well as two of the collar buttons, but he never saw the key before. These other four collar buttons are new, and common gold-rolled ones. The key don't look like it had had much use for a long time. What do you make of all that?"

I couldn't make anything out of it.

"How did the porter happen to turn the stuff in?"

"Oh, the whole story was in the morning papers—all about the missing shoe and collar buttons and all."

"What did you learn about the typewriter?" I asked.

"The letter and the list were written with it, right enough; but we haven't been able to find where it came from yet. We checked up the doc who owns the coupé, and he's in the clear. We accounted for all his time last night. Lagerquist, the grocer who found Gantvoort, seems to be all right, too. What did you do?"

"Haven't had any answers to the wires I sent last night. I dropped in at the Agency on my way down this morning, and got four operatives out covering the hotels and looking up all the people named

Bonfils they can find—there are two or three families by that name listed in the directory. Also I sent our New York branch a wire to have the steamship records searched to see if an Emil Bonfils had arrived recently; and I put a cable through to our Paris correspondent to see what he could dig up over there."

"I guess we ought to see Gantvoort's lawyer—Abernathy—and that Dexter woman before we do anything else," the detective-sergeant said.

"I guess so," I agreed, "let's tackle the lawyer first. He's the most important one, the way things now stand."

Murray Abernathy, attorney-at-law, was a long, stringy, slow-spoken old gentleman who still clung to starched-bosom shirts. He was too full of what he thought were professional ethics to give us as much help as we had expected; but by letting him talk—letting him ramble along in his own way—we did get a little information from him. What we got amounted to this:

The dead man and Creda Dexter had intended being married the coming Wednesday. His son and her brother were both opposed to the marriage, it seemed, so Gantvoort and the woman had planned to be married secretly in Oakland, and catch a boat for the Orient that same afternoon; figuring that by the time their lengthy honeymoon was over they could return to a son and brother who had become resigned to the marriage.

A new will had been drawn up, leaving half of Gantvoort's estate to his new wife and half to his son and daughter-in-law. But the new will had not been signed yet, and Creda Dexter knew it had not been signed. She knew—and this was one of the few points upon which Abernathy would make a positive statement—that under the old will, still in force, everything went to Charles Gantvoort and his wife.

The Gantvoort estate, we estimated from Abernathy's roundabout statements and allusions, amounted to about a million and a half in cash value. The attorney had never heard of Emil Bonfils, he said, and had never heard of any threats or attempts at murder directed toward the dead man. He knew nothing—or would tell us nothing—that threw any light upon the nature of the thing that the threatening letter had accused the dead man of stealing.

From Abernathy's office we went to Creda Dexter's apartment, in a new and expensively elegant building only a few minutes' walk from the Gantvoort residence.

Creda Dexter was a small woman in her early twenties. The first thing you noticed about her were her eyes. They were large and deep and the color of amber, and their pupils were never at rest. Continuously they changed size, expanded and contracted—slowly at times, suddenly at others—ranging incessantly from the size of pinheads to an extent that threatened to blot out the amber irises.

With the eyes for a guide, you discovered that she was pronouncedly feline throughout. Her every movement was the slow, smooth, sure one of a cat; and the contours of her rather pretty face, the shape of her mouth, her small nose, the set of her eyes, the swelling of her brows, were all cat-like. And the effect was heightened by the way she wore her hair, which was thick and tawny.

"Mr. Gantvoort and I," she told us after the preliminary explanations had been disposed of, "were to have been married the day after tomorrow. His son and daughter-in-law were both opposed to the marriage, as was my brother Madden. They all seemed to think that the difference between our ages was too great. So to avoid any unpleasantness, we had planned to be married quietly and then go abroad for a year or more, feeling sure that they would all have forgotten their grievances by the time we returned.

"That was why Mr. Gantvoort persuaded Madden to go to New York. He had some business there—something to do with the disposal of his interest in a steel mill—so he used it as an excuse to get Madden out of the way until we were off on our wedding trip. Madden lived here with me, and it would have been nearly impossible for me to have made any preparations for the trip without him seeing them."

"Was Mr. Gantvoort here last night?" I asked her.

"No, I expected him—we were going out. He usually walked

over—it's only a few blocks. When eight o'clock came and he hadn't arrived, I telephoned his house, and Whipple told me that he had left nearly an hour before. I called up again, twice, after that. Then, this morning, I called up again before I had seen the papers, and I was told that he—"

She broke off with a catch in her voice—the only sign of sorrow she displayed throughout the interview. The impression of her we had received from Charles Gantvoort and Whipple had prepared us for a more or less elaborate display of grief on her part. But she disappointed us. There was nothing crude about her work—she didn't even turn on the tears for us.

"Was Mr. Gantvoort here night before last?"

"Yes. He came over at a little after eight and stayed until nearly twelve. We didn't go out."

"Did he walk over and back?"

"Yes, so far as I know."

"Did he ever say anything to you about his life being threatened?"

"No."

She shook her head decisively.

"Do you know Emil Bonfils?"

"No."

"Ever hear Mr. Gantvoort speak of him?"

"No."

"At what hotel is your brother staying in New York?"

The restless black pupils spread out abruptly, as if they were about to overflow into the white areas of her eyes. That was the first clear indication of fear I had seen. But, outside of those telltale pupils, her composure was undisturbed.

"I don't know."

"When did he leave San Francisco?"

"Thursday—four days ago."

O'Gar and I walked six or seven blocks in thoughtful silence after we left Creda Dexter's apartment, and then he spoke.

"A sleek kitten—that dame! Rub her the right way, and she'll purr pretty. Rub her the wrong way—and look out for the claws!"

"What did that flash of her eyes when I asked about her brother tell you?" I asked.

"Something—but I don't know what! It wouldn't hurt to look him up and see if he's really in New York. If he is there today it's a cinch he wasn't here last night—even the mail planes take twenty-six or twenty-eight hours for the trip."

"We'll do that," I agreed. "It looks like this Creda Dexter wasn't any too sure that her brother wasn't in on the killing. And there's nothing to show that Bonfils didn't have help. I can't figure Creda being in on the murder, though. She knew the new will hadn't been signed. There'd be no sense in her working herself out of that three-quarters of a million berries."

We sent a lengthy telegram to the Continental's New York branch, and then dropped in at the Agency to see if any replies had come to the wires I had got off the night before.

They had.

None of the people whose names appeared on the typewritten list with Gantvoort's had been found; not the least trace had been found of any of them. Two of the addresses given were altogether wrong. There were no houses with those numbers on those streets—and there never had been.

CHAPTER IV

"Maybe that ain't so foolish!"

What was left of the afternoon, O'Gar and I spent going over the street between Gantvoort's house on Russian Hill and the building in which the Dexters lived. We questioned everyone we could find—man, woman and child—who lived, worked, or played along any of the three routes the dead man could have taken.

We found nobody who had heard the shot that had been fired by Bonfils on the night before the murder. We found nobody who had seen anything suspicious on the night of the murder. Nobody who remembered having seen him picked up in a coupé.

Then we called at Gantvoort's house and questioned Charles Gantvoort again, his wife, and all the servants—and we learned nothing. So far as they knew, nothing belonging to the dead man was missing—nothing small enough to be concealed in the heel of a shoe.

The shoes he had worn the night he was killed were one of three pairs made in New York for him two months before. He could have removed the heel of the left one, hollowed it out sufficiently to hide a small object in it, and then nailed it on again; though Whipple insisted that he would have noticed the effects of any tampering with the shoe unless it had been done by an expert repairman.

This field exhausted, we returned to the Agency. A telegram had just come from the New York branch, saying that none of the steamship companies' records showed the arrival of an Emil Bonfils from either England, France, or Germany within the past six months.

The operatives who had been searching the city for Bonfils had all come in empty-handed. They had found and investigated eleven persons named Bonfils in San Francisco, Oakland, Berkeley, and Alameda. Their investigations had definitely cleared all eleven. None of these Bonfilses knew an Emil Bonfils. Combing the hotels had yielded nothing.

O'Gar and I went to dinner together—a quiet grouchy sort of meal during which we didn't speak six words apiece—and then came back to the Agency to find that another wire had come in from New York.

> Madden Dexter arrived McAlpin Hotel this morning with Power of Attorney to sell Gantvoort interest in B. F. and F. Iron Corporation. Denies knowledge of Emil Bonfils or of murder. Expects to finish business and leave for San Francisco tomorrow.

THE TENTH CLEW

I let the sheet of paper upon which I had decoded the telegram slide out of my fingers, and we sat listlessly facing each other across my desk looking vacantly each at the other, listening to the clatter of charwomen's buckets in the corridor.

"It's a funny one," O'Gar said softly to himself at last.

I nodded. It was.

"We got nine clews," he spoke again presently, "and none of them have got us a damned thing.

"Number one: the dead man called up you people and told you that he had been threatened and shot at by an Emil Bonfils that he'd had a run-in with in Paris a long time ago.

"Number two: the typewriter he was killed with and that the letter and list were written on. We're still trying to trace it, but with no breaks so far. What the hell kind of a weapon was that, anyway? It looks like this fellow Bonfils got hot and hit Gantvoort with the first thing he put his hand on. But what was the typewriter doing in a stolen car? And why were the numbers filed off it?"

I shook my head to signify that I couldn't guess the answer, and O'Gar went on enumerating our clews.

"Number three: the threatening letter, fitting in with what Gantvoort had said over the phone that afternoon.

"Number four: those two bullets with the crosses in their snoots.

"Number five: the jewel case.

"Number six: that bunch of yellow hair.

"Number seven: the fact that the dead man's shoe and collar buttons were carried away.

"Number eight: the wallet, with two ten-dollars bills, three clippings, and the list in it, found in the road.

"Number nine: finding the shoe next day, wrapped up in a five-day-old Philadelphia paper, and with the missing collar buttons, four more, and a rusty key in it.

"That's the list. If they mean anything at all, they mean that Emil Bonfils whoever he is—was flimflammed out of something by Gantvoort in Paris in 1902, and that Bonfils came to get it back. He picked Gantvoort up last night in a stolen car, bringing his typewriter with him—for God knows what reason! Gantvoort put up an argument, so Bonfils bashed in his noodle with the typewriter, and then went through his pockets, apparently not taking anything. He decided that what he was looking for was in Gantvoort's left shoe, so he took the shoe away with him. And then—but there's no sense to the collar button trick, or the phony list, or—"

"Yes there is!" I cut in, sitting up, wide awake now. "That's our tenth clew—the one we're going to follow from now on. That list was, except for Gantvoort's name and address, a fake. Our people would have found at least one of the five people whose names were on it if it had been on the level. But they didn't find the least trace of any of them. And two of the addresses were of street numbers that didn't exist!

"That list was faked up, put in the wallet with the clippings and twenty dollars—to make the play stronger—and planted in the road near the car to throw us off-track. And if that's so, then it's a hundred to one that the rest of the things were cooked up too.

"From now on I'm considering all those nine lovely clews as nine bum steers. And I'm going just exactly contrary to them. I'm looking for a man whose name isn't Emil Bonfils, and whose initials aren't either E or B; who isn't French, and who wasn't in Paris in 1902. A man who hasn't light hair, doesn't carry a .45-caliber pistol, and has no interest in Personal advertisements in newspapers. A man who didn't kill Gantvoort to recover anything that could have been hidden in a shoe or on a collar button. That's the sort of a guy I'm hunting for now!"

The detective-sergeant screwed up his little green eyes reflectively and scratched his head.

"Maybe that ain't so foolish!" he said. "You might be right at that. Suppose you are—what then? That Dexter kitten didn't do it—it cost her three-quarters of a million. Her brother didn't do it—he's

THE TENTH CLEW

in New York. And, besides, you don't croak a guy just because you think he's too old to marry your sister. Charles Gantvoort? He and his wife are the only ones who make any money out of the old man dying before the new will was signed. We have only their word for it that Charles was home that night. The servants didn't see him between eight and eleven. You were there, and you didn't see him until eleven. But me and you both believe him when he says he was home all that evening. And neither of us think he bumped the old man off—though of course he might. Who then?"

"This Creda Dexter," I suggested, "was marrying Gantvoort for his money, wasn't she? You don't think she was in love with him, do you?"

"No. I figure, from what I saw of her, that she was in love with the million and a half."

"All right," I went on. "Now she isn't exactly homely—not by a long shot. Do you reckon Gantvoort was the only man who ever fell for her?"

"I got you! I got you!" O'Gar exclaimed. "You mean there might have been some young fellow in the running who didn't have any million and a half behind him, and who didn't take kindly to being nosed out by a man who did. Maybe—maybe."

"Well, suppose we bury all this stuff we've been working on and try out that angle."

"Suits me," he said. "Starting in the morning, then, we spend our time hunting for Gantvoort's rival for the paw of this Dexter kitten."

CHAPTER V

"Meet Mr. Smith"

Right or wrong, that's what we did. We stowed all those lovely clews away in a drawer, locked the drawer, and forgot them. Then we set out to find Creda Dexter's masculine acquaintances and sift them for the murderer.

But it wasn't as simple as it sounded.

All our digging into her past failed to bring to light one man who could be considered a suitor. She and her brother had been in San Francisco three years. We traced them back the length of that period, from apartment to apartment. We questioned everyone we could find who even knew her by sight. And nobody could tell us of a single man who had shown an interest in her besides Gantvoort. Nobody, apparently, had ever seen her with any man except Gantvoort or her brother.

All of which, while not getting us ahead, at least convinced us that we were on the right trail. There must have been, we argued, at least one man in her life in those three years besides Gantvoort. She wasn't—unless we were very much mistaken—the sort of woman who would discourage masculine attention; and she was certainly endowed by nature to attract it. And if there was another man, then the very fact that he had been kept so thoroughly under cover strengthened the probability of him having been mixed up in Gantvoort's death.

We were unsuccessful in learning where the Dexters had lived before they came to San Francisco, but we weren't so very interested in their earlier life. Of course it was possible that some old-time lover had come upon the scene again recently; but in that case it should have been easier to find the recent connection than the old one.

There was no doubt, our explorations showed, that Gantvoort's son had been correct in thinking the Dexters were fortune hunters. All their activities pointed to that, although there seemed to be nothing downright criminal in their pasts.

I went up against Creda Dexter again, spending an entire afternoon in her apartment, banging away with question after question, all directed toward her former love affairs. Who had she thrown over for Gantvoort and his million and a half? And the answer was always *nobody*—an answer that I didn't choose to believe.

We had Creda Dexter shadowed night and day—and it car-

THE TENTH CLEW

ried us ahead not an inch. Perhaps she suspected that she was being watched. Anyway, she seldom left her apartment, and then on only the most innocent of errands. We had her apartment watched whether she was in it or not. Nobody visited it. We tapped her telephone—and all our listening-in netted us nothing. We had her mail covered—and she didn't receive a single letter, not even an advertisement.

Meanwhile, we had learned where the three clippings found in the wallet had come from—from the Personal columns of a New York, a Chicago, and a Portland newspaper. The one in the Portland paper had appeared two days before the murder, the Chicago one four days before, and the New York one five days before. All three of those papers would have been on the San Francisco newsstands the day of the murder—ready to be purchased and cut out by anyone who was looking for material to confuse detectives with.

The Agency's Paris correspondent had found no less than six Emil Bonfilses—all bloomers so far as our job was concerned—and had a line on three more.

But O'Gar and I weren't worrying over Emil Bonfils any more—that angle was dead and buried. We were plugging away at our new task—the finding of Gantvoort's rival.

Thus the days passed, and thus the matter stood when Madden Dexter was due to arrive home from New York.

Our New York branch had kept an eye on him until he left that city, and had advised us of his departure, so I knew what train he was coming on. I wanted to put a few questions to him before his sister saw him. He could tell me what I wanted to know, and he might be willing to if I could get to him before his sister had an opportunity to shut him up.

If I had known him by sight I could have picked him up when he left his train at Oakland, but I didn't know him; and I didn't want to carry Charles Gantvoort or anyone else along with me to pick him out for me.

DETECTIVE STORIES

So I went up to Sacramento that morning, and boarded his train there. I put my card in an envelope and gave it to a messenger boy in the station. Then I followed the boy through the train, while he called out:

"Mr. Dexter! Mr. Dexter!"

In the last car—the observation-club car—a slender, dark-haired man in well-made tweeds turned from watching the station platform through a window and held out his hand to the boy.

I studied him while he nervously tore open the envelope and read my card. His chin trembled slightly just now, emphasizing the weakness of a face that couldn't have been strong at its best. Between twenty-five and thirty, I placed him; with his hair parted in the middle and slicked down; large, too-expressive brown eyes; small well-shaped nose; neat brown mustache; very red, soft lips—that type.

I dropped into the vacant chair beside him when he looked up from the card.

"You are Mr. Dexter?"

"Yes," he said. "I suppose it's about Mr. Gantvoort's death that you want to see me?"

"Uh-huh. I wanted to ask you a few questions, and since I happened to be in Sacramento, I thought that by riding back on the train with you I could ask them without taking up too much of your time."

"If there's anything I can tell you," he assured me, "I'll be only too glad to do it. But I told the New York detectives all I knew, and they didn't seem to find it of much value."

"Well, the situation has changed some since you left New York." I watched his face closely as I spoke. "What we thought of no value then may be just what we want now."

I paused while he moistened his lips and avoided my eyes. He may not know anything, I thought, but he's certainly jumpy. I let him wait a few minutes while I pretended deep thoughtfulness. If I played him right, I was confident I could turn him inside out. He didn't seem to be made of very tough material.

THE TENTH CLEW

We were sitting with our heads close together, so that the four or five other passengers in the car wouldn't overhear our talk; and that position was in my favor. One of the things that every detective knows is that it's often easy to get information—even a confession—out of a feeble nature simply by putting your face close to his and talking in a loud tone. I couldn't talk loud here, but the closeness of our faces was by itself an advantage.

"Of the men with whom your sister was acquainted," I came out with it at last, "who, outside of Mr. Gantvoort, was the most attentive?"

He swallowed audibly, looked out of the window, fleetingly at me, and then out of the window again.

"Really, I couldn't say."

"All right. Let's get at it this way. Suppose we check off one by one all the men who were interested in her and in whom she was interested."

He continued to stare out of the window.

"Who's first?" I pressed him.

His gaze nickered around to meet mine for a second, with a sort of timid desperation in his eyes.

"I know it sounds foolish, but I, her brother, couldn't give you the name of even one man in whom Creda was interested before she met Gantvoort. She never, so far as I know, had the slightest feeling for any man before she met him. Of course it is possible that there may have been someone that I didn't know anything about, but—"

It did sound foolish, right enough! The Creda Dexter I had talked to—a sleek kitten as O'Gar had put it—didn't impress me as being at all likely to go very long without having at least one man in tow. This pretty little guy in front of me was lying. There couldn't be any other explanation.

I went at him tooth and nail. But when we reached Oakland early that night he was still sticking to his original statement—that Gantvoort was the only one of his sister's suitors that he knew anything about. And I knew that I had blundered, had underrated

Madden Dexter, had played my hand wrong in trying to shake him down too quickly—in driving too directly at the point I was interested in. He was either a lot stronger than I had figured him, or his interest in concealing Gantvoort's murderer was much greater than I had thought it would be.

But I had this much: if Dexter was lying—and there couldn't be much doubt of that—then Gantvoort had had a rival, and Madden Dexter believed or knew that this rival had killed Gantvoort.

When we left the train at Oakland I knew I was licked, that he wasn't going to tell me what I wanted to know—not this night, anyway. But I clung to him, stuck at his side when we boarded the ferry for San Francisco, in spite of the obviousness of his desire to get away from me. There's always a chance of something unexpected happening; so I continued to ply him with questions as our boat left the slip.

Presently a man came toward where we were sitting, a big burly man in a light overcoat, carrying a black bag.

"Hello, Madden!" he greeted my companion, striding over to him with outstretched hand. "Just got in and was trying to remember your phone number," he said, setting down his bag, as they shook hands warmly.

Madden Dexter turned to me.

"I want you to meet Mr. Smith," he told me, and then gave my name to the big man, adding, "he's with the Continental Detective Agency here."

That tag—clearly a warning for Smith's benefit—brought me to my feet, all watchfulness. But the ferry was crowded—a hundred persons were within sight of us, all around us. I relaxed, smiled pleasantly, and shook hands with Smith. Whoever Smith was, and whatever connection he might have with the murder—and if he hadn't any, why should Dexter have been in such a hurry to tip him off to my identity?—he couldn't do anything here. The crowd around us was all to my advantage.

That was my second mistake of the day.

THE TENTH CLEW

Smith's left hand had gone into his overcoat pocket—or rather, through one of those vertical slits that certain styles of overcoats have so that inside pockets may be reached without unbuttoning the overcoat. His hand had gone through that slit, and his coat had fallen away far enough for me to see a snub-nosed automatic in his hand—shielded from everyone's sight but mine—pointing at my waist-line.

"Shall we go on deck?" Smith asked—and it was an order.

I hesitated. I didn't like to leave all these people who were so blindly standing and sitting around us. But Smith's face wasn't the face of a cautious man. He had the look of one who might easily disregard the presence of a hundred witnesses.

I turned around and walked through the crowd. His right hand lay familiarly on my shoulder as he walked behind me; his left hand held his gun, under the overcoat, against my spine.

The deck was deserted. A heavy fog, wet as rain—the fog of San Francisco Bay's winter nights—lay over boat and water, and had driven everyone else inside. It hung about us, thick and impenetrable; I couldn't see so far as the end of the boat, in spite of the lights glowing overhead.

I stopped.

Smith prodded me in the back.

"Farther away, where we can talk," he rumbled in my ear.

I went on until I reached the rail.

The entire back of my head burned with sudden fire . . . tiny points of light glittered in the blackness before me . . . grew larger . . . came rushing toward me. . . .

CHAPTER VI

"Those damned horns!"

Semi-consciousness! I found myself mechanically keeping afloat somehow and trying to get out of my overcoat. The back of my head throbbed devilishly. My eyes burned. I felt heavy and logged, as if I had swallowed gallons of water.

The fog hung low and thick on the water—there was nothing else to be seen anywhere. By the time I had freed myself of the encumbering overcoat my head had cleared somewhat, but with returning consciousness came increased pain.

A light glimmered mistily off to my left, and then vanished. From out of the misty blanket, from every direction, in a dozen different keys, from near and far, fog-horns sounded. I stopped swimming and floated on my back, trying to determine my whereabouts.

After a while I picked out the moaning, evenly spaced blasts of the Alcatraz siren. But they told me nothing. They came to me out of the fog without direction—seemed to beat down upon me from straight above.

I was somewhere in San Francisco Bay, and that was all I knew, though I suspected the current was sweeping me out toward the Golden Gate.

A little while passed, and I knew that I had left the path of the Oakland ferries—no boat had passed close to me for some time. I was glad to be out of that track. In this fog a boat was a lot more likely to run me down than to pick me up.

The water was chilling me, so I turned over and began swimming, just vigorously enough to keep my blood circulating while I saved my strength until I had a definite goal to try for.

A horn began to repeat its roaring note nearer and nearer, and presently the lights of the boat upon which it was fixed came into sight. One of the Sausalito ferries, I thought.

It came quite close to me, and I hallooed until I was breathless and my throat was raw. But the boat's siren, crying its warning, drowned my shouts.

The boat went on and the fog closed in behind it.

The current was stronger now, and my attempts to attract the attention of the Sausalito ferry had left me weaker. I floated, letting the water sweep me where it would, resting.

THE TENTH CLEW

Another light appeared ahead of me suddenly—hung there for an instant—disappeared.

I began to yell, and worked my arms and legs madly, trying to drive myself through the water to where it had been.

I never saw it again.

Weariness settled upon me, and a sense of futility. The water was no longer cold. I was warm with a comfortable, soothing numbness. My head stopped throbbing; there was no feeling at all in it now. No lights, now, but the sound of fog-horns . . . fog-horns . . . fog-horns ahead of me, behind me, to either side; annoying me, irritating me.

But for the moaning horns I would have ceased all effort. They had become the only disagreeable detail of my situation—the water was pleasant, fatigue was pleasant. But the horns tormented me. I cursed them petulantly and decided to swim until I could no longer hear them, and then, in the quiet of the friendly fog, go to sleep. . . .

Now and then I would doze, to be goaded into wakefulness by the wailing voice of a siren.

"Those damned horns! Those damned horns!" I complained aloud, again and again.

One of them, I found presently, was bearing down upon me from behind, growing louder and stronger. I turned and waited. Lights, dun and steaming, came into view.

With exaggerated caution to avoid making the least splash, I swam off to one side. When this nuisance was past I could go to sleep. I sniggered softly to myself as the lights drew abreast, feeling a foolish triumph in my cleverness in eluding the boat. Those damned horns. . . .

Life—the hunger for life—all at once surged back into my being.

I screamed at the passing boat, and with every iota of my being struggled toward it. Between strokes I tilted up my head and screamed. . . .

DETECTIVE STORIES

CHAPTER VII

"You have a lot of fun, don't you?"

When I returned to consciousness for the second time that evening, I was lying on my back on a baggage truck, which was moving. Men and women were crowding around, walking beside the truck, staring at me with curious eyes. I sat up.

"Where are we?" I asked.

A little red-faced man in uniform answered my question.

"Just landing in Sausalito. Lay still. We'll take you over to the hospital."

I looked around.

"How long before this boat goes back to San Francisco?"

"Leaves right away."

I slid off the truck and started back aboard the boat.

"I'm going with it," I said.

Half an hour later, shivering and shaking in my wet clothes, keeping my mouth clamped tight so that my teeth wouldn't sound like a dice-game, I climbed into a taxi at the Ferry Building and went to my flat.

There, I swallowed half a pint of whisky, rubbed myself with a coarse towel until my skin was sore, and, except for an enormous weariness and a worse headache, I felt almost human again.

I reached O'Gar by phone, asked him to come up to my flat right away, and then called up Charles Gantvoort.

"Have you seen Madden Dexter yet?" I asked him.

"No, but I talked to him over the phone. He called me up as soon as he got in. I asked him to meet me in Mr. Abernathy's office in the morning, so we could go over that business he transacted for Father."

"Can you call him up now and tell him that you have been called out of town—will have to leave early in the morning—and that you'd like to run over to his apartment and see him tonight?"

"Why yes, if you wish."

"Good! Do that. I'll call for you in a little while and go over to see him with you."

"What is—"

"I'll tell you about it when I see you," I cut him off.

O'Gar arrived as I was finishing dressing.

"So he told you something?" he asked, knowing of my plan to meet Dexter on the train and question him.

"Yes," I said with sour sarcasm, "but I came near forgetting what it was. I grilled him all the way from Sacramento to Oakland, and couldn't get a whisper out of him. On the ferry coming over he introduces me to a man he calls Mr. Smith, and he tells Mr. Smith that I'm a gum-shoe. This, mind you, all happens in the middle of a crowded ferry! Mr. Smith puts a gun in my belly, marches me out on deck, raps me across the back of the head, and dumps me into the bay."

"You have a lot of fun, don't you?" O'Gar grinned, and then wrinkled his forehead. "Looks like Smith would be the man we want then—the buddy who turned the Gantvoort trick. But what the hell did he want to give himself away by chucking you overboard for?"

"Too hard for me," I confessed, while trying to find which of my hats and caps would sit least heavily upon my bruised head. "Dexter knew I was hunting for one of his sister's former lovers, of course. And he must have thought I knew a whole lot more than I do, or he wouldn't have made that raw play—tipping my mitt to Smith right in front of me.

"It may be that after Dexter lost his head and made that break on the ferry, Smith figured that I'd be on to him soon, if not right away; and so he'd take a desperate chance on putting me out of the way. But we'll know all about it in a little while," I said, as we went down to the waiting taxi and set out for Gantvoort's.

"You ain't counting on Smith being in sight, are you?" the detective-sergeant asked.

"No. He'll be holed up somewhere until he sees how things are going. But Madden Dexter will have to be out in the open to protect himself. He has an alibi, so he's in the clear so far as the actual killing is concerned. And with me supposed to be dead, the more he stays in the open, the safer he is. But it's a cinch that he knows what this is all about, though he wasn't necessarily involved in it. As near as I could see, he didn't go out on deck with Smith and me tonight. Anyway he'll be home. And this time he's going to talk—he's going to tell his little story!"

Charles Gantvoort was standing on his front steps when we reached his house. He climbed into our taxi and we headed for the Dexters' apartment. We didn't have time to answer any of the questions that Gantvoort was firing at us with every turning of the wheels.

"He's home and expecting you?" I asked him.

"Yes."

Then we left the taxi and went into the apartment building.

"Mr. Gantvoort to see Mr. Dexter," he told the Philippine boy at the switchboard.

The boy spoke into the phone.

"Go right up," he told us.

At the Dexters' door I stepped past Gantvoort and pressed the button.

Creda Dexter opened the door. Her amber eyes widened and her smile faded as I stepped past her into the apartment.

I walked swiftly down the little hallway and turned into the first room through whose open door a light showed.

And came face to face with Smith!

We were both surprised, but his astonishment was a lot more profound than mine. Neither of us had expected to see the other; but I had known he was still alive, while he had every reason for thinking me at the bottom of the bay.

I took advantage of his greater bewilderment to the extent of two steps toward him before he went into action.

One of his hands swept down.

THE TENTH CLEW

I threw my right fist at his face—threw it with every ounce of my 180 pounds behind it, re-enforced by the memory of every second I had spent in the water, and every throb of my battered head.

His hand, already darting down for his pistol, came back up too late to fend off my punch.

Something clicked in my hand as it smashed into his face, and my hand went numb.

But he went down—and lay where he fell.

I jumped across his body to a door on the opposite side of the room, pulling my gun loose with my left hand.

"Dexter's somewhere around!" I called over my shoulder to O'Gar, who with Gantvoort and Creda, was coming through the door by which I had entered. "Keep your eyes open!"

I dashed through the four other rooms of the apartment, pulling closet doors open, looking everywhere—and I found nobody.

Then I returned to where Creda Dexter was trying to revive Smith, with the assistance of O'Gar and Gantvoort.

The detective-sergeant looked over his shoulder at me.

"Who do you think this joker is?" he asked.

"My friend Mr. Smith."

"Gantvoort says he's Madden Dexter."

I looked at Charles Gantvoort, who nodded his head.

"This is Madden Dexter," he said.

CHAPTER VIII

"I hope you swing!"

We worked upon Dexter for nearly ten minutes before he opened his eyes.

As soon as he sat up we began to shoot questions and accusations at him, hoping to get a confession out of him before he recovered from his shakiness—but he wasn't that shaky.

All we could get out of him was:

"Take me in if you want to. If I've got anything to say I'll say it to my lawyer, and to nobody eke."

Creda Dexter, who had stepped back after her brother came to, and was standing a little way off, watching us, suddenly came forward and caught me by the arm.

"What have you got on him?" she demanded, imperatively.

"I wouldn't want to say," I countered, "but I don't mind telling you this much. We're going to give him a chance in a nice modern court-room to prove that he didn't kill Leopold Gantvoort."

"He was in New York!"

"He was not! He had a friend who went to New York as Madden Dexter and looked after Gantvoort's business under that name. But if this is the real Madden Dexter then the closest he got to New York was when he met his friend on the ferry to get from him the papers connected with the B. F. & F. Iron Corporation transaction; and learned that I had stumbled upon the truth about his alibi—even if I didn't know it myself at the time."

She jerked around to face her brother.

"Is that on the level?" she asked him.

He sneered at her, and went on feeling with the fingers of one hand the spot on his jaw where my fist had landed.

"I'll say all I've got to say to my lawyer," he repeated.

"You will?" she shot back at him. "Well, I'll say what I've got to say right now!"

She flung around to face me again.

"Madden is not my brother at all! My name is Ives. Madden and I met in St. Louis about four years ago, drifted around together for a year or so, and then came to Frisco. He was a con man—still is. He made Mr. Gantvoort's acquaintance six or seven months ago, and was getting him all ribbed up to unload a fake invention on him. He brought him here a couple of times, and introduced me to him as his sister. We usually posed as brother and sister.

"Then, after Mr. Gantvoort had been here a couple times, Madden decided to change his game. He thought Mr. Gantvoort liked

THE TENTH CLEW

me, and that we could get more money out of him by working a fancy sort of badger-game[2] on him. I was to lead the old man on until I had him wrapped around my finger—until we had him tied up so tight he couldn't get away—had something on him—something good and strong. Then we were going to shake him down for plenty of money.

"Everything went along fine for a while. He fell for me—fell hard. And finally he asked me to marry him. We had never figured on that. Blackmail was our game. But when he asked me to marry him I tried to call Madden off. I admit the old man's money had something to do with it—it influenced me—but I had come to like him a little for himself. He was mighty fine in lots of ways—nicer than anybody I had ever known.

"So I told Madden all about it, and suggested that we drop the other plan, and that I marry Gantvoort. I promised to see that Madden was kept supplied with money—I knew I could get whatever I wanted from Mr. Gantvoort. And I was on the level with Madden. I liked Mr. Gantvoort, but Madden had found him and brought him around to me; and so I wasn't going to run out on Madden. I was willing to do all I could for him.

"But Madden wouldn't hear of it. He'd have got more money in the long run by doing as I suggested—but he wanted his little handful right away. And to make him more unreasonable he got one of his jealous streaks. He beat me one night!

"That settled it. I made up my mind to ditch him. I told Mr. Gantvoort that my brother was bitterly opposed to our marrying, and he could see that Madden was carrying a grouch. So he arranged to send Madden East on that steel business, to get him out of the way until we were off on our wedding trip. And we thought Madden was completely deceived—but I should have known that he would see through our scheme. We planned to be gone about a year, and by that time I thought Madden would have forgotten me—

---

2   A confidence game in which a person in lured into a sexually compromising situation and then blackmailed.

or I'd be fixed to handle him if he tried to make any trouble.

"As soon as I heard that Mr. Gantvoort had been killed I had a hunch that Madden had done it. But then it seemed like a certainty that he was in New York the next day, and I thought I had done him an injustice. And I was glad he was out of it. But now—"

She whirled around to her erstwhile confederate.

"Now I hope you swing, you big sap!"

She spun around to me again. No sleek kitten, this, but a furious, spitting cat, with claws and teeth bared.

"What kind of looking fellow was the one who went to New York for him?"

I described the man I had talked to on the train.

"Evan Felter," she said, after a moment of thought. "He used to work with Madden. You'll probably find him hiding in Los Angeles. Put the screws on him and he'll spill all he knows—he's a weak sister! The chances are he didn't know what Madden's game was until it was all over."

"How do you like that?" she spat at Madden Dexter. "How do you like that for a starter? You messed up my little party, did you? Well, I'm going to spend every minute of my time from now until they pop you off helping them pop you!"

And she did, too—with her assistance it was no trick at all to gather up the rest of the evidence we needed to hang him. And I don't believe her enjoyment of her three-quarters of a million dollars is spoiled a bit by any qualms over what she did to Madden. She's a very respectable woman *now*, and glad to be free of the con man.

ZIGZAGS OF TREACHERY

ll I know about Dr. Estep's death," I said, "is the stuff in the papers." Vance Richmond's lean gray face took on an expression of distaste.

"The newspapers aren't always either thorough or accurate. I'll give you the salient points as I know them; though I suppose you'll want to go over the ground for yourself, and get your information first-hand."

I nodded, and the attorney went on, shaping each word precisely with his thin lips before giving it sound.

"Dr. Estep came to San Francisco in 1898 or 1899—a young man of twenty-five, just through qualifying for his license. He opened an office here, and, as you probably know, became in time a rather excellent surgeon. He married two or three years after he came here. There were no children. He and his wife seem to have been a bit happier together than the average.

"Of his life before coming to San Francisco, nothing is known. He told his wife briefly that he had been born and raised in Parkersburg, W. Va., but that his home life had been so unpleasant that he was trying to forget it, and that he did not like to talk—or even think—about it. Bear that in mind.

"Two weeks ago—on the third of the month—a woman came to his office, in the afternoon. His office was in his residence on

Pine Street. Lucy Coe, who was Dr. Estep's nurse and assistant, showed the woman into his office, and then went back to her own desk in the reception room.

"She didn't hear anything the doctor said to the woman, but through the closed door she heard the woman's voice now and then—a high and anguished voice, apparently pleading. Most of the words were lost upon the nurse, but she heard one coherent sentence. 'Please! Please!' she heard the woman cry. 'Don't turn me away!' The woman was with Dr. Estep for about fifteen minutes, and left sobbing into a handkerchief. Dr. Estep said nothing about the caller either to his nurse or to his wife, who didn't learn of it until after his death.

"The next day, toward evening, while the nurse was putting on her hat and coat preparatory to leaving for home, Dr. Estep came out of his office, with his hat on and a letter in his hand. The nurse saw that his face was pale—'white as my uniform,' she says—and he walked with the care of one who takes pains to keep from staggering.

"She asked him if he was ill. 'Oh, it's nothing!' he told her. 'I'll be all right in a very few minutes.' Then he went on out. The nurse left the house just behind him, and saw him drop the letter he had carried into the mailbox on the corner, after which he returned to the house.

"Mrs. Estep, coming downstairs ten minutes later—it couldn't have been any later than that—heard, just as she reached the first floor, the sound of a shot from her husband's office. She rushed into it, meeting nobody. Her husband stood by his desk, swaying, with a hole in his right temple and a smoking revolver in his hand. Just as she reached him and put her arms around him, he fell across the desk—dead."

"Anybody else—any of the servants, for instance—able to say that Mrs. Estep didn't go to the office until after the shot?" I asked.

The attorney shook his head sharply.

"No, damn it! That's where the rub comes in!"

His voice, after this one flare of feeling, resumed its level, incisive tone, and he went on with his tale.

"The next day's papers had accounts of Dr. Estep's death, and late that morning the woman who had called upon him the day before his death came to the house. She is Dr. Estep's first wife—which is to say, his legal wife! There seems to be no reason—not the slightest—for doubting it, as much as I'd like to. They were married in Philadelphia in 1896. She has a certified copy of the marriage record. I had the matter investigated in Philadelphia, and it's a certain fact that Dr. Estep and this woman—Edna Fife was her maiden name—were really married.

"She says that Estep, after living with her in Philadelphia for two years, deserted her. That would have been in 1898, or just before he came to San Francisco. She has sufficient proof of her identity—that she really is the Edna Fife who married him; and my agents in the East found positive proof that Estep had practiced for two years in Philadelphia.

"And here is another point. I told you that Estep had said he was born and raised in Parkersburg. I had inquiries made there, but found nothing to show that he had ever lived there, and found ample evidence to show that he had never lived at the address he had given his wife. There is, then, nothing for us to believe except that his talk of an unhappy early life was a ruse to ward off embarrassing questions."

"Did you do anything toward finding out whether the doctor and his first wife had ever been divorced?" I asked.

"I'm having that taken care of now, but I hardly expect to learn that they had. That would be too crude. To get on with my story: This woman—the first Mrs. Estep—said that she had just recently learned her husband's whereabouts, and had come to see him in an attempt to effect a reconciliation. When she called upon him the afternoon before his death, he asked for a little time to make up his mind what he should do. He promised to give her his decision in two days. My personal opinion, after talking to the woman several times, is that she had learned that he had accumulated some money, and that her interest was more in getting the money than in getting him. But that, of course, is neither here nor there.

"At first the authorities accepted the natural explanation of the doctor's death—suicide. But after the first wife's appearance, the second wife—my client—was arrested and charged with murder.

"The police theory is that after his first wife's visit, Dr. Estep told his second wife the whole story; and that she, brooding over the knowledge that he had deceived her, that she was not his wife at all, finally worked herself up into a rage, went to the office after his nurse had left for the day, and shot him with the revolver that she knew he always kept in his desk.

"I don't know, of course, just what evidence the prosecution has, but from the newspapers I gather that the case against her will be built upon her fingerprints on the revolver with which he was killed; an upset inkwell on his desk; splashes of ink on the dress she wore; and an inky print of her hand on a torn newspaper on his desk.

"Unfortunately, but perfectly naturally, one of the first things she did was to take the revolver out of her husband's hand. That accounts for her prints on it. He fell—as I told you—just as she put her arms around him, and, though her memory isn't very clear on this point, the probabilities are that he dragged her with him when he fell across the desk. That accounts for the upset inkwell, the torn paper, and the splashes of ink. But the prosecution will try to persuade the jury that those things all happened before the shooting—that they are proofs of a struggle."

"Not so bad," I gave my opinion.

"Or pretty damned bad—depending on how you look at it. And this is the worst time imaginable for a thing like this to come up! Within the past few months there have been no less than five widely advertised murders of men by women who were supposed to have been betrayed, or deceived, or one thing or another.

ZIGZAGS OF TREACHERY

"Not one of those five women was convicted. As a result, we have the press, the public, and even the pulpit, howling for a stricter enforcement of justice. The newspapers are lined up against Mrs. Estep as strongly as their fear of libel suits will permit. The women's clubs are lined up against her. Everybody is clamouring for an example to be made of her.

"Then, as if all that isn't enough, the prosecuting attorney has lost his last two big cases, and he'll be out for blood this time—election day isn't far off."

The calm, even, precise voice was gone now. In its place was a passionate eloquence.

"I don't know what you think," Richmond cried. "You're a detective. This is an old story to you. You're more or less callous, I suppose, and sceptical of innocence in general. But I *know* that Mrs. Estep didn't kill her husband. I don't say it because she's my client! I was Dr. Estep's attorney, and his friend, and if I thought Mrs. Estep guilty, I'd do everything in my power to help convict her. But I know as well as I know anything that she didn't kill him—couldn't have killed him.

"She's innocent. But I know too that if I go into court with no defence beyond what I now have, she'll be convicted! There has been too much leniency shown feminine criminals, public sentiment says. The pendulum will swing the other way—Mrs. Estep, if convicted, will get the limit. I'm putting it up to you! Can you save her?"

"Our best mark is the letter he mailed just before he died," I said, ignoring everything he said that didn't have to do with the facts of the case. "It's good betting that when a man writes and mails a letter and then shoots himself, that the letter isn't altogether unconnected with the suicide. Did you ask the wife about the letter?"

"I did, and she denies having received one."

"That wasn't right. If the doctor had been driven to suicide by her appearance, then according to all the rules there are, the letter should have been addressed to her. He might have written one to his second wife, but he would hardly have mailed it. Would she have any reason for lying about it?"

"Yes," the lawyer said slowly, "I think she would. His will leaves everything to the second wife. The first wife, being the only legal wife, will have no difficulty in breaking that will, of course; but if it is shown that the second wife had no knowledge of the first one's existence—that she really believed herself to be Dr. Estep's legal wife—then I think that she will receive at least a portion of the estate. I don't think any court would, under the circumstances, take everything away from her. But if she should be found guilty of murdering Dr. Estep, then no consideration will be shown her, and the first wife will get every penny."

"Did he leave enough to make half of it, say, worth sending an innocent person to the gallows for?"

"He left about half a million, roughly; two hundred and fifty thousand dollars isn't a mean inducement."

"Do you think it would be enough for the first wife—from what you have seen of her?"

"Candidly, I do. She didn't impress me as being a person of many very active scruples."

"Where does this first wife live?" I asked.

"She's staying at the Montgomery Hotel now. Her home is in Louisville, I believe. I don't think you will gain anything by talking to her, however. She has retained Somerset, Somerset and Quill to represent her—a very reputable firm, by the way—and she'll refer you to them. They will tell you nothing. But if there's anything dishonest about her affairs—such as the concealing of Dr. Estep's letter—I'm confident that Somerset, Somerset and Quill know nothing of it."

"Can I talk to the second Mrs. Estep—your client?"

"Not at present, I'm afraid; though perhaps in a day or two. She is on the verge of collapse just now. She has always been delicate; and the shock of her husband's death, followed by her own arrest and imprisonment, has been too much for her. She's in the city jail, you know, held without bail. I've tried to have her transferred to the prisoner's ward of the City Hospital, even; but the authorities seem to think that her illness is simply a ruse. I'm worried about her. She's really in a critical condition."

His voice was losing its calmness again, so I picked up my hat, said something about starting to work at once, and went out. I don't like eloquence: if it isn't effective enough to pierce your hide, it's tiresome; and if it is effective enough, then it muddles your thoughts.

II

I spent the next couple of hours questioning the Estep servants, to no great advantage. None of them had been near the front of the house at the time of the shooting, and none had seen Mrs. Estep immediately prior to her husband's death.

After a lot of hunting, I located Lucy Coe, the nurse, in an apartment on Vallejo Street. She was a small, brisk, businesslike woman of thirty or so. She repeated what Vance Richmond had told me, and could add nothing to it.

That cleaned up the Estep end of the job; and I set out for the Montgomery Hotel, satisfied that my only hope for success—barring miracles, which usually don't happen—lay in finding the letter that I believed Dr. Estep had written to his first wife.

My drag with the Montgomery Hotel management was pretty strong—strong enough to get me anything I wanted that wasn't too far outside the law. So as soon as I got there, I hunted up Stacey, one of the assistant managers.

"This Mrs. Estep who's registered here," I asked, "what do you know about her?"

"Nothing, myself, but if you'll wait a few minutes I'll see what I can learn."

The assistant manager was gone about ten minutes.

DETECTIVE STORIES

"No one seems to know much about her," he told me when he came back. "I've questioned the telephone girls, bellboys, maids, clerks, and the house detective; but none of them could tell me much.

"She registered from Louisville, on the second of the month. She has never stopped here before, and she seems unfamiliar with the city—asks quite a few questions about how to get around. The mail clerks don't remember handling any mail for her, nor do the girls on the switchboard have any record of phone calls for her.

"She keeps regular hours—usually goes out at ten or later in the morning, and gets in before midnight. She doesn't seem to have any callers or friends."

"Will you have her mail watched—let me know what postmarks and return addresses are on any letters she gets?"

"Certainly."

"And have the girls on the switchboard put their ears up against any talking she does over the wire?"

"Yes."

"Is she in her room now?"

"No, she went out a little while ago."

"Fine! I'd like to go up and take a look at her stuff."

Stacey looked sharply at me, and cleared his throat.

"Is it as—ah—important as all that? I want to give you all the assistance I can, but—"

"It's this important," I assured him, "that another woman's life depends on what I can learn about this one."

"All right!" he said. "I'll tell the clerk to let us know if she comes in before we are through; and we'll go right up."

The woman's room held two valises and a trunk, all unlocked, and containing not the least thing of importance—no letters—nothing. So little, in fact, that I was more than half convinced that she had expected her things to be searched.

Downstairs again, I planted myself in a comfortable chair within sight of the key-rack, and waited for a view of this first Mrs. Estep.

ZIGZAGS OF TREACHERY

She came in at 11:15 that night. A large woman of forty-five or fifty, well-dressed, and carrying herself with an air of assurance. Her face was a little too hard as to mouth and chin, but not enough to be ugly. A capable-looking woman—a woman who would get what she went after.

III

Eight o'clock was striking as I went into the Montgomery lobby the next morning and picked out a chair, this time within eye-range of the elevators.

At 10:30 Mrs. Estep left the hotel, with me in her wake. Her denial that a letter from her husband, written immediately before his death, had come to her didn't fit in with the possibilities as I saw them. And a good motto for the detective business is, "When in doubt—shadow 'em."

After eating breakfast at a restaurant on O'Farrell Street, she turned toward the shopping district; and for a long, long time—though I suppose it was a lot shorter than it seemed to me—she led me through the most densely packed portions of the most crowded department stores she could find.

She didn't buy anything, but she did a lot of thorough looking, with me muddling along behind her, trying to act like a little fat guy on an errand for his wife, while stout women bumped me and thin ones prodded me and all sorts got in my way and walked on my feet.

Finally, after I had sweated off a couple of pounds, she left the shopping district, and cut up through Union Square, walking along casually, as if out for a stroll.

Three-quarters way through, she turned abruptly, and retraced her steps, looking sharply at everyone she passed. I was on a bench, reading a stray page from a day-old newspaper, when she went by. She walked on down Post Street to Kearney, stopping every now and then to look—or to pretend to look—in store windows, while I ambled along sometimes behind her, sometimes almost by her side, and sometimes in front.

She was trying to check up the people around her, trying to determine whether she was being followed or not. But here, in the busy part of town, that gave me no cause for worry. On a less crowded street it might have been different, though not necessarily so.

There are four rules for shadowing: Keep behind your subject as much as possible; never try to hide from him; act in a natural manner no matter what happens; and never meet his eye. Obey them, and, except in unusual circumstances, shadowing is the easiest thing that a sleuth has to do.

Assured, after a while, that no one was following her, Mrs. Estep turned back toward Powell Street, and got into a taxicab at the St. Francis stand. I picked out a modest touring car from the rank of hire-cars along the Geary Street side of Union Square, and set out after her.

Our route was out Post Street to Laguna, where the taxi presently swung into the curb and stopped. The woman got out, paid the driver, and went up the steps of an apartment building. With idling engine my own car had come to rest against the opposite curb in the block above.

As the taxicab disappeared around a corner, Mrs. Estep came out of the apartment-building doorway, went back to the sidewalk, and started down Laguna Street.

"Pass her," I told my chauffeur, and we drew down upon her.

As we came abreast, she went up the front steps of another building, and this time she rang a bell. These steps belonged to a building apparently occupied by four flats, each with its separate door, and the button she had pressed belonged to the right-hand second-story flat.

Under cover of my car's rear curtains, I kept my eye on the doorway while my driver found a convenient place to park in the next block.

I kept my eye on the vestibule until 5:35 p.m., when she came out, walked to the Sutter Street car line, returned to the Montgomery, and went to her room.

I called up the Old Man—the Continental Detective Agency's San Francisco manager—and asked him to detail an operative to learn who and what were the occupants of the Laguna Street flat.

That night Mrs. Estep ate dinner at her hotel, and went to a show afterward, and she displayed no interest in possible shadowers. She went to her room at a little after eleven, and I knocked off for the day.

IV

The following morning I turned the woman over to Dick Foley, and went back to the Agency to wait for Bob Teal, the operative who had investigated the Laguna Street flat. He came in at a little after ten.

"A guy named Jacob Ledwich lives there," Bob said. "He's a crook of some sort, but I don't know just what. He and 'Wop' Healey are friendly, so he must be a crook! 'Porky' Grout says he's an ex-bunko man who is in with a gambling ring now; but Porky would tell you a bishop was a safe-ripper if he thought it would mean five bucks for himself.

"This Ledwich goes out mostly at night, and he seems to be pretty prosperous. Probably a high-class worker of some sort. He's got a Buick—license number 645-221—that he keeps in a garage around the corner from his flat. But he doesn't seem to use the car much."

"What sort of looking fellow is he?"

"A big guy—six feet or better—and he'll weigh a couple hundred easy. He's got a funny mug on him. It's broad and heavy around the cheeks and jaw, but his mouth is a little one that looks like it was made for a smaller man. He's no youngster—middle-aged."

"Suppose you tail him around for a day or two, Bob, and see what he's up to. Try to get a room or apartment in the neighborhood—a place that you can cover his front door from."

V

Vance Richmond's lean face lighted up as soon as I mentioned Ledwich's name to him.

"Yes!" he exclaimed. "He was a friend, or at least an acquaintance, of Dr. Estep's. I met him once—a large man with a peculiarly inadequate mouth. I dropped in to see the doctor one day, and Ledwich was in the office. Dr. Estep introduced us."

"What do you know about him?"

"Nothing."

"Don't you know whether he was intimate with the doctor, or just a casual acquaintance?"

"No. For all I know, he might have been a friend, a patient, or almost anything. The doctor never spoke of him to me, and nothing passed between them while I was there that afternoon. I simply gave the doctor some information he had asked for and left. Why?"

"Dr. Estep's first wife—after going to a lot of trouble to see that she wasn't followed—connected with Ledwich yesterday afternoon. And from what we can learn he seems to be a crook of some sort."

"What would that indicate?"

"I'm not sure what it means, but I can do a lot of guessing. Ledwich knew both the doctor and the doctor's first wife; then it's not a bad bet that *she* knew where her husband was all the time. If she did, then it's another good bet that she was getting money from him right along. Can you check up his accounts and see whether he was passing out any money that can't be otherwise accounted for?"

The attorney shook his head.

"No, his accounts are in rather bad shape, carelessly kept. He must have had more than a little difficulty with his income-tax statements."

"I see. To get back to my guesses: If she knew where he was all the time, and was getting money from him, then why did his first wife finally come to see her husband? Perhaps because—"

"I think I can help you there," Richmond interrupted. "A fortunate investment in lumber nearly doubled Dr. Estep's wealth two or three months ago."

"That's it, then! She learned of it through Ledwich. She demanded, either through Ledwich, or by letter, a rather large share of it—more than the doctor was willing to give. When he refused, she came to see him in person, to demand the money under threat—we'll say—of instant exposure. He thought she was in earnest. Either he couldn't raise the money she demanded, or he was tired of leading a double life. Anyway, he thought it all over, and decided to commit suicide. This is all a guess, or a series of guesses—but it sounds reasonable to me."

"To me, too," the attorney said. "What are you going to do now?"

"I'm still having both of them shadowed—there's no other way of tackling them just now. I'm having the woman looked up in Louisville. But, you understand, I might dig up a whole flock of things on them, and when I got through still be as far as ever from finding the letter Dr. Estep wrote before he died.

"There are plenty of reasons for thinking that the woman destroyed the letter—that would have been her wisest play. But if I can get enough on her, even at that, I can squeeze her into admitting that the letter was written, and that it said something about suicide—if it did. And that will be enough to spring your client. How is she today—any better?"

His thin face lost the animation that had come to it during our discussion of Ledwich, and became bleak.

"She went completely to pieces last night, and was removed to the hospital, where she should have been taken in the first place. To tell you the truth, if she isn't liberated soon, she won't need our help. I've done my utmost to have her released on bail—pulled every wire I know—but there's little likelihood of success in that direction.

"Knowing that she is a prisoner—charged with murdering her husband—is killing her. She isn't young, and she has always been subject to nervous disorders. The bare shock of her husband's death was enough to prostrate her—but now—You've *got* to get her out—and quickly!"

He was striding up and down his office, his voice throbbing with feeling. I left quickly.

VI

From the attorney's office, I returned to the Agency, where I was told that Bob Teal had phoned in the address of a furnished apartment he had rented on Laguna Street. I hopped on a street car, and went up to take a look at it.

But I didn't get that far.

Walking down Laguna Street, after leaving the car, I spied Bob Teal coming toward me. Between Bob and me—also coming toward me—was a big man whom I recognized as Jacob Ledwich: a big man with a big red face around a tiny mouth.

I walked on down the street, passing both Ledwich and Bob, without paying any apparent attention to either. At the next corner I stopped to roll a cigarette, and steal a look at the pair.

And then I came to life!

Ledwich had stopped at a vestibule cigar stand up the street to make a purchase. Bob Teal, knowing his stuff, had passed him and was walking steadily up the street.

He was figuring that Ledwich had either come out for the pur-

ZIGZAGS OF TREACHERY

pose of buying cigars or cigarettes, and would return to his flat with them; or that after making his purchase the big man would proceed to the car line, where, in either event, Bob would wait.

But as Ledwich had stopped before the cigar stand, a man across the street had stepped suddenly into a doorway, and stood there, back in the shadows. This man, I now remembered, had been on the opposite side of the street from Bob and Ledwich, and walking in the same direction.

He, too, was following Ledwich.

By the time Ledwich had finished his business at the stand, Bob had reached Sutter Street, the nearest car line. Ledwich started up the street in that direction. The man in the doorway stepped out and went after him. I followed that one.

A ferry-bound car came down Sutter Street just as I reached the corner. Ledwich and I got aboard together. The mysterious stranger fumbled with a shoe-string several pavements from the corner until the car was moving again, and then he likewise made a dash for it.

He stood beside me on the rear platform, hiding behind a large man in overalls, past whose shoulder he now and then peeped at Ledwich. Bob had gone to the corner above, and was already seated when Ledwich, this amateur detective—there was no doubting his amateur status—and I got on the car.

I sized up the amateur while he strained his neck peeping at Ledwich. He was small, this sleuth, and scrawny and frail. His most noticeable feature was his nose—a limp organ that twitched nervously all the time. His clothes were old and shabby, and he himself was somewhere in his fifties.

After studying him for a few minutes, I decided that he hadn't tumbled to Bob Teal's part in the game. His attention had been too firmly fixed upon Ledwich, and the distance had been too short thus far for him to discover that Bob was also tailing the big man.

So when the seat beside Bob was vacated presently, I chucked my cigarette away, went into the car, and sat down, my back toward the little man with the twitching nose.

"Drop off after a couple of blocks and go back to the apartment. Don't shadow Ledwich any more until I tell you. Just watch his place. There's a bird following him, and I want to see what he's up to," I told Bob in an undertone.

He grunted that he understood, and, after a few minutes, left the car.

At Stockton Street, Ledwich got off, the man with the twitching nose behind him and me in the rear. In that formation we paraded around town all afternoon.

The big man had business in a number of poolrooms, cigar stores, and soft-drink parlors—most of which I knew for places where you can get a bet down on any horse that's running in North America, whether at Tanforan, Tijuana, or Timonium.

Just what Ledwich did in these places, I didn't learn. I was bringing up the rear of the procession, and my interest was centered upon the mysterious little stranger. He didn't enter any of the places behind Ledwich, but loitered in their neighborhoods until Ledwich reappeared.

He had a rather strenuous time of it—laboring mightily to keep out of Ledwich's sight, and only succeeding because we were downtown, where you can get away with almost any sort of shadowing. He certainly made a lot of work for himself, dodging here and there.

After a while, Ledwich shook him.

The big man came out of a cigar store with another man. They got into an automobile that was standing beside the curb and drove away, leaving my man standing on the edge of the sidewalk twitching his nose in chagrin. There was a taxi stand just around the corner, but he either didn't know it or didn't have enough money to pay the fare.

I expected him to return to Laguna Street then, but he didn't. He led me down Kearny Street to Portsmouth, where he stretched himself out on the grass, facedown, lit a black pipe, and lay look-

ZIGZAGS OF TREACHERY

ing dejectedly at the Stevenson Monument,[3] probably without seeing it.

I sprawled on a comfortable piece of sod some distance away—between a Chinese woman with two perfectly round children and an ancient Portuguese in a gaily checkered suit—and we let the afternoon go by.

When the sun had gone low enough for the ground to become chilly, the little man got up, shook himself, and went back up Kearny Street to a cheap lunchroom, where he ate meagerly. Then he entered a hotel a few doors away, took a key from the row of hooks, and vanished down a dark corridor. Running through the register, I found that the key he had taken belonged to a room whose occupant was 'John Boyd, St. Louis, Mo.,' and that he had arrived the day before.

This hotel wasn't of the sort where it is safe to make inquiries, so I went down to the street again, and came to rest on the least conspicuous nearby corner.

Twilight came, and the street—and shop lights were turned on. It got dark. The night traffic of Kearny Street went up and down past me: Filipino boys in their too-dapper clothes, bound for the inevitable blackjack game; gaudy women still heavy-eyed from their day's sleep; plain-clothes men on their way to headquarters, to report before going off duty; Chinese going to or from Chinatown; sailors in pairs, looking for action of any sort; hungry people making for the Italian and French restaurants; worried people going into the bail-bond broker's office on the corner to arrange for the release of friends and relatives whom the police had nabbed; Italians on their homeward journeys from work; odds and ends of furtive-looking citizens on various shady errands.

Midnight came, and no John Boyd, and I called it a day, and went home.

Before going to bed, I talked with Dick Foley over the wire. He

---

3 A monument to Robert Louis Stevenson in Portsmouth Square, San Francisco.

said that Mrs. Estep had done nothing of any importance all day, and had received neither mail nor phone calls. I told him to stop shadowing her until I solved John Boyd's game.

I was afraid Boyd might turn his attention to the woman, and I didn't want him to discover that she was being shadowed. I had already instructed Bob Teal to simply watch Ledwich's flat—to see when he came in and went out, and with whom—and now I told Dick to do the same with the woman.

My guess on this Boyd person was that he and the woman were working together—that she had him watching Ledwich for her, so that the big man couldn't double-cross her. But that was only a guess—and I don't gamble too much on my guesses.

VII

The next morning I dressed myself up in an army shirt and shoes, an old faded cap, and a suit that wasn't downright ragged, but was shabby enough not to stand out too noticeably beside John Boyd's old clothes.

It was a little after nine o'clock when Boyd left his hotel and had breakfast at the grease-joint where he had eaten the night before. Then he went up to Laguna Street, picked himself a corner, and waited for Jacob Ledwich.

He did a lot of waiting. He waited all day, because Ledwich didn't show until after dark. But the little man was well-stocked with patienc e—I'll say that for him. He fidgeted, and stood on one foot and then the other, and even tried sitting on the curb for a while, but he stuck it out.

I took it easy, myself. The furnished apartment Bob Teal had rented to watch Ledwich's flat from was a ground-floor one, across the street and just a little above the corner where Boyd waited. So we could watch him and the flat with one eye.

ZIGZAGS OF TREACHERY

Bob and I sat and smoked and talked all day, taking turns watching the fidgeting man on the corner and Ledwich's door.

Night had just definitely settled when Ledwich came out and started up toward the car line. I slid out into the street, and our parade was under way again—Ledwich leading, Boyd following him, and we following *him*.

Haif a block of this, and I got an idea!

I'm not what you'd call a brilliant thinker—such results as I get are usually the fruits of patience, industry, and unimaginative plugging, helped out now and then, maybe, by a little luck—but I do have my flashes of intelligence. And this was one of them.

Ledwich was about a block ahead of me; Boyd half that distance. Speeding up, I passed Boyd, and caught up with Ledwich. Then I slackened my pace so as to walk beside him, though with no appearance from the rear of having any interest in him.

"Jake," I said, without turning my head, "there's a guy following you!"

The big man almost spoiled my little scheme by stopping dead still, but he caught himself in time, and, taking his cue from me, kept walking.

"Who the hell are you?" he growled.

"Don't get funny!" I snapped back, still looking and walking ahead. "It ain't my funeral. But I was coming up the street when you came out, and I seen this guy duck behind a pole until you was past, and then follow you up."

That got him.

"You sure?"

"Sure! All you got to do to prove it is turn the next corner and wait."

I was two or three steps ahead of him by this time. I turned the corner, and halted, with my back against the brick building front. Ledwich took up the same position at my side.

"Want any help?" I grinned at him—a reckless sort of grin, unless my acting was poor.

"No."

His little lumpy mouth was set ugly, and his blue eyes were hard as pebbles.

I flicked the tail of my coat aside to show him the butt of my gun.

"Want to borrow the rod?" I asked.

"No."

He was trying to figure me out, and small wonder.

"Don't mind if I stick around to see the fun, do you?" I asked mockingly.

There wasn't time for him to answer that. Boyd had quickened his steps, and now he came hurrying around the corner, his nose twitching like a tracking dog's.

Ledwich stepped into the middle of the sidewalk, so suddenly that the little man thudded into him with a grunt. For a moment they stared at each other, and there was recognition between them.

Ledwich shot one big hand out and clamped the other by a shoulder.

"What are you snooping around me for, you rat? Didn't I tell you to keep away from 'Frisco?"

"Aw, Jake!" Boyd begged. "I didn't mean no harm. I just thought that—"

Ledwich silenced him with a shake that clicked his mouth shut, and turned to me.

"A friend of mine," he sneered.

His eyes grew suspicious and hard again and ran up and down me from cap to shoes.

"How'd you know my name?" he demanded.

"A famous man like you?" I asked, in burlesque astonishment.

"Never mind the comedy!" He took a threatening step toward me. "How'd you know my name?"

"None of your damned business," I snapped.

My attitude seemed to reassure him. His face became less suspicious.

"Well," he said slowly, "I owe you something for this trick, and—How are you fixed?"

"I have been dirtier." Dirty is Pacific Coast argot for prosperous.

He looked speculatively from me to Boyd, and back.

"Know 'The Circle?' " he asked me.

I nodded. The underworld calls "Wop" Healey's joint "The Circle."

"If you'll meet me there tomorrow night, maybe I can put a 'piece of change' your way."

"Nothing stirring!" I shook my head with emphasis. "I ain't circulating that prominent these days."

A fat chance I'd have of meeting him there! "Wop" Healey and half his customers knew me as a detective. So there was nothing to do but to try to get the impression over that I was a crook who had reasons for wanting to keep away from the more notorious hang-outs for a while. Apparently it got over. He thought a while, and then gave me his Laguna Street number.

"Drop in this time tomorrow and maybe I'll have a proposition to make you—if you've got the guts."

"I'll think it over," I said noncommittally, and turned as if to go down the street.

"Just a minute," he called, and I faced him again. "What's your name?"

"Wisher," I said. "Shine, if you want a front one."

"Shine Wisher," he repeated. "I don't remember ever hearing it before."

It would have surprised me if he had—I had made it up only about fifteen minutes before.

"You needn't yell it," I said sourly, "so that everybody in the burg *will* remember hearing it."

And with that I left him, not at all dissatisfied with myself. By tipping him off to Boyd, I had put him under obligations to me, and had led him to accept me, at least tentatively, as a fellow crook.

And by making no apparent effort to gain his good graces, I had strengthened my hand that much more.

I had a date with him for the next day, when I was to be given a chance to earn—illegally, no doubt—'a piece of change.'

There was a chance that this proposition he had in view for me had nothing to do with the Estep affair, but then again it might; and whether it did or not, I had my entering wedge at least a little way into Jake Ledwich's business.

I strolled around for about half an hour, and then went back to Bob Teal's apartment.

"Ledwich come back?"

"Yes," Bob said, "with that little guy of yours. They went in about half an hour ago."

"Good! Haven't seen a woman go in?"

"No."

I expected to see the first Mrs. Estep arrive sometime during the evening, but she didn't. Bob and I sat around and talked and watched Ledwich's doorway, and the hours passed.

At one o'clock Ledwich came out alone.

"I'm going to tail him, just for luck," Bob said, and caught up his cap.

Ledwich vanished around a corner, and then Bob passed out of sight behind him.

Five minutes later Bob was with me again.

"He's getting his machine out of the garage."

I jumped for the telephone and put in a rush order for a fast touring car.

Bob, at the window, called out, "Here he is!"

I joined Bob in time to see Ledwich going into his vestibule. His car stood in front of the house. A very few minutes, and Boyd and Ledwich came out together. Boyd was leaning heavily on Ledwich, who was supporting the little man with an arm across his back. We couldn't see their faces in the dark, but the little man was plainly either sick, drunk, or drugged!

ZIGZAGS OF TREACHERY

Ledwich helped his companion into the touring car. The red tail-light laughed back at us for a few blocks, and then disappeared. The automobile I had ordered arrived twenty minutes later, so we sent it back unused.

At a little after three that morning, Ledwich, alone and afoot, returned from the direction of his garage. He had been gone exactly two hours.

VIII

Neither Bob nor I went home that night, but slept in the Laguna Street apartment.

Bob went down to the corner grocer's to get what we needed for breakfast in the morning, and he brought a morning paper back with him.

I cooked breakfast while he divided his attention between Ledwich's front door and the newspaper.

"Hey!" he called suddenly, "look here!"

I ran out of the kitchen with a handful of bacon.

"What is it?"

"Listen! 'Park Murder Mystery!' " he read. " 'Early this morning the body of an unidentified man was found near a driveway in Golden Gate Park. His neck had been broken, according to the police, who say that the absence of any considerable bruises on the body, as well as the orderly condition of the clothes and the ground nearby, show that he did not come to his death through falling, or being struck by an automobile. It is believed that he was killed and then carried to the park in an automobile, to be left there.' "

"Boyd!" I said.

"I bet you!" Bob agreed.

And at the morgue a very little while later, we learned that we were correct. The dead man was John Boyd.

"He was dead when Ledwich brought him out of the house," Bob said.

I nodded.

"He was! He was a little man, and it wouldn't have been much of a stunt for a big bruiser like Ledwich to have dragged him along with one arm the short distance from the door to the curb, pretending to be holding him up, like you do with a drunk. Let's go over to the Hall of Justice and see what the police have got on it—if anything."

At the detective bureau we hunted up O'Gar, the detective-sergeant in charge of the Homicide Detail, and a good man to work with.

"This dead man found in the park," I asked, "know anything about him?"

O'Gar pushed back his village constable's hat—a big black hat with a floppy brim that belonged in vaudeville—scratched his bullet-head, and scowled at me as if he thought I had a joke up my sleeve.

"Not a damned thing except that he's dead!" he said at last.

"How'd you like to know who he was last seen with?"

"It wouldn't hinder me any in finding out who bumped him off, and that's a fact."

"How do you like the sound of this?" I asked. "His name was John Boyd and he was living at a hotel down in the next block. The last person he was seen with was a guy who is tied up with Dr. Estep's first wife. You know—the Dr. Estep whose second wife is the woman you people are trying to prove a murder on. Does that sound interesting?"

"It does," he said. "Where do we go first?"

"This Ledwich—he's the fellow who was last seen with Boyd—is going to be a hard bird to shake down. We better try to crack the woman first—the first Mrs. Estep. There's a chance that Boyd was a pal of hers, and in that case when she finds out that Ledwich rubbed him out, she may open up and spill the works to us.

"On the other hand, if she and Ledwich are stacked up against Boyd together, then we might as well get her safely placed before we tie into him. I don't want to pull him before night, anyway. I got a date with him, and I want to try to rope him first."

Bob Teal made for the door.

"I'm going up and keep my eye on him until you're ready for him," he called over his shoulder.

"Good," I said. "Don't let him get out of town on us. If he tries to blow, have him chucked in the can."

In the lobby of the Montgomery Hotel, O'Gar and I talked to Dick Foley first. He told us that the woman was still in her room—had had her breakfast sent up. She had received neither letters, telegrams, nor phone calls since we began to watch her.

I got hold of Stacey again.

"We're going up to talk to this Estep woman, and maybe we'll take her away with us. Will you send up a maid to find out whether she's up and dressed yet? We don't want to announce ourselves ahead of time, and we don't want to burst in on her while she's in bed, or only partly dressed."

He kept us waiting about fifteen minutes, and then told us that Mrs. Estep was up and dressed.

We went up to her room, taking the maid with us.

The maid rapped on the door.

"What is it?" an irritable voice demanded.

"The maid; I want to—"

The key turned on the inside, and an angry Mrs. Estep jerked the door open. O'Gar and I advanced, O'Gar flashing his "buzzer."

"From headquarters," he said. "We want to talk to you."

O'Gar's foot was where she couldn't slam the door on us, and we were both walking ahead, so there was nothing for her to do but to retreat into the room, admitting us—which she did with no pretence of graciousness.

We closed the door, and then I threw our big load at her.

"Mrs. Estep, why did Jake Ledwich kill John Boyd?"

The expressions ran over her face like this: Alarm at Ledwich's name, fear at the word "kill," but the name John Boyd brought only bewilderment.

"Why did what?" she stammered meaninglessly, to gain time.

"Exactly," I said. "Why did Jake kill him last night in his flat, and then take him in the park and leave him?"

Another set of expressions: Increased bewilderment until I had almost finished the sentence, and then the sudden understanding of something, followed by the inevitable groping for poise. These things weren't as plain as billboards, you understand, but they were there to be read by anyone who had ever played poker—either with cards or people.

What I got out of them was that Boyd hadn't been working with or for her, and that, though she knew Ledwich had killed somebody at some time, it wasn't Boyd and it wasn't last night. Who, then? And when? Dr. Estep? Hardly! There wasn't a chance in the world that—if he had been murdered—anybody except his wife had done it—his second wife. No possible reading of the evidence could bring any other answer.

Who, then, had Ledwich killed before Boyd? Was he a wholesale murderer?

These things were flitting through my head in flashes and odd scraps while Mrs. Estep was saying:

"This is absurd! The idea of your coming up here and—"

She talked for five minutes straight, the words fairly sizzling from between her hard lips; but the words themselves didn't mean anything. She was talking for time—talking while she tried to hit upon the safest attitude to assume.

And before we could head her off, she had hit upon it—silence!

We got not another word out of her; and that is the only way in the world to beat the grilling game. The average suspect tries to talk himself out of being arrested; and it doesn't matter how shrewd a man is, or how good a liar, if he'll talk to you, and you play your cards right, you can hook him—can make him help you convict him. But if he won't talk you can't do a thing with him.

And that's how it was with this woman. She refused to pay any attention to our questions—she wouldn't speak, nod, grunt, or wave an arm in reply. She gave us a fine assortment of facial expressions, true enough, but we wanted verbal information—and we got none.

We weren't easily licked, however. Three beautiful hours of it we gave her without rest. We stormed, cajoled, threatened, and at times I think we danced; but it was no go. So in the end we took her away with us. We didn't have anything on her, but we couldn't afford to have her running around loose until we nailed Ledwich.

At the Hall of Justice we didn't book her; but simply held her as a material witness, putting her in an office with a matron and one of O'Gar's men, who were to see what they could do with her while we went after Ledwich. We had had her frisked as soon as she reached the Hall, of course; and, as we expected, she hadn't a thing of importance on her.

O'Gar and I went back to the Montgomery and gave her room a thorough overhauling—and found nothing.

"Are you sure you know what you're talking about?" the detective-sergeant asked as we left the hotel. "It's going to be a pretty joke on somebody if you're mistaken."

I let that go by without an answer.

"I'll meet you at six-thirty," I said, "and we'll go up against Ledwich."

He grunted an approval, and I set out for Vance Richmond's office.

IX

The attorney sprang up from his desk as soon as his stenographer admitted me. His face was leaner and grayer than ever; its lines had deepened, and there was a hollowness around his eyes.

"You've *got* to do something!" he cried huskily. "I have just come from the hospital. Mrs. Estep is on the point of death! A day more of this—two days at the most—and she will—"

I interrupted him, and swiftly gave him an account of the day's happenings, and what I expected, or hoped, to make out of them. But he received the news without brightening, and shook his head hopelessly.

"But don't you see," he exclaimed when I had finished, "that that won't do? I know you can find proof of her innocence in time. I'm not complaining—you've done all that could be expected, and more! But all that's no good! I've got to have—well—a miracle, perhaps.

"Suppose that you do finally get the truth out of Ledwich and the first Mrs. Estep or it comes out during their trials for Boyd's murder? Or that you even get to the bottom of the matter in three or four days? That will be too late! If I can go to Mrs. Estep and tell her she's free now, she may pull herself together, and come through. But another day of imprisonment—two days, or perhaps even two hours—and she won't need anybody to clear her. Death will have done it! I tell you, she's—"

I left Vance Richmond abruptly again. This lawyer was bound upon getting me worked up; and I like my jobs to be simply jobs—emotions are nuisances during business hours.

X

At a quarter to seven that evening, while O'Gar remained down the street, I rang Jacob Ledwich's bell. As I had stayed with Bob Teal in our apartment the previous night, I was still wearing the clothes in which I had made Ledwich's acquaintance as Shine Wisher.

Ledwich opened the door.

"Hello, Wisher!" he said without enthusiasm, and led me upstairs.

His flat consisted of four rooms, I found, running the full length and half the breadth of the building, with both front and rear exits. It was furnished with the ordinary none-too-spotless appoint-

ZIGZAGS OF TREACHERY

ments of the typical moderately priced furnished flat—alike the world over.

In his front room we sat down and talked and smoked and sized one another up. He seemed a little nervous. I thought he would have been just as well satisfied if I had forgotten to show up.

"About this job you mentioned?" I asked presently.

"Sorry," he said, moistening his little lumpy mouth, "but it's all off." And then he added, obviously as an afterthought, "For the present, at least."

I guessed from that that my job was to have taken care of Boyd—but Boyd had been taken care of for good.

He brought out some whisky after a while, and we talked over it for some time, to no purpose whatever. He was trying not to appear too anxious to get rid of me, and I was cautiously feeling him out.

Piecing together things he let fall here and there, I came to the conclusion that he was a former con man who had fallen into an easier game of late years. That was in line, too, with what "Porky" Grout had told Bob Teal.

I talked about myself with the evasiveness that would have been natural to a crook in my situation; and made one or two carefully planned slips that would lead him to believe that I had been tied up with the "Jimmy the Riveter" hold-up mob, most of whom were doing long hitches at Walla Walla then.

He offered to lend me enough money to tide me over until I could get on my feet again. I told him I didn't need chicken feed so much as a chance to pick up some real jack.

The evening was going along, and we were getting nowhere.

"Jake," I said casually—outwardly casual, that is—"you took a big chance putting that guy out of the way like you did last night."

I meant to stir things up, and I succeeded.

His face went crazy.

A gun came out of his coat.

Firing from my pocket, I shot it out of his hand.

"Now behave!" I ordered.

He sat rubbing his benumbed hand and staring with wide eyes at the smouldering hole in my coat.

Looks like a great stunt, this shooting a gun out of a man's hand, but it's a thing that happens now and then. A man who is a fair shot (and that is exactly what I am—no more, no less) naturally and automatically shoots pretty close to the spot upon which his eyes are focused. When a man goes for his gun in front of you, you shoot at *him*—not at any particular part of him. There isn't time for that— you shoot at *him*. However, you are more than likely to be looking at his gun, and in that case it isn't altogether surprising if your bullet should hit his gun—as mine had done. But it looks impressive.

I beat out the fire around the bullet-hole in my coat, crossed the room to where his revolver had been knocked, and picked it up. I started to eject the bullets from it, but, instead, I snapped it shut again and stuck it in my pocket. Then I returned to my chair, opposite him.

"A man oughtn't to act like that," I kidded him; "he's likely to hurt somebody."

His little mouth curled up at me.

"An elbow, huh?" putting all the contempt he could in his voice; and somehow any synonym for detective seems able to hold a lot of contempt.

I might have tried to talk myself back into the Wisher role. It could have been done, but I doubted that it would be worth it; so I nodded my confession.

His brain was working now, and the passion left his face, while he sat rubbing his right hand, and his little mouth and eyes began to screw themselves up calculatingly.

I kept quiet, waiting to see what the outcome of his thinking would be. I knew he was trying to figure out just what my place in this game was. Since, to his knowledge, I had come into it no later than the previous evening, then the Boyd murder hadn't brought me in. That would leave the Estep affair—unless he was tied up in

ZIGZAGS OF TREACHERY

a lot of other crooked stuff that I didn't know anything about.

"You're not a city dick, are you?" he asked finally, and his voice was on the verge of friendliness now: the voice of one who wants to persuade you of something, or sell you something.

The truth, I thought, wouldn't hurt.

"No," I said, "I'm with the Continental."

He hitched his chair a little closer to the muzzle of my automatic.

"What are you after, then? Where do you come in on it?"

I tried the truth again.

"The second Mrs. Estep. She didn't kill her husband."

"You're trying to dig up enough dope to spring her?"

"Yes."

I waved him back as he tried to hitch his chair still nearer.

"How do you expect to do it?" he asked, his voice going lower and more confidential with each word.

I took still another flier at the truth.

"He wrote a letter before he died."

"Well?"

But I called a halt for the time.

"Just that," I said.

He leaned back in his chair, and his eyes and mouth grew small in thought again.

"What's your interest in the man who died last night?" he asked slowly.

"It's something on you," I said, truthfully again. "It doesn't do the second Mrs. Estep any direct good, maybe; but you and the first wife are stacked up together against her. Anything, therefore, that hurts you two will help her, somehow. I admit I'm wandering around in the dark; but I'm going ahead wherever I see a point of light—and I'll come through to daylight in the end. Nailing you for Boyd's murder is one point of light."

He leaned forward suddenly, his eyes and mouth popping open as far as they would go.

"You'll come out all right," he said very softly, "if you use a little judgment."

"What's that supposed to mean?"

"Do you think," he asked, still very softly, "that you can nail me for Boyd's murder—that you can convict me of murder?"

"I do."

But I wasn't any too sure. In the first place, though we were morally certain of it, neither Bob Teal nor I could swear that the man who had got in the machine with Ledwich was John Boyd.

We knew it was, of course, but the point is that it had been too dark for us to see his face. And, again, in the dark, we had thought him alive; it wasn't until later that we knew he had been dead when he came down the steps.

Little things, those, but a private detective on the witness stand—unless he is absolutely sure of every detail—has an unpleasant and ineffectual time of it.

"I do," I repeated, thinking these things over, "and I'm satisfied to go to the bat with what I've got on you and what I can collect between now and the time you and your accomplice go to trial."

"Accomplice?" he said, not very surprised. "That would be Edna. I suppose you've already grabbed her?"

"Yes."

He laughed.

"You'll have one sweet time getting anything out of her. In the first place, she doesn't know much, and in the second—well, I suppose you've tried, and have found out what a helpful sort she is! So don't try the old gag of pretending that she has talked!"

"I'm not pretending anything."

Silence between us for a few seconds, and then—

"I'm going to make you a proposition," he said. "You can take it or leave it. The note Dr. Estep wrote before he died was to me, and it is positive proof that he committed suicide. Give me a chance to get away—just a chance—a half-hour start—and I'll give you my word of honor to send you the letter."

ZIGZAGS OF TREACHERY

"I know I can trust you," I said sarcastically.

"I'll trust you, then!" he shot back at me. "I'll turn the note over to you if you'll give me your word that I'm to have half an hour's start."

"For what?" I demanded. "Why shouldn't I take both you and the note?"

"If you can get them! But do I look like the kind of sap who would leave the note where it would be found? Do you think it's here in the room maybe?"

I didn't, but neither did I think that because he had hidden it, it couldn't be found.

"I can't think of any reason why I should bargain with you," I told him. "I've got you cold, and that's enough."

"If I can show you that your only chance of freeing the second Mrs. Estep is through my voluntary assistance, will you bargain with me?"

"Maybe—I'll listen to your persuasion, anyway."

"All right," he said, "I'm going to come clean with you. But most of the things I'm going to tell you can't be proven in court without my help; and if you turn my offer down I'll have plenty of evidence to convince the jury that these things are all false, that I never said them, and that you are trying to frame me."

That part was plausible enough. I've testified before juries all the way from the city of Washington to the state of Washington, and I've never seen one yet that wasn't anxious to believe that a private detective is a double-crossing specialist who goes around with a cold deck in one pocket, a complete forger's outfit in another, and who counts that day lost in which he railroads no innocent to the hoosegow.

XI

"There was once a young doctor in a town a long way from here,"

Ledwich began. "He got mixed up in a scandal—a pretty rotten one—and escaped the pen only by the skin of his teeth. The state medical board revoked his license.

"In a large city not far away, this young doc, one night when he was drunk—as he usually was in those days—told his troubles to a man he had met in a dive. The friend was a resourceful sort; and he offered, for a price, to fix the doc up with a fake diploma, so he could set up in practice in some other state.

"The young doctor took him up, and the friend got the diploma for him. The doc was the man you know as Dr. Estep, and I was the friend. The real Dr. Estep was found dead in the park this morning!"

That was news—if true!

"You see," the big man went on, "when I offered to get the phoney diploma for the young doc—whose real name doesn't matter—I had in mind a forged one. Nowadays they're easy to get—there's a regular business in them—but twenty-five years ago, while you could manage it, they were hard to get. While I was trying to get one, I ran across a woman I used to work with—Edna Fife. That's the woman you know as the first Mrs. Estep.

"Edna had married a doctor—the real Dr. Humbert Estep. He was a hell of a doctor, though; and after starving with him in Philadelphia for a couple of years, she made him close up his office, and she went back to the bunko game, taking him with her. She was good at it, I'm telling you—a real cleaner—and, keeping him under her thumb all the time, she made him a pretty good worker himself.

"It was shortly after that that I met her, and when she told me all this, I offered to buy her husband's medical diploma and other credentials. I don't know whether he wanted to sell them or not—but he did what she told him, and I got the papers.

"I turned them over to the young doc, who came to San Francisco and opened an office under the name of Humbert Estep. The real Esteps promised not to use that name any more—not much of an inconvenience for them, as they changed names every time they changed addresses.

"I kept in touch with the young doctor, of course, getting my regular rake-off from him. I had him by the neck, and I wasn't foolish enough to pass up any easy money. After a year or so, I learned that he had pulled himself together and was making good. So I jumped on a train and came to San Francisco. He was doing fine; so I camped here, where I could keep my eye on him and watch out for my own interests.

"He got married about then, and, between his practice and his investments, he began to accumulate a roll. But he tightened up on me—damn him! He wouldn't be bled. I got a regular percentage of what he made, and that was all.

"For nearly twenty-five years I got it—but not a nickel over the percentage. He knew I wouldn't kill the goose that laid the golden eggs, so no matter how much I threatened to expose him, he sat tight, and I couldn't budge him. I got my regular cut, and not a nickel more.

"That went along, as I say, for years. I was getting a living out of him, but I wasn't getting any big money. A few months ago I learned that he had cleaned up heavily in a lumber deal so I made up my mind to take him for what he had.

"During all these years I had got to know the doc pretty well. You do when you're bleeding a man—you get a pretty fair idea of what goes on in his head, and what he's most likely to do if certain things should happen. So I knew the doc pretty well.

"I knew, for instance, that he had never told his wife the truth about his past; that he had stalled her with some lie about being born in West Virginia. That was fine—for me! Then I knew that he kept a gun in his desk, and I knew why. It was kept there for the purpose of killing himself if the truth ever came out about his diploma. He figured that if, at the first hint of exposure, he wiped himself out, the authorities, out of respect for the good reputation he had built up, would hush things up.

"And his wife—even if she herself learned the truth—would be spared the shame of a public scandal. I can't see myself dying just to spare some woman's feelings, but the doc was a funny guy in some ways—and he was nutty about his wife.

"That's the way I had him figured out, and that's the way things turned out.

"My plan might sound complicated, but it was simple enough. I got hold of the real Esteps—it took a lot of hunting, but I found them at last. I brought the woman to San Francisco, and told the man to stay away.

"Everything would have gone fine if he had done what I told him; but he was afraid that Edna and I were going to double-cross him, so he came here to keep an eye on us. But I didn't know that until you put the finger on him for me.

"I brought Edna here and, without telling her any more than she had to know, drilled her until she was letter-perfect in her part.

"A couple days before she came I had gone to see the doc, and had demanded a hundred thousand cool smacks. He laughed at me, and I left, pretending to be as hot as hell.

"As soon as Edna arrived, I sent her to call on him. She asked him to perform an illegal operation on her daughter. He, of course, refused. Then she pleaded with him, loud enough for the nurse or whoever else was in the reception room to hear. And when she raised her voice she was careful to stick to words that could be interpreted the way we wanted them to. She ran off her end to perfection, leaving in tears.

"Then I sprung my other trick! I had a fellow—a fellow who's a whiz at that kind of stuff—make me a plate: an imitation of newspaper printing. It was all worded like the real article, and said that the state authorities were investigating information that a prominent surgeon in San Francisco was practicing under a license secured by false credentials. This plate measured four and an eighth by six and three-quarter inches. If you'll look at the first inside page of the *Evening Times* any day in the week you'll see a photograph just that size.

ZIGZAGS OF TREACHERY

"On the day after Edna's call, I bought a copy of the first edition of the *Times*—on the street at ten in the morning. I had this scratcher friend of mine remove the photograph with acid, and print this fake article in its place.

"That evening I substituted a 'home edition' outer sheet for the one that had come with the paper we had cooked up, and made a switch as soon as the doc's newsboy made his delivery. There was nothing to that part of it. The kid just tossed the paper into the vestibule. It's simply a case of duck into the doorway, trade papers, and go on, leaving the loaded one for the doc to read."

I was trying not to look too interested, but my ears were cocked for every word. At the start, I had been prepared for a string of lies. But I knew now that he was telling me the truth! Every syllable was a boast; he was half-drunk with appreciation of his own cleverness—the cleverness with which he had planned and carried out his program of treachery and murder.

I knew that he was telling the truth, and I suspected that he was telling more of it than he had intended. He was fairly bloated with vanity—the vanity that fills the crook almost invariably after a little success, and makes him ripe for the pen.

His eyes glistened, and his little mouth smiled triumphantly around the words that continued to roll out of it.

"The doc read the paper, all right—and shot himself. But first he wrote and mailed a note—to me. I didn't figure on his wife's being accused of killing him. That was plain luck.

"I figured that the fake piece in the paper would be overlooked in the excitement. Edna would then go forward, claiming to be his first wife; and his shooting himself after her first call, with what the nurse had overheard, would make his death seem a confession that Edna was his wife.

"I was sure that she would stand up under any sort of an investigation. Nobody knew anything about the doc's real past; except what he had told them, which would be found false.

"Edna had really married a Dr. Humbert Estep in Philadelphia in 1896; and the twenty-seven years that had passed since then would do a lot to hide the fact that that Dr. Humbert Estep wasn't this Dr. Humbert Estep.

"All I wanted to do was convince the doc's real wife and her lawyers that she wasn't really his wife at all. And we did that! Everybody took it for granted that Edna was the legal wife.

"The next play would have been for Edna and the real wife to have reached some sort of an agreement about the estate, whereby Edna would have got the bulk—or at least half—of it; and nothing would have been made public.

"If worse came to worst, we were prepared to go to court. We were sitting pretty! But I'd have been satisfied with half the estate. It would have come to a few hundred thousand at the least, and that would have been plenty for me—even deducting the twenty thousand I had promised Edna.

"But when the police grabbed the doc's wife and charged her with his murder, I saw my way into the whole roll. All I had to do was sit tight and wait until they convicted her. Then the court would turn the entire pile over to Edna.

"I had the only evidence that would free the doc's wife: the note he had written me. But I couldn't—even if I had wanted to—have turned it in without exposing my hand. When he read that fake piece in the paper, he tore it out, wrote his message to me across the face of it, and sent it to me. So the note is a dead give-away. However, I didn't have any intention of publishing it, anyhow.

"Up to this point everything had gone like a dream. All I had to do was wait until it was time to cash in on my brains. And that's the time that the real Humbert Estep picked out to mess up the works.

"He shaved his mustache off, put on some old clothes, and came snooping around to see that Edna and I didn't run out on him. As if he could have stopped us! After you put the finger on him for me, I brought him up here.

"I intended salving him along until I could find a place to keep him until all the cards had been played. That's what I was going to hire you for—to take care of him.

"But we got to talking, and wrangling, and I had to knock him down. He didn't get up, and I found that he was dead. His neck was broken. There was nothing to do but take him out to the park and leave him.

"I didn't tell Edna. She didn't have a lot of use for him, as far as I could see, but you can't tell how women will take things. Anyhow, she'll stick, now that it's done. She's on the up and up all the time. And if she should talk, she can't do a lot of damage. She only knows her own part of the lay.

"All this long-winded story is so you'll know just exactly what you're up against. Maybe you think you can dig up the proof of these things I have told you. You can this far. You can prove that Edna wasn't the doc's wife. You can prove that I've been blackmailing him. But you can't prove that the doc's wife didn't *believe* that Edna was his real wife! It's her word against Edna's and mine.

"We'll swear that we had convinced her of it, which will give her a motive. You can't prove that the phoney news article I told you about ever existed. It'll sound like a hophead's dream to a jury.

"You can't tie last night's murder on me—I've got an alibi that will knock your hat off! I can prove that I left here with a friend of mine who was drunk, and that I took him to his hotel and put him to bed, with the help of a night clerk and a bellboy. And what have you got against that? The word of two private detectives. Who'll believe you?

"You can convict me of conspiracy to defraud, or something—maybe. But, regardless of that, you can't free Mrs. Estep without my help.

"Turn me loose and I'll give you the letter the doc wrote me. It's the goods, right enough! In his own handwriting, written across the face of the fake newspaper story—which ought to fit the torn place in the paper that the police are supposed to be holding—and he wrote that he was going to kill himself, in words almost that plain."

That would turn the trick—there was no doubt of it. And I believed Ledwich's story. The more I thought it over the better I liked it. It fitted into the facts everywhere. But I wasn't enthusiastic about giving this big crook his liberty.

"Don't make me laugh!" I said. "I'm going to put you away and free Mrs Estep—both."

"Go ahead and try it! You're up against it without the letter; and you don't think a man with brains enough to plan a job like this one would be foolish enough to leave the note where it could be found, do you?"

I wasn't especially impressed with the difficulty of convicting this Ledwich and freeing the dead man's widow. His scheme—that cold-blooded zigzag of treachery for everybody he had dealt with, including his latest accomplice, Edna Estep—wasn't as airtight as he thought it. A week in which to run out a few lines in the East, and—But a week was just what I didn't have!

Vance Richmond's words were running through my head: "But another day of imprisonment—two days, or perhaps even two hours—and she won't need anybody to clear her. Death will have done it!"

If I was going to do Mrs. Estep any good, I had to move quick. Law or no law, her life was in my fat hands. This man before me—his eyes bright and hopeful now and his mouth anxiously pursed—was thief, blackmailer, double-crosser, and at least twice a murderer. I hated to let him walk out. But there was the woman dying in a hospital....

XII

Keeping my eye on Ledwich, I went to the telephone, and got Vance Richmond on the wire at his residence.

"How is Mrs. Estep?" I asked.

"Weaker! I talked with the doctor half an hour ago, and he says—"

I cut in on him; I didn't want to listen to the details.

ZIGZAGS OF TREACHERY

"Get over to the hospital, and be where I can reach you by phone. I may have news for you before the night is over."

"What—is there a chance? Are you—"

I didn't promise him anything. I hung up the receiver and spoke to Ledwich. "I'll do this much for you. Slip me the note, and I'll give you your gun and put you out the back door. There's a bull on the corner out front, and I can't take you past him."

He was on his feet, beaming.

"Your word on it?" he demanded.

"Yes—get going!"

He went past me to the phone, gave a number (which I made a note of), and then spoke hurriedly into the instrument.

"This is Shuler. Put a boy in a taxi with that envelope I gave you to hold for me, and send him out here right away."

He gave his address, said "Yes" twice, and hung up.

There was nothing surprising about his unquestioning acceptance of my word. He couldn't afford to doubt that I'd play fair with him. And, also, all successful bunko men come in time to believe that the world—except for themselves—is populated by a race of human sheep who may be trusted to conduct themselves with true sheeplike docility.

Ten minutes later the doorbell rang. We answered it together, and Ledwich took a large envelope from a messenger boy, while I memorized the number on the boy's cap. Then we went back to the front room.

Ledwich slit the envelope and passed its contents to me: a piece of rough-torn newspaper. Across the face of the fake article he had told me about was written a message in a jerky hand.

> I WOULDN'T HAVE SUSPECTED YOU, LEDWICH, OF SUCH PROFOUND STUPIDITY. MY LAST THOUGHT WILL BE—THIS BULLET THAT ENDS MY LIFE ALSO ENDS YOUR YEARS OF LEISURE. YOU'LL HAVE TO GO TO WORK NOW.
>
> ESTEP.

The doctor had died game!

I took the envelope from the big man, put the death note in it, and put them in my pocket. Then I went to a front window, flattening a cheek against the glass until I could see O'Gar, dimly outlined in the night, patiently standing where I had left him hours before.

"The city dick is still on the corner," I told Ledwich. "Here's your gat"—holding out the gun I had shot from his fingers a little while back—"take it, and blow through the back door. Remember, that's all I'm offering you—the gun and a fair start. If you play square with me, I'll not do anything to help find you—unless I have to keep myself in the clear."

"Fair enough!"

He grabbed the gun, broke it to see that it was still loaded, and wheeled toward the rear of the flat. At the door he pulled up, hesitated, and faced me again. I kept him covered with my automatic.

"Will you do me one favor I didn't put in the bargain?" he asked.

"What is it?"

"That note of the doc's is in an envelope with my handwriting and maybe my fingerprints on it. Let me put it in a fresh envelope, will you? I don't want to leave any broader trail behind than I have to."

With my left hand—my right being busy with the gun—I fumbled for the envelope and tossed it to him. He took a plain envelope from the table, wiped it carefully with his handkerchief, put the note in it, taking care not to touch it with the balls of his fingers, and passed it back to me; and I put it in my pocket.

I had a hard time to keep from grinning in his face.

That fumbling with the handkerchief told me that the envelope in my pocket was empty, that the death note was in Ledwich's possession—though I hadn't seen it pass there. He had worked one of his bunko tricks upon me.

"Beat it!" I snapped, to keep from laughing in his face.

He spun on his heel. His feet pounded against the floor. A door slammed in the rear.

I tore into the envelope he had given me. I needed to be sure he had double-crossed me.

The envelope was empty.

Our agreement was wiped out.

I sprang to the front window, threw it wide open, and leaned out. O'Gar saw me immediately—clearer than I could see him. I swung my arm in a wide gesture toward the rear of the house. O'Gar set out for the alley on the run. I dashed back through Ledwich's flat to the kitchen, and stuck my head out of an already open window.

I could see Ledwich against the white-washed fence—throwing the back gate open, plunging through it into the alley.

O'Gar's squat bulk appeared under a light at the end of the alley.

Ledwich's revolver was in his hand. O'Gar's wasn't—not quite.

Ledwich's gun swung up—the hammer clicked.

O'Gar's gun coughed fire.

Ledwich fell with a slow, revolving motion over against the white fence, gasped once or twice, and went down in a pile.

I walked slowly down the stairs to join O'Gar; slowly, because it isn't a nice thing to look at a man you've deliberately sent to his death. Not even if it's the surest way of saving an innocent life, and if the man who dies is a Jake Ledwich—altogether treacherous.

"How come?" O'Gar asked, when I came into the alley, where he stood looking down at the dead man.

"He got out on me," I said simply.

"He must've."

I stooped and searched the dead man's pockets until I found the suicide note, still crumpled in the handkerchief. O'Gar was examining the dead man's revolver.

"Lookit!" he exclaimed. "Maybe this ain't my lucky day! He snapped at me once, and his gun missed fire. No wonder! Somebody must've been using an ax on it—the firing pin's broke clean off!"

"Is that so?" I asked; just as if I hadn't discovered, when I first picked the revolver up, that the bullet which had knocked it out of Ledwich's hand had made it harmless.

THE ASSISTANT MURDERER

I
The Man in Gray

Gold on the door, edged with black, said *Alexander Rush, Private Detective*. Inside, an ugly man sat tilted back in a chair, his feet on a yellow desk.

The office was in no way lovely. Its furnishings were few and old with the shabby age of second-handdom. A shredding square of dun carpet covered the floor. On one buff wall hung a framed certificate that licensed Alexander Rush to pursue the calling of private detective in the city of Baltimore in accordance with certain red-numbered regulations. A map of the city hung on another wall. Beneath the map a frail bookcase, small as it was, gaped emptily around its contents: a yellowish railway guide, a smaller hotel directory, and street and telephone directories for Baltimore, Washington, and Philadelphia. An insecure oaken clothes-tree held up a black derby and a black overcoat beside a white sink in one corner. The four chairs in the room were unrelated to one another in everything except age. The desk's scarred top held, in addition to the proprietor's feet, a telephone, a black-clotted inkwell, a disarray of papers having generally to do with criminals who had escaped from one prison or another, and a grayed ashtray that held as much ash and as many black cigar stumps as a tray of its size could expect to hold.

An ugly office—the proprietor was uglier.

His head was squatly pear-shaped. Excessively heavy, wide, blunt at the jaw, it narrowed as it rose to the close-cropped, erect grizzled hair that sprouted above a low, slanting forehead. His complexion was of a rich darkish red, his skin tough in texture and rounded over thick cushions of fat.

These fundamental inelegancies were by no means all his ugliness. Things had been done to his features.

One way you looked at his nose, you said it was crooked. Another way, you said it could not be crooked; it had no shape at all. Whatever your opinion of its form, you could not deny its color. Veins had broken to pencil its already florid surface with brilliant red stars and curls and puzzling scrawls that looked as if they must have some secret meanings. His lips were thick, tough-skinned. Between them showed the brassy glint of two solid rows of gold teeth, the lower row lapping the upper, so undershot was the bulging jaw. His eyes—small, deep-set, and pale blue of iris—were bloodshot to a degree that made you think he had a heavy cold. His ears accounted for some of his earlier years: they were the thickened, twisted cauliflower ears of the pugilist.

A man of forty-something, ugly, sitting tilted back in his chair, feet on desk.

The gilt-labelled door opened and another man came into the office. Perhaps ten years younger than the man at the desk, he was, roughly speaking, everything that one was not. Fairly tall, slender, fair-skinned, brown-eyed, he would have been as little likely to catch your eye in a gambling-house as in an art gallery. His clothes—suit and hat were gray—were fresh and properly pressed, and even fashionable in that inconspicuous manner which is one sort of taste. His face was likewise unobtrusive, which was surprising when you considered how narrowly it missed handsomeness through the least meagerness of mouth—a mark of the too-cautious man.

THE ASSISTANT MURDERER

Two steps into the office he hesitated, brown eyes glancing from shabby furnishings to ill-visaged proprietor. So much ugliness seemed to disconcert the man in gray. An apologetic smile began on his lips, as if he were about to murmur, "I beg your pardon, I'm in the wrong office."

But when he finally spoke it was otherwise. He took another step forward, asking uncertainly:

"You are Mr. Rush?"

"Yeah." The detective's voice was hoarse with a choking harshness that seemed to corroborate the heavy-cold testimony of his eyes. He put his feet down on the floor and jerked a fat, red hand at a chair. "Sit down, sir."

The man in gray sat down, tentatively upright on the chair's front edge.

"Now what can I do for you?" Alec Rush croaked amiably.

"I want—I wish—I would like—" and further than that the man in gray said nothing.

"Maybe you'd better just tell me what's wrong," the detective suggested. "Then I'll know what you want of me." He smiled.

There was kindliness in Alec Rush's smile, and it was not easily resisted. True, his smile was a horrible grimace out of a nightmare, but that was its charm. When your gentle-countenanced man smiles there is small gain: his smile expresses little more than his reposed face. But when Alec Rush distorted his ogre's mask so that jovial friendliness peeped incongruously from his savage red eyes, from his brutal metal-studded mouth—then that was a heartening, a winning thing.

"Yes, I daresay that would be better." The man in gray sat back in his chair, more comfortably, less transiently. "Yesterday on Fayette Street, I met—a young woman I know. I hadn't—we hadn't met for several months. That isn't really pertinent, however. But after we separated—we had talked for a few minutes—I saw a man. That is, he came out of a doorway and went down the street in the same direction she had taken, and I got the idea he was following her. She turned into Liberty Street and he did likewise. Countless people walk along that same route, and the idea that he was following her seemed fantastic, so much so that I dismissed it and went on about my business.

"But I couldn't get the notion out of my head. It seemed to me there had been something peculiarly intent in his carriage, and no matter how much I told myself the notion was absurd, it persisted in worrying me. So last night, having nothing especial to do, I drove out to the neighborhood of—of the young woman's house. And I saw the same man again. He was standing on a corner two blocks from her house. It was the same man—I'm certain of it. I tried to watch him, but while I was finding a place for my car he disappeared and I did not see him again. Those are the circumstances. Now will you look into it, learn if he is actually following her, and why?"

"Sure," the detective agreed hoarsely, "but didn't you say anything to the lady or to any of her family?"

The man in gray fidgeted in his chair and looked at the stringy dun carpet.

"No, I didn't. I didn't want to disturb her, frighten her, and still don't. After all, it may be no more than a meaningless coincidence, and—and—well—I don't— That's impossible! What I had in mind was for you to find out what is wrong, if anything, and remedy it without my appearing in the matter at all."

"Maybe, but, mind you, I'm not saying I will. I'd want to know more first."

"More? You mean more—"

"More about you and her."

"But there is nothing about us!" the man in gray protested. "It is exactly as I have told you. I might add that the young woman is—is married, and that until yesterday I had not seen her since her marriage."

"Then your interest in her is—?" The detective let the husky interrogation hang incompleted in the air.

THE ASSISTANT MURDERER

"Of friendship—past friendship."

"Yeah. Now who is this young woman?"

The man in gray fidgeted again.

"See here, Rush," he said, coloring, "I'm perfectly willing to tell you, and shall, of course, but I don't want to tell you unless you are going to handle this thing for me. I mean I don't want to be bringing her name into it if—if you aren't. Will you?"

Alec Rush scratched his grizzled head with a stubby forefinger.

"I don't know," he growled. "That's what I'm trying to find out. I can't take a hold of a job that might be anything. I've got to know that you're on the up-and-up."

II

Two Names

Puzzlement disturbed the clarity of the younger man's brown eyes. "But I didn't think you'd be—" He broke off and looked away from the ugly man.

"Of course you didn't." A chuckle rasped in the detective's burly throat, the chuckle of a man touched in a once-sore spot that is no longer tender. He raised a big hand to arrest his prospective client in the act of rising from his chair. "What you did, on a guess, was to go to one of the big agencies and tell 'em your story. They wouldn't touch it unless you cleared up the fishy points. Then you ran across my name, remembered I was chucked out of the department a couple of years ago. 'There's my man,' you said to yourself, 'a baby who won't be so choicy!' "

The man in gray protested with head and gesture and voice that this was not so. But his eyes were sheepish.

Alec Rush laughed harshly again and said, "No matter. I ain't sensitive about it. I can talk about politics, and being made the goat, and all that, but the records show the Board of Police Commissioners gave me the air for a list of crimes that would stretch from here to Canton Hollow. All right, sir! I'll take your job. It sounds phoney, but maybe it ain't. It'll cost you fifteen a day and expenses."

"I can see that it sounds peculiar," the younger man assured the detective, "but you'll find that it's quite all right. You'll want a retainer, of course."

"Yes, say fifty."

The man in gray took five new ten-dollar bills from a pigskin billfold and put them on the desk. With a thick pen Alec Rush began to make muddy ink-marks on a receipt blank.

"Your name?" he asked.

"I would rather not. I'm not to appear in it, you know. My name would not be of importance, would it?"

Alec Rush put down his pen and frowned at his client.

"Now! Now!" he grumbled good-naturedly. "How am I going to do business with a man like you?"

The man in gray was sorry, even apologetic, but he was stubborn in his reticence. He would not give his name. Alec Rush growled and complained, but pocketed the five ten-dollar bills.

"It's in your favor, maybe," the detective admitted as he surrendered, "though it ain't to your credit. But if you were off-color I guess you'd have sense enough to fake a name. Now this young woman—who is she?"

"Mrs. Hubert Landow."

"Well, well, we've got a name at last! And where does Mrs. Landow live?"

"On Charles-Street Avenue," the man in gray said, and gave a number.

"Her description?"

"She is twenty-two or -three years old, rather tall, slender in an athletic way, with auburn hair, blue eyes, and very white skin."

"And her husband? You know him?"

"I have seen him. He is about my age—thirty—but larger than I, a tall, broad-shouldered man of the clean-cut blond type."

THE ASSISTANT MURDERER

"And your mystery man? What does he look like?"

"He's quite young, not more than twenty-two at the most, and not very large—medium size, perhaps, or a little under. He's very dark, with high cheek-bones and a large nose. High, straight shoulders, too, but not broad. He walks with small, almost mincing, steps."

"Clothes?"

"He was wearing a brown suit and a tan cap when I saw him on Fayette Street yesterday afternoon. I suppose he wore the same last night, but I'm not positive."

"I suppose you'll drop in here for my reports," the detective wound up, "since I won't know where to send them to you?"

"Yes." The man in gray stood up and held out his hand. "I'm very grateful to you for undertaking this, Mr. Rush."

Alec Rush said that was all right. They shook hands, and the man in gray went out.

The ugly man waited until his client had had time to turn off into the corridor that led to the elevators. Then the detective said, "Now, Mr. Man!" got up from his chair, took his hat from the clothes-tree in the corner, locked his office door behind him, and ran down the back stairs.

He ran with the deceptive heavy agility of a bear. There was something bearlike, too, in the looseness with which his blue suit hung on his stout body, and in the set of his heavy shoulders—sloping, limber-jointed shoulders whose droop concealed much of their bulk.

He gained the ground floor in time to see the gray back of his client issuing into the street. In his wake Alec Rush sauntered. Two blocks, a turn to the left, another block, and a turn to the right. The man in gray went into the office of a trust company that occupied the ground floor of a large office building.

The rest was the mere turning of a hand. Half a dollar to a porter: the man in gray was Ralph Millar, assistant cashier.

Darkness was settling in Charles-Street Avenue when Alec Rush, in a modest black coupé, drove past the address Ralph Millar had given him. The house was large in the dusk, spaced from its fellows as from the paving by moderate expanses of fenced lawn.

Alec Rush drove on, turned to the left at the first crossing, again to the left at the next, and at the next. For half an hour he guided his car along a many-angled turning and returning route until, when finally he stopped beside the curb at some distance from, but within sight of, the Landow house, he had driven through every piece of thoroughfare in the vicinity of that house.

He had not seen Millar's dark, high-shouldered young man.

Lights burned brightly in Charles-Street Avenue, and the night traffic began to purr southward into the city. Alec Rush's heavy body slumped against the wheel of his coupé while he filled its interior with pungent fog from a black cigar, and held patient, bloodshot eyes on what he could see of the Landow residence.

Three-quarters of an hour passed, and there was motion in the house. A limousine left the garage in the rear for the front door. A man and a woman, faintly distinguishable at that distance, left the house for the limousine. The limousine moved out into the cityward current. The third car behind it was Alec Rush's modest coupé.

III

The Man in the Doorway

Except for a perilous moment at North Avenue, when the interfering cross-stream of traffic threatened to separate him from his quarry, Alec Rush followed the limousine without difficulty. In front of a Howard Street theatre it discharged its freight: a youngish man and a young woman, both tall, evening-clad, and assuringly in agreement with the descriptions the detective had got from his client.

The Landows went into the already dark theatre while Alec Rush was buying his ticket. In the light of the first intermission

THE ASSISTANT MURDERER

he discovered them again. Leaving his seat for the rear of the auditorium, he found an angle from which he could study them for the remaining five minutes of illumination.

Hubert Landow's head was rather small for his stature, and the blond hair with which it was covered threatened each moment to escape from its imposed smoothness into crisp curls. His face, healthily ruddy, was handsome in a muscular, very masculine way, not indicative of any great mental nimbleness. His wife had that beauty which needs no cataloguing. However, her hair was auburn, her eyes blue, her skin white, and she looked a year or two older than the maximum twenty-three Millar had allowed her.

While the intermission lasted Hubert Landow talked to his wife eagerly, and his bright eyes were the eyes of a lover. Alec Rush could not see Mrs. Landow's eyes. He saw her replying now and again to her husband's words. Her profile showed no answering eagerness. She did not show she was bored.

Midway through the last act, Alec Rush left the theatre to maneuver his coupé into a handy position from which to cover the Landows' departure. But their limousine did not pick them up when they left the theatre. They turned down Howard Street afoot, going to a rather garish second-class restaurant, where an abbreviated orchestra succeeded by main strength in concealing its smallness from the ear.

His coupé conveniently parked, Alec Rush found a table from which he could watch his subjects without being himself noticeable. Husband still wooed wife with incessant, eager talking. Wife was listless, polite, unkindled. Neither more than touched the food before them. They danced once, the woman's face as little touched by immediate interest as when she listened to her husband's words. A beautiful face, but empty.

The minute hand of Alec Rush's nickel-plated watch had scarcely begun its last climb of the day from where 'VI' is inferred to 'XII' when the Landows left the restaurant. The limousine—against its side a young Norfolk-jacketed Negro smoking—was two doors away. It bore them back to their house. The detective having seen them into the house, having seen the limousine into the garage, drove his coupé again around and around through the neighboring thoroughfares. And saw nothing of Millar's dark young man.

Then Alec Rush went home and to bed.

At eight o'clock the next morning ugly man and modest coupé were stationary in Charles-Street Avenue again. Male Charles-Street Avenue went with the sun on its left toward its offices. As the morning aged and the shadows grew shorter and thicker, so, generally, did the individuals who composed this morning procession. Eight o'clock was frequently young and slender and brisk, Eight-thirty less so, Nine still less, and rear-guard Ten o'clock was preponderantly neither young nor slender, and more often sluggish than brisk.

Into this rear guard, though physically he belonged to no later period than eight-thirty, a blue roadster carried Hubert Landow. His broad shoulders were blue-coated, his blond hair gray-capped, and he was alone in the roadster. With a glance around to make sure Millar's dark young man was not in sight, Alec Rush turned his coupé in the blue car's wake.

They rode swiftly into the city, down into its financial center, where Hubert Landow deserted his roadster before a Redwood Street stockbroker's office. The morning had become noon before Landow was in the street again, turning his roadster northward.

When shadowed and shadower came to rest again they were in Mount Royal Avenue. Landow got out of his car and strode briskly into a large apartment building. A block distant, Alec Rush lighted a black cigar and sat still in his coupé. Half an hour passed. Alec Rush turned his head and sank his gold teeth deep into his cigar.

Scarcely twenty feet behind the coupé, in the doorway of a garage, a dark young man with high cheek-bones, high, straight shoulders, loitered. His nose was large. His suit was brown, as were the eyes with which he seemed to pay no especial attention to anything through the thin blue drift of smoke from the tip of a drooping cigarette.

THE ASSISTANT MURDERER

Alec Rush took his cigar from his mouth to examine it, took a knife from his pocket to trim the bitten end, restored cigar to mouth and knife to pocket, and thereafter was as indifferent to all Mount Royal Avenue as the dark youth behind him. The one drowsed in his doorway. The other dozed in his car. And the afternoon crawled past one o'clock, past one-thirty.

Hubert Landow came out of the apartment building, vanished swiftly in his blue roadster. His going stirred neither of the motionless men, scarcely their eyes. Not until another fifteen minutes had gone did either of them move.

Then the dark youth left his doorway. He moved without haste, up the street, with short, almost mincing, steps. The back of Alec Rush's black-derbied head was to the youth when he passed the coupé, which may have been chance, for none could have said that the ugly man had so much as glanced at the other since his first sight of him. The dark young man let his eyes rest on the detective's back without interest as he passed. He went on up the street toward the apartment building Landow had visited, up its steps, and out of sight into it.

When the dark young man had disappeared, Alec Rush threw away his cigar, stretched, yawned, and awakened the coupé's engine. Four blocks and two turnings from Mount Royal Avenue, he got out of the automobile, leaving it locked and empty in front of a graystone church. He walked back to Mount Royal Avenue, to halt on a corner two blocks above his earlier position.

He had another half-hour of waiting before the dark young man appeared. Alec Rush was buying a cigar in a glass-fronted cigar store when the other passed. The young man boarded a street car at North Avenue and found a seat. The detective boarded the same car at the next corner and stood on the rear platform. Warned by an indicative forward hitching of the young man's shoulders and head, Alec Rush was the first passenger off the car at Madison Avenue, and the first aboard a southbound car there. And again, he was off first at Franklin Street.

DETECTIVE STORIES

The dark youth went straight to a rooming-house in this street, while the detective came to rest beside the window of a corner drug store specializing in theatrical make-up. There he loafed until half-past three. When the dark young man came into the street again it was to walk—Alec Rush behind him—to Eutaw Street, board a car, and ride to Camden Station.

There, in the waiting-room, the dark young man met a young woman who frowned and asked:

"Where in the hell have you been at?"

IV
The Man in the Picture

Passing them, the detective heard the petulant greeting, but the young man's reply was pitched too low for him to catch, nor did he hear anything else the young woman said. They talked for perhaps ten minutes, standing together in a deserted end of the waiting-room, so that Alec Rush could not have approached them without making himself conspicuous.

The young woman seemed to be impatient, urgent. The young man seemed to explain, to reassure. Now and then he gestured with the ugly, deft hands of a skilled mechanic. His companion became more agreeable. She was short, square, as if carved economically from a cube. Consistently, her nose also was short and her chin square. She had, on the whole, now that her earlier displeasure was passing, a merry face, a pert, pugnacious, rich-blooded face that advertised inexhaustible vitality. That advertisement was in every feature, from the live ends of her cut brown hair to the earth-gripping pose of her feet on the cement flooring. Her clothes were dark, quiet, expensive, but none too gracefully worn, hanging just the least bit bunchily here and there on her sturdy body.

Nodding vigorously several times, the young man at length tapped his cap-visor with two careless fingers and went out into

THE ASSISTANT MURDERER

the street. Alec Rush let him depart unshadowed. But when, walking slowly out to the iron train-shed gates, along them to the baggage window, thence to the street door, the young woman passed out of the station, the ugly man was behind her. He was still behind her when she joined the four o'clock shopping crowd at Lexington Street.

The young woman shopped with the whole-hearted air of one with nothing else on her mind. In the second department store she visited, Alec Rush left her looking at a display of laces while he moved as swiftly and directly as intervening shoppers would permit toward a tall, thick-shouldered, gray-haired woman in black, who seemed to be waiting for someone near the foot of a flight of stairs.

"Hello, Alec!" she said when he touched her arm, and her humorous eyes actually looked with pleasure at his uncouth face. "What are you doing in my territory?"

"Got a booster for you," he mumbled. "The chunky girl in blue at the lace counter. Make her?"

The store detective looked and nodded.

"Yes. Thanks, Alec. You're sure she's boosting, of course?"

"Now, Minnie!" he complained, his rasping voice throttled down to a metallic growl. "Would I be giving you a bum rumble? She went south with a couple of silk pieces, and it's more than likely she's got herself some lace by now."

"Um-hmm," said Minnie. "Well, when she sticks her foot on the sidewalk, I'll be with her."

Alec Rush put his hand on the store detective's arm again.

"I want a line on her," he said. "What do you say we tail her around and see what she's up to before we knock her over?"

"If it doesn't take all day," the woman agreed. And when the chunky girl in blue presently left the lace counter and the store, the detectives followed, into another store, ranging too far behind her to see any thieving she might have done, content to keep her under surveillance. From this last store their prey went down to where Pratt Street was dingiest, into a dingy three-story house of furnished flats.

Two blocks away a policeman was turning a corner.

"Take a plant on the joint while I get a copper," Alex Rush ordered.

When he returned with the policeman the store detective was waiting in the vestibule.

"Second floor," she said.

Behind her the house's street door stood open to show a dark hallway and the foot of a tattered-carpeted flight of steps. Into this dismal hallway appeared a slovenly thin woman in rumpled gray cotton, saying whiningly as she came forward, "What do you want? I keep a respectable house, I'll have you understand, and I—"

"Chunky, dark-eyed girl living here," Alec Rush croaked. "Second floor. Take us up."

The woman's scrawny face sprang into startled lines, faded eyes wide, as if mistaking the harshness of the detective's voice for the harshness of great emotion.

"Why—why—" she stammered, and then remembered the first principle of shady rooming-house management—never to stand in the way of the police. "I'll take you up," she agreed, and, hitching her wrinkled skirt in one hand, led the way up the stairs.

Her sharp fingers tapped on a door near the head of the stairs.

"Who's that?" a casually curt feminine voice asked.

"Landlady."

The chunky girl in blue, without her hat now, opened the door. Alec Rush moved a big foot forward to hold it open, while the landlady said, "This is her," the policeman said, "You'll have to come along," and Minnie said, "Dearie, we want to come in and talk to you."

"My God!" exclaimed the girl. "There'd be just as much sense to it if you'd all jumped out at me and yelled 'Boo!'"

"This ain't any way," Alec Rush rasped, moving forward, grinning his hideous friendly grin. "Let's go in where we can talk it over."

THE ASSISTANT MURDERER

Merely by moving his loose-jointed bulk a step this way, a half-step that, turning his ugly face on this one and that one, he herded the little group as he wished, sending the landlady discontentedly away, marshalling the others into the girl's rooms.

"Remember, I got no idea what this is all about," said the girl when they were in her living-room, a narrow room where blue fought with red without ever compromising on purple. "I'm easy to get along with, and if you think this is a nice place to talk about whatever you want to talk about, go ahead! But if you're counting on me talking, too, you'd better smart me up."

"Boosting, dearie," Minnie said, leaning forward to pat the girl's arm. "I'm at Goodbody's."

"You think I've been shoplifting? Is that the idea?"

"Yeah. Exactly. Uh-huh. That's what." Alec Rush left her no doubt on the point.

The girl narrowed her eyes, puckered her red mouth, squinted sidewise at the ugly man.

"It's all right with me," she announced, "so long as Goodbody's is hanging the rap on me—somebody I can sue for a million when it flops. I've got nothing to say. Take me for my ride."

"You'll get your ride, sister," the ugly man rasped good-naturedly. "Nobody's going to beat you out of it. But do you mind if I look around your place a little first?"

"Got anything with a judge's name on it that says you can?"

"No."

"Then you don't get a peep!"

Alec Rush chuckled, thrust his hands into his trouser-pockets, and began to wander through the rooms, of which there were three. Presently he came out of the bedroom carrying a photograph in a silver frame.

"Who's this?" he asked the girl.

"Try and find out!"

"I am trying," he lied.

"You big bum!" said she. "You couldn't find water in the ocean!"

Alec Rush laughed with coarse heartiness. He could afford to. The photograph in his hand was of Hubert Landow.

V

The Overpaid Assassin

Twilight was around the graystone church when the owner of the deserted coupé returned to it. The chunky girl—Polly Vanness was the name she had given—had been booked and lodged in a cell in the Southwestern Police Station. Quantities of stolen goods had been found in her flat. Her harvest of that afternoon was still on her person when Minnie and a police matron searched her. She had refused to talk. The detective had said nothing to her about his knowledge of the photograph's subject, or of her meeting in the railroad station with the dark young man. Nothing found in her rooms threw any light on either of these things.

Having eaten his evening meal before coming back to his car, Alec Rush now drove out to Charles-Street Avenue. Lights glowed normally in the Landow house when he passed it. A little beyond it he turned his coupé so that it pointed toward the city, and brought it to rest in a tree-darkened curb-side spot within sight of the house.

The night went along and no one left or entered the Landow house.

Fingernails clicked on the coupé's glass door.

A man stood there. Nothing could be said of him in the darkness except that he was not large, and that to have escaped the detective's notice until now he must have stealthily stalked the car from the rear.

Alec Rush put out a hand and the door swung open.

"Got a match?" the man asked.

The detective hesitated, said, "Yeah," and held out a box.

A match scraped and flared into a dark young face: large nose, high cheekbones: the young man Alec Rush had shadowed that afternoon.

THE ASSISTANT MURDERER

But recognition, when it was voiced, was voiced by the dark young man.

"I thought it was you," he said simply as he applied the flaming match to his cigarette. "Maybe you don't know me, but I knew you when you were on the force."

The ex-detective sergeant gave no meaning at all to a husky "Yeah."

"I thought it was you in the heap on Mount Royal this afternoon, but I couldn't make sure," the young man continued, entering the coupé, sitting beside the detective, closing the door. "Scuttle Zeipp's me. I ain't as well known as Napoleon, so if you've never heard of me there's no hard feelings."

"Yeah."

"That's the stuff! When you once think up a good answer, stick to it." Scuttle Zeipp's face was a sudden bronze mask in the glow of his cigarette. "The same answer'll do for my next question. You're interested in these here Landows? Yeah," he added in hoarse mimicry of the detective's voice.

Another inhalation lighted his face, and his words came smokily out as the glow faded.

"You ought to want to know what I'm doing hanging around 'em. I ain't tight. I'll tell you. I've been slipped half a grand to bump off the girl—twice. How do you like that?"

"I hear you," said Alec Rush. "But anybody can talk that knows the words."

"Talk? Sure it's talk," Zeipp admitted cheerfully. "But so's it talk when the judge says 'hanged by the neck until dead and may God have mercy on your soul!' Lots of things are talk, but that don't always keep 'em from being real."

"Yeah?"

"Yeah, brother, yeah! Now listen to this: it's one for the cuff. A certain party comes to me a couple of days ago with a knock-down[4] from a party that knows me. See? This certain party asks me what

---

4 Introduction.

I want to bump off a broad. I thought a grand would be right, and said so. Too stiff. We come together on five hundred. I got two-fifty down and get the rest when the Landow twist is cold. Not so bad for a soft trick—a slug through the side of a car—huh?"

"Well, what are you waiting for?" the detective asked. "You want to make it a fancy caper—kill her on her birthday or a legal holiday?"

Scuttle Zeipp smacked his lips and poked the detective's chest with a finger in the dark.

"Not any, brother! I'm thinking way ahead of you! Listen to this: I pocket my two-fifty advance and come up here to give the ground a good casing, not wanting to lam into anything I didn't know was here. While I'm poking around, I run into another party that's poking around. This second party gives me a tumble, I talk smart, and bingo! First thing you know she's propositioning me. What do you guess? She wants to know what I want to bump off a broad! Is it the same one *she* wants stopped? I hope to tell you it is!

"It ain't so silly! I get my hands on another two hundred and fifty berries, with that much more coming when I put over the fast one. Now do you think I'm going to do anything to that Landow baby? You're dumb if you do. She's my meal ticket. If she lives till I pop her, she'll be older than either you or the bay. I've got five hundred out of her so far. What's the matter with sticking around and waiting for more customers that don't like her? If two of 'em want to buy her out of the world, why not more? The answer is 'Yeah!' And on top of that, here you are snooping around her. Now there it is, brother, for you to look at and taste and smell."

Silence held for several minutes, in the darkness of the coupé's interior, and then the detective's harsh voice put a sceptical question:

"And who are these certain parties that want her out of the way?"

"Be yourself!" Scuttle Zeipp admonished him. "I'm laying down on 'em, right enough, but I ain't feeding 'em to you."

"What are you giving me all this for then?"

"What for? Because you're in on the lay somewhere. Crossing each other, neither of us can make a thin dimmer. If we don't hook up we'll just ruin the racket for each other. I've already made half a grand off this Landow. That's mine, but there's more to be picked up by a couple of men that know what they're doing. All right. I'm offering to throw in with you on a two-way cut of whatever else we can get. But my parties are out! I don't mind throwing them down, but I ain't rat enough to put the finger on them for you."

Alec Rush grunted and croaked another dubious inquiry.

"How come you trust me so much, Scuttle?"

The hired killer laughed knowingly.

"Why not? You're a right guy. You can see a profit when it's showed to you. They didn't chuck you off the force for forgetting to hang up your stocking. Besides, suppose you want to double-cross me, what can you do? You can't prove anything. I told you I didn't mean the woman any harm. I ain't even packing a gun. But all that's the bunk. You're a wise head. You know what's what. Me and you, Alec, we can get plenty!"

Silence again, until the detectives spoke slowly, thoughtfully.

"The first thing would be to get a line on the reasons your parties want the girl put out. Got anything on that?"

"Not a whisper."

"Both of 'em women, I take it."

Scuttle Zeipp hesitated.

"Yes," he admitted. "But don't be asking me anything about 'em. In the first place, I don't know anything, and in the second, I wouldn't tip their mitts if I did."

"Yeah," the detective croaked, as if he quite understood his companion's perverted idea of loyalty. "Now if they're women, the chances are the racket hangs on a man. What do you think of Landow? He's a pretty lad."

Scuttle Zeipp leaned over to put his finger against the detective's chest again.

"You've got it, Alec! That could be it, damned if it couldn't!"

"Yeah," Alec Rush agreed, fumbling with the levers of his car. "We'll get away from here and stay away until I look into him."

At Franklin Street, half a block from the rooming-house into which he had shadowed the young man that afternoon, the detective stopped his coupé.

"You want to drop out here?" he asked.

Scuttle Zeipp looked sidewise, speculatively, into the elder man's ugly face.

"It'll do," the young man said, "but you're a damned good guesser, just the same." He stopped with a hand on the door. "It's a go, is it, Alec? Fifty-fifty?"

"I wouldn't say so." Alec Rush grinned at him with hideous good nature. "You're not a bad lad, Scuttle, and if there's any gravy you'll get yours, but don't count on me mobbing up with you."

Zeipp's eyes jerked to slits, his lips snarled back from yellow teeth that were set edge to edge.

"You sell me out, you damned gorilla, and I'll—" He laughed the threat out of being, his dark face young and careless again. "Have it your own way, Alec. I didn't make no mistake when I throwed in with you. What you say goes."

"Yeah," the ugly man agreed. "Lay off that joint out there until I tell you. Maybe you'd better drop in to see me tomorrow. The phone book'll tell you where my office is. So long, kid."

"So long, Alec."

VI

Cathedral Street

In the morning Alec Rush set about investigating Hubert Landow. First he went to the City Hall, where he examined the gray books in which marriage licenses are indexed. Hubert Britman Landow and Sara Falsoner had been married six months before, he learned.

The bride's maiden name thickened the red in the detective's bloodshot eyes. Air hissed sharply from his flattened nostrils. "Yeah! Yeah!" he said to himself, so raspingly that a lawyer's skinny clerk,

THE ASSISTANT MURDERER

fiddling with other records at his elbow, looked frightenedly at him and edged a little away.

From the City Hall, Alec Rush carried the bride's name to two newspaper offices, where, after studying the files, he bought an armful of six-month-old papers. He took the papers to his office, spread them on his desk, and attacked them with a pair of shears. When the last one had been cut and thrown aside, there remained on his desk a thick sheaf of clippings.

Arranging his clippings in chronological order, Alec Rush lighted a black cigar, put his elbows on the desk, his ugly head between his palms, and began to read a story with which newspaper-reading Baltimore had been familiar half a year before.

Purged of irrelevancies and earlier digressions, the story was essentially this:

Jerome Falsoner, aged forty-five, was a bachelor who lived alone in a flat in Cathedral Street, on an income more than sufficient for his comfort. He was a tall man, but of delicate physique, the result, it may have been, of excessive indulgence in pleasure on a constitution none too strong in the beginning. He was well-known, at least by sight, to all night-living Baltimoreans, and to those who frequented race-track, gambling-house, and the furtive cockpits that now and then materialize for a few brief hours in the forty miles of country that lie between Baltimore and Washington.

One Fanny Kidd, coming as was her custom at ten o'clock one morning to "do" Jerome Falsoner's rooms, found him lying on his back in his living-room, staring with dead eyes at a spot on the ceiling, a bright spot that was reflected sunlight—reflected from the metal hilt of his paper-knife, which protruded from his chest.

Police investigation established four facts:

First, Jerome Falsoner had been dead for fourteen hours when Fanny Kidd found him, which placed his murder at about eight o'clock the previous evening.

Second, the last persons known to have seen him alive were a woman named Madeline Boudin, with whom he had been intimate, and three of her friends. They had seen him, alive, at some time between seven-thirty and eight o'clock, or less than half an hour before his death. They had been driving down to a cottage on the Severn River, and Madeline Boudin had told the others she wanted to see Falsoner before she went. The others had remained in their car while she rang the bell. Jerome Falsoner opened the street door and she went in. Ten minutes later she came out and rejoined her friends. Jerome Falsoner came to the door with her, waving a hand at one of the men in the car—a Frederick Stoner, who knew Falsoner slightly, and who was connected with the district attorney's office. Two women, talking on the steps of a house across the street, had also seen Falsoner, and had seen Madeline Boudin and her friends drive away.

Third, Jerome Falsoner's heir and only near relative was his niece, Sara Falsoner, who, by some vagary of chance, was marrying Hubert Landow at the very hour that Fanny Kidd was finding her employer's dead body. Niece and uncle had seldom seen one another. The niece—for police suspicion settled on her for a short space—was definitely proved to have been at home, in her apartment in Carey Street, from six o'clock the evening of the murder until eight-thirty the next morning. Her husband, her fiancé then, had been there with her from six until eleven that evening. Prior to her marriage, the girl had been employed as stenographer by the same trust company that employed Ralph Millar.

Fourth, Jerome Falsoner, who had not the most even of dispositions, had quarreled with an Icelander named Einar Jokumsson in a gambling-house two days before he was murdered. Jokumsson had threatened him. Jokumsson—a short, heavily built man, dark-haired, dark-eyed—had vanished from his hotel, leaving his bags there, the day the body was found, and had not been seen since.

The last of these clippings carefully read, Alec Rush rocked back in his chair and made a thoughtful monster's face at the ceiling. Presently he leaned forward again to look into the telephone directory, and to call the number of Ralph Millar's trust company. But when he got his number he changed his mind.

"Never mind," he said into the instrument, and called a number that was Goodbody's. Minnie, when she came to the telephone, told him that Polly Vanness had been identified as one Polly Bangs, arrested in Milwaukee two years ago for shoplifting, and given a two-year sentence. Minnie also said that Polly Bangs had been released on bail early that morning.

Alec Rush pushed back the telephone and looked through his clippings again until he found the address of Madeline Boudin, the woman who had visited Falsoner so soon before his death. It was a Madison Avenue number. Thither his coupé carried the detective.

No, Miss Boudin did not live there. Yes, she had lived there, but had moved four months ago. Perhaps Mrs. Blender, on the third floor, would know where she lived now. Mrs. Blender did not know. She knew Miss Boudin had moved to an apartment house in Garrison Avenue, but did not think she was living there now. At the Garrison Avenue house: Miss Boudin had moved away a month and a half ago—somewhere in Mount Royal Avenue, perhaps. The number was not known.

The coupé carried its ugly owner to Mount Royal Avenue, to the apartment building he had seen first Hubert Landow and then Scuttle Zeipp visit the previous day. At the manager's office he made inquiries about a Walter Boyden, who was thought to live there. Walter Boyden was not known to the manager. There was a Miss Boudin in 604, but her name was B-o-u-d-i-n, and she lived alone.

Alec Rush left the building and got in his car again. He screwed up his savage red eyes, nodded his head in a satisfied way, and with one finger described a small circle in the air. Then he returned to his office.

Calling the trust company's number again, he gave Ralph Millar's name, and presently was speaking to the assistant cashier.

"This is Rush. Can you come up to the office right away?"

"What's that? Certainly. But how—how—? Yes, I'll be up in a minute."

None of the surprise that had been in Millar's telephone voice was apparent when he reached the detective's office. He asked no questions concerning the detective's knowledge of his identity. In brown today, he was as neatly inconspicuous as he had been yesterday in gray.

"Come in," the ugly man welcomed him. "Sit down. I've got to have some more facts, Mr. Millar."

Millar's thin mouth tightened and his brows drew together with obstinate reticence.

"I thought we settled that point, Rush. I told you—"

Alec Rush frowned at his client with jovial, though frightful exasperation.

"I know what you told me," he interrupted. "But that was then and this is now. The thing's coming unwound on me, and I can see just enough to get myself tangled up if I don't watch Harvey. I found your mysterious man, talked to him. He was following Mrs. Landow, right enough. According to the way he tells it, he's been hired to kill her."

Millar leaped from his chair to lean over the yellow desk, his face close to the detective's.

"My God, Rush, what are you saying? To kill her?"

"Now, now! Take it easy. He's not going to kill her. I don't think he ever meant to. But he claims he was hired to do it."

"You've arrested him? You've found the man who hired him?"

The detective squinted up his bloodshot eyes and studied the younger man's passionate face.

"As a matter of fact," he croaked calmly when he had finished his examination, "I haven't done either of those things. She's in no danger just now. Maybe the lad was stringing me, maybe he wasn't, but either way he wouldn't have spilled it to me if he meant to do anything. And when it comes right down to it, Mr. Millar, do you want him arrested?"

"Yes! That is—" Millar stepped back from the desk, sagged limply down on the chair again, and put shaking hands over his face. "My God, Rush, I don't know!" he gasped.

VII
Millar Talks

"Exactly," said Alec Rush. "Now here it is. Mrs. Landow was Jerome Falsoner's niece and heir. She worked for your trust company. She married Landow the morning her uncle was found dead. Yesterday Landow visited the building where Madeline Boudin lives. She was the last person known to have been in Falsoner's rooms before he was killed. But her alibi seems to be as air-tight as the Landows'. The man who claims he was hired to kill Mrs. Landow also visited Madeline Boudin's building yesterday. I saw him go in. I saw him meet another woman. A shoplifter, the second one. In her rooms I found a photograph of Hubert Landow. Your dark man claims he was hired twice to kill Mrs. Landow—by two women neither knowing the other had hired him. He won't tell me who they are, but he doesn't have to."

The hoarse voice stopped and Alec Rush waited for Millar to speak. But Millar was for the time without a voice. His eyes were wide and despairingly empty. Alec Rush raised one big hand, folded it into a fist that was almost perfectly spherical, and thumped his desk softly.

"There it is, Mr. Millar," he rasped. "A pretty tangle. If you'll tell me what you know, we'll get it straightened out, never fear. If you don't—I'm out!"

Now Millar found words, however jumbled.

"You couldn't, Rush! You can't desert me—us—her! It's not—You're not—"

But Alec Rush shook his ugly pear-shaped head with slow emphasis.

"There's murder in this and the Lord knows what all. I've got no liking for a blindfolded game. How do I know what you're up to? You can tell me what you know—everything—or you can find yourself another detective. That's flat."

Ralph Millar's fingers picked at each other, his teeth pulled at his lips, his harassed eyes pleaded with the detective.

"You can't, Rush," he begged. "She's still in danger. Even if you are right about that man not attacking her, she's not safe. The women who hired him can hire another. You've got to protect her, Rush."

"Yeah? Then you've got to talk."

"I've got to—? Yes, I'll talk, Rush. I'll tell you anything you ask. But there's really nothing—or almost nothing—I know beyond what you've already learned."

"She worked for your trust company?"

"Yes, in my department."

"Left there to be married?"

"Yes. That is—No, Rush, the truth is she was discharged. It was an outrage, but—"

"When was this?"

"It was the day before the—before she was married."

"Tell me about it."

"She had—I'll have to explain her situation to you first, Rush. She is an orphan. Her father, Ben Falsoner, had been wild in his youth—and perhaps not only in his youth—as I believe all the Falsoners have been. However, he had quarreled with his father—old Howard Falsoner—and the old man had cut him out of the will. But not altogether out. The old man hoped Ben would mend his ways, and he didn't mean to leave him with nothing in that event. Unfortunately he trusted it to his other son, Jerome.

"Old Howard Falsoner left a will whereby the income from his estate was to go to Jerome during Jerome's life. Jerome was to provide for his brother, Ben, as he saw fit. That is, he had an absolutely free hand. He could divide the income equally with his brother, or he could give him a pittance, or he could give him nothing, as

THE ASSISTANT MURDERER

Ben's conduct deserved. On Jerome's death the estate was to be divided equally among the old man's grandchildren.

"In theory, that was a fairly sensible arrangement, but not in practice—not in Jerome Falsoner's hands. You didn't know him? Well, he was the last man you'd ever trust with a thing of that sort. He exercised his power to the utmost. Ben Falsoner never got a cent from him. Three years ago Ben died, and so the girl, his only daughter, stepped into his position in relation to her grandfather's money. Her mother was already dead. Jerome Falsoner never paid her a cent.

"That was her situation when she came to the trust company two years ago. It wasn't a happy one. She had at least a touch of the Falsoner recklessness and extravagance. There she was: heiress to some two million dollars—for Jerome had never married and she was the only grandchild—but without any present income at all, except her salary, which was by no means a large one.

"She got in debt. I suppose she tried to economize at times, but there was always that two million dollars ahead to make scrimping doubly distasteful. Finally, the trust company officials heard of her indebtedness. A collector or two came to the office, in fact. Since she was employed in my department, I had the disagreeable duty of warning her. She promised to pay her debts and contract no more, and I suppose she did try, but she wasn't very successful. Our officials are old-fashioned, ultra-conservative. I did everything I could to save her, but it was no good. They simply would not have an employee who was heels over head in debt."

Millar paused a moment, looked miserably at the floor, and went on:

"I had the disagreeable task of telling her her services were no longer needed. I tried to—It was awfully unpleasant. That was the day before she married Landow. It—" He paused and, as if he could think of nothing else to say, repeated, "Yes, it was the day before she married Landow," and fell to staring miserably at the floor again.

Alec Rush, who had sat as still through the recital of this history as a carven monster on an old church, now leaned over his desk and put a husky question:

"And who is this Hubert Landow? What is he?"

Ralph Millar shook his downcast head.

"I don't know him. I've seen him. I know nothing of him."

"Mrs. Landow ever speak of him? I mean when she was in the trust company?"

"It's likely, but I don't remember."

"So you didn't know what to make of it when you heard she'd married him?"

The younger man looked up with frightened brown eyes.

"What are you getting at, Rush? You don't think—Yes, as you say, I was surprised. What are you getting at?"

"The marriage license," the detective said, ignoring his client's repeated question, "was issued to Landow four days before the wedding-day, four days before Jerome Falsoner's body was found."

Millar chewed a fingernail and shook his head hopelessly.

"I don't know what you're getting at," he mumbled around the finger. "The whole thing is bewildering."

"Isn't it a fact, Mr. Millar," the detective's voice filled the office with hoarse insistence, "that you were on more friendly terms with Sara Falsoner than with anyone else in the trust company?"

The younger man raised his head and looked Alec Rush in the eye—held his gaze with brown eyes that were doggedly level.

"The fact is," he said quietly, "that I asked Sara Falsoner to marry me the day she left."

"Yeah. And she—?"

"And she—I suppose it was my fault. I was clumsy, crude, whatever you like. God knows what she thought—that I was asking her to marry me out of pity, that I was trying to force her into marriage by discharging her when I knew she was over her head in debt! She might have thought anything. Anyhow, it was—it was disagreeable."

"You mean she not only refused you, but was—well—disagreeable about it?"

"I do mean that."

Alec Rush sat back in his chair and brought fresh grotesqueries into his face by twisting his thick mouth crookedly up at one corner. His red eyes were evilly reflective on the ceiling.

"The only thing for it," he decided, "is to go to Landow and give him what we've got."

"But are you sure he—?" Millar objected indefinitely.

"Unless he's one whale of an actor, he's a lot in love with his wife," the detective said with certainty. "That's enough to justify taking the story to him."

Millar was not convinced.

"You're sure it would be wisest?"

"Yeah. We've got to go to one of three people with the tale—him, her, or the police. I think he's the best bet, but take your choice."

The younger man nodded reluctantly.

"All right. But you don't have to bring me into it, do you?" he said with quick alarm. "You can handle it so I won't be involved. You understand what I mean? She's his wife, and it would be—"

"Sure," Alec Rush promised; "I'll keep you covered up."

VIII
Sara Talks

Hubert Landow, twisting the detective's card in his fingers, received Alec Rush in a somewhat luxuriously furnished room in the second story of the Charles-Street Avenue house. He was standing—tall, blond, boyishly handsome—in the middle of the floor, facing the door, when the detective—fat, grizzled, battered, and ugly—was shown in.

"You wish to see me? Here, sit down."

Hubert Landow's manner was neither restrained nor hearty. It was precisely the manner that might be expected of a young man receiving an unexpected call from so savage-visaged a detective.

"Yeah," said Alec Rush as they sat in facing chairs. "I've got something to tell you. It won't take much time, but it's kind of wild. It might be a surprise to you, and it might not. But it's on the level. I don't want you to think I'm kidding you."

Hubert Landow bent forward, his face all interest.

"I won't," he promised. "Go on."

"A couple of days ago I got a line on a man who might be tied up in a job I'm interested in. He's a crook. Trailing him around, I discovered he was interested in your affairs, and your wife's. He's shadowed you and he's shadowed her. He was loafing down the street from a Mount Royal Avenue apartment that you went in yesterday, and he went in there later himself."

"But what the devil is he up to?" Landow exclaimed. "You think he's—"

"Wait," the ugly man advised. "Wait until you've heard it all, and then you can tell me what you make of it. He came out of there and went to Camden Station, where he met a young woman. They talked a bit, and later in the afternoon she was picked up in a department store—shoplifting. Her name is Polly Bangs, and she's done a hitch in Wisconsin for the same racket. Your photograph was on her dresser."

"My photograph?"

Alec Rush nodded placidly up into the face of the young man, who was now standing.

"Yours. You know this Polly Bangs? A chunky, square-built girl of twenty-six or so, with brown hair and eyes—saucy looking?"

Hubert Landow's face was a puzzled blank.

"No! What the devil could she be doing with my picture?" he demanded. "Are you sure it was mine?"

"Not dead sure, maybe, but sure enough to need proof that it wasn't. Maybe she's somebody you've forgotten, or maybe she ran across the picture somewhere and kept it because she liked it."

"Nonsense!" The blond man squirmed at this tribute to his face, and blushed a vivid red beside which Alec Rush's complexion was almost colorless. "There must be some sensible reason. She has been arrested, you say?"

"Yeah, but she's out on bail now. But let me get along with my story. Last night this thug I've told you about and I had a talk. He claims he has been hired to kill your wife."

Hubert Landow, who had returned to his chair, now jerked in it so that its joints creaked strainingly. His face, crimson a second ago, drained paper-white. Another sound than the chair's creaking was faint in the room: the least of muffled gasps. The blond young man did not seem to hear it, but Alec Rush's bloodshot eyes flicked sidewise for an instant to focus fleetingly on a closed door across the room.

Landow was out of his chair again, leaning down to the detective, his fingers digging into the ugly man's loose muscular shoulders.

"This is horrible!" he was crying. "We've got to—"

The door at which the detective had looked a moment ago opened. A beautiful tall girl came through—Sara Landow. Her rumpled hair was an auburn cloud around her white face. Her eyes were dead things. She walked slowly toward the men, her body inclined a little forward, as if against a strong wind.

"It's no use, Hubert." Her voice was as dead as her eyes. "We may as well face it. It's Madeline Boudin. She has found out that I killed my uncle."

"Hush, darling, hush!" Landow caught his wife in his arms and tried to soothe her with a caressing hand on her shoulder. "You don't know what you're saying."

"Oh, but I do." She shrugged herself listlessly out of his arms and sat in the chair Alec Rush had just vacated. "It's Madeline Boudin, you know it is. She knows I killed Uncle Jerome."

Landow whirled to the detective, both hands going out to grip the ugly man's arm.

"You won't listen to what she's saying, Rush?" he pleaded. "She hasn't been well. She doesn't know what she's saying."

Sara Landow laughed with weary bitterness.

"Haven't been well?" she said. "No, I haven't been well, not since I killed him. How could I be well after that? You are a detective." Her eyes lifted their emptiness to Alec Rush. "Arrest me. I killed Jerome Falsoner."

Alec Rush, standing arms akimbo, legs apart, scowled at her, saying nothing.

"You can't, Rush!" Landow was tugging at the detective's arm again. "You can't, man. It's ridiculous! You—"

"Where does this Madeline Boudin fit in?" Alec Rush's harsh voice demanded. "I know she was chummy with Jerome, but why should she want your wife killed?"

Landow hesitated, shifting his feet, and when he replied it was reluctantly.

"She was Jerome's mistress, had a child by him. My wife, when she learned of it, insisted on making her a settlement out of the estate. It was in connection with that that I went to see her yesterday."

"Yeah. Now to get back to Jerome: you and your wife were supposed to be in her apartment at the time he was killed, if I remember right?"

Sara Landow sighed with spiritless impatience.

"Must there be all this discussion?" she asked in a small, tired voice. "I killed him. No one else killed him. No one else was there when I killed him. I stabbed him with the paper-knife when he attacked me, and he said, 'Don't! Don't!' and began to cry, down on his knees, and I ran out."

Alec Rush looked from the girl to the man. Landow's face was wet with perspiration, his hands were white fists, and something quivered in his chest. When he spoke his voice was as hoarse as the detective's, if not so loud.

"Sara, will you wait here until I come back? I'm going out for a little while, possibly an hour. You'll wait here and not do anything until I return?"

"Yes," the girl said, neither curiosity nor interest in her voice. "But it's no use, Hubert. I should have told you in the beginning. It's no use."

"Just wait for me, Sara," he pleaded, and then bent his head to the detective's deformed ear. "Stay with her, Rush, for God's sake!" he whispered, and went swiftly out of the room.

The front door banged shut. An automobile purred away from the house. Alec Rush spoke to the girl.

"Where's the phone?"

"In the next room," she said, without looking up from the handkerchief her fingers were measuring.

The detective crossed to the door through which she had entered the room, found that it opened into a library, where a telephone stood in a corner. On the other side of the room a clock indicated 3:35. The detective went to the telephone and called Ralph Millar's office, asked for Millar, and told him:

"This is Rush. I'm at the Landows'. Come up right away."

"But I can't, Rush. Can't you understand my—"

"Can't hell!" croaked Alec Rush. "Get here quick!"

IX
The Shadow

The young woman with dead eyes, still playing with the hem of her handkerchief, did not look up when the ugly man returned to the room. Neither of them spoke. Alec Rush, standing with his back to a window, twice took out his watch to glare savagely at it.

The faint tingling of the doorbell came from below. The detective went across to the hall door and down the front stairs, moving with heavy swiftness. Ralph Millar, his face a field in which fear and embarrassment fought, stood in the vestibule, stammering something unintelligible to the maid who had opened the door. Alec Rush put the girl brusquely aside, brought Millar in, guided him upstairs.

"She says she killed Jerome," he muttered into his client's ear as they mounted.

Ralph Millar's face went dreadfully white, but there was no surprise in it.

"You knew she killed him?" Alec Rush growled.

Millar tried twice to speak and made no sound. They were on the second-floor landing before the words came.

"I saw her on the street that night, going toward his flat!"

Alec Rush snorted viciously and turned the younger man toward the room where Sara Landow sat.

"Landow's out," he whispered hurriedly. "I'm going out. Stay with her. She's shot to hell—likely to do anything if she's left alone. If Landow gets back before I do, tell him to wait for me."

Before Millar could voice the confusion in his face they were across the sill and into the room. Sara Landow raised her head. Her body was lifted from the chair as if by an invisible power. She came up tall and erect on her feet. Millar stood just inside the door. They looked eye into eye, posed each as if in the grip of a force pushing them together, another holding them apart.

Alec Rush hurried clumsily and silently down to the street.

In Mount Royal Avenue, Alec Rush saw the blue roadster at once. It was standing empty before the apartment building in which Madeline Boudin lived. The detective drove past it and turned his coupé in to the curb three blocks below. He had barely come to rest there when Landow ran out of the apartment building, jumped into his car, and drove off. He drove to a Charles Street hotel. Behind him went the detective.

In the hotel, Landow walked straight to the writing-room. For half an hour he sat there, bending over a desk, covering sheet after sheet of paper with rapidly written words, while the detective sat behind a newspaper in a secluded angle of the lobby, watching the writing-room exit. Landow came out of the room stuffing a thick envelope in his pocket, left the hotel, got into his machine, and drove to the office of a messenger service company in St. Paul Street.

He remained in this office for five minutes. When he came out he ignored his roadster at the curb, walking instead to Calvert Street, where he boarded a northbound street car. Alec Rush's coupé rolled along behind the car. At Union Station, Landow left the street car and went to the ticket-window. He had just asked for a one-way ticket to Philadelphia when Alec Rush tapped him on the shoulder.

Hubert Landow turned slowly, the money for his ticket still in his hand. Recognition brought no expression to his handsome face.

"Yes," he said coolly, "what is it?"

Alec Rush nodded his ugly head at the ticket-window, at the money in Landow's hand.

"This is nothing for you to be doing," he growled.

"Here you are," the ticket-seller said through his grille. Neither of the men in front paid any attention to him. A large woman in pink, red, and violet, jostling Landow, stepped on his foot and pushed past him to the window. Landow stepped back, the detective following.

"You shouldn't have left Sara alone," said Landow. "She's—"

"She's not alone. I got somebody to stay with her."

"Not—?"

"Not the police, if that's what you're thinking."

Landow began to pace slowly down the long concourse, the detective keeping step with him. The blond man stopped and looked sharply into the other's face.

"Is it that fellow Millar who's with her?" he demanded.

"Yeah."

"Is he the man you're working for, Rush?"

"Yeah."

Landow resumed his walking. When they had reached the northern extremity of the concourse, he spoke again.

"What does he want, this Millar?"

Alec Rush shrugged his thick, limber shoulders and said nothing.

"Well, what do you want?" the young man asked with some heat, facing the detective squarely now.

"I don't want you going out of town."

Landow pondered that, scowling.

"Suppose I insist on going," he asked, "how will you stop me?"

"Accomplice after the fact in Jerome's murder would be a charge I could hold you on."

Silence again, until broken by Landow.

"Look here, Rush. You're working for Millar. He's out at my house. I've just sent a letter out to Sara by messenger. Give them time to read it, and then phone Millar there. Ask him if he wants me held or not."

Alec Rush shook his head decidedly.

"No good," he rasped. "Millar's too rattle-brained for me to take his word for anything like that over the phone. We'll go back there and have a talk all around."

Now it was Landow who balked.

"No," he snapped. "I won't!" He looked with cool calculation at the detective's ugly face. "Can I buy you, Rush?"

"No, Landow. Don't let my looks and my record kid you."

"I thought not." Landow looked at the roof and at his feet, and he blew his breath out sharply. "We can't talk here. Let's find a quiet place."

"The heap's outside," Alec Rush said, "and we can sit in that."

x
Bangs

Seated in Alec Rush's coupé, Hubert Landow lighted a cigarette, the detective one of his black cigars.

"That Polly Bangs you were talking about, Rush," the blond man said without preamble, "is my wife. My name is Henry Bangs.

You won't find my fingerprints anywhere. When Polly was picked up in Milwaukee a couple of years ago and sent over, I came east and fell in with Madeline Boudin. We made a good team. She had brains in chunks, and if I've got somebody to do my thinking for me, I'm a pretty good worker myself."

He smiled at the detective, pointing at his own face with his cigarette. While Alec Rush watched, a tide of crimson surged into the blond man's face until it was as rosy as a blushing school-girl's. He laughed again and the blush began to fade.

"That's my best trick," he went on. "Easy if you have the gift and keep in practice: fill your lungs, try to force the air out while keeping it shut off at the larynx. It's a gold mine for a grifter! You'd be surprised how people will trust me after I've turned on a blush or two for 'em. So Madeline and I were in the money. She had brains, nerve, and a good front. I have everything but brains. We turned a couple of tricks—one con and one blackmail—and then she ran into Jerome Falsoner. We were going to give him the squeeze at first. But when Madeline found out that Sara was his heiress, that she was in debt, and that she and her uncle were on the outs, we ditched that racket and cooked a juicier one. Madeline found somebody to introduce me to Sara. I made myself agreeable, playing the boob—the shy but worshipful young man.

"Madeline had brains, as I've said. She used 'em all this time. I hung around Sara, sending her candy, books, flowers, taking her to shows and dinner. The books and shows were part of Madeline's work. Two of the books mentioned the fact that a husband can't be made to testify against his wife in court, nor wife against husband. One of the plays touched the same thing. That was planting the seeds. We planted another with my blushing and mumbling—persuaded Sara, or rather let her discover for herself, that I was the clumsiest liar in the world.

"The planting done, we began to push the game along. Madeline kept on good terms with Jerome. Sara was getting deeper in debt. We helped her in still deeper. We had a burglar clean out her apartment one night—Ruby Sweeger, maybe you know him. He's in stir now for another caper. He got what money she had and most of the things she could have hocked in a pinch. Then we stirred up some of the people she owed, sent them anonymous letters warning them not to count too much on her being Jerome's heir. Foolish letters, but they did the trick. A couple of her creditors sent collectors to the trust company.

"Jerome got his income from the estate quarterly. Madeline knew the dates, and Sara knew them. The day before the next one, Madeline got busy on Sara's creditors again. I don't know what she told them this time, but it was enough. They descended on the trust company in a flock, with the result that the next day Sara was given two weeks' pay and discharged. When she came out I met her—by chance—yes, I'd been watching for her since morning. I took her for a drive and got her back to her apartment at six o'clock. There we found more frantic creditors waiting to pounce on her. I chased them out, played the big-hearted boy, making embarrassed offers of all sorts of help. She refused them, of course, and I could see decision coming into her face. She knew this was the day on which Jerome got his quarterly check. She determined to go see him, to demand that he pay her debts at least. She didn't tell me where she was going, but I could see it plain enough, since I was looking for it.

"I left her and waited across the street from her apartment, in Franklin Square, until I saw her come out. Then I found a telephone, called up Madeline, and told her Sara was on her way to her uncle's flat."

Landow's cigarette scorched his fingers. He dropped it, crushed it under his foot, lighted another.

"This is a long-winded story, Rush," he apologized, "but it'll soon be over now."

"Keep talking, son," said Alec Rush.

"There were some people in Madeline's place when I phoned her—people trying to persuade her to go down the country on a party. She agreed now. They would give her an even better alibi than the one she had cooked up. She told them she had to see Jerome before she left, and they drove her over to his place and waited in their car while she went in with him.

"She had a pint bottle of cognac with her, all doped and ready. She poured out a drink of it for Jerome, telling him of the new bootlegger she had found who had a dozen or more cases of this cognac to sell at a reasonable price. The cognac was good enough and the price low enough to make Jerome think she had dropped in to let him in on something good. He gave her an order to pass on to the bootlegger. Making sure his steel paper-knife was in full view on the table, Madeline rejoined her friends, taking Jerome as far as the door so they would see he was still alive, and drove off.

"Now I don't know what Madeline had put in that cognac. If she told me, I've forgotten. It was a powerful drug—not a poison, you understand, but an excitant. You'll see what I mean when you hear the rest. Sara must have reached her uncle's flat ten or fifteen minutes after Madeline's departure. Her uncle's face, she says, was red, inflamed, when he opened the door for her. But he was a frail man, while she was strong, and she wasn't afraid of the devil himself, for that matter. She went in and demanded that he settle her debts, even if he didn't choose to make her an allowance out of his income.

"They were both Falsoners, and the argument must have grown hot. Also the drug was working on Jerome, and he had no will with which to fight it. He attacked her. The paper-knife was on the table, as Madeline had seen. He was a maniac. Sara was not one of your corner-huddling, screaming girls. She grabbed the paper-knife and let him have it. When he fell, she turned and ran.

"Having followed her as soon as I'd finished telephoning to Madeline, I was standing on Jerome's front steps when she dashed out. I stopped her and she told me she'd killed her uncle. I made her wait there while I went in, to see if he was really dead. Then I took her home, explaining my presence at Jerome's door by saying, in my boobish, awkward way, that I had been afraid she might do something reckless and had thought it best to keep an eye on her.

"Back in her apartment, she was all for giving herself up to the police. I pointed out the danger in that, arguing that, in debt, admittedly going to her uncle for money, being his heiress, she would most certainly be convicted of having murdered him so she would get the money. Her story of his attack, I persuaded her, would be laughed at as a flimsy yarn. Dazed, she wasn't hard to convince. The next step was easy. The police would investigate her, even if they didn't especially suspect her. I was, so far as we knew, the only person whose testimony could convict her. I was loyal enough, but wasn't I the clumsiest liar in the world? Didn't the mildest lie make me blush like an auctioneer's flag? The way around that difficulty lay in what two of the books I had given her, and one of the plays we had seen, had shown: if I was her husband I couldn't be made to testify against her. We were married the next morning, on a license I had been carrying for nearly a week.

"Well, there we were. I was married to her. She had a couple of million coming when her uncle's affairs were straightened out. She couldn't possibly, it seemed, escape arrest and conviction. Even if no one had seen her entering or leaving her uncle's flat, everything still pointed to her guilt, and the foolish course I had persuaded her to follow would simply ruin her chance of pleading self-defence. If they hanged her, the two million would come to me. If she got a long term in prison, I'd have the handling of the money at least."

Landow dropped and crushed his second cigarette and stared for a moment straight ahead into distance.

"Do you believe in God, or Providence, or Fate, or any of that, Rush?" he asked. "Well, some believe in one thing and some in another, but listen. Sara was never arrested, never even really suspected. It seems there was some sort of Finn or Swede who had had a run-in with Jerome and threatened him. I suppose he couldn't account for his whereabouts the night of the killing, so he went into hiding when he heard of Jerome's murder. The police suspicion settled on him. They looked Sara up, of course, but not very thoroughly. No one seems to have seen her in the street, and the people in her apartment house, having seen her come in at six o'clock with me, and not having seen her—or not remembering if they did—go out or in again, told the police she had been in all evening. The police were too much interested in the missing Finn, or whatever he was, to look any further into Sara's affairs.

"So there we were again. I was married into the money, but I wasn't fixed so I could hand Madeline her cut. Madeline said we'd let things run along as they were until the estate was settled up, and then we could tip Sara off to the police. But by the time the money was settled up there was another hitch. This one was my doing. I—I—well, I wanted to go on just as we were. Conscience had nothing to do with it, you understand? It was simply that—well—that living on with Sara was the only thing I wanted. I wasn't even sorry for what I'd done, because if it hadn't been for that I would never have had her.

"I don't know whether I can make this clear to you, Rush, but even now I don't regret any of it. If it could have been different—but it couldn't. It had to be this way or none. And I've had those six months. I can see that I've been a chump. Sara was never for me. I got her by a crime and a trick, and while I held on to a silly hope that some day she'd—she'd look at me as I did at her, I knew in my heart all the time it was no use. There had been a man—your Millar. She's free now that it's out about my being married to Polly, and I hope she—I hope— Well, Madeline began to howl for action. I told Sara that Madeline had had a child by Jerome, and Sara agreed to settle some money on her. But that didn't satisfy Madeline. It wasn't sentiment with her. I mean, it wasn't any feeling for me, it was just the money. She wanted every cent she could get, and she couldn't get enough to satisfy her in a settlement of the kind Sara wanted to make.

"With Polly, it was that too, but maybe a little more. She's fond of me, I think. I don't know how she traced me here after she got out of the Wisconsin big house, but I can see how she figured things. I was married to a wealthy woman. If the woman died—shot by a bandit in a hold-up attempt—then I'd have money, and Polly would have both me and money. I haven't seen her, wouldn't know she was in Baltimore if you hadn't told me, but that's the way it would work out in her mind. The killing idea would have occurred just as easily to Madeline. I had told her I wouldn't stand for pushing the game through on Sara. Madeline knew that if she went ahead on her own hook and hung the Falsoner murder on Sara I'd blow up the whole racket. But if Sara died, then I'd have the money and Madeline would draw her cut. So that was it.

"I didn't know that until you told me, Rush. I don't give a damn for your opinion of me, but it's God's truth that I didn't know that either Polly or Madeline was trying to have Sara killed. Well, that's about all. Were you shadowing me when I went to the hotel?"

"Yeah."

"I thought so. That letter I wrote and sent home told just about what I've told you, spilled the whole story. I was going to run for it, leaving Sara in the clear. She's clear, all right, but now I'll have to face it. But I don't want to see her again, Rush."

"I wouldn't think you would," the detective agreed. "Not after making a killer of her."

"But I didn't," Landow protested. "She isn't. I forgot to tell you that, but I put it in the letter. Jerome Falsoner was not dead, not even dying, when I went past her into the flat. The knife was too high in his chest. I killed him, driving the knife into the same wound again, but downward. That's what I went in for, to make sure he was finished!"

Alec Rush screwed up his savage bloodshot eyes, looked long into the confessed murderer's face.

THE ASSISTANT MURDERER

"That's a lie," he croaked at last, "but a decent one. Are you sure you want to stick to it? The truth will be enough to clear the girl, and maybe won't swing you."

"What difference does it make?" the younger man asked. "I'm a gone baby anyhow. And I might as well put Sara in the clear with herself as well as with the law. I'm caught to rights and another rap won't hurt. I told you Madeline had brains. I was afraid of them. She'd have had something up her sleeve to spring on us—to ruin Sara with. She could out-smart me without trying. I couldn't take any chances."

He laughed into Alec Rush's ugly face and, with a somewhat theatrical gesture, jerked one cuff an inch or two out of his coat-sleeve. The cuff was still damp with a maroon stain.

"I killed Madeline an hour ago," said Henry Bangs, alias Hubert Landow.

THE MAN WHO KILLED DAN ODAMS

When the light that came through the barred square foot of the cell's one high window had dwindled until he could no longer clearly make out the symbols and initials his predecessors had scratched and penciled on the opposite wall, the man who had killed Dan Odams got up from the cot and went to the steel-slatted door.

"Hey, chief!" he called, his voice rumbling within the narrow walls.

A chair scraped across a floor in the front of the building, deliberate footsteps approached, and the marshal of Jingo came into the passage between his office and the cell.

"I got something I want to tell you," the man in the cell said.

Then the marshal was near enough to see in the dim light the shiny muzzle of a short, heavy revolver threatening him from just in front of the prisoner's right hip.

Without waiting for the time-honored order the marshal raised his hands until their palms were level with his ears.

The man behind the bars spoke in a curt whisper.

"Turn around! Push your back against the door!"

When the marshal's back pressed against the bars a hand came up under his left armpit, pulled aside his unbuttoned vest, and plucked his revolver from its holster. "Now unlock this here door!"

THE MAN WHO KILLED DAN ODAMS

The prisoner's own weapon had disappeared and the captured one had taken its place. The marshal turned around, lowered one hand, keys jingled in it, and the cell door swung open.

The prisoner backed across the cell, inviting the other in with a beckoning flip of the gun in his hand. "Flop on the bunk, face-down."

In silence the marshal obeyed. The man who had killed Dan Odams bent over him. The long black revolver swept down in a swift arc that ended at the base of the prone official's head.

His legs jerked once, and he lay still.

With unhurried deftness the prisoner's fingers explored the other's pockets, appropriating money, tobacco, and cigarette papers. He removed the holster from the marshal's shoulder and adjusted it to his own. He locked the cell door behind him when he left.

The marshal's office was unoccupied. Its desk gave up two sacks of tobacco, matches, an automatic pistol, and a double handful of cartridges. The wall yielded a hat that sat far down on the prisoner's ears, and a too-tight, too-long, black rubber slicker.

Wearing them, he essayed the street.

The rain, after three days of uninterrupted sovereignty, had stopped for the time. But Jingo's principal thoroughfare was deserted—Jingo ate between five and six in the evening.

His deep-set maroon eyes—their animality emphasized by the absence of lashes—scanned the four blocks of wooden-sidewalked street. A dozen automobiles were to be seen, but no horses.

At the first corner he left the street and half a block below turned into a muddy alley that paralleled it. Under a shed in the rear of a poolroom he found four horses, their saddles and bridles hanging near by. He selected a chunky, well-muscled roan—the race is not to the swift through the mud of Montana—saddled it, and led it to the end of the alley.

Then he climbed into the saddle and turned his back on the awakening lights of Jingo.

Presently he fumbled beneath the slicker and took from his hip pocket the weapon with which he had held up the marshal: a dummy pistol of moulded soap, covered with tinfoil from cigarette packages. He tore off the wrapping, squeezed the soap into a shapeless handful, and threw it away.

The sky cleared after a while and the stars came out. He found that the road he was traveling led south. He rode all night, pushing the roan unrelentingly through the soft, viscid footing.

At daylight the horse could go no farther without rest. The man led it up a coulee—safely away from the road—and hobbled it beneath a clump of cottonwoods.

Then he climbed a hill and sprawled on the soggy ground, his lashless red eyes on the country through which he had come: rolling hills of black and green and gray, where wet soil, young grass, and dirty snow divided dominion—the triple rule trespassed here and there by the sepia ribbon of county road winding into and out of sight.

He saw no man while he lay there, but the landscape was too filled with the marks of man's proximity to bring any feeling of security. Shoulder-high wire fencing edged the road, a footpath cut the side of a near-by hill, telephone poles held their short arms stiffly against the gray sky.

At noon he saddled the roan again and rode on along the coulee. Several miles up he came to a row of small poles bearing a line of telephone wire. He left the coulee bottom, found the ranch house to which the wire ran, circled it, and went on.

Late in the afternoon he was not so fortunate.

With lessening caution—he had seen no wires for more than an hour—he rode across a hill to stumble almost into the center of a cluster of buildings. Into the group, from the other side, ran a line of wire.

The man who had killed Dan Odams retreated, crossed to another hill, and as he dropped down, on the far side, a rifle snapped from the slope he had just quit.

He bent forward until his nose was deep in the roan's mane, and worked upon the horse with hand and foot. The rifle snapped again.

THE MAN WHO KILLED DAN ODAMS

He rolled clear of the horse as it fell, and continued to roll until bunch grass and sagebrush screened him from behind. Then he crawled straight away, rounded the flank of a hill, and went on. The rifle did not snap again. He did not try to find it.

He turned from the south now, toward the west, his short, heavy legs pushing him on toward where Tiger Butte bulked against the leaden sky like a great crouching cat of black and green, with dirty white stripes where snow lay in coulee and fissure.

His left shoulder was numb for a while, and then the numbness was replaced by a searing ache. Blood trickled down his arm, staining his mud-caked hand. He stopped to open coat and shirt and readjust the bandage over the wound in his shoulder—the fall from the horse had broken it open and started it bleeding again. Then he went on.

The first road he came to bent up toward Tiger Butte. He followed it, ploughing heavily through the sticky, clinging mud.

Only once did he break the silence he had maintained since his escape from the Jingo jail. He stopped in the middle of the road and stood with legs far apart, turned his bloodshot eyes from right to left and from ground to sky, and without emotion but with utter finality cursed the mud, the fence, the telephone wires, the man whose rifle had set him afoot, and the meadow larks whose taunting flutelike notes mocked him always from just ahead.

Then he went on, pausing after each few miles to scrape the ever-accumulating mud from his boots, using each hilltop to search the country behind for signs of pursuit.

The rain came down again, matting his thin, clay-plastered hair—his hat had gone with his mount. The ill-fitting slicker restricted his body and flapped about his ankles, impeding his progress, but his wounded shoulder needed its protection from the rain.

Twice he left the road to let vehicles pass—once a steaming Ford, once a half-load of hay creeping along behind four straining horses.

DETECTIVE STORIES

His way was still through fenced land that offered scant concealment. Houses dotted the country, with few miles between them; and the loss of his horse was ample evidence that the telephone wires had not been idle. He had not eaten since noon of the previous day but—notwithstanding the absence of visible pursuit—he could not forage here.

Night was falling as he left the road for the slope of Tiger Butte. When it was quite dark he stopped. The rain kept up all night. He sat through it—his back against a boulder, the slicker over his head.

The shack, unpainted and ramshackle, groveled in a fork of the coulee. Smoke hung soddenly, lifelessly above its roof, not trying to rise, until beaten into nothingness by the rain. The structures around the chimneyed shack were even less lovely. The group seemed asprawl in utter terror of the great cat upon whose flank it found itself.

But to the red eyes of the man who had killed Dan Odams—he lay on his belly on the crest of the hill around which the coulee split—the lack of telephone wires gave this shabby homestead a wealth of beauty beyond reach of architect or painter.

Twice within the morning hour that he lay there a woman came into view. Once she left the shack, went to one of the other sheds, and then returned. The other time she came to the door, to stand a while looking down the coulee. She was a small woman, of age and complexion indeterminable through the rain, in a limp, grayish dress.

Later, a boy of ten or twelve came from the rear of the house, his arms piled high with kindling, and passed out of sight.

Presently the watcher withdrew from his hill, swung off in a circle, and came within sight of the shack again from the rear.

Half an hour passed. He saw the boy carrying water from a spring below, but he did not see the woman again.

The fugitive approached the building stealthily, his legs car-

THE MAN WHO KILLED DAN ODAMS

rying him stiffly, their elasticity gone. Now and then his feet faltered under him. But under its layers of clay and three-day beard his jaw jutted with nothing of weakness.

Keeping beyond them, he explored the outbuildings—wretched, flimsy structures, offering insincere pretences of protection to an abject sorrel mare and a miscellaneous assortment of farm implements, all of which had come off second-best in their struggle with the earth. Only the generous, though not especially skillful, application of the material which has given to establishments of this sort the local sobriquet 'hay-wire outfit' held the tools from frank admission of defeat.

Nowhere did the ground hold the impression of feet larger than a small woman's or a ten—or twelve—year-old boy's.

The fugitive crossed the yard to the dwelling, moving with wide-spread legs to offset the unsteadiness of his gait. With the unhurried, unresting spacing of clock-ticks, fat drops of blood fell from the fingers of his limp left hand to be hammered by the rain into the soggy earth.

Through the dirty pane of a window he saw the woman and boy, sitting together on a cot, facing the door.

The boy's face was white when the man threw the door open and came into the unpartitioned interior, and his mouth trembled; but the woman's thin, sallow face showed nothing—except, by its lack of surprise, that she had seen him approaching. She sat stiffly on the cot, her hands empty and motionless in her lap, neither fear nor interest in her faded eyes.

The man stood for a time where he had halted—just within the door to one side—a grotesque statue modeled of mud. Short, sturdy-bodied, with massive sagging shoulders. Nothing of clothing or hair showed through his husk of clay, and little of face and hands. The marshal's revolver in his hand, clean and dry, took on by virtue of that discordant immaculateness an exaggerated deadliness.

His eyes swept the room: two cots against the undressed board side walls, a plain deal table in the center, rickety kitchen chairs here and there, a battered and scratched bureau, a trunk, a row of hooks holding an indiscriminate assembly of masculine and feminine clothing, a pile of shoes in a corner, an open door giving access to a lean-to kitchen.

He crossed to the kitchen door, the woman's face turning to follow.

The lean-to was empty. He confronted the woman.

"Where's your man?"

"Gone."

"When'll he be back?"

"Ain't coming back."

The flat, expressionless voice of the woman seemed to puzzle the fugitive, as had her lack of emotion at his entrance. He scowled, and turned his eyes—now redder than ever with flecks of blood—from her face to the boy's and back to hers.

"Meaning what?" he demanded.

"Meaning he got tired of homesteading."

He pursed his lips thoughtfully. Then he went to the corner where the shoes were piled. Two pairs of men's worn shoes were there—dry and without fresh mud.

He straightened, slipped the revolver back into its holster, and awkwardly took off the slicker. "Get me some grub."

The woman left the cot without a word and went into the kitchen. The fugitive pushed the boy after her, and stood in the doorway while she cooked coffee, flapjacks, and bacon. Then they returned to the living-room. She put the food on the table and with the boy beside her resumed her seat on the cot.

The man wolfed the meal without looking at it—his eyes busy upon door, window, woman, and boy, his revolver beside his plate. Blood still dripped from his left hand, staining table and floor. Bits of earth were dislodged from his hair and face and hands and fell into his plate, but he did not notice them.

His hunger appeased, he rolled and lit a cigarette, his left hand fumbling stiffly through its part.

THE MAN WHO KILLED DAN ODAMS

For the first time the woman seemed to notice the blood. She came around to his side. "You're bleeding. Let me fix it."

His eyes—heavy now with the weights of fatigue and satisfied hunger—studied her face suspiciously. Then he leaned back in his chair and loosened his clothes, exposing the week-old bullet-hole.

She brought water and cloths, and bathed and bandaged the wound. Neither of them spoke again until she had returned to the cot.

Then: "Had any visitors lately?"

"Ain't seen nobody for six or seven weeks."

"How far's the nearest phone?"

"Nobel's—eight miles up the coulee."

"Got any horses besides the one in the shed?"

"No."

He got up wearily and went to the bureau, pulling the drawers out and plunging his hands into them. In the top one he found a revolver, and pocketed it. In the trunk he found nothing. Behind the clothes on the wall he found a rifle. The cots concealed no weapons.

He took two blankets from one of the cots, the rifle, and his slicker. He staggered as he walked to the door.

"I'm going to sleep a while," he said thickly, "out in the shed where the horse is at. I'll be turning out every now and then for a look around, and I don't want to find nobody missing. Understand?"

She nodded, and made a suggestion.

"If any strangers show up, I guess you want to be woke up before they see you?"

His sleep-dull eyes became alive again, and he came unsteadily back to thrust his face close to hers, trying to peer behind the faded surfaces of her eyes.

"I killed a fellow in Jingo last week," he said after a while, talking slowly, deliberately, in a monotone that was both cautioning and menacing. "It was fair shooting. He got me in the shoulder before I downed him. But he belonged in Jingo and I don't. The best I could expect is the worst of it. I got a chance to get away before they took me to Great Falls, and I took it. And I ain't figuring on being took back there and hung. I ain't going to be here long, but while I am—"

The woman nodded again.

He scowled at her and left the shack.

He tied the horse in one corner of the hut with shortened rope and spread his blankets between it and the door. Then, with the marshal's revolver in his hand, he lay down and slept.

The afternoon was far gone when he woke, and the rain was still falling. He studied the bare yard carefully, and reconnoitred the house before re-entering it.

The woman had swept and tidied the room; had put on a fresh dress, which much washing had toned down to a soft pink; had brushed and fluffed her hair. She looked up at his entrance from the sewing that occupied her, and her face, still young in spite of the harshness that work had laid upon it, was less sallow than before.

"Where's the kid?" the man snapped.

She jerked a thumb over her shoulder.

"Up on the hill. I sent him up to watch the coulee."

His eyes narrowed and he left the building. Studying the hill through the rain, he discerned the outline of the boy, lying face-down under a stunted red cedar, looking toward the east. The man returned indoors.

"How's the shoulder?" she asked.

He raised an experimental arm.

"Better. Pack me some grub. I'm moving on."

"You're a fool," she said without spirit as she went into the kitchen. "You'd do better to stay here until your shoulder's fit to travel."

"Too close to Jingo."

"Ain't nobody going to fight all that mud to come after you. A horse couldn't get through, let alone a car. And you don't think

THE MAN WHO KILLED DAN ODAMS

they'd foot it after you even if they knew where to find you, do you? And this rain ain't going to do your shoulder no good."

She bent to pick up a sack from the floor. Under the thin pink dress the line of back and hips and legs stood out sharply against the wall.

As she straightened she met his gaze, her lids dropped, her face flushed, her lips parted a little.

The man leaned against the jamb of the door and caressed the muddy stubble of his chin with a thick thumb.

"Maybe you're right," he said.

She put away the food she had been bundling, took a galvanized pail from the corner, and made three trips to the spring, filling an iron tub that she had set on the stove. He stood in the doorway watching.

She stirred the fire, went into the living-room, and took a suit of underwear, a blue shirt, and a pair of socks from the bureau, a pair of gray trousers from one of the hooks, and a pair of carpet slippers from the pile of footwear. She put the clothing on a chair in the kitchen.

Then she returned to the living-room, closing the connecting door.

As the man undressed and bathed, he heard her humming softly. Twice he tiptoed to the connecting door and put an eye to the crack between it and the jamb. Each time he saw her sitting on the cot, bending over her sewing, her face still flushed.

He had one leg in the trousers she had given him when the humming stopped suddenly.

His right hand swept up the revolver from a convenient chair, and he moved to the door, the trousers trailing across the floor behind the ankle he had thrust through them. Flattening himself against the wall, he put an eye to the crack.

In the front door of the shack stood a tall youth in a slicker that was glistening with water. In the youth's hands was a double-barreled shotgun, the twin muzzles of which, like dull, malignant eyes, were focused on the center of the connecting door.

The man in the kitchen swung his revolver up, his thumb drawing back the hammer with the mechanical precision of the man who is accustomed to single-action pistols.

The lean-to's rear door slammed open. "Drop it!"

The fugitive, wheeling with the sound of the door's opening, was facing this new enemy before the order was out.

Two guns roared together.

But the fugitive's feet, as he wheeled, had become entangled in the trailing trousers. The trousers had tripped him. He had gone to his knees at the very instant of the two guns' roaring.

His bullet had gone out into space over the shoulder of the man in the doorway. That one's bullet had driven through the wall a scant inch over the falling fugitive's head.

Floundering on his knees, the fugitive fired again.

The man in the door swayed and spun half around.

As he righted himself, the fugitive's forefinger tightened again around the trigger—

From the connecting doorway a shotgun thundered.

The fugitive came straight up on his feet, his face filled with surprise, stood bolt upright for a moment, and wilted to the floor.

The youth with the shotgun crossed to the man who leaned against the door with a hand clapped to his side. "Did he get you, Dick?"

"Just through the flesh, I reckon—don't amount to nothing. Reckon you killed him, Bob?"

"I reckon I did. I hit him fair!"

The woman was in the lean-to. "Where's Buddy?"

"The kid's all right, Mrs. Odams," Bob assured her. "But he was all in from running through the mud, so Ma put him to bed."

The man who lay still on the floor made a sound then, and they saw that his eyes were open.

Mrs. Odams and Bob knelt beside him, but he stopped them when they tried to move him to examine the wreckage the shot-

THE MAN WHO KILLED DAN ODAMS

gun had made of his back.

"No use," he protested, blood trickling thinly from the corners of his mouth as he spoke. "Let me alone."

Then his eyes—their red savageness glazed—sought the woman's.

"You—Dan—Odams's—woman?" he managed.

There was something of defiance—a hint that she felt the need of justification—in her answer. "Yes."

His face—thick-featured and deep—lined without the mud—told nothing of what was going on in his mind.

"Dummy," he murmured to himself presently, his eyes flickering toward the hill on whose top he had seen what he had believed to be a reclining boy.

She nodded.

The man who had killed Dan Odams turned his head away and spat his mouth empty of blood. Then his eyes returned to hers.

"Good girl," he said clearly—and died.

WOMEN, POLITICS AND MURDER

A plump maid with bold green eyes and a loose, full-lipped mouth led me up two flights of steps and into an elaborately furnished boudoir, where a woman in black sat at a window. She was a thin woman of a little more than thirty, this murdered man's widow, and her face was white and haggard.

"You are from the Continental Detective Agency?" she asked before I was two steps inside the room.

"Yes."

"I want you to find my husband's murderer." Her voice was shrill, and her dark eyes had wild lights in them. "The police have done nothing. Four days, and they have done nothing. They say it was a robber, but they haven't found him. They haven't found anything!"

"But, Mrs. Gilmore," I began, not exactly tickled to death with this explosion, "you must—"

"I know! I know!" she broke in. "But they have done nothing, I tell you—nothing. I don't believe they've made the slightest effort. I don't believe they want to find h-him!"

"Him?" I asked, because she had started to say *her*. "You think it was a man?"

She bit her lip and looked away from me, out of the window to where San Francisco Bay, the distance making toys of its boats, was blue under the early afternoon sun.

"I don't know," she said hesitantly; "it might have—"

Her face spun toward me—a twitching face—and it seemed impossible that anyone could talk so fast, hurl words out so rapidly one after the other.

"I'll tell you. You can judge for yourself. Bernard wasn't faithful to me. There was a woman who calls herself Cara Kenbrook. She wasn't the first. But I learned about her last month. We quarreled. Bernard promised to give her up. Maybe he didn't. But if he did, I wouldn't put it past her—a woman like that would do anything—anything. And down in my heart I really believe she did it!"

"And you think the police don't want to arrest her?"

"I didn't mean exactly that. I'm all unstrung, and likely to say anything. Bernard was mixed up in politics, you know; and if the police found, or thought, that politics had anything to do with his death, they might—I don't know just what I mean. I'm a nervous, broken woman, and full of crazy notions." She stretched a thin hand out to me. "Straighten this tangle out for me! Find the person who killed Bernard!"

I nodded with empty assurance, still not any too pleased with my client.

"Do you know this Kenbrook woman?" I asked.

"I've seen her on the street, and that's enough to know what sort of person she is!"

"Did you tell the police about her?"

"No-o." She looked out of the window again, and then, as I waited, she added, defensively:

"The police detectives who came to see me acted as if they thought I might have killed Bernard. I was afraid to tell them that I had cause for jealousy. Maybe I shouldn't have kept quiet about that woman, but I didn't think she had done it until afterward, when the police failed to find the murderer. Then I began to think she had done it; but I couldn't make myself go to the police and tell them that I had withheld information. I knew what they'd think. So

I—You can twist it around so it'll look as if I hadn't known about the woman, can't you?"

"Possibly. Now as I understand it, your husband was shot on Pine Street, between Leavenworth and Jones, at about three o'clock Tuesday morning. That right?"

"Yes."

"Where was he going?"

"Coming home, I suppose; but I don't know where he had been. Nobody knows. The police haven't found out, if they have tried. He told me Monday evening that he had a business engagement. He was a building contractor, you know. He went out at about half-past eleven, saying he would probably be gone four or five hours."

"Wasn't that an unusual hour to be keeping a business engagement?"

"Not for Bernard. He often had men come to the house at midnight."

"Can you make any guess at all where he was going that night?"

She shook her head with emphasis.

"No. I knew nothing at all about his business affairs, and even the men in his office don't seem to know where he went that night."

That wasn't unlikely. Most of the B. F. Gilmore Construction Company's work had been on city and state contracts, and it isn't altogether unheard-of for secret conferences to go with that kind of work. Your politician-contractor doesn't always move in the open.

"How about enemies?" I asked.

"I don't know anybody that hated him enough to kill him."

"Where does this Kenbrook woman live, do you know?"

"Yes—in the Garford Apartments on Bush Street."

"Nothing you've forgotten to tell me, is there?" I asked, stressing the *me* a little.

"No, I've told you everything I know—every single thing."

WOMEN, POLITICS AND MURDER

CHAPTER II

Walking over to California Street, I shook down my memory for what I had heard here and there of Bernard Gilmore. I could remember a few things—the opposition papers had been in the habit of exposing him every election year—but none of them got me anywhere. I had known him by sight: a boisterous, red-faced man who had hammered his way up from hod-carrier to the ownership of a half-million-dollar business and a pretty place in politics. "A roughneck with a manicure," somebody had called him; a man with a lot of enemies and more friends; a big, good-natured, hard-hitting rowdy.

Odds and ends of a dozen graft scandals in which he had been mixed up, without anybody ever really getting anything on him, flitted through my head as I rode downtown on the too-small outside seat of a cable car. Then there had been some talk of a bootlegging syndicate of which he was supposed to be the head...

I left the car at Kearny Street and walked over to the Hall of Justice. In the detectives' assembly-room I found O'Gar, the detective-sergeant in charge of the Homicide Detail: a squat man of fifty who went in for wide-brimmed hats of the movie-sheriff sort, but whose little blue eyes and bullet-head weren't handicapped by the trick headgear.

"I want some dope on the Gilmore killing," I told him.

"So do I," he came back. "But if you'll come along I'll tell you what little I know while I'm eating. I ain't had lunch yet."

Safe from eavesdroppers in the clatter of a Sutter Street lunchroom, the detective-sergeant leaned over his clam chowder and told me what he knew about the murder, which wasn't much.

"One of the boys, Kelly, was walking his beat early Tuesday morning, coming down the Jones Street hill from California Street to Pine. It was about three o'clock—no fog or nothing—a clear night. Kelly's within maybe twenty feet of Pine Street when he hears a shot. He whisks around the corner, and there's a man dying on the north sidewalk of Pine Street, halfway between Jones and Leavenworth. Nobody else is in sight. Kelly runs up to the man and finds it's Gilmore. Gilmore dies before he can say a word. The doctors say he was knocked down and then shot; because there's a bruise on his forehead, and the bullet slanted upward in his chest. See what I mean? He was lying on his back when the bullet hit him, with his feet pointing toward the gun it came from. It was a thirty-eight."

"Any money on him?"

O'Gar fed himself two spoons of chowder and nodded.

"Six hundred smacks, a coupla diamonds, and a watch. Nothing touched."

"What was he doing on Pine Street at that time in the morning?"

"Damned if I know, brother. Chances are he was going home, but we can't find out where he'd been. Don't even know what direction he was walking in when he was knocked over. He was lying across the sidewalk with his feet to the curb; but that don't mean nothing—he could of turned around three or four times after he was hit."

"All apartment buildings in that block, aren't there?"

"Uh-huh. There's an alley or two running off from the south side; but Kelly says he could see the mouths of both alleys when the shot was fired—before he turned the corner—and nobody got away through them."

"Reckon somebody who lives in that block did the shooting?" I asked.

O'Gar tilted his bowl, scooped up the last drops of the chowder, put them in his mouth, and grunted.

"Maybe. But we got nothing to show that Gilmore knew anybody in that block."

"Many people gather around afterward?"

"A few. There's always people on the street to come running if anything happens. But Kelly says there wasn't anybody that looked wrong—just the ordinary night crowd. The boys gave the neighborhood a combing, but didn't turn up anything."

"Any cars around?"

"Kelly says there wasn't, that he didn't see any, and couldn't of missed seeing it if there'd been one."

"What do you think?" I asked.

He got to his feet, glaring at me.

"I don't think," he said disagreeably; "I'm a police detective."

I knew by that that somebody had been panning him for not finding the murderer.

"I have a line on a woman," I told him. "Want to come along and talk to her with me?"

"I want to," he growled, "but I can't. I got to be in court this afternoon—in half an hour."

CHAPTER III

In the vestibule of the Garford Apartments, I pressed the button tagged Miss Cara Kenbrook several times before the door clicked open. Then I mounted a flight of stairs and walked down a hall to her door. It was opened presently by a tall girl of twenty-three or -four in a black and white crepe dress.

"Miss Cara Kenbrook?"

"Yes."

I gave her a card—one of those that tell the truth about me.

"I'd like to ask you a few questions; may I come in?"

"Do."

Languidly she stepped aside for me to enter, closed the door behind me, and led me back into a living room that was littered with newspapers, cigarettes in all stages of consumption from unlighted freshness to cold ash, and miscellaneous articles of feminine clothing. She made room for me on a chair by dumping off a pair of pink silk stockings and a hat, and herself sat on some magazines that occupied another chair.

"I'm interested in Bernard Gilmore's death," I said, watching her face.

It wasn't a beautiful face, although it should have been. Everything was there—perfect features; smooth, white skin; big, almost enormous, brown eyes—but the eyes were dead-dull, and the face was as empty of expression as a china doorknob, and what I said didn't change it.

"Bernard Gilmore," she said without interest. "Oh, yes."

"You and he were pretty close friends, weren't you?" I asked, puzzled by her blankness.

"We had been—yes."

"What do you mean by *had been*?"

She pushed back a lock of her short-cut brown hair with a lazy hand.

"I gave him the air last week," she said casually, as if speaking of something that had happened years ago.

"When was the last time you saw him?"

"Last week—Monday, I think—a week before he was killed."

"Was that the time when you broke off with him?"

"Yes."

"Have a row, or part friends?"

"Not exactly either. I just told him that I was through with him."

"How did he take it?"

"It didn't break his heart. I guess he'd heard the same thing before."

"Where were you the night he was killed?"

"At the Coffee Cup, eating and dancing with friends until about one o'clock. Then I came home and went to bed."

"Why did you split with Gilmore?"

"Couldn't stand his wife."

"Huh?"

"She was a nuisance." This without the faintest glint of either annoyance or humor. "She came here one night and raised a racket; so I told Bernie that if he couldn't keep her away from me he'd have to find another playmate."

"Have you any idea who might have killed him?" I asked.

"Not unless it was his wife—these excitable women always do silly things."

"If you had given her husband up, what reason would she have for killing him, do you think?"

"I'm sure I don't know," she replied with complete indifference. "But I'm not the only girl that Bernie ever looked at."

"Think there were others, do you? Know anything, or are you just guessing?"

"I don't know any names," she said, "but I'm not just guessing."

I let that go at that and switched back to Mrs. Gilmore, wondering if this girl could be full of dope.

"What happened the night his wife came here?"

"Nothing but that. She followed Bernie here, rang the bell, rushed past me when I opened the door, and began to cry and call Bernie names. Then she started on me, and I told him that if he didn't take her away I'd hurt her, so he took her home."

Admitting I was licked for the time, I got up and moved to the door. I couldn't do anything with this baby just now. I didn't think she was telling the whole truth, but on the other hand it wasn't reasonable to believe that anybody would lie so woodenly—with so little effort to be plausible.

"I may be back later," I said as she let me out.

"All right."

Her manner didn't even suggest that she hoped I wouldn't.

CHAPTETR IV

From this unsatisfactory interview I went to the scene of the killing, only a few blocks away, to get a look at the neighborhood. I found the block just as I had remembered it and as O'Gar had described it: lined on both sides by apartment buildings, with two blind alleys—one of which was dignified with a name, Touchard Street—running from the south side.

The murder was four days old; I didn't waste any time snooping around the vicinity; but, after strolling the length of the block, boarded a Hyde Street car, transferred at California Street, and went up to see Mrs. Gilmore again. I was curious to know why she hadn't told me about her call on Cara Kenbrook.

The same plump maid who had admitted me earlier in the afternoon opened the door.

"Mrs. Gilmore is not at home," she said. "But I think she'll be back in half an hour or so."

"I'll wait," I decided.

The maid took me into the library, an immense room on the second floor, with barely enough books in it to give it that name. She switched on a light—the windows were too heavily curtained to let in much daylight—crossed to the door, stopped, moved over to straighten some books on a shelf, and looked at me with a half-questioning, half-inviting look in her green eyes, started for the door again, and halted.

By that time I knew she wanted to say something, and needed encouragement. I leaned back in my chair and grinned at her, and decided I had made a mistake—the smile into which her slack lips curved held more coquetry than anything else. She came over to me, walking with an exaggerated swing of the hips, and stood close in front of me.

"What's on your mind?" I asked.

"Suppose—suppose a person knew something that nobody else knew; what would it be worth to them?"

"That," I stalled, "would depend on how valuable it was."

"Suppose I knew who killed the boss?" She bent her face close down to mine, and spoke in a husky whisper. "What would that be worth?"

WOMEN, POLITICS AND MURDER

"The newspapers say that one of Gilmore's clubs has offered a thousand-dollar reward. You'd get that."

Her green eyes went greedy, and then suspicious.

"If *you* didn't."

I shrugged. I knew she'd go through with it—whatever it was—now; so I didn't even explain to her that the Continental doesn't touch rewards, and doesn't let its hired men touch them.

"I'll give you my word," I said; "but you'll have to use your own judgment about trusting me."

She licked her lips.

"You're a good fellow, I guess. I wouldn't tell the police, because I know they'd beat me out of the money. But you look like I can trust you." She leered into my face. "I used to have a gentleman friend who was the very image of you, and he was the grandest—"

"Better speak your piece before somebody comes in," I suggested.

She shot a look at the door, cleared her throat, licked her loose mouth again, and dropped on one knee beside my chair.

"I was coming home late Monday night—the night the boss was killed—and was standing in the shadows saying good night to my friend, when the boss came out of the house and walked down the street. And he had hardly got to the corner, when she—Mrs. Gilmore—came out, and went down the street after him. Not trying to catch up with him, you understand; but following him. What do you think of that?"

"What do *you* think of it?"

"*I* think that she finally woke up to the fact that all of her Bernie's dates didn't have anything to do with the building business."

"Do you know that they didn't?"

"Do I know it? I knew that man! He liked 'em—liked 'em all." She smiled into my face, a smile that suggested all evil. "I found *that* out soon after I first came here."

"Do you know when Mrs. Gilmore came back that night—what time?"

"Yes," she said, "at half-past three."

"Sure?"

"Absolutely! After I got undressed I got a blanket and sat at the head of the front stairs. My room's in the rear of the top floor. I wanted to see if they came home together, and if there was a fight. After she came in alone I went back to my room, and it was just twenty-five minutes to four then. I looked at my alarm clock."

"Did you see her when she came in?"

"Just the top of her head and shoulders when she turned toward her room at the landing."

"What's your name?" I asked.

"Lina Best."

"All right, Lina," I told her. "If this is the goods I'll see that you collect on it. Keep your eyes open, and if anything else turns up you can get in touch with me at the Continental office. Now you'd better beat it, so nobody will know we've had our heads together."

Alone in the library, I cocked an eye at the ceiling and considered the information Lina Best had given me. But I soon gave that up—no use trying to guess at things that will work out for themselves in a while. I found a book, and spent the next half-hour reading about a sweet young she-chump and a big strong he-chump and all their troubles.

Then Mrs. Gilmore came in, apparently straight from the street.

I got up and closed the door behind her, while she watched me with wide eyes.

"Mrs. Gilmore," I said, when I faced her again, "why didn't you tell me that you followed your husband the night he was killed?"

"That's a lie!" she cried; but there was no truth in her voice. "That's a lie!"

"Don't you think you're making a mistake?" I urged. "Don't you think you'd better tell me the whole thing?"

She opened her mouth, but only a dry sobbing sound came out; and she began to sway with a hysterical rocking motion, the fingers of one black-gloved hand plucking at her lower lip, twisting and pulling it.

I stepped to her side and set her down in the chair I had been sitting in, making foolish clucking sounds—meant to soothe her—with my tongue. A disagreeable ten minutes—and gradually she pulled herself together; her eyes lost their glassiness, and she stopped clawing at her mouth.

"I did follow him." It was a hoarse whisper, barely audible.

Then she was out of the chair, kneeling, with arms held up to me, and her voice was a thin scream.

"But I didn't kill him! I didn't! Please believe that I didn't!"

I picked her up and put her back in the chair.

"I didn't say you did. Just tell me what did happen."

"I didn't believe him when he said he had a business engagement," she moaned. "I didn't trust him. He had lied to me before. I followed him to see if he went to that woman's rooms."

"Did he?"

"No. He went into an apartment house on Pine Street, in the block where he was killed. I don't know exactly which house it was—I was too far behind him to make sure. But I saw him go up the steps and into one—near the middle of the block."

"And then what did you do?"

"I waited, hiding in a dark doorway across the street. I knew the woman's apartment was on Bush Street, but I thought she might have moved, or be meeting him here. I waited a long time, shivering and trembling. It was chilly and I was frightened—afraid somebody would come into the vestibule where I was. But I made myself stay. I wanted to see if he came out alone, or if that woman came out. I had a right to do it—he had deceived me before.

"It was terrible, horrible—crouching there in the dark—cold and scared. Then—it must have been about half-past two—I couldn't stand it any longer. I decided to telephone the woman's apartment' and find out if she was home. I went down to an all-night lunch-room on Ellis Street and called her up."

"Was she home?"

"No! I tried for fifteen minutes, or maybe longer, but nobody answered the phone. So I *knew* she was in that Pine Street building."

"And what did you do then?"

"I went back there, determined to wait until he came out. I walked up Jones Street. When I was between Bush and Pine I heard a shot. I thought it was a noise made by an automobile then, but now I know that it was the shot that killed Bernie.

"When I reached the corner of Pine and Jones, I could see a policeman bending over Bernie on the sidewalk, and I saw people gathering around. I didn't know then that it was Bernie lying on the sidewalk. In the dark and at that distance I couldn't even see whether it was a man or a woman.

"I was afraid that Bernard would come out to see what was going on, or look out of a window, and discover me; so I didn't go down that way. I was afraid to stay in the neighborhood now, for fear the police would ask me what I was doing loitering in the street at three in the morning—and have it come out that I had been following my husband. So I kept on walking up Jones Street, to California, and then straight home."

"And then what?" I led her on.

"Then I went to bed. I didn't go to sleep—lay there worrying over Bernie; but still not thinking it was he I had seen lying in the street. At nine o'clock that morning two police detectives came and told me Bernie had been killed. They questioned me so sharply that I was afraid to tell them the whole truth. If they had known I had reason for being jealous, and had followed my husband that night, they would have accused me of shooting him. And what could I have done? Everybody would have thought me guilty.

"So I didn't say anything about the woman. I thought they'd find the murderer, and then everything would be all right. I didn't think *she* had done it then, or I would have told you the whole thing the first time you were here. But four days went by without the police finding the murderer, and I began to think they suspected *me!* It was terrible! I couldn't go to them and confess that I had lied to them, and I was sure that the woman had killed him and that the police had failed to suspect her because I hadn't told them about her.

"So I employed you. But I was afraid to tell even you the whole truth. I thought that if I just told you there had been another woman and who she was, you could do the rest without having to know that I had followed Bernie that night. I was afraid *you* would think I had killed him, and would turn me over to the police if I told you everything. And now you *do* believe it! And you'll have me arrested! And they'll hang me! I know it! I know it!"

She began to rock crazily from side to side in her chair.

"Sh-h-h," I soothed her. "You're not arrested yet. Sh-h-h."

I didn't know what to make of her story. The trouble with these nervous, hysterical women is that you can't possibly tell when they're lying and when telling the truth unless you have outside evidence—half of the time they themselves don't know.

"When you heard the shot," I went on when she had quieted down a bit, "you were walking north on Jones, between Bush and Pine? You could see the corner of Pine and Jones?"

"Yes—clearly."

"See anybody?"

"No—not until I reached the corner and looked down Pine Street. Then I saw a policeman bending over Bernie, and two men walking toward them."

"Where were the two men?"

"On Pine Street east of Jones. They didn't have hats on—as if they had come out of a house when they heard the shot."

"Any automobiles in sight either before or after you heard the shot?"

"I didn't see or hear any."

"I have some more questions, Mrs. Gilmore," I said, "but I'm in a hurry now. Please don't go out until you hear from me again."

"I won't," she promised, "but—"

I didn't have any answers for anybody's questions, so I ducked my head and left the library.

Near the street door Lina Best appeared out of a shadow, her eyes bright and inquisitive.

"Stick around," I said without any meaning at all, stepped around her, and went on out into the street.

CHAPTER V

I returned then to the Garford Apartments, walking, because I had a lot of things to arrange in my mind before I faced Cara Kenbrook again. And, even though I walked slowly, they weren't all exactly filed in alphabetical order when I got there. She had changed the black and white dress for a plushlike gown of bright green, but her empty doll's face hadn't changed.

"Some more questions," I explained when she opened the door.

She admitted me without word or gesture, and led me back into the room where we had talked before.

"Miss Kenbrook," I asked, standing beside the chair she had offered me, "why did you tell me you were home in bed when Gilmore was killed?"

"Because it's so." Without the flicker of a lash.

"And you wouldn't answer the doorbell?"

I had to twist the facts to make my point. Mrs. Gilmore had phoned, but I couldn't afford to give this girl a chance to shunt the blame for her failure to answer off on central.

She hesitated for a split second.

"No—because I didn't hear it."

One cool article, this baby! I couldn't figure her. I didn't know then, and I don't know now, whether she was the owner of the world's best poker face or was just naturally stupid. But whichever

she was, she was thoroughly and completely it!
I stopped trying to guess and got on with my probing.

"And you wouldn't answer the phone either?"

"It didn't ring—or not enough to awaken me."

I chuckled—an artificial chuckle—because central could have been ringing the wrong number. However...

"Miss Kenbrook," I lied, "your phone rang at two-thirty and at two-forty that morning. And your doorbell rang almost continually from about two-fifty until after three."

"Perhaps," she said, "but I wonder who'd be trying to get me at that hour."

"You didn't hear either?"

"No."

"But you were here?"

"Yes—who was it?" carelessly.

"Get your hat," I bluffed, "and I'll show them to you down at headquarters."

She glanced down at the green gown and walked toward an open bedroom door.

"I suppose I'd better get a cloak, too," she said.

"Yes," I advised her, "and bring your toothbrush."

She turned around then and looked at me, and for a moment it seemed that some sort of expression—surprise, maybe—was about to come into her big brown eyes; but none actually came. The eyes stayed dull and empty.

"You mean you're arresting me?"

"Not exactly. But if you stick to your story about being home in bed at three o'clock last Tuesday morning, I can promise you you *will* be arrested. If I were you I'd think up another story."

She left the doorway slowly and came back into the room, as far as a chair that stood between us, put her hands on its back, and leaned over it to look at me. For perhaps a minute neither of us spoke—just stood there staring at each other, while I tried to keep my face as expressionless as hers.

"Do you really think," she asked at last, "that I wasn't here when Bernie was killed?"

"I'm a busy man, Miss Kenbrook." I put all the certainty I could fake into my voice. "If you want to stick to your funny story, it's all right with me. But please don't expect me to stand here and argue about it. Get your hat and cloak."

She shrugged, and came around the chair on which she had been leaning.

"I suppose you *do* know something," she said, sitting down. "Well, it's tough on Stan, but women and children first."

My ears twitched at the name *Stan*, but I didn't interrupt her.

"I was in the Coffee Cup until one o'clock," she was saying, her voice still flat and emotionless. "And I *did* come home afterward. I'd been drinking *vino* all evening, and it always makes me blue. So after I came home I got to worrying over things. Since Bernie and I split, finances haven't been so good. I took stock that night—or morning—and found only four dollars in my purse. The rent was due, and the world looked damned blue.

"Half-lit on dago wine as I was, I decided to run over and see Stan, tell him all my troubles, and make a touch. Stan is a good egg and he's always willing to go the limit for me. Sober, I wouldn't have gone to see him at three in the morning; but it seemed a perfectly sensible thing to do at the time.

"It's only a few minutes' walk from here to Stan's. I went down Bush Street to Leavenworth, and up Leavenworth to Pine. I was in the middle of that last block when Bernie was shot—I heard it. And when I turned the corner into Pine Street I saw a copper bending over a man on the pavement right in front of Stan's. I hesitated for a couple of minutes, standing in the shadow of a pole, until three or four men had gathered around the man on the sidewalk. Then I went over.

"It was Bernie. And just as I got there I heard the copper tell one of the men that he had been shot. It was an awful shock to me. You know how things like that will hit you!"

I nodded, though God knows there was nothing in this girl's face, manner, or voice to suggest shock. She might have been talking about the weather.

"Dumbfounded, not knowing what to do," she went on, "I didn't even stop. I went on, passing as close to Bernie as I am to you now, and rang Stan's bell. He let me in. He had been half-undressed when I rang. His rooms are in the rear of the building, and he hadn't heard the shot, he said. He didn't know Bernie had been killed until I told him. It sort of knocked the wind out of him. He said Bernie had been there—in Stan's rooms—since midnight, and had just left.

"Stan asked me what I was doing there, and I told him my tale of woe. That was the first time Stan knew that Bernie and I were so thick. I met Bernie through Stan, but Stan didn't know we had got so chummy.

"Stan was worried for fear it would come out that Bernie had been to see him that night, because it would make a lot of trouble for him—some sort of shady deal they had on, I guess. So he didn't go out to see Bernie. That's about all there is to it. I got some money from Stan, and stayed in his rooms until the police had cleared out of the neighborhood; because neither of us wanted to get mixed up in anything. Then I came home. That's straight—on the level."

"Why didn't you get this off your chest before?" I demanded, knowing the answer.

It came.

"I was afraid. Suppose I told about Bernie throwing me down, and said I was close to him—a block or so away—when he was killed, and was half-full of vino? The first thing everybody would have said was that I had shot him! I'd lie about it still if I thought you'd believe me."

"So Bernie was the one who broke off, and not you?"

"Oh, yes," she said lightly.

DETECTIVE STORIES

CHAPTER VI

I lit a Fatima and breathed smoke in silence for a while, and the girl sat placidly watching me.

Here I had two women—neither normal. Mrs. Gilmore was hysterical, abnormally nervous. This girl was dull, subnormal. One was the dead man's wife; the other his mistress; and each with reason for believing she had been thrown down for the other. Liars, both; and both finally confessing that they had been near the scene of the crime at the time of the crime, though neither admitted seeing the other. Both, by their own accounts, had been at that time even further from normal than usual—Mrs. Gilmore filled with jealousy; Cara Kenbrook, half-drunk.

What was the answer? Either could have killed Gilmore; but hardly both—unless they had formed some sort of crazy partnership, and in that event—

Suddenly all the facts I had gathered—true and false—clicked together in my head. I had the answer—the one simple, satisfying answer!

I grinned at the girl, and set about filling in the gaps in my solution.

"Who is Stan?" I asked.

"Stanley Tennant—he has something to do with the city."

Stanley Tennant. I knew him by reputation, a—

A key rattled in the hall door.

The hall door opened and closed, and a man's footsteps came toward the open doorway of the room in which we were. A tall, broad-shouldered man in tweeds filled the doorway—a ruddy-faced man of thirty-five or so, whose appearance of athletic blond wholesomeness was marred by close-set eyes of an indistinct blue.

Seeing me, he stopped—a step inside the room.

"Hello, Stan!" the girl said lightly. "This gentleman is from the Continental Detective Agency. I've just emptied myself to him about Bernie. Tried to stall him at first, but it was no good."

The man's vague eyes switched back and forth between the girl and me. Around the pale irises his eyeballs were pink.

He straightened his shoulders and smiled too jovially.

"And what conclusion have you come to?" he inquired.

The girl answered for me.

"I've already had *my* invitation to take a ride."

Tennant bent forward. With an unbroken swing of his arms, he swept a chair up from the floor into my face. Not much force behind it, but quick.

I went back against the wall, fending off the chair with both arms—threw it aside—and looked into the muzzle of a nickeled revolver.

A table drawer stood open—the drawer from which he had grabbed the gun while I was busy with the chair. The revolver, I noticed, was of .38 caliber.

"Now"—his voice was thick, like a drunk's—"turn around."

I turned my back to him, felt a hand moving over my body, and my gun was taken away.

"All right," he said, and I faced him again.

He stepped back to the girl's side, still holding the nickel-plated revolver on me. My own gun wasn't in sight—in his pocket perhaps. He was breathing noisily, and his eyeballs had gone from pink to red. His face, too, was red, with veins bulging in the forehead.

"You know me?" he snapped.

"Yes, I know you. You're Stanley Tennant, assistant city engineer, and your record is none too lovely." I chattered away on the theory that conversation is always somehow to the advantage of the man who is looking into the gun. "You're supposed to be the lad who supplied the regiment of well-trained witnesses who turned last year's investigation of graft charges against the engineer's office into a comedy. Yes, Mr. Tennant, I know you. You're the answer to why Gilmore was so lucky in landing city contracts with bids only a few dollars beneath his competitors. Yes, Mr. Tennant, I know you. You're the bright boy who—"

I had a lot more to tell him, but he cut me off.

"That will do out of you!" he yelled. "Unless you want me to knock a corner off your head with this gun."

Then he addressed the girl, not taking his eyes from me.

"Get up, Cara."

She got out of her chair and stood beside him. His gun was in his right hand, and that side was toward her. He moved around to the other side.

The fingers of his left hand hooked themselves inside the girl's green gown where it was cut low over the swell of her breasts. His gun never wavered from me. He jerked his left hand, ripping her gown down to the waistline.

"*He* did that, Cara," Tennant said.

She nodded.

His fingers slid inside the flesh-colored undergarment that was now exposed, and he tore that as he had torn the gown.

"*He* did that."

She nodded again.

His bloodshot eyes darted little measuring glances at her face—swift glances that never kept his eyes from me for the flash of time I would have needed to tie into him.

Then—eyes and gun on me—he smashed his left fist into the girl's blank white face.

One whimper—low and not drawn out—came from her as she went down in a huddle against the wall. Her face—well, there wasn't *much* change in it. She looked dumbly up at Tennant from where she had fallen.

"*He* did that," Tennant was saying.

She nodded, got up from the floor, and returned to her chair.

"Here's our story." The man talked rapidly, his eyes alert on me. "Gilmore was never in my rooms in his life, Cara, and neither were you. The night he was killed you were home shortly after one o'clock, and stayed here. You were sick—probably from the wine you had been drinking—and called a doctor. His name is Howard. I'll see that he's fixed. He got here at two-thirty and stayed until three-thirty.

"Today, this gumshoe, learning that you had been intimate with Gilmore, came here to question you. He knew you hadn't killed Gilmore, but he made certain suggestions to you—you can play them up as strong as you like; maybe say that he's been annoying you for months—and when you turned him down he threatened to frame you.

"You refused to have anything to do with him, and he grabbed you, tearing your clothes, and bruising your face when you resisted. I happened to come along then, having an engagement with you, and heard you scream. Your front door was unlocked, so I rushed in, pulled this fellow away, and disarmed him. Then we held him until the police—whom we will phone for—came. Got that?"

"Yes, Stan."

"Good! Now listen: When the police get here this fellow will spill all he knows of course, and the chances are that all three of us will be taken in. That's why I want you to know what's what right now. I ought to have enough pull to get you and me out on bail tonight, or, if worse comes to worst, to see that my lawyer gets to me tonight—so I can arrange for the witnesses we'll need. Also I ought to be able to fix it so our little fat friend will be held for a day or two, and not allowed to see anybody until late tomorrow—which will give us a good start on him. I don't know how much he knows, but between your story and the stories of a couple of other smart little ladies I have in mind, I'll fix him up with a rep that will keep any jury in the world from ever believing him about anything."

"How do you like that?" he asked me, triumphantly.

"You big clown," I laughed at him, "I think it's funny!"

But I didn't really think so. In spite of what I thought I knew about Gilmore's murder—in spite of my simple, satisfactory solution—something was crawling up my back, my knees felt jerky, and my hands were wet with sweat. I had had people try to frame me before—no detective stays in the business long without having it happen—but I had never got used to it. There's a peculiar deadliness about the thing—especially if you know how erratic juries can be—that makes your flesh crawl, no matter how safe your judgment tells you you are.

"Phone the police," Tennant told the girl, "and for God's sake keep your story straight!"

As he tried to impress that necessity on the girl his eyes left me.

I was perhaps five feet from him and his level gun.

A jump—not straight at him—off to one side—put me close.

The gun roared under my arm. I was surprised not to feel the bullet. It seemed that he *must* have hit me.

There wasn't a second shot.

I looped my right fist over as I jumped. It landed when I landed. It took him too high—up on the cheek-bone—but it rocked him back a couple of steps.

I didn't know what had happened to his gun. It wasn't in his hand any more. I didn't stop to look for it. I was busy, crowding him back—not letting him set himself—staying close to him—driving at him with both hands.

He was a head taller than I, and had longer arms, but he wasn't any heavier or stronger. I suppose he hit me now and then as I hammered him across the room. He must have. But I didn't feel anything.

I worked him into a corner. Jammed him back in a corner with his legs cramped under him—which didn't give him much leverage to hit from. I got my left arm around his body, holding him where I wanted him. And I began to throw my right fist into him.

I liked that. His belly was flabby, and it got softer every time I hit it. I hit it often.

He was chopping at my face, but by digging my nose into his chest and holding it there I kept my beauty from being altogether ruined. Meanwhile I threw my right fist into him.

Then I became aware that Cara Kenbrook was moving around behind me; and I remembered the revolver that had fallen somewhere when I had charged Tennant. I didn't like that; but there was nothing I could do about it—except put more weight in my punches. My own gun, I thought, was in one of his pockets. But neither of us had time to hunt for it now.

Tennant's knees sagged the next time I hit him.

Once more, I said to myself, and then I'll step back, let him have one on the button, and watch him fall.

But I didn't get that far.

Something that I knew was the missing revolver struck me on the top of the head. An ineffectual blow—not clean enough to stun me—but it took the steam out of my punches.

Another.

They weren't hard; these taps, but to hurt a skull with a hunk of metal you don't have to hit it hard.

I tried to twist away from the next bump, and failed. Not only failed, but let Tennant wiggle away from me.

That was the end.

I wheeled on the girl just in time to take another rap on the head, and then one of Tennant's fists took me over the ear.

I went down in one of those falls that get pugs called quitters—my eyes were open, my mind was alive, but my legs and arms wouldn't lift me up from the floor.

Tennant took my own gun out of a pocket, and with it held on me, sat down in a Morris chair, to gasp for the air I had pounded out of him. The girl sat in another chair; and I, finding I could manage it, sat up in the middle of the floor and looked at them.

Tennant spoke, still panting.

"This is fine—all the signs of a struggle we need to make our story good!"

"If they don't believe you were in a fight," I suggested sourly, pressing my aching head with both hands, "you can strip and show them your little tummy."

"And you can show them this!"

He leaned down and split my lip with a punch that spread me on my back.

Anger brought my legs to life. I got up on them. Tennant moved around behind the Morris chair. My black gun was steady in his hand.

"Go easy," he warned me. "My story will work if I have to kill you—maybe work better."

That was sense. I stood still.

"Phone the police, Cara," he ordered.

She went out of the room, closing the door behind her; and all I could hear of her talk was a broken murmur.

CHAPTER VII

Ten minutes later three uniformed policemen arrived. All three knew Tennant, and they treated him with respect. Tennant reeled off the story he and the girl had cooked up, with a few changes to take care of the shot that had been fired from the nickeled gun and our rough-house. She nodded her head vigorously whenever a policeman looked at her. Tennant turned both guns over to the white-haired sergeant in charge.

I didn't argue, didn't deny anything, but told the sergeant:

"I'm working with Detective Sergeant O'Gar on a job. I want to talk to him over the phone and then I want you to take all three of us down to the detective bureau."

Tennant objected to that, of course; not because he expected to gain anything, but on the off-chance that he might. The white-haired sergeant looked from one of us to the other in puzzlement. Me, with my skinned face and split lip; Tennant, with a red lump under one eye where my first wallop had landed; and the girl, with most of the clothes above the waistline ripped off and a bruised cheek.

"It has a queer look, this thing," the sergeant decided aloud, "and I shouldn't wonder but what the detective bureau was the place for the lot of you."

One of the policemen went into the hall with me, and I got O'Gar on the phone at his home. It was nearly ten o'clock by now, and he was preparing for bed.

"Cleaning up the Gilmore murder," I told him. "Meet me at the Hall. Will you get hold of Kelly, the patrolman who found Gilmore, and bring him down there? I want him to look at some people."

"I will that," O'Gar promised, and I hung up.

The "wagon" in which the three policemen had answered Cara Kenbrook's call carried us down to the Hall of Justice, where we all went into the captain of detectives' office. McTighe, a lieutenant, was on duty.

I knew McTighe, and we were on pretty good terms, but I wasn't an influence in local politics, and Tennant was. I don't mean that McTighe would have knowingly helped Tennant frame me; but with me stacked up against the assistant city engineer, I knew who would get the benefit of any doubt there might be.

My head was thumping and roaring just now, with knots all over it where the girl had beaned me. I sat down, kept quiet, and nursed my head while Tennant and Cara Kenbrook, with a lot of details that they had not wasted on the uniformed men, told their tale and showed their injuries.

Tennant was talking—describing the terrible scene that had met his eyes when, drawn by the girl's screams, he had rushed into her apartment—when O'Gar came into the office. He recognized Tennant with a lifted eyebrow, and came over to sit beside me.

"What the hell is all this?" he muttered.

"A lovely mess," I whispered back. "Listen—in that nickel gun on the desk there's an empty shell. Get it for me."

He scratched his head doubtfully, listened to the next few words of Tennant's yarn, glanced at me out of the corner of his eye, and then went over to the desk and picked up the revolver.

McTighe looked at him—a sharp, questioning look.

"Something on the Gilmore killing," the detective-sergeant said, breaking the gun.

The lieutenant started to speak, changed his mind, and O'Gar brought the shell over and handed it to me.

"Thanks," I said, putting it in my pocket. "Now listen to my friend there. It's a good act, if you like it."

Tennant was winding up his history.

"... Naturally a man who tried a thing like that on an unprotected woman would be yellow, so it wasn't very hard to handle him after I got his gun away from him. I hit him a couple of times, and he quit—begging me to stop, getting down on his knees. Then we called the police."

McTighe looked at me with eyes that were cold and hard. Tennant had made a believer of him, and not only of him—the police-sergeant and his two men were glowering at me. I suspected that even O'Gar—with whom I had been through a dozen storms—would have been half-convinced if the engineer hadn't added the neat touches about my kneeling.

"Well, what have *you* got to say?" McTighe challenged me in a tone which suggested that it didn't make much difference what I said.

"I've got nothing to say about this dream," I said shortly. "I'm interested in the Gilmore murder—not in this stuff." I turned to O'Gar. "Is the patrolman here?"

The detective-sergeant went to the door, and called: "Oh, Kelly!"

Kelly came in—a big, straight-standing man, with iron-gray hair and an intelligent fat face.

"You found Gilmore's body?" I asked.

"I did."

I pointed at Cara Kenbrook.

"Ever see her before?"

His gray eyes studied her carefully.

"Not that I remember," he answered.

"Did she come up the street while you were looking at Gilmore, and go into the house he was lying in front of?"

"She did not."

I took out the empty shell O'Gar had got for me, and chucked it down on the desk in front of the patrolman.

"Kelly," I asked, "*why did you kill Gilmore?*"

Kelly's right hand went under his coat-tail at his hip.

I jumped for him.

Somebody grabbed me by the neck. Somebody else piled on my back. McTighe aimed a big fist at my face, but it missed. My legs had been suddenly kicked from under me, and I went down hard with men all over me.

When I was yanked to my feet again, big Kelly stood straight up by the desk, weighing his service revolver in his hand. His clear eyes met mine, and he laid the weapon on the desk. Then he unfastened his shield and put it with the gun.

"It was an accident," he said simply.

By this time the birds who had been manhandling me woke up to the fact that maybe they were missing part of the play—that maybe I wasn't a maniac. Hands dropped off me, and presently everybody was listening to Kelly.

He told his story with unhurried evenness, his eyes never wavering or clouding. A deliberate man, though unlucky.

"I was walkin' my beat that night, an' as I turned the corner of Jones into Pine I saw a man jump back from the steps of a buildin' into the vestibule. A burglar, I thought, an' cat-footed it down there. It was a dark vestibule, an' deep, an' I saw somethin' that looked like a man in it, but I wasn't sure.

" 'Come out o' there!' I called, but there was no answer. I took my gun in my hand an' started up the steps. I saw him move just then, comin' out. An' then my foot slipped. It was worn smooth, the bottom step, an' my foot slipped. I fell forward, the gun went off, an' the bullet hit him. He had come out a ways by then, an' when the bullet hit him he toppled over frontwise, tumblin' down the steps onto the sidewalk.

"When I looked at him I saw it was Gilmore. I knew him to say 'howdy' to, an' he knew me—which is why he must o' ducked out of sight when he saw me comin' around the corner. He didn't want me to see him comin' out of a buildin' where I knew Mr. Tennant lived, I suppose, thinkin' I'd put two an' two together, an' maybe talk.

"I don't say that I did the right thing by lyin', but it didn't hurt anybody. It was an accident, but he was a man with a lot of friends up in high places, an'—accident or no—I stood a good chance of bein' broke, an' maybe sent over for a while. So I told my story the way you people know it. I couldn't say I'd seen anything suspicious without maybe puttin' the blame on some innocent party, an' I didn't want that. I'd made up my mind that if anybody was arrested for the murder, an' things looked bad for them, I'd come out an' say I'd done it. Home, you'll find a confession all written out—written out in case somethin' happened to me—so nobody else'd ever be blamed.

"That's why I had to say I'd never seen the lady here. I did see her—saw her go into the buildin' that night—the buildin' Gilmore had come out of. But I couldn't say so without makin' it look bad for her; so I lied. I could have thought up a better story if I'd had more time, I don't doubt, but I had to think quick. Anyways, I'm glad it's all over."

CHAPTER VIII

Kelly and the other uniformed policeman had left the office, which now held McTighe, O'Gar, Cara Kenbrook, Tennant, and me. Tennant had crossed to my side, and was apologizing.

"I hope you'll let me square myself for this evening's work. But you know how it is when somebody you care for is in a jam. I'd have killed you if I had thought it would help Cara—on the level. Why didn't you tell us that you didn't suspect her?"

"But I did suspect the pair of you," I said. "It looked as if Kelly had to be the guilty one; but you people carried on so much that I began to feel doubtful. For a while it was funny—you thinking she had done it, and she thinking you had, though I suppose each had sworn to his or her innocence. But after a time it stopped being funny. You carried it too far."

"How did you rap to Kelly?" O'Gar, at my shoulder, asked.

"Miss Kenbrook was walking north on Leavenworth—and was halfway between Bush and Pine—when the shot was fired. She saw nobody, no cars, until she rounded the corner. Mrs. Gilmore, walking north on Jones, was about the same distance away when *she* heard the shot, and she saw nobody until she reached Pine Street. If Kelly had been telling the truth, she would have seen him on Jones Street. He said he didn't turn the corner until after the shot was fired.

"Either of the women could have killed Gilmore, but hardly both; and I doubted that either could have shot him and got away without running into Kelly or the other. Suppose both of them were telling the truth—what then? Kelly must have been lying! He was the logical suspect anyway—the nearest known person to the murdered man when the shot was fired.

"To back all this up, he had let Miss Kenbrook go into the apartment building at three in the morning, in front of which a man had just been killed, without questioning her or mentioning her in his report. That looked as if he *knew* who had done the killing. So I took a chance with the empty-shell trick, it being a good bet that he would have thrown his away, and would think that—"

McTighe's heavy voice interrupted my explanation.

"How about this assault charge?" he asked, and had the decency to avoid my eye when I turned toward him with the others.

Tennant cleared his throat.

"Er—ah—in view of the way things have turned out, and knowing that Miss Kenbrook doesn't want the disagreeable publicity that would accompany an affair of this sort, why, I'd suggest that we drop the whole thing." He smiled brightly from McTighe to me. "You know nothing has gone on the records yet."

"Make the big heap play his hand out," O'Gar growled in my ear. "Don't let him drop it."

"Of course if Miss Kenbrook doesn't want to press the charge," McTighe was saying, watching me out of the tail of his eye, "I suppose—"

"If everybody understands that the whole thing was a plant," I said, "and if the policemen who heard the story are brought in here now and told by Tennant and Miss Kenbrook that it was all a lie—then I'm willing to let it go at that. Otherwise, I won't stand for a hush-up."

"You're a damned fool!" O'Gar whispered. "Put the screws on them!"

But I shook my head. I didn't see any sense in making a lot of trouble for myself just to make some for somebody else—and suppose Tennant *proved* his story...

So the policemen were found, and brought into the office again, and told the truth.

And presently Tennant, the girl, and I were walking together like three old friends through the corridors toward the door, Tennant still asking me to let him make amends for the evening's work.

"You've *got* to let me do something!" he insisted. "It's only right!"

His hand dipped into his coat, and came out with a thick billfold.

"Here," he said, "let me—"

We were going, at that happy moment, down the stone vestibule steps that lead to Kearny Street—six or seven steps there are.

"No," I said, "let me—"

He was on the next to the top step, when I reached up and let go. He settled in a rather limp pile at the bottom.

WOMEN, POLITICS AND MURDER

Leaving his empty-faced lady love to watch over him, I strolled up through Portsmouth Square toward a restaurant where the steaks come thick.

WHO KILLED BOB TEAL?

"Teal was killed last night."

The Old Man—the Continental Detective Agency's San Francisco manager—spoke without looking at me. His voice was as mild as his smile, and gave no indication of the turmoil that was seething in his mind.

If I kept quiet, waiting for the Old Man to go on, it wasn't because the news didn't mean anything to me. I had been fond of Bob Teal—we all had. He had come to the Agency fresh from college two years before; and if ever a man had the makings of a crack detective in him, this slender, broad-shouldered lad had. Two years is little enough time in which to pick up the first principles of sleuthing, but Bob Teal, with his quick eye, cool nerve, balanced head, and whole-hearted interest in the work, was already well along the way to expertness. I had an almost fatherly interest in him, since I had given him most of his early training.

The Old Man didn't look at me as he went on. He was talking to the open window at his elbow.

"He was shot with a thirty-two, twice, through the heart. He was shot behind a row of signboards on the vacant lot on the northwest corner of Hyde and Eddy Streets, at about ten last night. His body was found by a patrolman a little after eleven. The gun was found about fifteen feet away. I have seen him and I have gone

WHO KILLED BOB TEAL?

over the ground myself. The rain last night wiped out any leads the ground may have held, but from the condition of Teal's clothing and the position in which he was found, I would say that there was no struggle, and that he was shot where he was found, and not carried there afterward. He was lying behind the signboards, about thirty feet from the sidewalk, and his hands were empty. The gun was held close enough to him to singe the breast of his coat. Apparently no one either saw or heard the shooting. The rain and wind would have kept pedestrians off the street, and would have deadened the reports of a thirty-two, which are not especially loud, anyway."

The Old Man's pencil began to tap the desk, its gentle clicking setting my nerves on edge. Presently it stopped, and the Old Man went on:

"Teal was shadowing a Herbert Whitacre—had been shadowing him for three days. Whitacre is one of the partners in the firm Ogburn and Whitacre, farm-development engineers. They have options on a large area of land in several of the new irrigation districts. Ogburn handles the sales end, while Whitacre looks after the rest of the business, including the bookkeeping.

"Last week Ogburn discovered that his partner had been making false entries. The books show certain payments made on the land, and Ogburn learned that these payments had not been made. He estimates that the amount of Whitacre's thefts may be anywhere from one hundred fifty to two hundred fifty thousand dollars. He came in to see me three days ago and told me all this, and wanted to have Whitacre shadowed in an endeavour to learn what he has done with the stolen money. Their firm is still a partnership, and a partner cannot be prosecuted for stealing from the partnership, of course. Thus, Ogburn could not have his partner arrested, but he hoped to find the money, and then recover it through civil action. Also he was afraid that Whitacre might disappear.

"I sent Teal out to shadow Whitacre, who supposedly didn't know that his partner suspected him. Now I am sending you out

DETECTIVE STORIES

to find Whitacre. I'm determined to find him and convict him if I have to let all regular business go and put every man I have on this job for a year. You can get Teal's reports from the clerks. Keep in touch with me."

All that, from the Old Man, was more than an ordinary man's oath written in blood.

In the clerical office I got the two reports Bob had turned in. There was none for the last day, of course, as he would not have written that until after he had quit work for the night. The first of these two reports had already been copied and a copy sent to Ogburn; a typist was working on the other now.

In his reports Bob had described Whitacre as a man of about thirty-seven, with brown hair and eyes, a nervous manner, a smooth-shaven, medium-complexioned face, and rather small feet. He was about five feet eight inches tall, weighed about a hundred and fifty pounds, and dressed fashionably, though quietly. He lived with his wife in an apartment on Gough Street. They had no children. Ogburn had given Bob a description of Mrs. Whitacre: a short, plump, blond woman of something less than thirty.

Those who remember this affair will know that the city, the detective agency, and the people involved all had names different from the ones I have given them. But they will know also that I have kept the facts true. Names of some sort are essential to clearness, and when the use of the real names might cause embarrassment, or pain even, pseudonyms are the most satisfactory alternative.

In shadowing Whitacre, Bob had learned nothing that seemed to be of any value in finding the stolen money. Whitacre had gone about his usual business, apparently, and Bob had seen him do nothing downright suspicious. But Whitacre had seemed nervous, had often stopped to look around, obviously suspecting that he was being shadowed without being sure of it. On several occasions Bob had had to drop him to avoid being recognized. On one of these occasions, while waiting in the vicinity of Whitacre's residence for him to return, Bob had seen Mrs. Whitacre—or a woman who

WHO KILLED BOB TEAL?

fit the description Ogburn had given—leave in a taxicab. Bob had not tried to follow her, but he made a memorandum of the taxi's license number.

These two reports read and practically memorized, I left the Agency and went down to Ogburn & Whitacre's suite in the Packard Building. A stenographer ushered me into a tastefully furnished office, where Ogburn sat at a desk signing mail. He offered me a chair. I introduced myself to him, a medium-sized man of perhaps thirty-five, with sleek brown hair and the cleft chin that is associated in my mind with orators, lawyers, and salesmen.

"Oh, yes!" he said, pushing aside the mail, his mobile, intelligent face lighting up. "Has Mr. Teal found anything?"

"Mr. Teal was shot and killed last night."

He looked at me blankly for a moment out of wide brown eyes, and then repeated: "Killed?"

"Yes," I replied, and told him what little I knew about it.

"You don't think—" he began when I had finished, and then stopped. "You don't think Herb would have done that?"

"What do you think?"

"I don't think Herb would commit murder! He's been jumpy the last few days, and I was beginning to think he suspected I had discovered his thefts, but I don't believe he would have gone that far, even if he knew Mr. Teal was following him. I honestly don't!"

"Suppose," I suggested, "that sometime yesterday Teal found where he had put the stolen money, and then Whitacre learned that Teal knew it. Don't you think that under those circumstances Whitacre might have killed him?"

"Perhaps," he said slowly, "but I'd hate to think so. In a moment of panic Herb might—but I really don't think he would."

"When did you see him last?"

"Yesterday. We were here in the office together most of the day. He left for home a few minutes before six. But I talked to him over the phone later. He called me up at home at a little after seven, and said he was coming down to see me, wanted to tell me something.

DETECTIVE STORIES

I thought he was going to confess his dishonesty, and that maybe we would be able to straighten out this miserable affair. His wife called up at about ten. She wanted him to bring something from downtown when he went home, but of course he was not there. I stayed in all evening waiting for him, but he didn't—"

He stuttered, stopped talking, and his face drained white.

"My God, I'm wiped out!" he said faintly, as if the thought of his own position had just come to him. "Herb gone, money gone, three years' work gone for nothing! And I'm legally responsible for every cent he stole. God!"

He looked at me with eyes that pleaded for contradiction, but I couldn't do anything except assure him that everything possible would be done to find both Whitacre and the money. I left him trying frantically to get his attorney on the telephone.

From Ogburn's office I went up to Whitacre's apartment. As I turned the corner below into Gough Street I saw a big, hulking man going up the apartment house steps, and recognized him as George Dean. Hurrying to join him, I regretted that he had been assigned to the job instead of some other member of the police detective Homicide Detail. Dean isn't a bad sort, but he isn't so satisfactory to work with as some of the others; that is, you can never be sure that he isn't holding out some important detail so that George Dean would shine as the clever sleuth in the end. Working with a man of that sort, you're bound to fall into the habit—which doesn't make for teamwork.

I arrived in the vestibule as Dean pressed Whitacre's bell-button.

"Hello," I said. "You in on this?"

"Uh-huh. What d'you know?"

"Nothing. I just got it."

The front door clicked open, and we went together up to the Whitacres' apartment on the third floor. A plump, blond woman in a light blue house-dress opened the apartment door. She was rather pretty in a thick-featured, stolid way.

"Mrs. Whitacre?" Dean inquired.

"Yes."

"Is Mr. Whitacre in?"

"No. He went to Los Angeles this morning," she said, and her face was truthful.

"Know where we can get in touch with him there?"

"Perhaps at the Ambassador, but I think he'll be back by tomorrow or the next day."

Dean showed her his badge.

"We want to ask you a few questions," he told her, and with no appearance of astonishment she opened the door wide for us to enter. She led us into a blue and cream living-room where we found a chair apiece. She sat facing us on a big blue settle.

"Where was your husband last night?" Dean asked.

"Home. Why?" Her round blue eyes were faintly curious.

"Home all night?"

"Yes, it was a rotten rainy night. Why?" She looked from Dean to me.

Dean's glance met mine, and I nodded an answer to the question that I read there.

"Mrs. Whitacre," he said bluntly, "I have a warrant for your husband's arrest."

"A warrant? For what?"

"Murder."

"Murder?" It was a stifled scream.

"Exactly, an' last night."

"But—but I told you he was—"

"And Ogburn told me," I interrupted, leaning forward, "that you called up his apartment last night, asking if your husband was there."

She looked at me blankly for a dozen seconds, and then she laughed, the clear laugh of one who has been the victim of some slight joke.

"You win," she said, and there was neither shame nor humiliation in either face or voice. "Now listen"—the amusement had left her—"I don't know what Herb has done, or how I stand, and I oughtn't to talk until I see a lawyer. But I like to dodge all the trouble I can. If you folks will tell me what's what, on your word of honor, I'll maybe tell you what I know, if anything. What I mean is, if talking will make things any easier for me, if you can show me it will, maybe I'll talk—provided I know anything."

That seemed fair enough, if a little surprising. Apparently this plump woman who could lie with every semblance of candour, and laugh when she was tripped up, wasn't interested in anything much beyond her own comfort.

"You tell it," Dean said to me.

I shot it out all in a lump.

"Your husband had been cooking the books for some time, and got into his partner for something like two hundred thousand dollars before Ogburn got wise to it. Then he had your husband shadowed, trying to find the money. Last night your husband took the man who was shadowing him over on a lot and shot him."

Her face puckered thoughtfully. Mechanically she reached for a package of popular-brand cigarettes that lay on a table behind the settle, and proffered them to Dean and me. We shook our heads. She put a cigarette in her mouth, scratched a match on the sole of her slipper, lit the cigarette, and stared at the burning end. Finally she shrugged, her face cleared, and she looked up at us.

"I'm going to talk," she said. "Never got any of the money, and I'd be a chump to make a goat of myself for Herb. He was all right, but if he's run out and left me flat, there's no use of me making a lot of trouble for myself over it. Here goes: I'm not Mrs. Whitacre, except on the register. My name is Mae Landis. Maybe there is a real Mrs. Whitacre, and maybe not. I don't know. Herb and I have been living together here for over a year.

"About a month ago he began to get jumpy, nervous, even worse than usual. He said he had business worries. Then a couple of days ago I discovered that his pistol was gone from the drawer where it had been kept ever since we came here, and that he was carrying it. I asked him: 'What's the idea?' He said he thought he was being followed, and asked me if I'd seen anybody hanging around the neighborhood as if watching our place. I told him no; I thought he was nutty.

"Night before last he told me that he was in trouble, and might have to go away, and that he couldn't take me with him, but would give me enough money to take care of me for a while. He seemed excited, packed his bags so they'd be ready if he needed them in a hurry, and burned up all his photos and a lot of letters and papers. His bags are still in the bedroom, if you want to go through them. When he didn't come home last night I had a hunch that he had beat it without his bags and without saying a word to me, much less giving me any money—leaving me with only twenty dollars to my name and not even much that I could hock, and with the rent due in four days."

"When did you see him last?"

"About eight o'clock last night. He told me he was going down to Mr. Ogburn's apartment to talk some business over with him, but he didn't go there. I know that. I ran out of cigarettes—I like Elixir Russians, and I can't get them uptown here—so I called up Mr. Ogburn's to ask Herb to bring some home with him when he came, and Mr. Ogburn said he hadn't been there."

"How long have you known Whitacre?" I asked.

"Couple of years, I guess. I think I met him first at one of the beach resorts."

"Has he got any people?"

"Not that I know of. I don't know a whole lot about him. Oh, yes! I do know that he served three years in prison in Oregon for forgery. He told me that one night when he was lushed up. He served them under the name of Barber, or Barbee, or something like that. He said he was walking the straight and narrow now."

Dean produced a small automatic pistol, fairly new-looking in spite of the mud that clung to it, and handed it to the woman.

"Ever see that?"

She nodded her blond head. "Yep! That's Herb's or its twin."

Dean pocketed the gun again, and we stood up.

"Where do I stand now?" she asked. "You're not going to lock me up as a witness or anything, are you?"

"Not just now," Dean assured her. "Stick around where we can find you if we want you, and you won't be bothered. Got any idea which direction Whitacre'd be likely to go in?"

"No."

"We'd like to give the place the once-over. Mind?"

"Go ahead," she invited. "Take it apart if you want to. I'm coming all the way with you people."

We very nearly did take the place apart, but we found not a thing of value. Whitacre, when he had burned the things that might have given him away, had made a clean job of it.

"Did he ever have any pictures taken by a professional photographer?" I asked just before we left.

"Not that I know of."

"Will you let us know if you hear anything or remember anything else that might help?"

"Sure," she said heartily; "sure."

Dean and I rode down in the elevator in silence, and walked out into Gough Street.

"What do you think of all that?" I asked when we were outside.

"She's a lil, huh?" He grinned. "I wonder how much she knows. She identified the gun an' gave us that dope about the forgery sentence up north, but we'd of found out them things anyway. If she was wise she'd tell us everything she knew we'd find out, an' that would make her other stuff go over stronger. Think she's dumb or wise?"

"We won't guess," I said. "We'll slap a shadow on her and cover her mail. I have the number of a taxi she used a couple days ago. We'll look that up too."

At a corner drug store I telephoned the Old Man, asking him to detail a couple of the boys to keep Mae Landis and her apart-

WHO KILLED BOB TEAL?

ment under surveillance night and day; also to have the Post Office Department let us know if she got any mail that might have been addressed by Whitacre. I told the Old Man I would see Ogburn and get some specimens of the fugitive's writing for comparison with the woman's mail.

Then Dean and I set about tracing the taxi in which Bob Teal had seen the woman ride away. Half an hour in the taxi company's office gave us the information that she had been driven to a number on Greenwich Street. We went to the Greenwich Street address.

It was a ramshackle building, divided into apartments or flats of a dismal and dingy sort. We found the landlady in the basement: a gaunt woman in soiled gray, with a hard, thin-lipped mouth and pale, suspicious eyes. She was rocking vigorously in a creaking chair and sewing on a pair of overalls, while three dirty kids tussled with a mongrel puppy up and down the room.

Dean showed his badge, and told her that we wanted to speak to her in privacy. She got up to chase the kids and their dog out, and then stood with hands on hips facing us.

"Well, what do you want?" she demanded sourly.

"Want to get a line on your tenants," Dean said. "Tell us about them."

"Tell you about them?" She had a voice that would have been harsh enough even if she hadn't been in such a peevish mood. "What do you think I got to say about 'em? What do you think I am? I'm a woman that minds her own business! Nobody can't say that I don't run a respectable—"

This was getting us nowhere.

"Who lives in number one?" I asked.

"The Auds—two old folks and their grandchildren. If you know anything against them, it's more'n them that has lived with 'em for ten years does!"

"Who lives in number two?"

"Mrs. Codman and her boys, Frank and Fred. They been here three years, and—"

I carried her from apartment to apartment, until finally we reached a second-floor one that didn't bring quite so harsh an indictment of my stupidity for suspecting its occupants of whatever it was that I suspected them of.

"The Quirks live there." She merely glowered now, whereas she had had a snippy manner before. "And they're decent people, if you ask me!"

"How long have they been here?"

"Six months or more."

"What does he do for a living?"

"I don't know." Sullenly: "Travels, maybe."

"How many in the family?"

"Just him and her, and they're nice quiet people, too."

"What does he look like?"

"Like an ordinary man. I ain't a detective, I don't go 'round snoopin' into folks' faces to see what they look like, and prying into their business. I ain't—"

"How old a man is he?"

"Maybe between thirty-five and forty, if he ain't younger or older."

"Large or small?"

"He ain't as short as you and he ain't as tall as this feller with you," glaring scornfully from my short stoutness to Dean's big hulk, "and he ain't as fat as neither of you."

"Mustache?"

"No."

"Light hair?"

"No." Triumphantly: "Dark."

"Dark eyes, too?"

"I guess so."

Dean, standing off to one side, looked over the woman's shoulder at me. His lips framed the name "Whitacre."

"Now how about Mrs. Quirk—what does she look like?" I went on.

WHO KILLED BOB TEAL?

"She's got light hair, is short and chunky, and maybe under thirty."

Dean and I nodded our satisfaction at each other; that sounded like Mae Landis, right enough.

"Are they home much?" I continued.

"I don't know," the gaunt woman snarled sullenly, and I knew she did know, so I waited, looking at her, and presently she added grudgingly: "I think they're away a lot, but I ain't sure."

"I know," I ventured, "they are home very seldom, and then only in the daytime—and you know it."

She didn't deny it, so I asked: "Are they in now?"

"I don't think so, but they might be."

"Let's take a look at the joint," I suggested to Dean.

He nodded and told the woman: "Take us up to their apartment an' unlock the door for us."

"I won't!" she said with sharp emphasis. "You got no right goin' into folks' homes unless you got a search warrant. You got one?"

"We got nothin'." Dean grinned at her. "But we can get plenty if you want to put us to the trouble. You run this house; you can go into any of the flats any time you want, an' you can take us in. Take us up, an' we'll lay off you; but if you're going to put us to a lot of trouble, then you'll take your chances of bein' tied up with the Quirks, an' maybe sharin' a cell with 'em. Think that over."

She thought it over, and then, grumbling and growling with each step, took us up to the Quirks' apartment. She made sure they weren't at home, then admitted us.

The apartment consisted of three rooms, a bath, and a kitchen, furnished in the shabby fashion that the ramshackle exterior of the building had prepared us for. In these rooms we found a few articles of masculine and feminine clothing, toilet accessories, and so on. But the place had none of the marks of a permanent abode: there were no pictures, no cushions, none of the dozens of odds and ends of personal belongings that are usually found in homes. The kitchen had the appearance of long disuse; the interiors of the coffee, tea, spice, and flour containers were clean.

Two things we found that meant something: a handful of Elixir Russian cigarettes on a table; and a new box of .32 cartridges—ten of which were missing—in a dresser drawer.

All through our searching the landlady hovered over us, her pale eyes sharp and curious; but now we chased her out, telling her that, law or no law, we were taking charge of the apartment.

"This was or is a hide-out for Whitacre and his woman all right," Dean said when we were alone. "The only question is whether he intended to lay low here or whether it was just a place where he made preparations for his getaway. I reckon the best thing is to have the captain put a man in here night and day until we turn up Brother Whitacre."

"That's safest," I agreed, and he went to the telephone in the front room to arrange it.

After Dean was through phoning, I called up the Old Man to see if anything new had developed.

"Nothing new," he told me. "How are you coming along?"

"Nicely. Maybe I'll have news for you this evening."

"Did you get those specimens of Whitacre's writing from Ogburn? Or shall I have someone else take care of it?"

"I'll get them this evening," I promised.

I wasted ten minutes trying to reach Ogburn at his office before I looked at my watch and saw that it was after six o'clock. I found his residence listed in the telephone directory, and called him there.

"Have you anything in Whitacre's writing at home?" I asked. "I want to get a couple of samples—would like to get them this evening, though if necessary I can wait until tomorrow."

"I think I have some of his letters here. If you come over now I'll give them to you."

"Be with you in fifteen minutes," I told him.

"I'm going down to Ogburn's," I told Dean, "to get some of Whitacre's scribbling while you're waiting for your man to come from headquarters to take charge of this place. I'll meet you at the States as soon as you can get away. We'll eat there, and make our plans for the night."

"Uh-huh," he grunted, making himself comfortable in one chair, with his feet on another, as I let myself out.

Ogburn was dressing when I reached his apartment, and had his collar and tie in his hand when he came to the door to let me in.

"I found quite a few of Herb's letters," he said as we walked back to his bedroom.

I looked through the fifteen or more letters that lay on a table, selecting the ones I wanted, while Ogburn went on with his dressing.

"How are you progressing?" he asked presently.

"So-so. Heard anything that might help?"

"No, but just a few minutes ago I happened to remember that Herb used to go over to the Mills Building quite frequently. I've seen him going in and out often, but never thought anything of it. I don't know whether it is of any importance or—"

I jumped out of my chair.

"That does it!" I cried. "Can I use your phone?"

"Certainly. It's in the hallway, near the door." He looked at me in surprise. "It's a slot phone; have you a nickel in change?"

"Yes." I was going through the bedroom door.

"The switch is near the door," he called after me, "if you want a light. Do you think—"

But I didn't stop to listen to his questions. I was making for the telephone, searching my pockets for a nickel. And, fumbling hurriedly with the nickel, I muffed it—not entirely by accident, for I had a hunch that I wanted to work out. The nickel rolled away down the carpeted hallway. I switched on the light, recovered the nickel, and called the "Quirks'" number. I'm glad I played that hunch.

Dean was still there.

"That joint's dead." I sang. "Take the landlady down to headquarters, and grab the Landis woman, too. I'll meet you there—at headquarters."

"You mean it?" he rumbled.

"Almost," I said, and hung up the receiver.

I switched off the hall light and, whistling a little tune to myself, walked back to the room where I had left Ogburn. The door was not quite closed. I walked straight up to it, kicked it open with one foot, and jumped back, hugging the wall.

Two shots—so close together that they were almost one—crashed.

Flat against the wall, I pounded my feet against the floor and wainscot, and let out a medley of shrieks and groans that would have done credit to a carnival wild-man.

A moment later Ogburn appeared in the doorway, a revolver in his hand, his face wolfish. He was determined to kill me. It was my life or his, so—

I slammed my gun down on the sleek, brown top of his head.

When he opened his eyes, two policemen were lifting him into the back of a patrol wagon.

I found Dean in the detectives' assembly-room in the Hall of Justice.

"The landlady identified Mae Landis as Mrs. Quirk," he said. "Now what?"

"Where is she now?"

"One of the policewomen is holding both of them in the captain's office."

"Ogburn is over in the Pawnshop Detail office," I told him. "Let's take the landlady in for a look at him."

Ogburn sat leaning forward, holding his head in his hands' and staring sullenly at the feet of the uniformed man who guarded him, when we took the gaunt landlady in to see him.

"Ever see him before?" I asked her.

"Yes"—reluctantly—"that's Mr. Quirk."

Ogburn didn't look up, and he paid not the least attention to any of us.

WHO KILLED BOB TEAL?

After we had told the landlady that she could go home, Dean led me back to a far corner of the assembly-room, where we could talk without disturbance.

"Now spill it!" he burst out. "How come all the startling developments, as the newspaper boys call 'em?"

"Well, first-off, I knew that the question 'Who killed Bob Teal?' could have only one answer. Bob wasn't a boob! He might possibly have let a man he was trailing lure him behind a row of billboards on a dark night, but he would have gone prepared for trouble. He wouldn't have died with empty hands, from a gun that was close enough to scorch his coat. The murderer had to be somebody Bob trusted, so it couldn't be Whitacre. Now Bob was a conscientious sort of lad, and he wouldn't have stopped shadowing Whitacre to go over and talk with some friend. There was only one man who could have persuaded him to drop Whitacre for a while, and that one man was the one he was working for—Ogburn.

"If I hadn't known Bob, I might have thought he had hidden behind the billboards to watch Whitacre; but Bob wasn't an amateur. He knew better than to pull any of that spectacular gumshoe stuff. So there was nothing to it but Ogburn!

"With all that to go on, the rest was duck soup. All the stuff Mae Landis gave us—identifying the gun as Whitacre's, and giving Ogburn an alibi by saying she had talked to him on the phone at ten o'clock—only convinced me that she and Ogburn were working together. When the landlady described 'Quirk' for us, I was fairly certain of it. Her description would fit either Whitacre or Ogburn, but there was no sense to Whitacre's having the apartment on Greenwich Street, while if Ogburn and the Landis woman were thick, they'd need a meeting-place of some sort. The rest of the box of cartridges there helped some too.

"Then tonight I put on a little act in Ogburn's apartment, chasing a nickel along the floor and finding traces of dried mud that had escaped the cleaning-up he no doubt gave the carpet and clothes after he came home from walking through the lot in the rain. We'll let the experts decide whether it could be mud from the lot on which Bob was killed, and the jury can decide whether it is.

"There are a few more odds and ends—like the gun. The Landis woman said Whitacre had had it for more than a year, but in spite of being muddy it looks fairly new to me. We'll send the serial number to the factory, and find when it was turned out.

"For motive, just now all I'm sure of is the woman, which should be enough. But I think that when Ogburn and Whitacre's books are audited, and their finances sifted, we'll find something there. What I'm banking on strong is that Whitacre will come in, now that he is cleared of the murder charge."

And that is exactly what happened.

Next day Herbert Whitacre walked into Police Headquarters at Sacramento and surrendered.

Neither Ogburn nor Mae Landis ever told what they knew, but with Whitacre's testimony, supported by what we were able to pick up here and there, we went into court when the time came and convinced the jury that the facts were these:

Ogburn and Whitacre had opened their farm-development business as a plain swindle. They had options on a lot of land, and they planned to sell as many shares in their enterprise as possible before the time came to exercise their options. Then they intended packing up their bags and disappearing. Whitacre hadn't much nerve, and he had a clear remembrance of the three years he had served in prison for forgery; so to bolster his courage, Ogburn had told his partner that he had a friend in the Post Office Department in Washington, D.C., who would tip him off the instant official suspicion was aroused.

The two partners made a neat little pile out of their venture, Ogburn taking charge of the money until the time came for the split-up. Meanwhile, Ogburn and Mae Landis—Whitacre's supposed wife—had become intimate, and had rented the apartment on Greenwich Street, meeting there afternoons when Whitacre was busy at the office, and when Ogburn was supposed to be out

WHO KILLED BOB TEAL?

hunting fresh victims. In this apartment Ogburn and the woman had hatched their little scheme, whereby they were to get rid of Whitacre, keep all the loot, and clear Ogburn of criminal complicity in the affairs of Ogburn & Whitacre.

Ogburn had come into the Continental office and told his little tale of his partner's dishonesty, engaging Bob Teal to shadow him. Then he had told Whitacre that he had received a tip from his friend in Washington that an investigation was about to be made. The two partners planned to leave town on their separate ways the following week. The next night Mae Landis told Whitacre she had seen a man loitering in the neighborhood, apparently watching the building in which they lived. Whitacre—thinking Bob a Post Office inspector—had gone completely to pieces, and it had taken the combined efforts of the woman and his partner—apparently working separately—to keep him from bolting immediately. They persuaded him to stick it out another few days.

On the night of the murder, Ogburn, pretending scepticism of Whitacre's story about being followed, had met Whitacre for the purpose of learning if he really was being shadowed. They had walked the streets in the rain for an hour. Then Ogburn, convinced, had announced his intention of going back and talking to the supposed Post Office inspector, to see if he could be bribed. Whitacre had refused to accompany his partner, but had agreed to wait for him in a dark doorway.

Ogburn had taken Bob Teal over behind the billboards on some pretext, and had murdered him. Then he had hurried back to his partner, cryirig: "My God! He grabbed me and I shot him. We'll have to leave!"

Whitacre, in blind panic, had left San Francisco without stopping for his bags or even notifying Mae Landis. Ogburn was supposed to leave by another route. They were to meet in Oklahoma City ten days later, where Ogburn—after getting the loot out of the Los Angeles banks where he had deposited it under various names—was to give Whitacre his share, and then they were to part for good.

DETECTIVE STORIES

In Sacramento next day Whitacre had read the newspapers, and had understood what had been done to him. He had done all the bookkeeping; all the false entries in Ogburn & Whitacre's books were in his writing. Mae Landis had revealed his former criminal record, and had fastened the ownership of the gun—really Ogburn's—upon him. He was framed completely! He hadn't a chance of clearing himself.

He had known that his story would sound like a far-fetched and flimsy lie; he had a criminal record. For him to have surrendered and told the truth would have been merely to get himself laughed at.

As it turned out, Ogburn went to the gallows, Mae Landis is now serving a fifteen-year sentence, and Whitacre, in return for his testimony and restitution of the loot, was not prosecuted for his share in the land swindle.

MIKE, ALEC, OR RUFUS

I don't know whether Frank Toplin was tall or short. All of him I ever got a look at was his round head—naked scalp and wrinkled face, both of them the color and texture of Manila paper—propped up on white pillows in a big four-poster bed. The rest of him was buried under a thick pile of bedding.

Also in the room that first time were his wife, a roly-poly woman with lines in a plump white face like scratches in ivory; his daughter Phyllis, a smart popular-member-of-the-younger-set type; and the maid who had opened the door for me, a big-boned blond girl in apron and cap.

I had introduced myself as a representative of the North American Casualty Company's San Francisco office, which I was in a way. There was no immediate profit in admitting I was a Continental Detective Agency sleuth, just now in the casualty company's hire, so I held back that part.

"I want a list of the stuff you lost," I told Toplin, "but first—"

"Stuff?" Toplin's yellow sphere of a skull bobbed off the pillows, and he wailed to the ceiling, "A hundred thousand dollars if a nickel, and he calls it stuff!"

Mrs. Toplin pushed her husband's head down on the pillows again with a short-fingered fat hand.

"Now, Frank, don't get excited," she soothed him.

Phyllis Toplin's dark eyes twinkled, and she winked at me.

The man in bed turned his face to me again, smiled a bit shamefacedly, and chuckled.

"Well, if you people want to call your seventy-five-thousand-dollar loss stuff, I guess I can stand it for twenty-five thousand."

"So it adds up to a hundred thousand?" I asked.

"Yes. None of them were insured to their full value, and some weren't insured at all."

That was very usual. I don't remember ever having anybody admit that anything stolen from them was insured to the hilt—always it was half, or at most, three-quarters covered by the policy.

"Suppose you tell me exactly what happened," I suggested, and added, to head off another speech that usually comes, "I know you've already told the police the whole thing, but I'll have to have it from you."

"Well, we were getting dressed to go to the Bauers' last night. I brought my wife's and daughter's jewellery—the valuable pieces—home with me from the safe-deposit box. I had just got my coat on and had called to them to hurry up when the doorbell rang."

"What time was this?"

"Just about half-past eight. I went out of this room into the sitting-room across the passageway and was putting some cigars in my case when Hilda"—nodding at the blond maid—"came walking into the room, backward. I started to ask her if she had gone crazy, walking around backward, when I saw the robber. He—"

"Just a moment." I turned to the maid. "What happened when you answered the bell?"

"Why, I opened the door, of course, and this man was standing there, and he had a revolver in his hand, and he stuck it against my—my stomach, and pushed me back into the room where Mr. Toplin was, and he shot Mr. Toplin, and—"

"When I saw him and the revolver in his hand"—Toplin took the story away from his servant—"it gave me a fright, sort of, and I let my cigar case slip out of my hand. Trying to catch it again—

no sense in ruining good cigars even if you are being robbed—he must have thought I was trying to get a gun or something. Anyway, he shot me in the leg. My wife and Phyllis came running in when they heard the shot and he pointed the revolver at them, took all their jewels, and had them empty my pockets. Then he made them drag me back into Phyllis's room, into the closet, and he locked us all in there. And mind you, he didn't say a word all the time, not a word—just made motions with his gun and his left hand."

"How bad did he bang your leg?"

"Depends on whether you want to believe me or the doctor. He says it's nothing much. Just a scratch, he says, but it's my leg that's shot, not his!"

"Did he say anything when you opened the door?" I asked the maid.

"No, sir."

"Did any of you hear him say anything while he was here?"

None of them had.

"What happened after he locked you in the closet?"

"Nothing that we knew about," Toplin said, "until McBirney and a policeman came and let us out."

"Who's McBirney?"

"The janitor."

"How'd he happen along with a policeman?"

"He heard the shot and came upstairs just as the robber was starting down after leaving here. The robber turned around and ran upstairs, then into an apartment on the seventh floor, and stayed there—keeping the woman who lives there, a Miss Eveleth, quiet with his revolver—until he got a chance to sneak out and get away. He knocked her unconscious before he left, and—and that's all. McBirney called the police right after he saw the robber, but they got here too late to be any good."

"How long were you in the closet?"

"Ten minutes—maybe fifteen."

"What sort of looking man was the robber?"

"Short and thin and—"

"How short?"

"About your height, or maybe shorter."

"About five feet five or six, say? What would he weigh?"

"Oh, I don't know—maybe a hundred and fifteen or twenty. He was kind of puny."

"How old?"

"Not more than twenty-two or -three."

"Oh, Papa," Phyllis objected, "he was thirty, or near it!"

"What do you think?" I asked Mrs. Toplin.

"Twenty-five, I'd say."

"And you?" to the maid.

"I don't know exactly, sir, but he wasn't very old."

"Light or dark?"

"He was light," Toplin said. "He needed a shave and his beard was yellowish."

"More of a light brown," Phyllis amended.

"Maybe, but it was light."

"What color eyes?"

"I don't know. He had a cap pulled down over them. They looked dark, but that might have been because they were in the shadow."

"How would you describe the part of his face you could see?"

"Pale, and kind of weak-looking—small chin. But you couldn't see much of his face; he had his coat collar up and his cap pulled down."

"How was he dressed?"

"A blue cap pulled down over his eyes, a blue suit, black shoes, and black gloves—silk ones."

"Shabby or neat?"

"Kind of cheap-looking clothes, awfully wrinkled."

"What sort of gun?"

Phyllis Toplin put in her word ahead of her father.

"Papa and Hilda keep calling it a revolver, but it was an automatic—a thirty-eight."

MIKE, ALEC OR RUFUS

"Would you folks know him if you saw him again?"

"Yes," they agreed.

I cleared a space on the bedside table and got out a pencil and paper.

"I want a list of what he got, with as thorough a description of each piece as possible, and the price you paid for it, where you bought it, and when." I got the list half an hour later.

"Do you know the number of Miss Eveleth's apartment?" I asked.

"702, two floors above."

I went up there and rang the bell. The door was opened by a girl of twenty-something, whose nose was hidden under adhesive tape. She had nice clear hazel eyes, dark hair, and athletics written all over her.

"Miss Eveleth?"

"Yes."

"I'm from the insurance company that insured the Toplin jewellery, and I'm looking for information about the robbery."

She touched her bandaged nose and smiled ruefully.

"This is some of my information."

"How did it happen?"

"A penalty of femininity. I forgot to mind my own business. But what you want, I suppose, is what I know about the scoundrel. The doorbell rang a few minutes before nine last night and when I opened the door he was there. As soon as I got the door opened he jabbed a pistol at me and said, 'Inside, kid!'

"I let him in with no hesitancy at all; I was quite instantaneous about it and he kicked the door to behind him.

" 'Where's the fire escape?' he asked.

"The fire escape doesn't come to any of my windows, and I told him so, but he wouldn't take my word for it. He drove me ahead of him to each of the windows; but of course he didn't find his fire escape, and he got peevish about it, as if it were my fault. I didn't like some of the things he called me, and he was such a little half-portion of a man so I tried to take him in hand. But—well, man is still the dominant animal so far as I'm concerned. In plain American, he busted me in the nose and left me where I fell. I was dazed, though not quite all the way out, and when I got up he had gone. I ran out into the corridor then, and found some policemen on the stairs. I sobbed out my pathetic little tale to them and they told me of the Toplin robbery. Two of them came back here with me and searched the apartment. I hadn't seen him actually leave, and they thought he might be foxy enough or desperate enough to jump into a closet and stay there until the coast was clear. But they didn't find him here."

"How long do you think it was after he knocked you down that you ran out into the corridor?"

"Oh, it couldn't have been five minutes. Perhaps only half that time."

"What did Mr. Robber look like?"

"Small, not quite so large as I; with a couple of days' growth of light hair on his face; dressed in shabby blue clothes, with black cloth gloves."

"How old?"

"Not very. His beard was thin, patchy, and he had a boyish face."

"Notice his eyes?"

"Blue; his hair, where it showed under the edge of his cap, was very light yellow, almost white."

"What sort of voice?"

"Very deep bass, though he may have been putting that on."

"Know him if you'd see him again?"

"Yes, indeed!" She put a gentle finger on her bandaged nose. "My nose would know, as the ads say, anyway!"

From Miss Eveleth's apartment I went down to the office on the first floor, where I found McBirney, the janitor, and his wife, who managed the apartment building. She was a scrawny little woman with the angular mouth and nose of a nagger; he was big, broad-shouldered, with sandy hair and mustache, good-humored, shiftless red face, and genial eyes of a pale and watery blue.

He drawled out what he knew of the looting.

"I was fixin' a spigot on the fourth floor when I heard the shot. I went up to see what was the matter, an' just as I got far enough up the front stairs to see the Toplins' door, the fella came out. We seen each other at the same time, an' he aims his gun at me. There's a lot o' things I might of done, but what I did do was to duck down an' get my head out o' range. I heard him run upstairs, an' I got up just in time to see him make the turn between the fifth and sixth floors.

"I didn't go after him. I didn't have a gun or nothin', an' I figured we had him cooped. A man could get out o' this buildin' to the roof of the next from the fourth floor, an' maybe from the fifth, but not from any above that; an' the Toplins' apartment is on the fifth. I figured we had this fella. I could stand in front of the elevator an' watch both the front an' back stairs; an' I rang for the elevator, an' told Ambrose, the elevator boy, to give the alarm an' run outside an' keep his eye on the fire escape until the police came.

"The missus came up with my gun in a minute or two, an' told me that Martinez—Ambrose's brother, who takes care of the switchboard an' the front door—was callin' the police. I could see both stairs plain, an' the fella didn't come down them; an' it wasn't more'n a few minutes before the police—a whole pack of 'em—came from the Richmond Station. Then we let the Toplins out of the closet where they were, an' started to search the buildin'. An' then Miss Eveleth came runnin' down the stairs, her face an' dress all bloody, an' told about him bein' in her apartment; so we were pretty sure we'd land him. But we didn't. We searched every apartment in the buildin', but didn't find hide nor hair of him."

"Of course you didn't!" Mrs. McBirney said unpleasantly. "But if you had—"

"I know," the janitor said with the indulgent air of one who has learned to take his pannings as an ordinary part of married life, "if

I'd been a hero an' grabbed him, an' got myself all mussed up. Well, I ain't foolish like old man Toplin, gettin' himself plugged in the foot, or Blanche Eveleth, gettin' her nose busted. I'm a sensible man that knows when he's licked—an' I ain't jumpin' at no guns!"

"No! You're not doing anything that—"

This Mr. and Mrs. stuff wasn't getting me anywhere, so I cut in with a question to the woman. "Who is the newest tenant you have?"

"Mr. and Mrs. Jerald—they came the day before yesterday."

"What apartment?"

"704—next door to Miss Eveleth."

"Who are these Jeralds?"

"They come from Boston. He told me he came out here to open a branch of a manufacturing company. He's a man of at least fifty, thin and dyspeptic-looking."

"Just him and his wife?"

"Yes. She's poorly too—been in a sanatorium for a year or two."

"Who's the next newest tenant?"

"Mr. Heaton, in 535. He's been here a couple of weeks, but he's down in Los Angeles right now. He went away three days ago and said he would be gone for ten or twelve days."

"What does he look like and what does he do?"

"He's with a theatrical agency and he's kind of fat and red-faced."

"Who's the next newest?"

"Miss Eveleth. She's been here about a month."

"And the next?"

"The Wageners in 923. They've been here going on two months."

"What are they?"

"He's a retired real-estate agent. The others are his wife and son Jack—a boy of maybe nineteen. I see him with Phyllis Toplin a lot."

"How long have the Toplins been here?"

MIKE, ALEC OR RUFUS

"It'll be two years next month."

I turned from Mrs. McBirney to her husband.

"Did the police search all these people's apartments?"

"Yeah," he said. "We went into every room, every alcove, an' every closet from cellar to roof."

"Did you get a good look at the robber?"

"Yeah. There's a light in the hall outside of the Toplins' door, an' it was shinin' full on his face when I saw him."

"Could he have been one of your tenants?"

"No, he couldn't."

"Know him if you saw him again?"

"You bet."

"What did he look like?"

"A little runt, a light-complected youngster of twenty-three or -four in an old blue suit."

"Can I get hold of Ambrose and Martinez—the elevator and door boys who were on duty last night—now?"

The janitor looked at his watch.

"Yeah. They ought to be on the job now. They come on at two."

I went out into the lobby and found them together, matching nickels.

They were brothers, slim, bright-eyed Filipino boys. They didn't add much to my dope.

Ambrose had come down to the lobby and told his brother to call the police as soon as McBirney had given him his orders, and then he had to beat it out the back door to take a plant on the fire escapes. The fire escapes ran down the back and one side wall. By standing a little off from the corner of those walls, the Filipino had been able to keep his eyes on both of them, as well as on the back door.

There was plenty of illumination, he said, and he could see both fire escapes all the way to the roof, and he had seen nobody on them.

Martinez had given the police a rap on the phone and had then watched the front door and the foot of the front stairs. He had seen nothing.

DETECTIVE STORIES

I had just finished questioning the Filipinos when the street door opened and two men came in. I knew one of them: Bill Garren, a police detective on the Pawnshop Detail. The other was a small blond youth all flossy in pleated pants, short, square-shouldered coat, and patent-leather shoes with fawn spats to match his hat and gloves. His face wore a sullen pout. He didn't seem to like being with Garren.

"What are you up to around here?" the detective hailed me.

"The Toplin doings for the insurance company," I explained.

"Getting anywhere?" he wanted to know.

"About ready to make a pinch," I said, not altogether in earnest and not altogether joking.

"The more the merrier," he grinned. "I've already made mine," nodding at the dressy youth. "Come on upstairs with us."

The three of us got into the elevator and Ambrose carried us to the fifth floor. Before pressing the Toplin bell, Garren gave me what he had.

"This lad tried to soak a ring in a Third Street shop a little while ago—an emerald and diamond ring that looks like one of the Toplin lot. He's doing the clam now; he hasn't said a word—yet. I'm going to show him to these people; then I'm going to take him down to the Hall of Justice and get words out of him—words that fit together in nice sentences and everything!"

The prisoner looked sullenly at the floor and paid no attention to this threat. Garren rang the bell and the maid Hilda opened the door. Her eyes widened when she saw the dressy boy, but she didn't say anything as she led us into the sitting-room, where Mrs. Toplin and her daughter were. They looked up at us.

"Hello, Jack!" Phyllis greeted the prisoner.

"'Lo, Phyl," he mumbled, not looking at her.

"Among friends, huh? Well, what's the answer?" Garren demanded of the girl.

She put her chin in the air and although her face turned red, she looked haughtily at the police detective.

"Would you mind removing your hat?" she asked.

Bill isn't a bad bimbo, but he hasn't any meekness. He answered her by tilting his hat over one eye and turning to her mother.

"Ever see this lad before?"

"Why, certainly!" Mrs. Toplin exclaimed. "That's Mr. Wagener who lives upstairs."

"Well," said Bill, "Mr. Wagener was picked up in a hock shop trying to get rid of this ring." He fished a gaudy green and white ring from his pocket. "Know it?"

"Certainly!" Mrs. Toplin said, looking at the ring. "It belongs to Phyllis, and the robber—" Her mouth dropped open as she began to understand. "How could Mr. Wagener—?"

"Yes, how?" Bill repeated.

The girl stepped between Garren and me, turning her back on him to face me. "I can explain everything," she announced.

That sounded too much like a movie subtitle to be very promising, but—

"Go ahead," I encouraged her.

"I found that ring in the passageway near the front door after the excitement was over. The robber must have dropped it. I didn't say anything to Papa and Mamma about it, because I thought nobody would ever know the difference, and it was insured, so I thought I might as well sell it and be in that much money. I asked Jack last night if he could sell it for me and he said he knew just how to go about it. He didn't have anything to do with it outside of that, but I did think he'd have sense enough not to try to pawn it right away!"

She looked scornfully at her accomplice.

"See what you've done!" she accused him.

He fidgeted and pouted at his feet.

"Ha! Ha! Ha!" Bill Garren said sourly. "That's a nifty! Did you ever hear the one about the two Irishmen that got in the Y.W.C.A. by mistake?"

She didn't say whether she had heard it or not.

"Mrs. Toplin," I asked, "making allowances for the different clothes and the unshaven face, could this lad have been the robber?"

She shook her head with emphasis. "No! He could not!"

"Set your prize down, Bill," I suggested, "and let's go over in a corner and whisper things at each other."

"Right."

He dragged a heavy chair to the center of the floor, sat Wagener on it, anchored him there with handcuffs—not exactly necessary, but Bill was grouchy at not getting his prisoner identified as the robber—and then he and I stepped out into the passageway. We could keep an eye on the sitting-room from there without having our low-voiced conversation overheard.

"This is simple," I whispered into his big red ear. "There are only five ways to figure the lay. First: Wagener stole the stuff for the Toplins. Second: the Toplins framed the robbery themselves and got Wagener to peddle it. Third: Wagener and the girl engineered the deal without the old folks being in on it. Fourth: Wagener pulled it on his own hook and the girl is covering him up. Fifth: she told us the truth. None of them explains why your little playmate should have been dumb enough to flash the ring downtown this morning, but that can't be explained by any system. Which of the five do you favor?"

"I like 'em all," he grumbled. "But what I like most is that I've got this baby right—got him trying to pass a hot ring. That suits me fine. You do the guessing. I don't ask for any more than I've got."

"It doesn't irritate me any either," I agreed. "The way it stands the insurance company can welsh on the policies—but I'd like to smoke it out a little further, far enough to put away anybody who has been trying to run a hooligan on the North American. We'll clean up all we can on this kid, stow him in the can, and then see what further damage we can do."

"All right," Garren said. "Suppose you get hold of the janitor and that Eveleth woman while I'm showing the boy to old man Toplin and getting the maid's opinion."

MIKE, ALEC OR RUFUS

I nodded and went out into the corridor, leaving the door unlocked behind me. I took the elevator to the seventh floor and told Ambrose to get hold of McBirney and send him to the Toplins' apartment. Then I rang Blanche Eveleth's bell.

"Can you come downstairs for a minute or two?" I asked her. "We've a prize who might be your friend of last night."

"Will I?" She started toward the stairs with me. "And if he's the right one, can I pay him back for my battered beauty?"

"You can," I promised. "Go as far as you like, so you don't maul him too badly to stand trial."

I took her into the Toplins' apartment without ringing the bell, and found everybody in Frank Toplin's bedroom. A look at Garren's glum face told me that neither the old man nor the maid had given him a nod on the prisoner.

I put the finger on Jack Wagener. Disappointment came into Blanche Eveleth's eyes. "You're wrong," she said. "That's not he."

Garren scowled at her. It was a pipe that if the Toplins were tied up with young Wagener, they wouldn't identify him as the robber. Bill had been counting on that identification coming from the two outsiders—Blanche Eveleth and the janitor—and now one of them had flopped.

The other one rang the bell just then and the maid brought him in.

I pointed at Jack Wagener, who stood beside Garren staring sullenly at the floor.

"Know him, McBirney?"

"Yeah, Mr. Wagener's son, Jack."

"Is he the man who shooed you away with a gun last night?"

McBirney's watery eyes popped in surprise.

"No," he said with decision, and began to look doubtful.

"In an old suit, cap pulled down, needing a shave—could it have been him?"

"No-o-o-o," the janitor drawled, "I don't think so, though it— You know, now that I come to think about it, there was something familiar about that fella, an' maybe—By cracky, I think maybe you're right—though I couldn't exactly say for sure."

"That'll do!" Garren grunted in disgust.

An identification of the sort the janitor was giving isn't worth a damn one way or the other. Even positive and immediate identifications aren't always the goods. A lot of people who don't know any better—and some who do, or should—have given circumstantial evidence a bad name. It is misleading sometimes. But for genuine, undiluted, pre-war untrustworthiness, it can't come within gunshot of human testimony. Take any man you like—unless he is the one in a hundred thousand with a mind trained to keep things straight, and not always even then—get him excited, show him something, give him a few hours to think it over and talk it over, and then ask him about it. It's dollars to doughnuts that you'll have a hard time finding any connection between what he saw and what he says he saw. Like this McBirney—another hour and he'd be ready to gamble his life on Jack Wagener's being the robber.

Garren wrapped his fingers around the boy's arm and started for the door.

"Where to, Bill?" I asked.

"Up to talk to his people. Coming along?"

"Stick around a while," I invited. "I'm going to put on a party. But first, tell me, did the coppers who came here when the alarm was turned in do a good job?"

"I didn't see it," the police detective said. "I didn't get here until the fireworks were pretty well over, but I understand the boys did all that could be expected of them."

I turned to Frank Toplin. I did my talking to him chiefly because we—his wife and daughter, the maid, the janitor, Blanche Eveleth, Garren and his prisoner, and I—were grouped around the old man's bed and by looking at him I could get a one-eyed view of everybody else.

"Somebody has been kidding me somewhere," I began my speech. "If all the things I've been told about this job are right, then so is Prohibition. Your stories don't fit together, not even almost. Take the bird who stuck you up. He seems to have been pretty well acquainted with your affairs. It might be luck that he hit your apartment at a time when all of your jewellery was on hand, instead of another apartment, or your apartment at another time. But I don't like luck. I'd rather figure that he knew what he was doing. He nicked you for your pretties, and then he galloped up to Miss Eveleth's apartment. He may have been about to go downstairs when he ran into McBirney, or he may not. Anyway, he went upstairs, into Miss Eveleth's apartment, looking for a fire escape. Funny, huh? He knew enough about the place to make a push-over out of the stick-up, but he didn't know there were no fire escapes on Miss Eveleth's side of the building.

"He didn't speak to you or to McBirney, but he talked to Miss Eveleth, in a bass voice. A very, very deep voice. Funny, huh? From Miss Eveleth's apartment he vanished with every exit watched. The police must have been here before he left her apartment and they would have blocked the outlets first thing, whether McBirney and Ambrose had already done that or not. But he got away. Funny, huh? He wore a wrinkled suit, which might have been taken from a bundle just before he went to work, and he was a small man. Miss Eveleth isn't a small woman, but she would be a small man. A guy with a suspicious disposition would almost think Blanche Eveleth was the robber."

Frank Toplin, his wife, young Wagener, the janitor, and the maid were gaping at me. Garren was sizing up the Eveleth girl with narrowed eyes, while she glared white-hot at me. Phyllis Toplin was looking at me with a contemptuous sort of pity for my feeble-mindedness.

Bill Garren finished his inspection of the girl and nodded slowly.

"She could get away with it," he gave his opinion, "indoors and if she kept her mouth shut."

"Exactly," I said.

"Exactly, my eye!" Phyllis Toplin exploded. "Do you two correspondence-school detectives think we wouldn't know the difference between a man and a woman dressed in man's clothes? He had a day or two's growth of hair on his face—real hair, if you know what I mean. Do you think he could have fooled us with false whiskers? This happened, you know, it's not in a play!"

The others stopped gaping, and heads bobbed up and down.

"Phyllis is right." Frank Toplin backed up his offspring. "He was a man—no woman dressed like one."

His wife, the maid, and the janitor nodded vigorous endorsements.

But I'm a bull-headed sort of bird when it comes to going where the evidence leads. I spun to face Blanche Eveleth.

"Can you add anything to the occasion?" I asked her.

She smiled very sweetly at me and shook her head.

"All right, bum," I said. "You're pinched. Let's go."

Then it seemed she could add something to the occasion. She had something to say, quite a few things to say, and they were all about me. They weren't nice things. In anger her voice was shrill, and just now she was madder than you'd think anybody could get on short notice. I was sorry for that. This job had run along peacefully and gently so far, hadn't been marred by any rough stuff, had been almost ladylike in every particular; and I had hoped it would go that way to the end. But the more she screamed at me the nastier she got. She didn't have any words I hadn't heard before, but she fitted them together in combinations that were new to me. I stood as much of it as I could.

Then I knocked her over with a punch in the mouth.

"Here! Here!" Bill Garren yelled, grabbing my arm.

"Save your strength, Bill," I advised him, shaking his hand off and going over to yank the Eveleth person up from the floor. "Your gallantry does you credit, but I think you'll find Blanche's real name is Mike, Alec, or Rufus."

I hauled her (or him, whichever you like) to his or her feet and asked it: "Feel like telling us about it?"

MIKE, ALEC OR RUFUS

For answer I got a snarl.

"All right," I said to the others, "in the absence of authoritative information I'll give you my dope. If Blanche Eveleth could have been the robber except for the beard and the difficulty of a woman passing for a man, why couldn't the robber have been Blanche Eveleth before and after the robbery by using a—what do you call it?—strong depilatory on his face, and a wig? It's hard for a woman to masquerade as a man, but there are lots of men who can get away with the feminine role. Couldn't this bird, after renting his apartment as Blanche Eveleth and getting everything lined up, have stayed in his apartment for a couple of days letting his beard grow? Come down and knock the job over? Beat it upstairs, get the hair off his face, and get into his female rig in, say, fifteen minutes? My guess is that he could. And he had fifteen minutes. I don't know about the smashed nose. Maybe he stumbled going up the stairs and had to twist his plans to account for it—or maybe he smacked himself intentionally."

My guesses weren't far off, though his name was Fred—Frederick Agnew Rudd. He was known in Toronto, having done a stretch in the Ontario Reformatory as a boy of nineteen, caught shoplifting in his she-make-up. He wouldn't come through, and we never turned up his gun or the blue suit, cap, and black gloves, although we found a cavity in his mattress where he had stuffed them out of the police's sight until later that night, when he could get rid of them. But the Toplin sparklers came to light piece by piece when we had plumbers take apart the drains and radiators in apartment 702.

NIGHTMARE TOWN

CHAPTER I
A Sensational Arrival

A Ford—whitened by desert travel until it was almost indistinguishable from the dust-clouds that swirled around it—came down Izzard's Main Street. Like the dust, it came swiftly, erratically, zigzagging the breadth of the roadway.

A small woman—a girl of twenty in tan flannel—stepped into the street. The wavering Ford missed her by inches, missing her at all only because her backward jump was bird-quick. She caught her lower lip between white teeth, dark eyes flashed annoyance at the rear of the passing machine, and she essayed the street again.

Near the opposite curb the Ford charged down upon her once more. But turning had taken some of its speed. She escaped it this time by scampering the few feet between her and the sidewalk ahead.

Out of the moving automobile a man stepped. Miraculously he kept his feet, stumbling, sliding, until an arm crooked around an iron awning-post jerked him into an abrupt halt. He was a large man in bleached khaki, tall, broad, and thick-armed; his gray eyes were bloodshot; face and clothing were powdered heavily with dust. One of his hands clutched a thick, black stick, the other swept off his hat, and he bowed with exaggerated lowness before the girl's angry gaze.

The bow completed, he tossed his hat carelessly into the street, and grinned grotesquely through the dirt that masked his face—a grin that accented the heaviness of a begrimed and hair-roughened jaw.

"I *beg* y'r par'on," he said. " 'F I hadn't been careful I believe I'd a'most hit you. 'S unreli'ble, tha' wagon. Borr'ed it from an engi—eng'neer. Don't ever borrow one from eng'neer. They're unreli'ble."

The girl looked at the place where he stood as if no one stood there, as if, in fact, no one had ever stood there, turned her small back on him, and walked very precisely down the street.

He stared after her with stupid surprise in his eyes until she had vanished through a doorway in the middle of the block. Then he scratched his head, shrugged, and turned to look across the street, where his machine had pushed its nose into the red-brick side wall of the Bank of Izzard and now shook and clattered as if in panic at finding itself masterless.

"Look at the son-of-a-gun," he exclaimed.

A hand fastened upon his arm. He turned his head, and then, though he stood a good six feet himself, had to look up to meet the eyes of the giant who held his arm.

"We'll take a little walk," the giant said.

The man in bleached khaki examined the other from the tips of his broad-toed shoes to the creased crown of his black hat, examined him with a whole-hearted admiration that was unmistakable in his red-rimmed eyes. There were nearly seven massive feet of the speaker. Legs like pillars held up a great hogshead of a body, with wide shoulders that sagged a little, as if with their own excessive weight. He was a man of perhaps forty-five, and his face was thick-featured, phlegmatic, with sunlines around small light eyes—the face of a deliberate man.

"My God, you're big!" the man in khaki exclaimed when he had finished his examination; and then his eyes brightened. "Let's wrestle. Bet you ten bucks against fifteen I can throw you. Come on!"

The giant chuckled deep in his heavy chest, took the man in khaki by the nape of the neck and an arm, and walked down the street with him.

CHAPTER II
Justice and a Slapped Face

Steve Threefall awakened without undue surprise at the unfamiliarity of his surroundings as one who has awakened in strange places before. Before his eyes were well open he knew the essentials of his position. The feel of the shelf-bunk on which he lay and the sharp smell of disinfectant in his nostrils told him that he was in jail. His head and his mouth told him that he had been drunk; and the three-day growth of beard on his face told him he had been very drunk.

As he sat up and swung his feet down to the floor details came back to him. The two days of steady drinking in Whitetufts on the other side of the Nevada-California line, with Harris, the hotel proprietor, and Whiting, an irrigation engineer. The boisterous arguing over desert travel, with his own Gobi experience matched against the American experiences of the others. The bet that he could drive from Whitetufts to Izzard in daylight with nothing to drink but the especially bitter white liquor they were drinking at the time. The start in the grayness of imminent dawn, in Whiting's Ford, with Whiting and Harris staggering down the street after him, waking the town with their drunken shouts and roared-out mocking advice, until he had reached the desert's edge. Then the drive through the desert, along the road that was hotter than the rest of the desert, with—He chose not to think of the ride. He had made it, though—had won the bet. He couldn't remember the amount of the latter.

NIGHTMARE TOWN

"So you've come out of it at last?" a rumbling voice inquired.

The steel-slatted door swung open and a man filled the cell's door. Steve grinned up at him. This was the giant who would not wrestle. He was coatless and vestless now, and loomed larger than before. One suspender strap was decorated with a shiny badge that said MARSHAL.

"Feel like breakfast?" he asked.

"I could do things to a can of black coffee," Steve admitted.

"All right. But you'll have to gulp it. Judge Denvir is waiting to get a crack at you, and the longer you keep him waiting, the tougher it'll be for you."

The room in which Tobin Denvir, J.P., dealt justice was a large one on the third floor of a wooden building. It was scantily furnished with a table, an ancient desk, a steel engraving of Daniel Webster, a shelf of books sleeping under the dust of weeks, a dozen uncomfortable chairs, and half as many cracked and chipped china cuspidors.

The judge sat between desk and table, with his feet on the latter. They were small feet, and he was a small man. His face was filled with little irritable lines, his lips were thin and tight, and he had the bright, lidless eyes of a bird.

"Well, what's he charged with?" His voice was thin, harshly metallic. He kept his feet on the table.

The marshal drew a deep breath, and recited:

"Driving on the wrong side of the street, exceeding the speed limit, driving while under the influence of liquor, driving without a driver's license, endangering the lives of pedestrians by taking his hands off the wheel, and I parking improperly—on the sidewalk up against the bank."

The marshal took another breath, and added, with manifest regret:

"There was a charge of attempted assault, too, but that Vallance girl won't appear, so that'll have to be dropped."

The justice's bright eyes turned upon Steve.

"What's your name?" he growled.

"Steve Threefall."

"Is that your real name?" the marshal asked.

"Of course it is," the justice snapped. "You don't think anybody'd be damn fool enough to give a name like that unless it was his, do you?" Then to Steve: "What have you got to say—guilty or not?"

"I was a little—"

"Are you guilty or not?"

"Oh, I suppose I did—"

"That's enough! You're fined a hundred and fifty dollars and costs. The costs are fifteen dollars and eighty cents, making a total of a hundred and sixty-five dollars and eighty cents. Will you pay it or will you go to jail?"

"I'll pay it if I've got it," Steve said, turning to the marshal. "You took my money. Have I got that much?"

The marshal nodded his massive head.

"You have," he said, "exactly—to the nickel. Funny it should have come out like that—huh?"

"Yes—funny," Steve repeated.

While the justice of the peace was making out a receipt for the fine, the marshal restored Steve's watch, tobacco and matches, pocket-knife, keys, and last of all the black walking-stick. The big man weighed the stick in his hand and examined it closely before he gave it up. It was thick and of ebony, but heavy even for that wood, with a balanced weight that hinted at loaded ferrule and knob. Except for a space the breadth of a man's hand in its middle, the stick was roughened, cut and notched with the marks of hard use—marks that much careful polishing had failed to remove or conceal. The unscarred hand's-breadth was of a softer black than the rest—as soft a black as the knob—as if it had known much contact with a human palm.

"Not a bad weapon in a pinch," the marshal said meaningly as he handed the stick to its owner. Steve took it with the grasp a man reserves for a favorite and constant companion.

"Not bad," he agreed. "What happened to the flivver?"

"It's in the garage around the corner on Main Street. Pete said it wasn't altogether ruined, and he thinks he can patch it up if you want."

The justice held out the receipt.

"Am I all through here now?" Steve asked.

"I hope so," Judge Denvir said sourly.

"Both of us," Steve echoed. He put on his hat, tucked the black stick under his arm, nodded to the big marshal, and left the room.

Steve Threefall went down the wooden stairs toward the street in as cheerful a frame of mind as his body—burned out inwardly with white liquor and outwardly by a day's scorching desert-riding—would permit. That justice had emptied his pockets of every last cent disturbed him little. That, he knew, was the way of justice everywhere with the stranger, and he had left the greater part of his money with the hotel proprietor in Whitetufts. He had escaped a jail sentence, and he counted himself lucky. He would wire Harris to send him some of his money, wait here until the Ford was repaired, and then drive back to Whitetufts—but not on a whisky ration this time.

"You will not!" a voice cried in his ear.

He jumped, and then laughed at his alcohol-jangled nerves. The words had not been meant for him. Beside him, at a turning of the stairs, was an open window, and opposite it, across a narrow alley, a window in another building was open. This window belonged to an office in which two men stood facing each other across a flat-topped desk.

One of them was middle-aged and beefy, in a black broadcloth suit out of which a white-vested stomach protruded. His face was purple with rage. The man who faced him was younger—a man of perhaps thirty, with a small dark mustache, finely chiseled features, and satiny brown hair. His slender athlete's body was immaculately clothed in gray suit, gray shirt, gray and silver tie, and on the desk before him lay a Panama hat with gray band. His face was as white as the other's was purple.

The beefy man spoke—a dozen words pitched too low to catch.

The younger man slapped the speaker viciously across the face with an open hand—a hand that then flashed back to its owner's coat and flicked out a snub-nosed automatic pistol.

"You big lard-can," the younger man cried, his voice sibilant; "you'll lay off or I'll spoil your vest for you!"

He stabbed the protuberant vest with the automatic, and laughed into the scared fat face of the beefy man—laughed with a menacing flash of even teeth and dark slitted eyes. Then he picked up his hat, pocketed the pistol, and vanished from Steve's sight. The fat man sat down.

Steve went on down to the street.

CHAPTER III
Izzard Gains a Citizen

Steve Unearthed the garage to which the Ford had been taken, found a greasy mechanic who answered to the name of Pete, and was told that Whiting's automobile would be in condition to move under its own power within two days.

"A beautiful snootful you had yesterday," Pete grinned.

Steve grinned back and went on out. He went down to the telegraph office, next door to the Izzard Hotel, pausing for a moment on the sidewalk to look at a glowing, cream-colored Vauxhall-Velox roadster that stood at the curb—as out of place in this grimy factory town as a harlequin opal in a grocer's window.

In the doorway of the telegraph office Steve paused again, abruptly.

Behind the counter was a girl in tan flannel—the girl he had nearly run down twice the previous afternoon—the "Vallance girl" who had refrained from adding to justice's account against Steve Threefall. In front of the counter, leaning over it, talking to her with every appearance of intimacy was one of the two men he had seen from the staircase window half an hour before—the slender dandy in gray who had slapped the other's face and threatened him with an automatic.

The girl looked up, recognized Steve, and stood very erect. He took off his hat, and advanced smiling.

"I'm awfully sorry about yesterday," he said. "I'm a crazy fool when I—"

"Do you wish to send a telegram?" she asked frigidly.

"Yes," Steve said; "I also wish to—"

"There are blanks and pencils on the desk near the window," and she turned her back on him.

Steve felt himself coloring, and since he was one of the men who habitually grin when at a loss, he grinned now, and found himself looking into the dark eyes of the man in gray.

That one smiled back under his little brown mustache, and said:

"Quite a time you had yesterday."

"Quite," Steve agreed, and went to the table the girl had indicated. He wrote his telegram:

> HENRY HARRIS
> HARRIS HOTEL, WHITETUFTS:
> ARRIVED RIGHT SIDE UP, BUT AM IN HOCK. WIRE ME TWO HUNDRED DOLLARS. WILL BE BACK SATURDAY.
>   THREEFALL.

But he did not immediately get up from the desk. He sat there holding the piece of paper in his fingers, studying the man and girl, who were again engaged in confidential conversation over the counter. Steve studied the girl most.

She was quite a small girl, no more than five feet in height, if that;

and she had that peculiar rounded slenderness which gives a deceptively fragile appearance. Her face was an oval of skin whose fine whiteness had thus far withstood the grimy winds of Izzard; her nose just missed being upturned, her violet-black eyes just missed being too theatrically large, and her black-Brown hair just missed being too bulky for the small head it crowned; but in no respect did she miss being as beautiful as a figure from a Monticelli canvas.

All these things Steve Threefall, twiddling his telegram in sun-brown fingers, considered and as he considered them he came to see the pressing necessity of having his apologies accepted. Explain it as you will—he carefully avoided trying to explain it to himself—the thing was there. One moment there was nothing, in the four continents he knew, of any bothersome importance to Steve Threefall; the next moment he was under an inescapable compulsion to gain the favor of this small person in tan flannel with brown ribbons at wrists and throat.

At this point the man in gray leaned farther over the counter, to whisper something to the girl. She flushed, and her eyes flinched. The pencil in her hand fell to the counter, and she picked it up with small fingers that were suddenly incongruously awkward. She made a smiling reply, and went on with her writing, but the smile seemed forced.

Steve tore up his telegram and composed another:

> I MADE IT, SLEPT IT OFF IN THE COOLER, AND I AM GOING TO SETTLE HERE A WHILE. THERE ARE THINGS ABOUT THE PLACE I LIKE. WIRE MY MONEY AND SEND MY CLOTHES TO HOTEL HERE. BUY WHITING'S FORD FROM HIM AS CHEAP AS YOU CAN FOR ME.

He carried the blank to the counter and laid it down. The girl ran her pencil over it, counting the words.

"Forty-seven," she said, in a tone that involuntarily rebuked the absence of proper telegraphic brevity.

"Long, but it's all right," Steve assured her. "I'm sending it collect."

She regarded him icily.

"I can't accept a collect message unless I know that the sender can pay for it if the addressee refuses it. It's against the rules."

"You'd better make an exception this time," Steve told her solemnly, "because if yon don't you'll have to lend me the money to pay for it."

"I'll have—?"

"You will," he insisted. "You got me into this jam, and it's up to you to help me get out. The Lord knows you've cost me enough as it is—nearly two hundred dollars! The whole thing was your fault."

"*My fault?*"

"It was! Now I'm giving you a chance to square yourself. Hurry it off, please, because I'm hungry and I need a shave. I'll be waiting on the bench outside." And he spun on his heel and left the office.

CHAPTER IV
A Thin, Sad-Faced Man

One end of the bench in front of the telegraph office was occupied when Steve, paying no attention to the man who sat there, made himself comfortable on the other. He put his black stick between his legs and rolled a cigarette with thoughtful slowness, his mind upon the just completed scene in the office.

Why, he wondered, whenever there was some special reason for gravity, did he always find himself becoming flippant? Why, whenever he found himself face to face with a situation that was important, that meant something to him, did he slip uncontrollably into banter—play the clown? He lit his cigarette and decided scornfully—as he had decided a dozen times before—that it all came from a childish attempt to conceal his self-consciousness;

that for all his thirty-three years of life and his eighteen years of rubbing shoulders with the world—its rough corners as well as its polished—he was still a green boy underneath—a big kid.

"A neat package you had yesterday," the man who sat on the other end of the bench remarked.

"Yeah," Steve admitted without turning his head. He supposed he'd be hearing about his crazy arrival as long as he stayed in Izzard.

"I reckon old man Denvir took you to the cleaner's as usual?"

"Uh-huh!" Steve said, turning now for a look at the other.

He saw a very tall and very lean man in rusty brown, slouched down on the small of his back, angular legs thrust out across the sidewalk. A man past forty, whose gaunt, melancholy face was marked with lines so deep that they were folds in the skin rather than wrinkles. His eyes were the mournful chestnut eyes of a basset hound, and his nose was as long and sharp as a paper-knife. He puffed on a black cigar, getting from it a surprising amount of smoke, which he exhaled upward, his thin nose splitting the smoke into two gray plumes.

"Ever been to our fair young city before?" this melancholy individual asked next. His voice held a monotonous rhythm that was not unpleasant to the ear.

"No, this is my first time."

The thin man nodded ironically.

"You'll like it if you stay," he said. "It's very interesting."

"What's it all about?" Steve asked, finding himself mildly intrigued by his benchmate.

"Soda niter. You scoop it up off the desert, and boil and otherwise cook it, and sell it to fertilizer manufacturers, and nitric acid manufacturers, and any other kind of manufacturers who can manufacture something out of soda niter. The factory in which, for which, and from which you do all this lies yonder, beyond the railroad tracks."

He waved a lazy arm down the street, to where a group of square concrete buildings shut out the desert at the end of the thoroughfare.

"Suppose you don't play with this soda?" Steve asked, more to keep the thin man talking than to satisfy any thirst for local knowledge. "What do you do then?"

The thin man shrugged his sharp shoulders.

"That depends," he said, "on who you are. If you're Dave Brackett"—he wiggled a finger at the red bank across the street—"you gloat over your mortgages, or whatever it is a banker does; if you're Grant Fernie, and too big for a man without being quite big enough for a horse, you pin a badge on your bosom and throw rough-riding strangers into the can until they sober up; or if you're Larry Ormsby, and your old man owns the soda works, then you drive trick cars from across the pond"—nodding at the cream Vauxhall—"and spend your days pursuing beautiful telegraph operators. But I take it that you're broke, and have just wired for money, and are waiting for the more or less doubtful results. Is that it?"

"It is," Steve answered absent-mindedly. So the dandy in gray was named Larry Ormsby and was the factory owner's son.

The thin man drew in his feet and stood up on them.

"In that case it's lunchtime, and my name is Roy Kamp, and I'm hungry, and I don't like to eat alone, and I'd be glad to have you face the greasy dangers of a meal at the Finn's with me."

Steve got up and held out his hand.

"I'll be glad to," he said. "The coffee I had for breakfast could stand company. My name's Steve Threefall."

They shook hands, and started up the street together. Coming toward them were two men in earnest conversation; one of them was the beefy man whose face Larry Ormsby had slapped. Steve waited until they had passed, and then questioned Kamp casually:

"And who are those prominent-looking folks?"

"The little round one in the checkered college-boy suit is Conan Elder, real estate, insurance, and securities. The Wallingford-looking personage at his side is W. W. himself—the town's founder, owner, and whatnot—W. W. Ormsby, the Hon. Larry's papa."

DETECTIVE STORIES

The scene in the office, with its slapping of a face and flourish of a pistol, had been a family affair, then; a matter between father and son, with the son in the more forcible rôle. Steve, walking along with scant attention just now for the words Kamp's baritone voice was saying, felt a growing dissatisfaction in the memory of the girl and Larry Ormsby talking over the counter with their heads close together.

The Finn's lunchroom was little more than a corridor squeezed in between a poolroom and a hardware store, of barely sufficient width for a counter and a row of revolving stools. Only one customer was there when the two men entered. "Hello, Mr. Rymer," said Kamp.

"How are you, Mr. Kamp?" the man at the counter said, and as he turned his head toward them, Steve saw that he was blind. His large blue eyes were filmed over with a gray curtain which gave him the appearance of having dark hollows instead of eyes.

He was a medium-sized man who looked seventy, but there was a suggestion of fewer years in the suppleness of his slender white hands. He had a thick mane of white hair about a face that was crisscrossed with wrinkles, but it was a calm face, the face of a man at peace with his world. He was just finishing his meal, and left shortly, moving to the door with the slow accuracy of the blind man in familiar surroundings.

"Old man Rymer," Kamp told Steve, "lives in a shack behind where the new fire house is going to be, all alone. Supposed to have tons of gold coins under his floor—thus local gossip. Some day we're going to find him all momicked up. But he won't listen to reason. Says nobody would hurt him. Says that in a town as heavy with assorted thugs as this!"

"A tough town, is it?" Steve asked.

"Couldn't help being! It's only three years old—and a desert boom town draws the tough boys."

Kamp left Steve after their meal, saying he probably would run across him later in the evening, and suggesting that there were games of a sort to be found in the next-door poolroom.

NIGHTMARE TOWN

"I'll see you there then," Steve said, and went back to the telegraph office. The girl was alone. "Anything for me?" he asked her.

She put a green check and a telegram on the counter and returned to her desk. The telegram read:

> COLLECTED BET. PAID WHITING TWO HUNDRED FOR FORD. SENDING BALANCE SIX HUNDRED FORTY. SHIPPING CLOTHES. WATCH YOUR STEP.
>
> HARRIS.

"Did you send the wire collect, or do I owe—"

"Collect." She did not look up.

Steve put his elbows on the counter and leaned over; his jaw, still exaggerated by its growth of hair, although he had washed the dirt from it, jutted forward with his determination to maintain a properly serious attitude until he had done this thing that had to be done.

"Now listen, Miss Vallance," he said deliberately. "I was all kinds of a damned fool yesterday, and I'm sorrier than I can say. But, after all, nothing terrible happened, and—"

"Nothing terrible!" she exploded. "Is it nothing to be humiliated by being chased up and down the street like a rabbit by a drunken man with a dirty face in a worse car?"

"I wasn't chasing you. I came back that second time to apologize. But, anyway"—in the uncomfortable face of her uncompromising hostility his determination to be serious went for nothing, and he relapsed into his accustomed defensive mockery—"no matter how scared you were you ought to accept my apology now and let bygones be bygones."

"Scared? Why—"

"I wish you wouldn't repeat words after me," he complained. "This morning you did it, and now you're at it again. Don't you ever think of anything to say on your own account?"

She glared at him, opened her mouth, shut it with a little click. Her angry face bent sharply over the papers on the desk, and she began to add a column of figures.

Steve nodded with pretended approval, and took his check across the street to the bank.

The only man in sight in the bank when Steve came in was a little plump fellow with carefully trimmed salt-and-pepper whiskers hiding nearly all of a jovial round face except the eyes—shrewd, friendly eyes.

This man came to the window in the grille, and said: "Good afternoon. Can I do something for you?"

Steve laid down the telegraph company's check. "I want to open an account."

The banker picked up the slip of green paper and flicked it with a fat finger. "You are the gentleman who assaulted my wall with an automobile yesterday?"

Steve grinned. The banker's eyes twinkled, and a smile ruffled his whiskers. "Are you going to stay in Izzard?"

"For a while."

"Can you give me references?" the banker asked.

"Maybe Judge Denvir or Marshal Fernie will put in a word for me," Steve said. "But if you'll write the Seaman's Bank in San Francisco they'll tell you that so far as they know I'm all right."

The banker stuck a plump hand through the window in the grille.

"I'm very glad to make your acquaintance. My name is David Brackett, and anything I can do to help you get established—call on me."

Outside of the bank ten minutes later, Steve met the huge marshal, who stopped in front of him. "You still here?" Fernie asked.

"I'm an Izzardite now," Steve said. "For a while, anyhow. I like your hospitality."

"Don't let old man Denvir see you coming out of a bank," Fernie advised him, "or he'll soak you plenty next time."

NIGHTMARE TOWN

"There isn't going to be any next time."

"There always is—in Izzard," the marshal said enigmatically as he got his bulk in motion again.

CHAPTER V

A Man Leaves Izzard

That night, shaved and bathed, though still wearing his bleached khaki, Steve, with his black stick beside him, played stud poker with Roy Kamp and four factory workers. They played in the poolroom next door to the Finn's lunchroom. Izzard apparently was a wide-open town. Twelve tables given to craps, poker, red dog, and twenty-one occupied half of the poolroom, and white-hot liquor was to be had at the cost of fifty cents and a raised finger. There was nothing surreptitious about the establishment; obviously its proprietor—a bullet-headed Italian whose customers called him "Gyp"—was in favor with the legal powers of Izzard.

The game in which Steve sat went on smoothly and swiftly, as play does when adepts participate. Though, as most games are, always potentially crooked, it was, in practice, honest. The six men at the table were, without exception, men who knew their way around—men who played quietly and watchfully, winning and losing without excitement or inattention. Not one of the six—except Steve, and perhaps Kamp—would have hesitated to favor himself at the expense of honesty had the opportunity come to him; but where knowledge of trickery is evenly distributed honesty not infrequently prevails.

Larry Ormsby came into the poolroom at a little after eleven and sat at a table some distance from Steve. Faces he had seen in the street during the day were visible through the smoke. At five minutes to twelve the four factory men at Steve's table left for work—they were in the "graveyard" shift—and the game broke up with their departure. Steve, who had kept about even throughout the play, found that he had won something less than ten dollars; Kamp had won fifty-some.

Declining invitations to sit in another game, Steve and Kamp left together, going out into the dark and night-cool street, where the air was sweet after the smoke and alcohol of the poolroom. They walked slowly down the dim thoroughfare toward the Izzard Hotel, neither in a hurry to end their first evening together; for each knew by now that the unpainted bench in front of the telegraph office had given him a comrade. Not a thousand words had passed between the two men, but they had as surely become brothers-in-arms as if they had tracked a continent together.

Strolling thus, a dark doorway suddenly vomited men upon them.

Steve rocked back against a building front from a blow on his head, arms were around him, the burning edge of a knife blade ran down his left arm. He chopped his black stick up into a body, freeing himself from encircling grip. He used the moment's respite this gave him to change his grasp on the stick; so that he held it now horizontal, his right hand grasping its middle, its lower half flat against his forearm, its upper half extending to the left.

He put his left side against the wall, and the black stick became a whirling black arm of the night. The knob darted down at a man's head. The man threw an arm up to fend the blow. Spinning back on its axis, the stick reversed—the ferruled end darted up under warding arm, hit jaw-bone with a click, and no sooner struck than slid forward, jabbing deep into throat. The owner of that jaw and throat turned his broad, thick-featured face to the sky, went backward out of the fight, and was lost to sight beneath the curbing.

Kamp, struggling with two men in the middle of the sidewalk, broke loose from them, whipped out a gun; but before he could use it his assailants were on him again.

Lower half of stick against forearm once more, Steve whirled in time to take the impact of a blackjack-swinging arm upon it. The stick spun sidewise with thud of knob on temple—spun back with loaded ferrule that missed opposite temple only because the first blow had brought its target down on knees. Steve saw suddenly that Kamp had gone down. He spun his stick and battered a passage to the thin man, kicked a head that bent over the prone, thin form, straddled it; and the ebony stick whirled swifter in his hand—spun as quarter-staves once spun in Sherwood Forest. Spun to the clicking tune of wood on bone, on metal weapons; to the duller rhythm of wood on flesh. Spun never in full circles, but always in short arcs—one end's recovery from a blow adding velocity to the other's stroke. Where an instant ago knob had swished from left to right, now weighted ferrule struck from right to left—struck under upthrown arms, over low-thrown arms—put into space a forty-inch sphere, whose radii were whirling black flails.

Behind his stick that had become a living part of him, Steve Threefall knew happiness—that rare happiness which only the expert ever finds—the joy in doing a thing that he can do supremely well. Blows he took—blows that shook him, staggered him—but he scarcely noticed them. His whole consciousness was in his right arm and the stick it spun. A revolver, tossed from a smashed hand, exploded ten feet over his head, a knife tinkled like a bell on the brick sidewalk, a man screamed as a stricken horse screams.

As abruptly as it had started, the fight stopped. Feet thudded away, forms vanished into the more complete darkness of a side street; and Steve was standing alone—alone except for the man stretched out between his feet and the other man who lay still in the gutter.

Kamp crawled from beneath Steve's legs and scrambled briskly to his feet.

"Your work with a bat is what you might call adequate," he drawled.

Steve stared at the thin man. This was the man he had accepted on an evening's acquaintance as a comrade! A man who lay on the street and let his companion do the fighting for both. Hot words formed in Steve's throat.

"You—"

The thin man's face twisted into a queer grimace, as if he were listening to faint, far-off sounds. He caught his hands to his chest, pressing the sides together. Then he turned half around, went down on one knee, went over backward with a leg bent over him.

"Get—word—to—"

The fourth word was blurred beyond recognition. Steve knelt beside Kamp, lifted his head from the bricks, and saw that Kamp's thin body was ripped open from throat to waistline.

"Get—word—to—" The thin man tried desperately to make the last word audible.

A hand gripped Steve's shoulder.

"What the hell's all this?" The roaring voice of Marshal Grant Fernie blotted out Kamp's words.

"Shut up a minute!" Steve snapped, and put his ear again close to Kamp's mouth.

But now the dying man could achieve no articulate sound. He tried with an effort that bulged his eyes; then he shuddered horribly, coughed, the slit in his chest gaped open, and he died.

"What's all this?" the marshal repeated.

"Another reception committee," Steve said bitterly, easing the dead body lo the sidewalk, and standing up. "There's one of them in the street; the others beat it around the corner."

He tried to point with his left hand, then let it drop to his side. Looking at it, he saw that his sleeve was black with blood.

The marshal bent to examine Kamp, grunted, "He's dead, all right," and moved over to where the man Steve had knocked into the gutter lay.

"Knocked out," the marshal said, straightening up; "but he'll be coming around in a while. How'd you make out?"

"My arm's slashed, and I've got some sore spots, but I'll live through it."

Fernie took hold of the wounded arm.

"Not bleeding so bad," he decided. "But you better get it patched up. Doc MacPhail's is only a little way up the street. Can you make it, or do you want me to give you a lift?"

"I can make it. How do I find the place?"

"Two blocks up this street, and four to the left. You can't miss it—it's the only house in town with flowers in front of it. I'll get in touch with you when I want you."

CHAPTER VI
The House with Flowers

Steve Threefall found Dr. MacPhail's house without difficulty—a two-story building set back from the street, behind a garden that did its best to make up a floral profusion for Izzard's general barrenness. The fence was hidden under twining virgin's bower, clustered now with white blossoms, and the narrow walk wound through roses, trillium, poppies, tulips, and geraniums that were ghosts in the starlight. The air was heavily sweet with the fragrance of saucer-like moon flowers, whose vines covered the doctor's porch.

Two steps from the latter Steve stopped, and his right hand slid to the middle of his stick. From one end of the porch had come a rustling, faint but not of the wind, and a spot that was black between vines had an instant before been paler, as if framing a peeping face.

"Who is—" Steve began, and went staggering back.

From the vine-blackened porch a figure had flung itself on his chest.

"Mr. Threefall," the figure cried in the voice of the girl of the telegraph office, "there's somebody in the house!"

"You mean a burglar?" he asked stupidly, staring down into the small white face that was upturned just beneath his chin.

"Yes! He's upstairs—in Dr. MacPhail's room!"

"Is the doctor up there?"

"No, no! He and Mrs. MacPhail haven't come home yet."

He patted her soothingly on a velvet-coated shoulder, selecting a far shoulder, so that he had to put his arm completely around her to do the patting.

"We'll fix that," he promised. "You stick here in the shadows, and I'll be back as soon as I have taken care of our friend."

"No, no!" She clung to his shoulder with both hands. "I'll go with you. I couldn't stay here alone; but I won't be afraid with you."

He bent his head to look into her face, and cold metal struck his chin, clicking his teeth together. The cold metal was the muzzle of a big nickel-plated revolver in one of the hands that clung to his shoulder.

"Here, give me that thing," he exclaimed; "and I'll let you come with me."

She gave him the gun and he put it in his pocket.

"Hold on to my coattails," he ordered; "keep as close to me as you can, and when I say 'Down,' let go, drop flat to the floor, and stay there."

Thus, the girl whispering guidance to him, they went through the door she had left open, into the house, and mounted to the second floor. From their right, as they stood at the head of the stairs, came cautious rustlings.

Steve put his face down until the girl's hair was on his lips.

"How do you get to that room?" he whispered.

"Straight down the hall. It ends there."

They crept down the hall. Steve's outstretched hand touched a doorframe.

"Down!" he whispered to the girl.

Her fingers released his coat. He flung the door open, jumped through, slammed it behind him. A head-sized oval was black against the gray of a window. He spun his stick at it. Something caught the stick overhead; glass crashed, showering him with fragments. The oval was no longer visible against the window. He wheeled to the left, flung out an arm toward a sound of motion. His fingers found a neck—a thin neck with skin as dry and brittle as paper.

A kicking foot drove into his shin just below the knee. The paperish neck slid out of his hand. He dug at it with desperate fingers, but his fingers, weakened by the wound in his forearm, failed to hold. He dropped his stick and flashed his right hand to the left's assistance. Too late. The weakened hand had fallen away from the paperish neck, and there was nothing for the right to clutch.

A misshapen blot darkened the center of an open window, vanished with a thud of feet on the roof of the rear porch. Steve sprang to the window in time to see the burglar scramble up from the ground, where he had slid from the porch roof, and make for the low back fence. One of Steve's legs was over the sill when the girl's arms came around his neck.

"No, no!" she pleaded. "Don't leave me! Let him go!"

"All right," he said reluctantly, and then brightened.

He remembered the gun he had taken from the girl, got it out of his pocket as the fleeing shadow in the yard reached the fence; and as the shadow, one hand on the fence top, vaulted high over it, Steve squeezed the trigger. The revolver clicked. Again—another click. Six clicks, and the burglar was gone into the night.

Steve broke the revolver in the dark, and ran his fingers over the back of the cylinder—six empty chambers.

"Turn on the lights," he said brusquely.

CHAPTER VII
Blind Rymer

When the girl had obeyed, Steve stepped back into the room and looked first for his ebony stick. That in his hand, he faced the girl. Her eyes were jet black with excitement and pale lines of strain were around her mouth. As they stood looking into each other's eyes something of a bewilderment began to show through her fright. He turned away abruptly and gazed around the room.

The place had been ransacked thoroughly if not expertly. Drawers stood out, their contents strewn on the floor; the bed had been stripped of clothing, and pillows had been dumped out of their cases. Near the door a broken wall light—the obstruction that had checked Steve's stick—hung crookedly. In the center of the, floor lay a gold watch and half a length of gold chain. He picked them up and held them out to the girl.

"Dr. MacPhail's?"

She shook her head in denial before she took the watch, and then, examining it closely, she gave a little gasp. "It's Mr. Rymer's!"

"Rymer?" Steve repeated, and then he remembered. Rymer was the blind man who had been in the Finn's lunchroom, and for whom Kamp had prophesied trouble.

"Yes! Oh, I know something has happened to him!"

She put a hand on Steve's left arm.

"We've got to go see! He lives all alone, and if any harm has—"

She broke off, and looked down at the arm under her hand.

"Your arm! You're hurt!"

"Not as bad as it looks," Steve said. "That's what brought me here. But it has stopped bleeding. Maybe by the time we get back from Rymer's the doctor will be home."

They left the house by the back door, and the girl led him through dark streets and across darker lots. Neither of them spoke during the five-minute walk. The girl hurried at a pace that left her little breath for conversation, and Steve was occupied with uncomfortable thinking.

The blind man's cabin was dark when they reached it, but the front door was ajar. Steve knocked his stick against the frame, got no answer, and struck a match. Rymer lay on the floor, sprawled on his back, his arms outflung.

The cabin's one room was topsy-turvy. Furniture lay in upended confusion, clothing was scattered here and there, and boards had been torn from the floor. The girl knelt beside the unconscious man while Steve hunted for a light. Presently he found an oil lamp that had escaped injury, and got it burning just as Rymer's filmed eyes opened and he sat up. Steve righted an overthrown rocking chair and, with the girl, assisted the blind man to it, where he sat panting. He had recognized the girl's voice at once, and he smiled bravely in her direction.

"I'm all right, Nova," he said; "not hurt a bit. Someone knocked at the door, and when I opened it I heard a swishing sound in my ear—and that was all I knew until I came to to find you here."

He frowned with sudden anxiety, got to his feet, and moved across the room. Steve pulled a chair and an upset table from his path, and the blind man dropped on his knees in a corner, fumbling beneath the loosened floor boards. His hands came out empty, and he stood up with a tired droop to his shoulders. "Gone," he said softly.

Steve remembered the watch then, took it from his pocket, and put it into one of the blind man's hands.

"There was a burglar at our house," the girl explained. "After he had gone we found that on the floor. This is Mr. Threefall."

The blind man groped for Steve's hand, pressed it, then his flexible fingers caressed the watch, his face lighting up happily.

"I'm glad," he said, "to have this back—gladder than I can say. The money wasn't so much—less than three hundred dollars. I'm not the Midas I'm said to be. But this watch was my father's."

He tucked it carefully into his vest, and then, as the girl started to straighten up the room, he remonstrated.

"You'd better run along home, Nova; it's late, and I'm all right. I'll go to bed now, and let the place go as it is until tomorrow."

The girl demurred, but presently she and Steve were walking back to the MacPhails' house, through the black streets; but they did not hurry now. They walked two blocks in silence, Steve looking ahead into dark space with glum thoughtfulness, the girl eyeing him covertly.

"What is the matter?" she asked abruptly.

Steve smiled pleasantly down at her.

"Nothing. Why?"

"There is," she contradicted him. "You're thinking of something unpleasant, something to do with me."

He shook his head.

"That's wrong, wrong on the face of it—they don't go together."

But she was not to be put off with compliments. "You're— you're—" She stood still in the dim street, searching for the right word.

"You're on your guard—you don't trust me—that's what it is!"

Steve smiled again, but with narrowed eyes. This reading of his mind might have been intuitive, or it might have been something else.

He tried a little of the truth:

"Not distrustful—just wondering. You know you *did* give me an empty gun to go after the burglar with, and you know you wouldn't let me chase him."

Her eyes flashed, and she drew herself up to the last inch of her slender five feet.

"So you think—" she began indignantly. Then she drooped toward him, her hands fastening upon the lapels of his coat. "Please, please, Mr. Threefall, you've got to believe that I didn't know the revolver was empty. It was Dr. MacPhail's. I took it when I ran out of the house, never dreaming that it wasn't loaded. And as for not letting you chase the burglar—I was afraid to be left alone again. I'm a little coward. I—I—Please believe in me, Mr. Threefall. Be friends with me. I need friends. I—"

Womanhood had dropped from her. She pleaded with the small white face of a child of twelve—a lonely, frightened child. And because his suspicions would not capitulate immediately to her appeal, Steve felt dumbly miserable, with an obscure shame in himself, as if he were lacking in some quality he should have had.

She went on talking, very softly, so that he had to bend his head to catch the words. She talked about herself, as a child would talk.

"It's been terrible! I came here three months ago because there

NIGHTMARE TOWN

was a vacancy in the telegraph office. I was suddenly alone in the world, with very little money, and telegraphy was all I knew that could be capitalized. It's been terrible here! The town—I can't get accustomed to it. It's so bleak. No children play in the streets. The people are different from those I've known—cruder, more brutal. Even the houses—street after street of them without curtains in the windows, without flowers. No grass in the yards, No trees.

"But I had to stay—there was nowhere else to go. I thought I could stay until I had saved a little money—enough to take me away. But saving money takes so long. Dr. MacPhail's garden has been like a piece of paradise to me. If it hadn't been for that I don't think I could have—I'd have; gone crazy! The doctor and his wife have been nice to me; some people have been nice to me, but most of them are people I can't understand. And not all have been nice. At first it was awful. Men would say things, and women would say things, and when I was afraid of them they thought I was stuck up. Larry—Mr. Ormsby—saved me from that. He made them let me alone, and he persuaded the MacPhails to let me live with them. Mr. Rymer has helped me, too, given me courage; but I lose it again as soon as I'm away from the sight of his face and the sound of his voice.

"I'm scared—scared of everything! Of Larry Ormsby especially! And he's been wonderfully helpful to me. But I can't help it. I'm afraid of him—of the way he looks at me sometimes, of things he says when he has been drinking. It's as if there was something inside of him waiting for something. I shouldn't say that—because I owe him gratitude for— But I'm so afraid! I'm afraid of every person, of every house, of every doorstep even. It's a nightmare!"

Steve found that one of his hands was cupped over the white cheek that was not flat against his chest, and that his other arm was around her shoulders, holding her close.

"New towns are always like this, or worse," he began to tell her. "You should have seen Hopewell, Virginia, when the Du Ponts first opened it. It takes time for the undesirables who come with the first rush to be weeded out. And, stuck out here in the desert, Izzard would naturally fare a little worse than the average new town. As for being friends with you—that's why I stayed here instead of going back to Whitetufts. We'll be great friends. We'll—"

He never knew how long he talked, or what he said; though he imagined afterward that he must have made a very long-winded and very stupid speech. But he was not talking for the purpose of saying anything; he was tallking to soothe the girl, and to keep her small face between his hand and chest, and her small body close against his for as long a time as possible.

So, he talked on and on and on—

CHAPTER VIII
A Pair of Threats

The MacPhails were at home when Nova Vallance and Steve came through the flowered yard again, and they welcomed the girl with evident relief. The doctor was a short man with a round bald head, and a round jovial face, shiny and rosy except where a sandy mustache drooped over his mouth. His wife was perhaps ten years younger than he, a slender blond woman with much of the feline in the set of her blue eyes and the easy grace of her movements.

"The car broke down with us about twenty miles out," the doctor explained in a mellow rumbling voice with a hint of a burr lingering around the r's. "I had to perform a major operation on it before we could get going again. When we got home we found you gone, and were just about to rouse thee town."

The girl introduced Steve to the MacPhails, and then told them about the burglar, and of what they had found in the blind man's cabin.

Dr. MacPhail shook his round naked head and clicked his tongue on teeth. "Seems to me Fernie doesn't do all that could be done to tone Izzard down," he said.

Then the girl remembered Steve's wounded arm, and the doctor examined, washed, and bandaged it.

"You won't have to wear the arm in a sling," he said, "if you take a reasonable amount of care of it. It isn't a deep cut, and fortunately it went between the *supinator tongus* and the *great palmar* without injury to either. Get it from our burglar?"

"No. Got it in the street. A man named Kamp and I were walking toward the hotel tonight and were jumped. Kamp was killed. I got this."

An asthmatic clock somewhere up the street was striking three as Steve passed through the MacPhails' front gate and set out for the hotel again. He felt tired and sore in every muscle, and he walked close to the curb.

"If anything else happens tonight," he told himself, "I'm going to run like hell from it. I've had enough for one evening."

At the first cross-street he had to pause to let an automobile race by. As it passed him he recognized it—Larry Ormsby's cream Vauxhall. In its wake sped five big trucks, with a speed that testified to readjusted gears. In a roar of engines, a cloud of dust, and a rattling of windows, the caravan vanished toward the desert.

Steve went on toward the hotel, thinking. The factory worked twenty-four hours a day, he knew; but surely no necessity of niter manufacturing would call for such excessive speed in its trucks—if they were factory trucks. He turned into Main Street and faced another surprise. The cream Vauxhall stood near the corner, its owner at the wheel. As Steve came abreast of it Larry Ormsby let its near door swing open, and held out an inviting hand.

Steve stopped and stood by the door.

"Jump in and I'll give you a lift as far as the hotel."

"Thanks."

Steve looked quizzically from the man's handsome, reckless face to the now dimly lighted hotel, less than two blocks away. Then he looked at the man again, and got into the automobile beside him.

"I hear you're a more or less permanent fixture among us," Ormsby said, proffering Steve cigarettes in a lacquered leather case, and shutting off his idling engine.

"For a while."

Steve declined the cigarettes and brought out tobacco and papers from his pocket, adding, "There are things about the place I like."

"I also hear you had a little excitement tonight."

"Some," Steve admitted, wondering whether the other meant the fight in which Kamp had been killed, the burglary at the MacPhails', or both.

"If you keep up the pace you've set," the factory owner's son went on, "it won't take you long to nose me out of my position as Izzard's brightest light."

Tautening nerves tickled the nape of Steve's neck. Larry Ormsby's words and tones seemed idle enough, but underneath them was a suggestion that they were not aimless—that they were leading to some definite place. It was not likely that he had circled around to intercept Steve merely to exchange meaningless chatter with him. Steve, lighting his cigarette, grinned and waited.

"The only thing I ever got from the old man, besides money," Larry Ormsby was saying, "is a deep-rooted proprietary love for my own property. I'm a regular burgher for insisting that my property is mine and must stay mine. I don't know exactly how to feel about a stranger coming in and making himself the outstanding black sheep of the town in two days. A reputation—even for recklessness—is property, you know; and I don't feel that I should give it up—*or any other rights*—without a struggle."

There it was. Steve's mind cleared. He disliked subtleties. But now he knew what the talk was about. He was being warned to keep away from Nova Vallance.

"I knew a fellow once in Onehunga," he drawled, "who thought he owned all of the Pacific south of the Tropic of Capricorn—and had papers to prove it. He'd been that way ever since a Maori bashed in his head with a stone *mere.*[5] Used to accuse us of stealing our drinking water from his ocean."

Larry Ormsby flicked his cigarette into the street and started the engine.

"But the point is"—he was smiling pleasantly—"that a man is moved to protect what he thinks belongs to him. He may be wrong, of course, but that wouldn't affect the—ah—vigor of his protecting efforts."

Steve felt himself growing warm and angry.

"Maybe you're right," he said slowly, with deliberate intent to bring this thing between them to a crisis, "but I've never had enough experience with property to know how I'd feel about being deprived of it. But suppose I had a—well, say—a white vest that I treasured. And suppose a man slapped my face and threatened to spoil the vest. I reckon I'd forget all about protecting the vest in my hurry to tangle with him."

Larry laughed sharply.

Steve caught the wrist that flashed up, and pinned it to Ormsby's side with a hand that much spinning of a heavy stick had muscled with steel.

"Easy," he said into the slitted, dancing eyes; "easy now."

Larry Ormsby's white teeth flashed under his mustache.

"Righto," he smiled. "If you'll turn my wrist loose, I'd like to shake hands with you—a sort of antebellum gesture. I like you, Threefall; you're going to add materially to the pleasures of Izzard."

In his room on the third floor of the Izzard Hotel, Steve Threefall undressed slowly, hampered by a stiff left arm and much thinking. Matter for thought he had in abundance. Larry Ormsby slapping his father's face and threatening him with an automatic; Larry Ormsby and the girl in confidential conversation; Kamp dying in a dark street, his last words lost in the noise of the marshal's arrival;

---

5 A short club often made of jade.

Nova Vallance giving him an empty revolver, and persuading him to let a burglar escape; the watch on the floor and the looting of the blind man's savings; the caravan Larry Ormsby had led toward the desert; the talk in the Vauxhall, with its exchange of threats.

Was there any connection between each of these things and the others? Or were they simply disconnected happenings? If there was a connection—and the whole of that quality in mankind which strives toward simplification of life's phenomena, unification, urged him to belief in a connection—just what was it? Still puzzling, he got into bed; and then out again quickly. An uneasiness that had been vague until now suddenly thrust itself into his consciousness. He went to the door, opened and closed it. It was a cheaply carpentered door, but it moved easily and silently on well-oiled hinges.

"I reckon I'm getting to be an old woman," he growled to himself; "but I've had all I want tonight."

He blocked the door with the dresser, put his stick where he could reach it quickly, got into bed again, and went to sleep.

CHAPTER IX
"What Next?"

A pounding on the door awakened Steve at nine o'clock the next morning. The pounder was one of Fernie's subordinates, and he told Steve that he was expected to be present at the inquest into Kamp's death within an hour. Steve found that his wounded arm bothered him little; not so much as a bruised area on one shoulder—another souvenir of the fight in the street.

He dressed, ate breakfast in the hotel cafe, and went up to Ross Amthor's "undertaking parlor," where the inquest was to be held.

The coroner was a tall man with high, narrow shoulders and a sallow, puffy face, who sped proceedings along regardless of the finer points of legal technicality. Steve told his story; the marshal told his, and then produced a prisoner—a thickset Austrian who seemingly neither spoke nor understood English. His throat and lower face were swathed in white bandages.

"Is this the one you knocked down?" the coroner asked.

Steve looked at as much of the Austrian's face as was visible above the bandages.

"I don't know. I can't see enough of him."

"This is the one I picked out of the gutter," Grant Fernie volunteered; "whether you knocked him there or not. I don't suppose you got a good look at him. But this is he all right."

Steve frowned doubtfully. "I'd know him," he said, "if he turned his face up and I got a good look at him."

"Take off some of his bandages so the witness can see him," the coroner ordered. Fernie unwound the Austrian's bandages, baring a bruised and swollen jaw.

Steve stared at the man. This fellow may have been one of his assailants, but he most certainly wasn't the one he had knocked into the street. He hesitated. Could he have confused faces in the fight?

"Do you identify him?" the coroner asked impatiently.

Steve shook his head.

"I don't remember ever seeing him."

"Look here, Threefall"—the giant marshal scowled down at Steve—"this is the man I hauled out of the gutter—one of the men you said jumped you and Kamp. Now what's the game? What's the idea of forgetting?"

Steve answered slowly, stubbornly:

"I don't know. All I know is that this isn't the first one I hit, the one I knocked out. He was an American—had an American face. He was about this fellow's size, but this isn't he."

The coroner exposed broken yellow teeth in a snarl, the marshal glowered at Steve, the jurors regarded him with frank suspicion. The marshal and the coroner withdrew to a far corner of the room, where they whispered together, casting frequent glances at Steve.

"All right," the coroner told Steve when this conference was over; "that's all."

From the inquest Steve walked slowly back to the hotel, his mind puzzled by this newest addition to Izzard's mysteries. What was the explanation of the certain fact that the man the marshal had produced at the inquest was not the man he had taken from the gutter the previous night? Another thought: the marshal had arrived immediately after the fight with the men who had attacked him and Kamp, had arrived noisily, drowning the dying man's last words. That opportune arrival and the accompanying noise—were they accidental? Steve didn't know; and because he didn't know he strode back to the hotel in frowning meditation.

At the hotel he found that his bag had arrived from Whitetufts. He took it up to his room and changed his clothes. Then he carried his perplexity to the window, where he sat smoking cigarette after cigarette, staring into the alley below, his forehead knotted beneath his tawny hair. Was it possible that so many things should explode around one man in so short a time, in a small city of Izzard's size, without there being a connection between them—and between them and him? And if he was being involved in a vicious maze of crime and intrigue, what was it all about? What had started it? What was the key to it? The girl?

Confused thoughts fell away from him. He sprang to his feet.

Down the other side of the alley a man was walking—a thick-set man in soiled blue—a man with bandaged throat and chin. What was visible of his face was the face Steve had seen turned skyward in the fight—the face of the man he had knocked out.

Steve sprang to the door, out of the room, down three flights of stairs, past the desk, and out of the hotel's back door. He gained the alley in time to see a blue trouser-leg disappearing into a doorway in the block below. Thither he went.

The doorway opened into an office building. He searched the corridors, upstairs and down, and did not find the bandaged man. He returned to the ground floor and discovered a sheltered corner near the back door, near the foot of the stairs. The corner was shielded from the stairs and from most of the corridor by a wooden closet in which brooms and mops were kept. The man had entered through the rear of the building; he would probably leave that way; Steve waited.

Fifteen minutes passed, bringing no one within sight of his hiding place. Then from the front of the building came a woman's soft laugh, and footsteps moved toward him. He shrank back in his dusky corner. The footsteps passed—a man and a woman laughing and talking together as they walked. They mounted the stairs. Steve peeped out at them, and then drew back suddenly, more in surprise than in fear of detection, for the two who mounted the stairs were completely engrossed in each other.

The man was Elder, the insurance and real-estate agent. Steve did not see his face, but the checkered suit on his round figure was unmistakable—"college-boy suit," Kamp had called it. Elder's arm was around the woman's waist as they went up the stairs, and her cheek leaned against his shoulder as she looked coquettishly into his face. The woman was Dr. MacPhail's feline wife.

"What next?" Steve asked himself, when they had passed from his sight. "Is the whole town wrong? What next, I wonder?"

The answer came immediately—the pounding of crazy footsteps directly over Steve's head—footsteps that might have belonged to a drunken man, or to a man fighting a phantom. Above the noise of heels on wooden floor, a scream rose—a scream that blended horror and pain into a sound that was all the more unearthly because it was unmistakably of human origin.

Steve bolted out of his corner and up the steps three at a time, pivoted into the second-floor corridor on the newel, and came face to face with David Brackett, the banker.

Brackett's thick legs were far apart, and he swayed on them. His face was a pallid agony above his beard. Big spots of beard were gone, as if torn out or burned away. From his writhing lips thin wisps of vapor issued.

"They've poisoned me, the damned—"

He came suddenly up on the tips of his toes, his body arched, and he fell stiffly backward, as dead things fall.

Steve dropped on a knee beside him, but he knew nothing could be done—knew Brackett had died while still on his feet. For a moment, as he crouched there over the dead man, something akin to panic swept Steve Threefall's mind clean of reason. Was there never to be an end to this piling of mystery upon mystery, of violence upon violence? He had the sensation of being caught in a monstrous net—a net without beginning or end, and whose meshes were slimy with blood. Nausea—spiritual and physical—gripped him, held him impotent. Then a shot crashed.

He jerked erect—sprang down the corridor toward the sound; seeking in frenzy of physical activity escape from the sickness that had filled him.

At the end of the corridor a door was labelled ORMSBY NITER CORPORATION, W. W. ORMSBY, PRESIDENT. There was no need for hesitancy before deciding that the shot had come from behind that label. Even as he dashed toward it, another shot rattled the door and a falling body thudded behind it.

Steve flung the door open—and jumped aside to avoid stepping on the man who lay just inside. Over by a window, Larry Ormsby stood facing the door, a black automatic in his hand. His eyes danced with wild merriment, and his lips curled in a tight-lipped smile.

"Hello, Threefall," he said. "I see you're still keeping close to the storm centers."

Steve looked down at the man on the floor—W. W. Ormsby. Two bullet holes were in the upper left-hand pocket of his vest. The holes, less than an inch apart, had been placed with a precision that left no room for doubting that the man was dead. Steve remembered Larry's threat to his father: "I'll spoil your vest!"

He looked up from killed to killer. Larry Ormsby's eyes were hard and bright; the pistol in his hand was held lightly, with the loose alertness peculiar to professional gunmen.

"This isn't a—ah—personal matter with you, is it?" he asked.

Steve shook his head; and heard the trampling of feet and a confusion of excited voices in the corridor behind him.

"That's nice," the killer was saying; "and I'd suggest that you—"

He broke off as men came into the office. Grant Fernie, the marshal, was one of them.

"Dead?" he asked, with a bare glance at the man on the floor.

"Rather," Larry replied.

"How come?"

Larry Ormsby moistened his lips, not nervously, but thoughtfully. Then he smiled at Steve, and told his story.

"Threefall and I were standing down near the front door talking, when we heard a shot. I thought it had been fired up here, but he said it came from across the street. Anyhow, we came up here to make sure—making a bet on it first; so Threefall owes me a dollar. We came up here, and just as we got to the head of the steps we heard another shot, and Brackett came running out of here with this gun in his hand."

He gave the automatic to the marshal, and went on: "He took a few steps from the door, yelled, and fell down. Did you see him out there?"

"I did," Fernie said.

"Well, Threefall stopped to look at him while I came on in here to see if my father was all right—and found him dead. That's all there is to it."

CHAPTER X
"Y' Got To Get Out!"

Steve went slowly down to the street after the gathering in the dead man's office had broken up, without having either contradicted or corroborated Larry Ormsby's fiction. No one had questioned him.

At first he had been too astonished by the killer's boldness to say anything; and when his wits had resumed their functions, he had decided to hold his tongue for a while.

Suppose he had told the truth? Would it have helped justice? Would anything help justice in Izzard? If he had known what lay behind this piling-up of crime, he could have decided what to do; but he did not know—did not even know that there was anything behind it. So he had kept silent. The inquest would not be held until the following day—time enough to talk then, after a night's consideration.

He could not grasp more than a fragment of the affair at a time now; disconnected memories made a whirl of meaningless images in his brain. Elder and Mrs. MacPhail going up the stairs—to where? What had become of them? What had become of the man with the bandages on throat and jaw? Had those three any part in the double murder? Had Larry killed the hanker as well as his father? By what chance did the marshal appear on the scene immediately after murder had been done?

Steve carried his jumbled thoughts back to the hotel, and lay across his bed for perhaps an hour. Then he got up and went to the Bank of Izzard, drew out the money he had there, put it carefully in his pocket, and returned to his hotel room to lie across the bed again.

Nova Vallance, nebulous in yellow crepe, was sitting on the lower step of the MacPhails' porch when Steve went up the flowered walk that evening. She welcomed him warmly, concealing none of the impatience with which she had been waiting for him. He sat on the step beside her, twisting around a little for a better view of the dusky oval of her face.

"How is your arm?" she asked.

"Fine!" He opened and shut his left hand briskly. "I suppose you heard all about today's excitement?"

"Oh, yes! About Mr. Brackett's shooting Mr. Ormsby, and then dying with one of his heart attacks."

"Huh?" Steve demanded.

"But weren't you there?" she asked in surprise.

"I was, but suppose you tell me just what you heard."

"Oh, I've heard all sorts of things about it! But all I really know is what Dr. MacPhail, who examined both of them, said."

"And what was that?"

"That Mr. Brackert killed Mr. Ormsby—shot him—though nobody seems to know why; and then, before he could get out of the building, his heart failed him and he died."

"And he was supposed to have a bad heart?"

"Yes. Dr. MacPhail told him a year ago that he would have to be careful, that the least excitement might be fatal."

Steve caught her wrist in his hand.

"Think now," he commanded. "Did you ever hear Dr. MacPhail speak of Brackett's heart trouble until today?"

She looked curiously into his face, and a little pucker of bewilderment came between her eyes.

"No," she replied slowly. "I don't think so; but, of course, there was never any reason why he should have mentioned it. Why do you ask?"

"Because," he told, her, "Brackett did not shoot Ormsby; and any heart attack that killed Brackett was caused by poison—some poison that burned his face and beard."

She gave a little cry of horror.

"You think—" She stopped, glanced furtively over her shoulder at the front door of the house, and leaned close to him to whisper: "Didn't—didn't you say that the man who was killed in the fight last night was named Kamp?"

"Yes."

"Well, the report, or whatever it was that Dr. MacPhail made of his examination, reads Henry Cumberpatch."

"You sure? Sure it's the same man?"

"Yes. The wind blew it off the doctor's desk, and when I handed it back to him, he made some joke"—she colored with a little laugh—"some joke about it nearly being your death certificate instead of your companion's. I glanced down at it then, and saw that it was for a man named Henry Cumberpatch. What does it all mean? What is—"

The front gate clattered open, and a man swayed up the walk. Steve got up, picked up his black stick, and stepped between the girl and the advancing man. The man's face came out of the dark. It was Larry Ormsby; and when he spoke his words had a drunken thickness to match the unsteadiness—not quite a stagger, but nearly so—of his walk.

"Lis'en," he said; "I'm dam' near—"

Steve moved toward him. "If Miss Vallance will excuse us," he said, "we'll stroll to the gate and talk."

Without waiting for a reply from either of them, Steve linked an arm through one of Ormsby's and urged him down the path. At the gate Larry broke away, pulling his arm loose and confronting Steve.

"No time for foolishness," he snarled. "Y' got to get out! Get out o' Izzard!"

"Yes?" Steve asked. "And why?"

Larry leaned back against the fence and raised one hand in an impatient gesture.

"Your lives are not worth a nickel—neither of you."

He swayed and coughed. Steve grasped him by the shoulder and peered into his face.

"What's the matter with you?"

Larry coughed again and clapped a hand to his chest, up near the shoulder.

"Bullet—up high—Fernie's. But I got him—the big tramp. Toppled him out a window—down like a kid divin' for pennies." He laughed shrilly, and then became earnest again. "Get the girl—beat it—now! Now! Now! Ten minutes'll be too late. They're comin'!"

"Who? What? Why?" Steve snapped. "Talk turkey! I don't trust you. I've got to have reasons."

"Reasons, my God!" the wounded man cried. "You'll get your

reasons. You think I'm trying to scare you out o' town b'fore th' inquest." He laughed insanely. "Inquest! You fool! There won't be any inquest! There won't be any tomorrow—for Izzard! And you—"

He pulled himself sharply together and caught one of Steve's hands in both of his.

"Listen," he said. "I'll give it to you, but we're wasting time! But if you've got to have it—listen.

CHAPTER XI
The Naked Soul of Izzard

"Izzard is a plant! The whole damned town is queer. Booze—that's the answer. The man I knocked off this afternoon—the one you thought was my father—originated the scheme. You make soda niter by boiling the nitrate in tanks with heated coils. He got the idea that a niter plant would make a good front for a moonshine factory. And he got the idea that if you had a whole town working together it'd be impossible for the game ever to fall down.

"You can guess how much money there is in this country in the hands of men who'd be glad to invest it in a booze game that was airtight. Not only crooks, I mean, but men who consider themselves honest. Take your guess, whatever it is, and double it, and you still won't be within millions of the right answer. There are men with— But anyway, Ormsby took his scheme east and got his backing—a syndicate that could have raised enough money to build a dozen cities.

"Ormsby, Elder, and Brackett were the boys who managed the game. I was here to see that they didn't double-cross the syndicate; and then there's a flock of trusty lieutenants, like Fernie, and MacPhail, and Heman—he's postmaster—and Harker—another doctor, who got his last week—and Leslie, who posed as a minister. There was no trouble to getting the population we wanted. The word went around that the new town was a place where a crook would be safe so long as he did what he was told. The slums of all the cities of America, and half of 'em out of it, emptied themselves here. Every crook that was less than a step ahead of the police, and had car fare here, came and got cover.

"Of course, with every thug in the world blowing in here we had a lot of sleuths coming, too; but they weren't hard to handle, and if worse came to worst, we could let the law take an occasional man; but usually it wasn't hard to take care of the gumshoes. We have bankers, and ministers, and doctors, and postmasters, and prominent men of all sorts either to tangle the sleuths up with bum leads, or, if necessary, to frame them. You'll find a flock of men in the state pen who came here—most of them as narcotics agents or prohibition agents—and got themselves tied up before they knew what it was all about.

"God, there never was a bigger game! It couldn't flop—unless we spoiled it for ourselves. And that's what we've done. It was too big for us! There was too much money in it—it went to our heads! At first we played square with the syndicate. We made booze and shipped it out—shipped it in carload lots, in trucks, did everything but pipe it out, and we made money for the syndicate and for ourselves. Then we got the real idea—the big one! We kept on making the hooch; but we got the big idea going for our own profit. The syndicate wasn't in on that.

"First, we got the insurance racket under way. Elder managed that, with three or four assistants. Between them they became agents of half the insurance companies in the country, and they began to plaster Izzard with policies. Men who had never lived were examined, insured, and then killed—sometimes they were killed on paper, sometimes a real man who died was substituted, and there were times when a man or two was killed to order. It was soft! We had the insurance agents, the doctors, the coroner, the undertaker, and all the city officials. We had the machinery to swing any deal we wanted! You were with Kamp the night he was killed! That was a good one. He was an insurance company sleuth—the companies were getting suspicious. He came here and was foolish enough to trust his reports to the mail. There aren't many letters from strangers that get through the post office without being read. We read his reports, kept them, and sent phoney ones out in their places. Then we nailed Mr. Kamp, and changed his name on the records to fit a policy in the very company he represented. A rare joke, eh?

"The insurance racket wasn't confined to men—cars, houses, furniture, everything you can insure was plastered. In the last census—by distributing the people we could count on, one in a house, with a list of five or six names—we got a population on the records of at least five times as many as are really here. That gave us room for plenty of policies, plenty of deaths, plenty of property insurance, plenty of everything. It gave us enough political influence in the county and state to strengthen our hands a hundred per cent, make the game safer.

"You'll find street after street of houses with nothing in them out of sight of the front windows. They cost money to put up, but we've made the money right along, and they'll show a wonderful profit when the clean-up comes.

"Then, after the insurance stunt was on its feet, we got the promotion game going. There's a hundred corporations in Izzard that are nothing but addresses on letterheads—but stock certificates and bonds have been sold in them from one end of these United States to the other. And they have brought goods, paid for them, shipped them out to be got rid of—maybe at a loss—and put in larger and larger orders until they've built up a credit with the manufacturers that would make you dizzy to total. Easy! Wasn't Brackett's bank here to give them all the financial references they needed? There was nothing to it; a careful building-up of credit until they reached the highest possible point. Then, the goods shipped out to be sold through fences, and—bingo! The town is wiped out by fire. The stocks of goods are presumably burned; the expensive buildings that the out-of-town investors were told about are presumably destroyed; the books and records are burned.

DETECTIVE STORIES

"What a killing! I've had a hell of a time stalling off the syndicate, trying to keep them in the dark about the surprise we're going to give them. They're too suspicious as it is for us to linger much longer. But things are about ripe for the blow-off—the fire that's to start in the factory and wipe out the whole dirty town—and next Saturday was the day we picked. That's the day when Izzard becomes nothing but a pile of ashes—and a pile of collectable insurance policies.

"The rank and file in town won't know anything about the finer points of the game. Those that suspect anything take their money and keep quiet. When the town goes up in smoke there will be hundreds of bodies found in the ruins—all insured—and there will be proof of the death of hundreds of others—likewise insured—whose bodies can't be found.

"There never was a bigger game! But it was too big for us! My fault—some of it—but it would have burst anyway. We always weeded out those who came to town looking too honest or too wise, and we made doubly sure that nobody who was doubtful got into the post office, railroad depot, telegraph office, or telephone exchange. If the railroad company or the telegraph or telephone company sent somebody here to work, and we couldn't make them see things the way we wanted them seen, we managed to make the place disagreeable for them—and they usually flitted elsewhere in a hurry.

"Then the telegraph company sent Nova here and I flopped for her. At first it was just that I liked her looks. We had all sorts of women here—but they were mostly all sorts—and Nova was something different. I've done my share of dirtiness in this world, but I've never been able to get rid of a certain fastidiousness in my taste for women. I—well, the rest of them—Brackett, Ormsby, Elder, and the lot—were all for giving Nova the works. But I talked them out of it. I told them to let her alone and I'd have her on the inside in no time. I really thought I could do it. She liked me, or seemed to, but I couldn't get any further than that. I didn't make any headway. The others got impatient, but I kept putting them off, telling them that everything would be fine, that if necessary I'd marry her, and shut her up that way. They didn't like it. It wasn't easy to keep her from learning what was going on—working in the telegraph office—but we managed it somehow.

"Next Saturday was the day we'd picked for the big fireworks. Ormsby gave me the call yesterday—told me flatly that if I didn't sew Nova up at once they were going to pop her. They didn't know how much she had found out, and they were taking no chances. I told him I'd kill him if he touched her, but I knew I couldn't talk them out of it. Today the break came. I heard he had given the word that she was to be put out of the way tonight. I went to his office for a showdown. Brackett was there. Ormsby salved me along, denied he had given any order affecting the girl, and poured out drinks for the three of us. The drink looked wrong. I waited to see what was going to happen next. Brackett gulped his down. It was poisoned. He went outside to die, and I nailed Ormsby.

"The game has blown up! It was too rich for us. Everybody is trying to slit everybody else's throat. I couldn't find Elder—but Fernie tried to pot me from a window; and he's Elder's right-hand man. Or he was—he's a stiff now. I think this thing in my chest is the big one—I'm about—but you can get the girl out. You've got to! Elder will go through with the play—try to make the killing for himself. He'll have the town touched off tonight. It's now or never with him. He'll try to—"

A shriek cut through the darkness.

"Steve! Steve! Steve!!!"

CHAPTER XII
Pink Sky

Steve whirled away from the gate, leaped through flowerbeds, crossed the porch in a bound, and was in the house. Behind him Larry Ormsby's feet clattered. An empty hallway, an empty room, another. Nobody was in sight on the ground floor. Steve went up the stairs. A strip of golden light lay under a door. He went through the door, not knowing or caring whether it was locked or not. He simply hurled himself shoulder-first at it, and was in the room. Leaning back against a table in the center of the room, Dr. MacPhail was struggling with the girl. He was behind her, his arms around her, trying to hold her head still. The girl twisted and squirmed like a cat gone mad. In front of her Mrs. MacPhail poised an uplifted blackjack.

Steve flung his stick at the woman's white arm, flung it instinctively, without skill or aim. The heavy ebony struck arm and shoulder, and she staggered back. Dr. MacPhail, releasing the girl, dived at Steve's legs, got them, and carried him to the floor. Steve's fumbling fingers slid off the doctor's bald head, could get no grip on the back of his thick neck, found an ear, and gouged into the flesh under it.

The doctor grunted and twisted away from the digging fingers. Steve got a knee free—drove it at the doctor's face. Mrs. MacPhail bent over his head, raising the black leather billy she still held. He dashed an arm at her ankles, missed—but the down-crashing blackjack fell obliquely on his shoulder. He twisted away, scrambled to his knees and hands—and sprawled headlong under the impact of the doctor's weight on his back.

He rolled over, got the doctor under him, felt his hot breath on his neck. Sieve raised his head and snapped it back—hard. Raised it again, and snapped it down, hammering MacPhail's face with the back of his skull. The doctor's arms fell away and Steve lurched upright to find the fight over.

Larry Ormsby stood in the doorway grinning evilly over his pistol at Mrs. MacPhail, who stood sullenly by the table. The blackjack was on the floor at Larry's feet.

Against the other side of the table the girl leaned weakly, one hand on her bruised throat, her eyes dazed and blank with fear. Steve went around to her.

NIGHTMARE TOWN

"Get going, Steve! There's no time for playing. You got a car?" Larry Ormsby's voice was rasping.

"No," Steve said.

Larry cursed bitterly—an explosion of foul blasphemies. Then: "We'll go in mine—it can outrun anything in the state. But you can't wait here for me to get it. Take Nova over to blind Rymer's shack. I'll pick you up there. He's the only one in town you can trust. Go ahead, damn you!" he yelled.

Steve glanced at the sullen MacPhail woman, and at her husband, now getting up slowly from the floor, his face blood-smeared and battered.

"How about them?"

"Don't worry about them," Larry said. "Take the girl and make Rymer's place. I'll take care of this pair and be over there with the car in fifteen minutes. Get going!"

Steve's eyes narrowed and he studied the man in the doorway. He didn't trust him, but since all Izzard seemed equally dangerous, one place would be as safe as another—and Larry Ormsby might be honest this time.

"All right," he said, and turned to the girl. "Get a heavy coat."

Five minutes later they were hurrying through the same dark streets they had gone through on the previous night. Less than a block from the house, a muffled shot came to their ears, and then another. The girl glanced quickly at Steve but did not speak. He hoped she had not understood what the two shots meant.

They met nobody. Rymer had heard and recognized the girl's footsteps on the sidewalk, and he opened the door before they could knock.

"Come in, Nova," he welcomed her heartily, and then fumbled for Steve's hand. "This is Mr. Threefall, isn't it?"

He led them into the dark cabin, and then lighted the oil lamp on the table. Steve launched at once into a hurried summarizing of what Larry Ormsby had told him. The girl listened with wide eyes and wan face; the blind man's face lost its serenity, and he seemed to grow older and tired as he listened.

"Ormsby said he would come after us with his car," Steve wound up. "If he does, you will go with us, of course, Mr. Rymer. If you'll tell us what you want to take with you we'll get it ready; so that there will be no delay when he comes—if he comes." He turned to the girl. "What do you think, Nova? Will he come? And can we trust him if he does?"

"I—I hope so—he's not all bad, I think."

The blind man went to a wardrobe in the room's other end.

"I've got nothing to take," he said, "but I'll get into warmer clothes."

He pulled the wardrobe door open, so that it screened a corner of the room for him to change in. Steve went to a window, and stood there looking between blind and frame, into the dark street where nothing moved. The girl stood close to him, between his arm and side, her fingers twined in his sleeve.

"Will we—? Will we—?"

He drew her closer and answered the whispered question she could not finish.

"We'll make it," he said, "if Larry plays square, or if he doesn't. We'll make it."

A rifle cracked somewhere in the direction of Main Street. A volley of pistol shots. The cream-colored Vauxhall came out of nowhere to settle on the sidewalk, two steps from the door. Larry Ormsby, hatless and with his shirt torn loose to expose a hole under one of his collar-bones, tumbled out of the car and through the door that Steve threw open for him.

Larry kicked the door shut behind him, and laughed.

"Izzard's frying nicely!" he cried, and clapped his hands together. "Come, come! The desert awaits!"

Steve turned to call the blind man. Rymer stepped out from behind his screening door. In each of Rymer's hands was a heavy revolver. The film was gone from Rymer's eyes.

His eyes, cool and sharp now, held the two men and the girl.

"Put your hands up, all of you," he ordered curtly.

Larry Ormsby laughed insanely.

"Did you ever see a damned fool do his stuff, Rymer?" he asked.

"Put your hands up!"

"Rymer," Larry said, "I'm dying now. To hell with you!"

And without haste he took a black automatic pistol from an inside coat pocket.

The guns in Rymer's hands rocked the cabin with explosion after explosion.

Knocked into a sitting position on the floor by the heavy bullets that literally tore him apart, Larry steadied his back against the wall, and the crisp, sharp reports of his lighter weapon began to punctuate the roars of the erstwhile blind man's guns.

Instinctively jumping aside, pulling the girl with him, at the first shot, Sieve now hurled himself upon Rymer's flank. But just as he reached him the shooting stopped. Rymer swayed, the very revolvers in his hands seemed to go limp. He slid out of Steve's clutching hands—his neck scraping one hand with the brittle dryness of paper—and became a lifeless pile on the floor.

Steve kicked the dead man's guns across the floor a way, and then went over to where the girl knelt beside Larry Ormsby. Larry smiled up at Steve with a flash of white teeth.

"I'm gone, Steve," he said. "That Rymer—fooled us all—phoney films on eyes—painted on—spy for rum syndicate."

He writhed, and his smile grew stiff and strained.

"Mind shaking hands, Steve?" he asked a moment later.

"You're a good guy, Larry," was the only thing he could think to say.

The dying man seemed to like that. His smile became real again.

"Luck to you—you can get a hundred and ten out of the Vauxhall," he managed to say.

And then, apparently having forgotten the girl for whom he had given up his life, he flashed another smile at Steve and died.

The front door slammed open—two heads looked in. The heads' owners came in.

Steve bounded upright, swung his stick. A bone cracked like a whip, a man reeled back holding a hand to his temple.

"Behind me—close!" Steve cried to the girl, and felt her hands on his back.

Men filled the doorway. An invisible gun roared and a piece of the ceiling flaked down. Steve spun his stick and charged the door. The light from the lamp behind him glittered and glowed on the whirling wood. The stick whipped backward and forward, from left to right, from right to left. It writhed like a live thing—seemed to fold upon its grasped middle as if spring-hinged with steel. Flashing half-circles merged into a sphere of deadliness. The rhythm of incessant thudding against flesh and clicking on bone became a tune that sang through the grunts of fighting men, the groans and oaths of stricken men. Steve and the girl went through the door.

Between moving arms and legs and bodies the cream of the Vauxhall showed. Men stood upon the automobile, using its height for vantage in the fight. Steve threw himself forward, swinging his stick against shin and thigh, toppling men from the machine. With his left hand he swept the girl around to his side. His body shook and rocked under the weight of blows from men who were packed too closely for any effectiveness except the smothering power of sheer weight.

His stick was suddenly gone from him. One instant he held and spun it; the next, he was holding up a clenched fist that was empty—the ebony had vanished as if in a puff of smoke. He swung the girl up over the car door, hammered her down into the car—jammed her down upon the legs of a man who stood there—heard a bone break, and saw the man go down. Hands gripped him everywhere; hands pounded him. He cried aloud with joy when he saw the girl, huddled on the floor of the car, working with ridiculously small hands at the car's mechanism.

NIGHTMARE TOWN

The machine began to move. Holding with his hands, he lashed both feet out behind. Got them back on the step. Struck over the girl's head with a hand that had neither thought nor time to make a fist—struck stiff-fingered into a broad red face.

The car moved. One of the girl's hands came up to grasp the wheel, holding the car straight along a street she could not see. A man fell on her. Steve pulled him off—tore pieces from him—tore hair and flesh. The car swerved, scraped a building; scraped one side clear of men. The hands that held Steve fell away from him, taking most of his clothing with them. He picked a man off the back of the seat, and pushed him down into the street that was flowing past them. Then he fell into the car beside the girl.

Pistols exploded behind them. From a house a little ahead a bitter-voiced rifle emptied itself at them, sieving a mudguard. Then the desert—white and smooth as a gigantic hospital bed—was around them. Whatever pursuit there had been was left far behind.

Presently the girl slowed down, stopped.

"Are you all right?" Steve asked.

"Yes; but you're—"

"All in one piece," he assured her. "Let me take the wheel."

"No! No!" she protested. "You're bleeding. You're—"

"No! No!" he mocked her. "We'd better keep going until we hit something. We're not far enough from Izzard yet to call ourselves safe."

He was afraid that if she tried to patch him up he would fall apart in her hands. He felt like that.

She started the car, and they went on. A great sleepiness came to him. What a fight! What a fight!

"Look at the sky!" she exclaimed.

He opened his heavy eyes. Ahead of them, above them, the sky was lightening—from blue-black to violet, to mauve, to rose. He turned his head and looked back. Where they had left Izzard, a monstrous bonfire was burning, painting the sky with jewelled radiance.

"Good-bye, Izzard," he said drowsily, and settled himself more comfortably in the seat.

He looked again at the glowing pink in the sky ahead.

"My mother has primroses in her garden in Delaware that look like that sometimes," he said dreamily. "You'll like 'em."

His head slid over against her shoulder, and he went to sleep.

NIGHT SHOTS

The house was of red brick, large and square, with a green slate roof whose wide overhang gave the building an appearance of being too squat for its two stories; and it stood on a grassy hill, well away from the country road upon which it turned its back to look down on the Mokelumne River.

The Ford that I had hired to bring me out from Knownburg carried me into the grounds through a high steel-meshed gate, followed the circling gravel drive, and set me down within a foot of the screened porch that ran all the way around the house's first floor.

"There's Exon's son-in-law now," the driver told me as he pocketed the bill I had given him and prepared to drive away.

I turned to see a tall, loose-jointed man of thirty or so coming across the porch toward me—a carelessly dressed man with a mop of rumpled brown hair over a handsome sunburned face. There was a hint of cruelty in the lips that were smiling lazily just now, and more than a hint of recklessness in his narrow gray eyes.

"Mr. Gallaway?" I asked as he came down the steps.

'Yes." His voice was a drawling baritone. "You are—"

"From the Continental Detective Agency's San Francisco branch," I finished for him.

He nodded, and held the screen door open for me.

"Just leave your bag there. I'll have it taken up to your room."

He guided me into the house and—after I had assured him that I had already eaten luncheon—gave me a soft chair and an excellent cigar. He sprawled on his spine in an armchair opposite me—all loose-jointed angles sticking out of it in every direction—and blew smoke at the ceiling.

"First off," he began presently, his words coming out languidly, "I may as well tell you that I don't expect very much in the way of results. I sent for you more for the soothing effect of your presence on the household than because I expect you to do anything. I don't believe there's anything to do. However, I'm not a detective. I may be wrong. You may find out all sorts of more or less important things. If you do—fine! But I don't insist upon it."

I didn't say anything, though this beginning wasn't much to my taste. He smoked in silence for a moment, and then went on, "My father-in-law, Talbert Exon, is a man of fifty-seven, and ordinarily a tough, hard, active, and fiery old devil. But just now he's recovering from a rather serious attack of pneumonia, which has taken most of the starch out of him. He hasn't been able to leave his bed yet, and Dr. Rench hopes to keep him on his back for at least another week.

"The old man has a room on the second floor—the front, right-hand corner room—just over where we are sitting. His nurse, Miss Caywood, occupies the next room, and there is a connecting door between. My room is the other front one, just across the hall from the old man's; and my wife's bedroom is next to mine—across the hall from the nurse's. I'll show you around later. I just want to make the situation clear.

"Last night, or rather this morning at about half-past one, somebody shot at Exon while he was sleeping—and missed. The bullet went into the frame of the door that leads to the nurse's room, about six inches above his body as he lay in bed. The course the bullet took in the woodwork would indicate that it had been fired from one of the windows—either through it or from just inside.

"Exon woke up, of course, but he saw nobody. The rest of us—my wife, Miss Caywood, the Figgs, and myself—were also awakened by the shot. We all rushed into his room, and we saw nothing either. There's no doubt that whoever fired it left by the window. Otherwise some of us would have seen him—we came from every other direction. However, we found nobody on the grounds, and no traces of anybody."

"Who are the Figgs, and who else is there on the place besides you and your wife, Mr. Exon, and his nurse?"

"The Figgs are Adam and Emma—she is the housekeeper and he is a sort of handy man about the place. Their room is in the extreme rear, on the second floor. Besides them, there is Gong Lim, the cook, who sleeps in a little room near the kitchen, and the three farm hands. Joe Natara and Felipe Fadelia are Italians, and have been here for more than two years; Jesus Mesa, a Mexican, has been here a year or longer. The farm hands sleep in a little house near the barns. I think—if my opinion is of any value—that none of these people had anything to do with the shooting."

"Did you dig the bullet out of the doorframe?"

"Yes. Shand, the deputy sheriff at Knownburg, dug it out. He says it is a thirty-eight-caliber bullet."

"Any guns of that caliber in the house?"

"No. A twenty-two and my forty-four—which I keep in the car—are the only pistols on the place. Then there are two shotguns and a thirty-thirty rifle. Shand made a thorough search, and found nothing else in the way of firearms."

"What does Mr. Exon say?"

"Not much of anything, except that if we'll put a gun in bed with him he'll manage to take care of himself without bothering any policemen or detectives. I don't know whether he knows who shot at him or not—he's a close-mouthed old devil. From what I know of him, I imagine there are quite a few men who would think themselves justified in killing him. He was, I understand, far from being a lily in his youth—or in his mature years either, for that matter."

"Anything definite you know, or are you guessing?"

Gallaway grinned at me—a mocking grin that I was to see often before I was through with this Exon affair.

"Both," he drawled. "I know that his life has been rather more than sprinkled with swindled partners and betrayed friends, and that he saved himself from prison at least once by turning state's evidence and sending his associates there. And I know that his wife died under rather peculiar circumstances while heavily insured, and that he was for some time held on suspicion of having murdered her, but was finally released because of a lack of evidence against him. Those, I understand, are fair samples of the old boy's normal behavior, so there may be any number of people gunning for him."

"Suppose you give me a list of all the names you know of enemies he's made, and I'll have them checked up."

"The names I could give you would be only a few of many, and it might take you months to check up those few. It isn't my intention to go to all that trouble and expense. As I told you, I'm not insisting upon results. My wife is very nervous, and for some peculiar reason she seems to like the old man. So, to soothe her, I agreed to employ a private detective when she asked me to. My idea is that you hang around for a couple of days, until things quiet down and she feels safe again. Meanwhile, if you should stumble upon anything—go to it! If you don't—well and good."

My face must have shown something of what I was thinking, for his eyes twinkled and he chuckled.

"Don't, please," he drawled, "get the idea that you aren't to find my father-in-law's would-be assassin if you wish to. You're to have a free hand. Go as far as you like, except that I want you to be around the place as much as possible, so my wife will see you and feel that we are being adequately protected. Beyond that, I don't care what you do. You can apprehend criminals by the carload. As you may have gathered by now, I'm not exactly in love with my wife's father, and he's no more fond of me. To be frank, if hating

NIGHT SHOTS

weren't such an effort—I think I should hate the old devil. But if you want to, and can, catch the man who shot at him, I'd be glad to have you do it. But-"

"All right," I said. "I don't like this job much, but since I'm up here I'll take it on. But, remember, I'm trying all the time."

"Sincerity and earnestness"—he showed his teeth in a sardonic smile as we got to our feet—"are very praiseworthy traits."

"So I hear," I growled shortly. "Now let's take a look at Mr. Exon's room."

Gallaway's wife and the nurse were with the invalid, but I examined the room before I asked the occupants any questions.

It was a large room, with three wide windows opening over the porch, and two doors, one of which gave to the hall and the other to the adjoining room occupied by the nurse. This door stood open, with a green Japanese screen across it, and, I was told, was left that way at night, so that the nurse could hear readily if her patient was restless or if he wanted attention.

A man standing on the slate roof of the porch, I found, could have easily leaned across one of the window-sills (if he did not care to step over it into the room) and fired at the man in his bed. To get from the ground to the porch roof would have required but little effort, and the descent would be still easier—he could slide down the roof, let himself go feet-first over the edge, checking his speed with hands and arms spread out on the slate, and drop down to the gravel drive. No trick at all, either coming or going. The windows were unscreened.

The sick man's bed stood just beside the connecting doorway between his room and the nurse's, which, when he was lying down, placed him between the doorway and the window from which the shot had been fired. Outside, within long rifle range, there was no building, tree, or eminence of any character from which the bullet that had been dug out of the doorframe could have been fired.

I turned from the room to the occupants, questioning the invalid first. He had been a raw-boned man of considerable size in his health, but now he was wasted and stringy and dead-white. His face was thin and hollow; small beady eyes crowded together against the thin bridge of his nose; his mouth was a colorless gash above a bony projecting chin.

His statement was a marvel of petulant conciseness.

"The shot woke me. I didn't see anything. I don't know anything. I've got a million enemies, most of whose names I can't remember."

He jerked this out crossly, turned his face away, closed his eyes, and refused to speak again.

Mrs. Gallaway and the nurse followed me into the latter's room, where I questioned them. They were of as opposite types as you could find anywhere, and between them there was a certain coolness, an unmistakable hostility which I was able to account for later in the day.

Mrs. Gallaway was perhaps five years older than her husband; dark, strikingly beautiful in a statuesque way, with a worried look in her dark eyes that was particularly noticeable when those eyes rested on her husband. There was no doubt that she was very much in love with him, and the anxiety that showed in her eyes at times—the pains she took to please him in each slight thing during my stay at the Exon house—convinced me that she struggled always with a fear that she was about to lose him.

Mrs. Gallaway could add nothing to what her husband had told me. She had been awakened by the shot, had run to her father's room, had seen nothing—knew nothing—suspected nothing.

The nurse—Barbra Caywood was her name—told the same story, in almost the same words. She had jumped out of bed when awakened by the shot, pushed the screen away from the connecting doorway, and rushed into her patient's room. She was the first one to arrive there, and she had seen nothing but the old man sitting up in bed, shaking his feeble fists at the window.

This Barbra Caywood was a girl of twenty-one or -two, and just the sort that a man would pick to help him get well—a girl of little under the average height, with an erect figure wherein slimness and roundness got an even break under the stiff white of her uniform; with soft golden hair above a face that was certainly made to be looked at. But she was businesslike and had an air of efficiency, for all her prettiness. From the nurse's room, Gallaway led me to the kitchen, where I questioned the Chinese cook. Gong Lim was a sad-faced Oriental whose ever-present smile somehow made him look more gloomy than ever; and he bowed and smiled and yes-yes'd me from start to finish, and told me nothing.

Adam and Emma Figg—thin and stout, respectively, and both rheumatic—entertained a wide variety of suspicions, directed at the cook and the farm hands, individually and collectively, flitting momentarily from one to the other. They had nothing upon which to base these suspicions, however, except their firm belief that nearly all crimes of violence were committed by foreigners.

The farm hands—two smiling, middle-aged, and heavily mustached Italians, and a soft-eyed Mexican youth—I found in one of the fields. I talked to them for nearly two hours, and I left with a reasonable amount of assurance that none of the three had had any part in the shooting.

Dr. Rench had just come down from a visit to his patient when Gallaway and I returned from the fields. He was a little, wizened old man with mild manners and eyes, and a wonderful growth of hair on head, brows, cheeks, lips, chin, and nostrils.

The excitement, he said, had retarded Exon's recovery somewhat, but he did not think the setback would be serious. The invalid's temperature had gone up a little, but he seemed to be improving now.

I followed Dr. Rench out to his car after he left the others, for a few questions I wanted to put to him in privacy, but the questions might as well have gone unasked for all the good they did me. He could tell me nothing of any value. The nurse, Barbra Caywood, had been secured, he said, from San Francisco, through the usual channels, which made it seem unlikely that she had worked her way into the Exon house for any hidden purpose which might have some connection with the attempt upon Exon's life.

Returning from my talk with the doctor, I came upon Hilary Gallaway and the nurse in the hall, near the foot of the stairs. His arm was resting lightly across her shoulders, and he was smiling down at her. Just as I came through the door, she twisted away so that his arm slid off, laughed elfishly up into his face, and went on up the stairs.

I did not know whether she had seen me approaching before she eluded the encircling arm or not, nor did I know how long the arm had been there; and both of those questions would make a difference in how their positions were to be construed.

Hilary Gallaway was certainly not a man to allow a girl as pretty as the nurse to lack attention, and he was just as certainly attractive enough in himself to make his advances not too unflattering. Nor did Barbra Caywood impress me as being a girl who would dislike his admiration. But, at that, it was more than likely that there was nothing very serious between them, nothing more than a playful sort of flirtation.

But, no matter what the situation might be in that quarter, it didn't have any direct bearing upon the shooting—none that I could see, anyway. But I understood now the strained relations between the nurse and Gallaway's wife.

Gallaway was grinning quizzically at me while I was chasing these thoughts around in my head.

"Nobody's safe with a detective around," he complained.

I grinned back at him. That was the only sort of answer you could give this bird.

After dinner, Gallaway drove me to Knownburg in his roadster, and set me down on the doorstep of the deputy sheriff's house. He offered to drive me back to the Exon house when I had finished my investigations in town, but I did not know how long those investigations would take, so I told him I would hire a car when I was ready to return.

NIGHT SHOTS

Shand, the deputy sheriff, was a big, slow-spoken, slow-thinking, blond man of thirty or so—just the type best fitted for a deputy sheriff job in a San Joaquin County town.

"I went out to Exon's as soon as Gallaway called me up," he said. "About four-thirty in the morning, I reckon it was when I got there. I didn't find nothing. There weren't no marks on the porch roof, but that don't mean nothing. I tried climbing up and down it myself, and I didn't leave no marks neither. The ground around the house is too firm for footprints to be followed. I found a few, but they didn't lead nowhere; and everybody had run all over the place before I got there, so I couldn't tell who they belonged to.

"Far's I can learn, there ain't been no suspicious characters in the neighborhood lately. The only folks around here who have got any grudge against the old man are the Deemses—Exon beat 'em in a law suit a couple years back—but all of them—the father and both the boys—were at home when the shooting was done."

"How long has Exon been living here?"

"Four-five years, I reckon."

"Nothing at all to work on, then?"

"Nothing I know about."

"What do you know about the Exon Family?" I asked.

Shand scratched his head thoughtfully and frowned.

"I reckon it's Hilary Gallaway you're meaning," he said slowly. "I thought of that. The Gallaways showed up here a couple of years after her father had bought the place, and Hilary seems to spend most of his evenings up in Ady's back room, teaching the boys how to play poker. I hear he's fitted to teach them a lot. I don't know, myself. Ady runs a quiet game, so I let 'em alone. But naturally I don't never set in, myself.

"Outside of being a cardhound, and drinking pretty heavy, and making a lot of trips to the city, where he's supposed to have a girl on the string, I don't know nothing much about Hilary. But it's no secret that him and the old man don't hit it off together very well. And then Hilary's room is just across the hall from Exon's, and their windows open out on the porch roof just a little apart. But I don't know—"

Shand confirmed what Gallaway had told me about the bullet being .38 caliber, about the absence of any pistol of that caliber on the premises, and about the lack of any reason for suspecting the farm hands or servants.

I put in the next couple of hours talking to whomever I could find to talk to in Knownburge, and I learned nothing worth putting down on paper. Then I got a car and driver from the garage, and was driven out to Exon's.

Gallaway had not yet returned from town. His wife and Barbra Caywood were just about to sit down to a light dinner before retiring, so I joined them. Exon, the nurse said, was asleep, and had spent a quiet evening. We talked for a while—until about half-past twelve—and then went to our rooms.

My room was next to the nurse's, on the same side of the hall that divided the second story in half. I sat down and wrote my report for the day, smoked a cigar, and then, the house being quiet by this time, put a gun and a flashlight in my pockets, went downstairs, and out the kitchen door.

The moon was just coming up, lighting the grounds vaguely, except for the shadows cast by house, outbuildings, and the several clumps of shrubbery. Keeping in these shadows as much as possible, I explored the grounds, finding everything as it should be.

The lack of any evidence to the contrary pointed to last night's shot having been fired—either accidentally, or in fright at some fancied move of Exon's—by a burglar, who had been entering the sick man's room through a window. If that were so, then there wasn't one chance in a thousand of anything happening tonight. But I felt restless and ill at ease, nevertheless.

Gallaway's roadster was not in the garage. He had not returned from Knownburg. Beneath the farm hands' window I paused until snores in three distinct keys told me that they were all safely abed.

NIGHT SHOTS

After an hour of this snooping around, I returned to the house. The luminous dial of my watch registered 2:35 as I stopped outside the Chinese cook's door to listen to his regular breathing.

Upstairs, I paused at the door of the Figgs's room, until my ear told me that they were sleeping. At Mrs. Gallaway's door I had to wait several minutes before she sighed and turned in bed. Barbra Caywood was breathing deeply and strongly, with the regularity of a young animal whose sleep is without disturbing dreams. The invalid's breath came to me with the evenness of slumber and the rasping of the pneumonia convalescent.

This listening tour completed, I returned to my room.

Still feeling wide-awake and restless, I pulled a chair up to a window, and sat looking at the moonlight on the river which twisted just below the house so as to be visible from this side, smoking another cigar, and turning things over in my mind—to no great advantage.

Outside there was no sound.

Suddenly down the hall came the heavy explosion of a gun being fired indoors! I threw myself across the room, out into the hall.

A woman's voice filled the house with its shriek—high, frenzied.

Barbra Caywood's door was unlocked when I reached it. I slammed it open. By the light of the moonbeams that slanted past her window, I saw her sitting upright in the center of her bed. She wasn't beautiful now. Her face was twisted with terror. The scream was just dying in her throat.

All this I got in the flash of time that it took me to put a running foot across her sill.

Then another shot crashed out—in Exon's room.

The girl's face jerked up—so abruptly that it seemed her neck must snap—she clutched both hands to her breast—and fell facedown among the bedclothes.

I don't know whether I went through, over, or around the screen that stood in the connecting doorway. I was circling Exon's bed.

He lay on the floor on his side, facing a window. I jumped over him—leaned out the window.

In the yard that was bright now under the moon, nothing moved. There was no sound of flight. Presently, while my eyes still searched the surrounding country, the farm hands, in their underwear, came running barefooted from the direction of their quarters. I called down to them, stationing them at points of vantage.

Meanwhile, behind me, Gong Lim and Adam Figg had put Exon back in his bed, while Mrs. Gallaway and Emma Figg tried to check the blood that spurted from a hole in Barbra Caywood's side.

I sent Adam Figg to the telephone, to wake the doctor and the deputy sheriff, and then I hurried down to the grounds.

Stepping out of the door, I came face to face with Hilary Gallaway coming from the direction of the garage. His face was flushed, and his breath was eloquent of the refreshments that had accompanied the game in Ady's back room, but his step was steady enough, and his smile was as lazy as ever.

"What's the excitement?" he asked.

"Same as last night! Meet anybody on the road? Or see anybody leaving here?"

"No."

"All right. Get in that bus of yours, and bum up the road in the other direction. Stop anybody you meet going away from here or who looks wrong! Got a gun?"

He spun on his heel with nothing of indolence.

"One in my car," he called as he broke into a run.

The farm hands still at their posts, I combed the grounds from east to west and from north to south. I realized that I was spoiling my chance of finding footprints when it would be light enough to see them, but I was banking on the man I wanted still being close at hand. And then Shand had told me that the ground was unfavorable for tracing prints, anyway.

On the gravel drive in front of the house I found the pistol from which the shots had been fired—a cheap .38-caliber revolver, slightly rusty, smelling freshly of burned powder, with three empty shells and three that had not been fired in it.

Besides that I found nothing. The murderer—from what I had seen of the hole in the girl's side, I called him that—had vanished.

Shand and Dr. Rench arrived together, just as I was finishing my fruitless search. A little later, Hilary Gallaway came back—empty-handed.

Breakfast that morning was a melancholy meal, except to Hilary Gallaway. He refrained from jesting openly about the night's excitement, but his eyes twinkled whenever they met mine, and I knew he thought it a tremendously good joke for the shooting to have taken place right under my nose. During his wife's presence at the table, however, he was almost grave, as if not to offend her. Mrs. Gallaway left the table shortly, and Dr. Rench joined us. He said that both of his patients were in as good shape as could be expected, and he thought both would recover.

The bullet had barely grazed the girl's ribs and breast-bone, going through the flesh and muscles of her chest, in on the right side and out again, on the left. Except for the shock and the loss of blood, she was not in danger, although unconscious.

Exon was sleeping, the doctor said, so Shand and I crept up into his room to examine it. The first bullet had gone into the doorframe, about four inches above the one that had been fired the night before. The second bullet had pierced the Japanese screen, and, after passing through the girl, had lodged in the plaster of the wall. We dug out both bullets—they were of .38 caliber. Both had apparently been fired from the vicinity of one of the windows—either just inside or just outside.

Shand and I grilled the Chinese cook, the farm hands, and the Figgs unmercifully that day. But they came through it standing up—there was nothing to fix the shooting on any of them.

And all day long that damned Hilary Gallaway followed me

from pillar to post, with a mocking glint in his eyes that said plainer than words, "I'm the logical suspect. Why don't you put me through your little third degree?" But I grinned back, and asked him nothing.

Shand had to go to town that afternoon. He called me up on the telephone later, and told me that Gallaway had left Knownburg early enough that morning to have arrived home fully half an hour before the shooting, if he had driven at his usual fast pace.

The day passed—too rapidly—and I found myself dreading the coming of night. Two nights in succession Exon's life had been attempted—and now the third night was coming.

At dinner Hilary Gallaway announced that he was going to stay home this evening. Knownburg, he said, was tame in comparison; and he grinned at me.

Dr. Rench left after the meal, saying that he would return as soon as possible, but that he had two patients on the other side of town whom he must visit. Barbra Caywood had returned to consciousness, but had been extremely hysterical, and the doctor had given her an opiate. She was asleep now. Exon was resting easily except for a high temperature.

I went up to Exon's room for a few minutes after the meal and tried him out with a gentle question or two, but he refused to answer them, and he was too sick for me to press him.

He asked how the girl was.

"The doc says she's in no particular danger. Just loss of blood and shock. If she doesn't rip her bandages off and bleed to death in one of her hysterical spells, he says, he'll have her on her feet in a couple of weeks."

Mrs. Gallaway came in then, and I went downstairs again, where I was seized by Gallaway, who insisted with bantering gravity that I tell him about some of the mysteries I had solved. He was enjoying my discomfort to the limit. He kidded me for about an hour, and had me burning up inside; but I managed to grin back with a fair pretence of indifference.

NIGHT SHOTS

When his wife joined us presently—saying that both of the invalids were sleeping—I made my escape from her tormenting husband, saying that I had some writing to do. But I didn't go to my room.

Instead, I crept stealthily into the girl's room, crossed to a clothespress that I had noted earlier in the day, and planted myself in it. By leaving the door open the least fraction of an inch, I could see through the connecting doorway—from which the screen had been removed—across Exon's bed, and out of the window from which three bullets had already come, and the Lord only knew what else might come.

Time passed, and I was stiff from standing still. But I had expected that.

Twice Mrs. Gallaway came up to look at her father and the nurse. Each time I shut my closet door entirely as soon as I heard her tiptoeing steps in the hall. I was hiding from *everybody*.

She had just gone from her second visit, when, before I had time to open my door again, I heard a faint rustling, and a soft padding on the floor. Not knowing what it was or where it was, I was afraid to push the door open. In my narrow hiding place I stood still and waited.

The padding was recognizable now—quiet footsteps, coming nearer. They passed not far from my clothespress door.

I waited.

An almost inaudible rustling. A pause. The softest and faintest of tearing sounds.

I came out of the closet—my gun in my hand.

Standing beside the girl's bed, leaning over her unconscious form, was old Talbert Exon, his face flushed with fever, his nightshirt hanging limply around his wasted legs. One of his hands still rested upon the bedclothes he had turned down from her body. The other hand held a narrow strip of adhesive tape, with which her bandages had been fixed in place, and which he had just torn off.

DETECTIVE STORIES

He snarled at me, and both his hands went toward the girl's bandages.

The crazy, feverish glare of his eyes told me that the threat of the gun in my hand meant nothing to him. I jumped to his side, plucked his hands aside, picked him up in my arms, and carried him—kicking, clawing, and swearing—back to his bed. Then I called the others.

Hilary Gallaway, Shand—who had come out from town again—and I sat over coffee and cigarettes in the kitchen, while the rest of the household helped Dr. Rench battle for Exon's life. The old man had gone through enough excitement in the last three days to kill a healthy man, let alone a pneumonia convalescent.

"But why should the old devil want to kill her?" Gallaway asked me.

"Search me," I confessed, a little testily perhaps. "I don't know why he wanted to kill her, but it's a cinch that he did. The gun was found just about where he could have thrown it when he heard me coming. I was in the girl's room when she was shot, and I got to Exon's window without wasting much time, and I saw nothing. You, yourself, driving home from Knownburg, and arriving here right after the shooting, didn't see anybody leave by the road; and I'll take an oath that nobody could have left in any other direction without either one of the farm hands or me seeing them.

"And then, tonight, I told Exon that the girl would recover if she didn't tear off her bandages, which, while true enough, gave him the idea that she had been trying to tear them off. And from that he built up a plan of tearing them off himself—knowing that she had been given an opiate, perhaps—and thinking that everybody would believe she had torn them off herself. And he was putting that plan into execution—had torn off one piece of tape—when I stopped him. He shot her intentionally, and that's flat. Maybe I couldn't prove it in court without knowing why, but I know he did. But the doc says he'll hardly live to be tried; he killed himself trying to kill the girl."

"Maybe you're right"—Gallaway's mocking grin flashed at me—"but you're a hell of a detective. Why didn't you suspect me?"

"I did," I grinned back, "but not enough."

"Why not? You may be making a mistake," he drawled. "You know my room is just across the hall from his, and I could have left my window, crept across the porch, fired at him, and then run back to my room, on that first night.

"And on the second night—when you were here—you ought to know that I left Knownburg in plenty of time to have come out here, parked my car down the road a bit, fired those two shots, crept around in the shadow of the house, run back to my car, and then come driving innocently up to the garage. You should know also that my reputation isn't any too good—that I'm supposed to be a bad egg; and you do know that I don't like the old man. And for a motive, there is the fact that my wife is Exon's only heir. I hope"—he raised his eyebrows in burlesqued pain—"that you don't think I have any moral scruples against a well-placed murder now and then."

I laughed. "I don't."

"Well, then?"

"If Exon had been killed that first night, and I had come up here, you'd be doing your joking behind bars long before this. And if he'd been killed the second night, even, I might have grabbed you. But I don't figure you as a man who'd bungle so easy a job—not twice, anyway. You wouldn't have missed, and then run away, leaving him alive."

He shook my hand gravely.

"It is comforting to have one's few virtues appreciated."

Before Talbert Exon died he sent for me. He wanted to die, he said, with his curiosity appeased; and so we traded information. I told him how I had come to suspect him and he told me why he had tried to kill Barbra Caywood.

Fourteen years ago he had killed his wife, not for the insurance, as he had been suspected of doing, but in a fit of jealousy. However, he had so thoroughly covered up the proofs of his guilt that he had never been brought to trial; but the murder had weighed upon him, to the extent of becoming an obsession.

He knew that he would never give himself away consciously—he was too shrewd for that—and he knew that proof of his guilt could never be found. But there was always the chance that some time, in delirium, in his sleep, or when drunk, he might tell enough to bring him to the gallows.

He thought upon this angle too often, until it became a morbid fear that always hounded him. He had given up drinking—that was easy—but there was no way of guarding against the other things.

And one of them, he said, had finally happened. He had got pneumonia, and for a week he had been out of his head, and he had talked. Coming out of that week's delirium, he had questioned the nurse. She had given him vague answers, would not tell him what he had talked about, what he had said. And then, in unguarded moments, he had discovered that her eyes rested upon him with loathing—with intense repulsion.

He knew then that he had babbled of his wife's murder; and he set about laying plans for removing the nurse before she repeated what she had heard.

For so long as she remained in his house, he counted himself safe. She would not tell strangers, and it might be that for a while she would not tell anyone. Professional ethics would keep her quiet, perhaps; but he could not let her leave his house with her knowledge of his secret.

Daily and in secret, he had tested his strength until he knew himself strong enough to walk about the room a little, and to hold a revolver steady. His bed was fortunately placed for his purpose—directly in line with one of the windows, the connecting door, and the girl's bed. In an old bond box in his closet—and nobody but he had ever seen the things in that box—was a revolver; a revolver that could not possibly be traced to him.

NIGHT SHOTS

On the first night, he had taken this gun out, stepped back from his bed a little, and fired a bullet into the doorframe. Then he had jumped back into bed, concealing the gun under the blankets—where none thought to look for it—until he could return it to its box.

That was all the preparation he had needed. He had established an attempted murder directed against himself, and he had shown that a bullet fired at him could easily go near—and therefore through—the connecting doorway.

On the second night, he had waited until the house had seemed quiet. Then he had peeped through one of the cracks in the Japanese screen at the girl, whom he could see in the reflected light from the moon. He had found, though, that when he stepped far enough back from the screen for it to escape powder marks, he could not see the girl, not while she was lying down. So he had fired first into the doorframe—near the previous night's bullet—to awaken her.

She had sat up in bed immediately, screaming, and he had shot her. He had intended firing another shot into her body—to make sure of her death—but my approach had made that impossible, and had made concealment of the gun impossible; so, with what strength he had left, he had thrown the revolver out of the window.

He died that afternoon, and I returned to San Francisco.

But that was not quite the end of the story.

In the ordinary course of business, the Agency's bookkeeping department sent Gallaway a bill for my services. With the check that he sent by return mail, he enclosed a letter to me, from which I quote a paragraph:

I don't want to let you miss the cream of the whole affair. The lovely Caywood, when she recovered, denied that Exon had talked of murder or any other crime during his delirium. The cause of the distaste with which she might have looked at him afterward, and the reason she would not tell him what he had said, was that his entire conversation during that week of delirium had consisted of an uninterrupted stream of obscenities and blasphemies, which seem to have shocked the girl through and through.

ONE HOUR

I

"This is Mr. Chrostwaite," Vance Richmond said.

Chrostwaite, wedged between the arms of one of the attorney's large chairs, grunted what was perhaps meant for an acknowledgment of the introduction. I grunted back at him, and found myself a chair.

He was a big balloon of a man—this Chrostwaite—in a green plaid suit that didn't make him look any smaller than he was. His tie was a gaudy thing, mostly of yellow, with a big diamond set in the center of it, and there were more stones on his pudgy hands. Spongy fat blurred his features, making it impossible for his round purplish face to even hold any other expression than the discontented hoggishness that was habitual to it. He reeked of gin.

"Mr. Chrostwaite is the Pacific Coast agent for the Mutual Fire Extinguisher Manufacturing Company," Vance Richmond began, as soon as I had got myself seated. "His office is on Kearny Street, near California. Yesterday, at about two forty-five in the afternoon, he went to his office, leaving his machine—a Hudson touring car—standing in front, with the engine running. Then minutes later, he came out. The car was gone."

I looked at Chrostwaite. He was looking at his fat knees, show-

ONE HOUR

ing not the least interest in what his attorney was saying. I looked quickly back at Vance Richmond; his clean gray face and lean figure were downright beautiful beside his bloated client.

"A man named Newhouse," the lawyer was saying, "who was the proprietor of a printing establishment on California Street, just around the corner from Mr. Chrostwaite's office, was run down and killed by Mr. Chrostwaite's car at the corner of Clay and Kearny Streets, five minutes after Mr. Chrostwaite had left the car to go into his office. The police found the car shortly afterward, only a block away from the scene of the accident—on Montgomery near Clay.

"The thing is fairly obvious. Someone stole the car immediately after Mr. Chrostwaite left it; and in driving rapidly away, ran down Newhouse; and then, in fright, abandoned the car. But here is Mr. Chrostwaite's position; three nights ago, while driving perhaps a little recklessly out—"

"Drunk," Chrostwaite said, not looking up from his plaid knees; and though his voice was hoarse, husky—it was the hoarseness of a whisky-burned throat—there was no emotion in his voice.

"While driving perhaps a little recklessly out Van Ness Avenue," Vance Richmond went on, ignoring the interruption, "Mr. Chrostwaite knocked a pedestrian down. The man wasn't badly hurt, and he is being compensated very generously for his injuries. But we are to appear in court next Monday to face a charge of reckless driving, and I am afraid that this accident of yesterday, in which the printer was killed, may hurt us.

"No one thinks that Mr. Chrostwaite was in his car when it killed the printer—we have a world of evidence that he wasn't. But I am afraid that the printer's death may be made a weapon against us when we appear on the Van Ness Avenue charge. Being an attorney, I know just how much capital the prosecuting attorney—if he so chooses—can make out of the really, insignificant fact that the same car that knocked down the man on Van Ness Avenue killed another man yesterday. And, being an attorney, I know how likely the prosecuting attorney is to so choose. And he can handle it in such a way that we will be given little or no opportunity to tell our side.

"The worst that can happen, of course, is that, instead of the usual fine, Mr. Chrostwaite will be sent to the city jail for thirty or sixty days. That is bad enough, however, and that is what we wish to—"

Chrostwaite spoke again, still regarding his knees.

"Damned nuisance!" he said.

"That is what we wish to avoid," the attorney continued. "We are willing to pay a stiff fine, and expect to, for the accident on Van Ness Avenue was clearly Mr. Chrostwaite's fault. But we—"

"Drunk as a lord!" Chrostwaite said.

"But we don't want to have this other accident, with which we had nothing to do, given a false weight in connection with the slighter accident. What we want then, is to find the man or men who stole the car and ran down John Newhouse. If they are apprehended before we go to court, we won't be in danger of suffering for their act. Think you can find them before Monday?"

"I'll try," I promised; "though it isn't—"

The human balloon interrupted me by heaving himself to his feet, fumbling with his fat jewelled fingers for his watch.

"Three o'clock," he said. "Got a game of golf for three-thirty." He picked up his hat and gloves from the desk. "Find 'em, will you? Damned nuisance going to jail!"

And he waddled out.

II

From the attorney's office, I went down to the Hall of Justice, and, after hunting around a few minutes, found a policeman who had arrived at the corner of Clay and Kearny Streets a few seconds after Newhonse had been knocked down.

ONE HOUR

"I was just leaving the Hall when I seen a bus scoot around the corner at Clay Street," this patrolman—a big sandy-haired man named Coffee—told me. "Then I seen people gathering around, so I went up there and found this John Newhouse stretched out. He was already dead. Half a dozen people had seen him hit, and one of 'em had got the license number of the car that done it. We found the car standing empty just around the corner on Montgomery Street, pointing north. There was two fellows in the car when it hit Newhouse, but nobody saw what they looked like. Nobody was in it when we found it."

"In what direction was Newhouse walking?"

"North along Kearny Street, and he was about three-quarters across Clay when he was knocked. The car was coming north on Kearny, too, and turned east on Clay. It mightn't have been all the fault of the fellows in the car—according to them that seen the accident. Newhouse was walking across the street looking at a piece of paper in his hand. I found a piece of foreign money—paper money—in his hand, and I guess that's what he was looking at. The lieutenant tells me it was Dutch money—a hundred-florin note, he says."

"Found out anything about the men in the car?"

"Nothing! We lined up everybody we could find in the neighborhood of California and Kearny Streets—where the car was stolen from—and around Clay and Montgomery Streets—where it was left at. But nobody remembered seeing the fellows getting in it or getting out of it. The man that owns the car wasn't driving it—it was stole all right, I guess. At first I thought maybe there was something shady about the accident. This John Newhouse had a two—or three-day-old black eye on him. But we run that out and found that he had an attack of heart trouble or something a couple days ago, and fell, fetching his eye up against a chair. He'd been home sick for three days—just left his house half an hour or so before the accident."

"Where'd he live?"

DETECTIVE STORIES

"On Sacramento Street—way out. I got his address here somewhere."

He turned over the pages of a grimy memoranda book, and I got the dead man's house number, and the names and addresses of the witnesses to the accident that Coffee had questioned.

That exhausted the policeman's information, so I left him.

III

My next play was to canvass the vicinity of where the car had been stolen and where it had been deserted, and then interview the witnesses. The fact that the police had fruitlessly gone over this ground made it unlikely that I would find anything of value; but I couldn't skip these things on that account. Ninety-nine per cent of detective work is a patient collecting of details—and your details must be got as nearly first-hand as possible, regardless of who else has worked the territory before you.

Before starting on this angle, however, I decided to run around to the dead man's printing establishment—only three blocks from the Hall of Justice—and see if any of his employees had heard anything that might help me.

Newhouse's establishment occupied the ground floor of a small building on California, between Kearny and Montgomery. A small office was partitioned off in front, with a connecting doorway leading to the pressroom in the rear.

The only occupant of the small office, when I came in from the street, was a short, stocky, worried-looking blond man of forty or thereabouts, who sat at the desk in his shirt-sleeves, checking off figures in a ledger against others on a batch of papers before him.

I introduced myself, telling him that I was a Continental Detective Agency operative, interested in Newhouse's death. He told me his name was Ben Soules, and that he was Newhouse's foreman. We shook hands, and then he waved me to a chair across

ONE HOUR

the desk, pushed back the papers and book upon which he had been working, and scratched his head disgustedly with the pencil in his hand.

"This is awful!" he said. "What with one thing and another, we're heels over head in work, and I got to fool with these books that I don't know anything at all about, and—"

He broke off to pick up the telephone, which had jingled.

"Yes. ... This is Soules... We're working on them now. ... I'll give 'em to you by Monday noon at the least. ... I know! I know! But the boss's death set us back. Explain that to Mr. Chrostwaite. And ... And I'll promise you that we'll give them to you Monday morning, sure!" Soules slapped the receiver irritably on its hook and looked at me.

"You'd think that since it was his own car that killed the boss, he'd have decency enough not to squawk over the delay!"

"Chrostwaite?"

"Yes—that was one of his clerks. We're printing some leaflets for him—promised to have 'em ready yesterday—but between the boss's death and having a couple new hands to break in, we're behind with everything. I've been here eight years, and this is the first time we ever fell down on an order—and every damned customer is yelling his head off. If we were like most printers they'd be used to waiting; but we've been too good to them. But this Chrostwaite! You'd think he'd have some decency, seeing that his car killed the boss!"

I nodded sympathetically, slid a cigar across the desk, and waited until it was burning in Soules's mouth before I asked:

"You said something about having a couple new hands to break in. How come?"

"Yes. Mr. Newhouse fired two of our printers last week—Fincher and Keys. He found that they belonged to the I.W.W., so he gave them their time."

"Any trouble with them or anything against them except that they were Wobblies?"

"No—they were pretty good workers."

"Any trouble with them after he fired them?" I asked.

"No real trouble, though they were pretty hot. They made red speeches all over the place before they left."

"Remember what day that was?"

"Wednesday of last week, I think. Yes, Wednesday, because I hired two new men on Thursday."

"How many men do you work?"

"Three, besides myself."

"Was Mr. Newhouse sick very often?"

"Not sick enough to stay away very often, though every now and then his heart would go back on him, and he'd have to stay in bed for a week or ten days. He wasn't what you could call real well at any time. He never did anything but the office work—I run the shop."

"When was he taken sick this last time?"

"Mrs. Newhouse called up Tuesday morning and said he had had another spell, and wouldn't be down for a few days. He came in yesterday—which was Thursday—for about ten minutes in the afternoon, and said he would be back on the job this morning. He was killed just after he left."

"How did he look—very sick?"

"Not so bad. He never looked well, of course, but I couldn't see much difference from usual yesterday. This last spell hadn't been as bad as most, I reckon—he was usually laid up for a week or more."

"Did he say where he was going when he left? The reason I ask is that, living out on Sacramento Street, he would naturally have taken a car at that street if he had been going home, whereas he was run down on Clay Street."

"He said he was going up to Portsmouth Square to sit in the sun for half an hour or so. He had been cooped up indoors for two or three days, he said, and he wanted some sunshine before he went back home."

ONE HOUR

"He had a piece of foreign money in his hand when he was hit. Know anything about it?"

"Yes. He got it here. One of our customers—a man named Van Pelt—came in to pay for some work we had done yesterday afternoon while the boss was here. When Van Pelt pulled out his wallet to pay his bill, this piece of Holland money—I don't know what you call it—was among the bills. I think he said it was worth something like thirty-eight dollars. Anyway, the boss took it, giving Van Pelt his change. The boss said he wanted to show the Holland money to his boys—and he could have it changed back into American money later."

"Who is this Van Pelt?"

"He's a Hollander—is planning to open a tobacco importing business here in a month or two. I don't know much about him outside of that."

"Where's his home, or office?"

"His office is on Bush Street, near Sansome."

"Did he know that Newhouse had been sick?"

"I don't think so. The boss didn't look much different from usual."

"What's this Van Pelt's full name?"

"Hendrik Van Pelt."

"What does he look like?"

Before Soules could answer, three evenly spaced buzzes sounded above the rattle and whirring of the presses in the back of the shop.

I slid the muzzle of my gun—I had been holding it in my lap for five minutes—far enough over the edge of the desk for Ben Soules to see it.

"Put both of your hands on top of the desk," I said.

He put them there.

The pressroom door was directly behind him, so that, facing him across the desk, I could look over his shoulder at it. His stocky body served to screen my gun from the view of whoever came through the door, in response to Soules's signal.

I didn't have long to wait.

Three men—black with ink—came to the door, and through it into the little office. They strolled in careless and casual, laughing and joking to one another.

But one of them licked his lips as he stepped through the door. Another's eyes showed white circles all around the irises. The third was the best actor—but he held his shoulders a trifle too stiffly to fit his otherwise careless carriage.

"Stop right there!" I barked at them when the last one was inside the office—and I brought my gun up where they could see it.

They stopped as if they had all been mounted on the same pair of legs.

I kicked my chair back, and stood up.

I didn't like my position at all. The office was entirely too small for me. I had a gun, true enough, and whatever weapons may have been distributed among these other men were out of sight. But these four men were too close to me; and a gun isn't a thing of miracles. It's a mechanical contraption that is capable of just so much and no more.

If these men decided to jump me, I could down just one of them before the other three were upon me. I knew it, and they knew it.

"Put your hands up," I ordered, "and turn around!"

None of them moved to obey. One of the inked men grinned wickedly; Soules shook his head slowly; the other two stood and looked at me.

I was more or less stumped. You can't shoot a man just because he refuses to obey an order—even if he is a criminal. If they had turned around for me, I could have lined them up against the wall, and, being behind them, have held them safe while I used the telephone.

But that hadn't worked.

My next thought was to back across the office to the street door, keeping them covered, and then either stand in the door and yell

ONE HOUR

for help, or take them into the street, where I could handle them. But I put that thought away as quickly as it came to me.

These four men were going to jump me—there was no doubt of that. All that was needed was a spark of any sort to explode them into action. They were standing stiff-legged and tense, waiting for some move on my part. If I took a step backward—the battle would be on.

We were close enough for any of the four to have reached out and touched me. One of them I could shoot before I was smothered—one out of four. That meant that each of them had only one chance out of four of being the victim—low enough odds for any but the most cowardly of men.

I grinned what was supposed to be a confident grin—because I was up against it hard—and reached for the telephone: I had to do something! Then I cursed myself! I had merely changed the signal for the onslaught. It would come now when I picked up the receiver.

But I couldn't back down again—that, too, would be a signal—I had to go through with it.

The perspiration trickled across my temples from under my hat as I drew the phone closer with my left hand.

The street door opened! An exclamation of surprise came from behind me.

I spoke rapidly, without taking my eyes from the four men in front of me.

"Quick! The phone! The police!"

With the arrival of this unknown person—one of Newhouse's customers, probably—I figured I had the edge again. Even if he took no active part beyond calling the police in, the enemy would have to split to take care of him—and that would give me a chance to pot at least two of them before I was knocked over. Two out of four—each of them had an even chance of being dropped—which *is* enough to give even a nervy man cause for thinking a bit before he jumps.

"Hurry!" I urged the newcomer.

"Yes! Yes!" he said—and in the blurred sound of the "s" there was evidence of foreign birth.

Keyed up as I was, I didn't need any more warning than that.

I threw myself sidewise—a blind tumbling away from the spot where I stood. But I wasn't quite quick enough.

The blow that came from behind didn't hit me fairly, but I got enough of it to fold up my legs as if the knees were hinged with paper—and I slammed into a heap on the floor....

Something dark crashed toward me. I caught it with both hands. It may have been a foot kicking at my face. I wrung it as a washerwoman wrings a towel.

Down my spine ran jar after jar. Perhaps somebody was beating me over the head. I don't know. My head wasn't alive. The blow that had knocked me down had numbed me all over. My eyes were no good. Shadows swam to and fro in front of them—that was all. I struck, gouged, tore at the shadows. Sometimes I found nothing. Sometimes I found things that felt like parts of bodies. Then I would hammer at them, tear at them. My gun was gone.

I found presently that my feet were under me again, though some squirming thing was on my back, and kept me from standing upright: A hot, damp thing like a hand was across my face.

I put my teeth into it. I snapped my head back as far as it would go. Maybe it smashed into the face it was meant for. I don't know. Anyhow the squirming thing was no longer on my back.

Dimly I realized that I was being buffeted about by blows that I was too numb to feel. Ceaselessly, with head and shoulders and elbows and fists and knees and feet, I struck at the shadows that were around me...

Suddenly I could see again—not clearly—but the shadows were taking on colors; and my ears came back a little, so that grunts and growls and curses and the impact of blows sounded in them. My straining gaze rested upon a brass cuspidor six inches or so in front of my eyes. I knew then that I was down on the floor again.

ONE HOUR

As I twisted about to hurl a foot into a soft body above me, something that was like a burn, but wasn't a burn, ran down one leg—a knife. The sting of it brought consciousness back into me with a rush.

I grabbed the brass cuspidor and used it to club a way to my feet—to club a clear space in front of me. Men were hurling themselves upon me. I swung the cuspidor high and flung it over their heads through the frosted glass door into California Street.

Then we fought some more.

But you can't throw a brass cuspidor through a glass door into California Street between Montgomery and Kearny without attracting attention—it's too near the heart of daytime San Francisco. So presently—when I was on the floor again with six or eight hundred pounds of flesh hammering my face into the boards—we were pulled apart, and I was dug out of the bottom of the pile by a squad of policemen.

Big sandy-haired Coffee was one of them, but it took a lot of arguing to convince him that I was the Continental operative who had talked to him a little while before.

"Man! Man!" he said, when I finally convinced him. "Them lads sure—God!—have worked you over! You got a face like a wet geranium!"

I didn't laugh. It wasn't funny.

I looked out of the one eye which was working just now at the five men lined up across the office—Soules, the three inky printers, and the man with the blurred "s," who had started the slaughter by tapping me on the back of the head.

He was a rather tall man of thirty or so, with a round ruddy face that wore a few bruises now. He had been, apparently, rather well-dressed in expensive black clothing, but he was torn and ragged now. I knew who he was without asking—Hendrik Van Pelt.

"Well, man, what's the answer?" Coffee was asking me.

By holding one side of my jaw firmly with one hand I found that I could talk without too much pain.

"This is the crowd that ran down Newhouse," I said, "and it wasn't an accident. I wouldn't mind having a few more of the details myself, but I was jumped before I got around to all of them. Newhouse had a hundred-florin note in his hand when he was run down, and he was walking in the direction of police headquarters—was only half a block away from the Hall of Justice.

"Soules tells me that Newhouse said he was going up to Portsmouth Square to sit in the sun. But Soules didn't seem to know that Newhouse was wearing a black eye—the one you told me you had investigated. If Soules didn't see the shiner, then it's a good bet that Soules didn't see Newhouse's face that day!

"Newhouse was walking from his printing shop toward police headquarters with a piece of foreign paper money in his hand—remember that!

"He had frequent spells of sickness, which, according to friend Soules, always before kept him at home for a week or ten days at a time. This time he was laid up for only two and a half days.

"Soules tells me that the shop is three days behind with its orders, and he says that's the first time in eight years they've ever been behind. He blames Newhouse's death—which only happened yesterday. Apparently, Newhouse's previous sick spells never delayed things—why should this last spell?

"Two printers were fired last week, and two new ones hired the very next day—pretty quick work. The car with which Newhouse was run down was taken from just around the corner, and was deserted within quick walking distance of the shop. It was left facing north, which is pretty good evidence that its occupants went south after they got out. Ordinary car thieves wouldn't have circled back in the direction from which they came.

"Here's my guess: This Van Pelt is a Dutchman, and he had some plates for phoney hundred-florin notes. He hunted around until he found a printer who would go in with him. He found Soules, the foreman of a shop whose proprietor was now and then at home for a week or more at a time with a bad heart. One of the

ONE HOUR

printers under Soules was willing to go in with them. Maybe the other two turned the offer down. Maybe Soules didn't ask them at all. Anyhow, they were discharged, and two friends of Soules were given their places.

"Our friends then got everything ready, and waited for Newhouse's heart to flop again. It did—Monday night. As soon as his wife called up next morning and said he was sick, these birds started running off their counterfeits. That's why they fell behind with their regular work. But this spell of Newhouse's was lighter than usual. He was up and moving around within two days, and yesterday afternoon he came down here for a few minutes.

"He must have walked in while all of our friends were extremely busy in some far corner. He must have spotted some of the phoney money, immediately sized up the situation, grabbed one bill to show the police, and started out for police headquarters—no doubt thinking he had not been seen by our friends here.

"They must have got a glimpse of him as he was leaving, however. Two of them followed him out. They couldn't, afoot, safely knock him over within a block or two of the Hall of Justice. But, turning the corner, they found Chrostwaite's car standing there with idling engine. That solved their getaway problem. They got in the car and went on after Newhouse. I suppose the original plan was to shoot him—but he crossed Clay Street with his eyes fastened upon the phoney money in his hand. That gave them a golden chance. They piled the car into him. It was sure death, they knew his bum heart would finish the job if the actual collision didn't kill him. Then they deserted the car and came back here.

"There are a lot of loose ends to be gathered in—but this pipe-dream I've just told you fits in with all the facts we know—and I'll bet a month's salary I'm not far off anywhere. There ought be a three-day crop of Dutch notes cached somewhere! You people—"

I suppose I'd have gone on talking forever—in the giddy, head-swimming intoxication of utter exhaustion that filled me—if the big sandy-haired patrolman hadn't shut me off by putting a big hand across my mouth.

"Be quiet, man," he said, lifting me out the chair, and spreading me flat on my back on the desk. "I'll have an ambulance here in a second for you."

The office was swirling around in front of my one open eye—the yellow ceiling swung down toward me, rose again, disappeared, came back in odd shapes. I turned my head to one side to avoid it, and my glance rested upon the white dial of a spinning clock.

Presently the dial came to rest, and I read it—four o'clock.

I remembered that Chrostwaite had broken up our conference in Vance Richmond's office at three, and I had started to work.

"One full hour!" I tried to tell Coffee before I went to sleep.

The police wound up the job while I was lying on my back in bed. In Van Pelt's office on Bush Street they found a great bale of hundred-florin notes. Van Pelt, they learned, had a considerable reputation in Europe as a high-class counterfeiter. One of the printers came through, stating that Van Pelt and Soules were the two who followed Newhouse out of the shop, and killed him.

THE BODIES PILED UP

The Montgomery Hotel's regular detective had taken his last week's rake-off from the hotel bootlegger in merchandise instead of cash, had drunk it down, had fallen asleep in the lobby, and had been fired. I happened to be the only idle operative in the Continental Detective Agency's San Francisco branch at the time, and thus it came about that I had three days of hotel-coppering while a man was being found to take the job permanently.

The Montgomery is a quiet hotel of the better sort, and so I had a very restful time of it—until the third and last day. Then things changed.

I came down into the lobby that afternoon to find Stacey, the assistant manager, hunting for me.

"One of the maids just phoned that there's something wrong up in 906," he said.

We went up to that room together. The door was open. In the center of the floor stood a maid, staring goggle-eyed at the closed door of the clothespress. From under it, extending perhaps a foot across the floor toward us, was a snake-shaped ribbon of blood.

I stepped past the maid and tried the door. It was unlocked. I opened it. Slowly, rigidly, a man pitched out into my arms—pitched out backward—and there was a six-inch slit down the back of his coat, and the coat was wet and sticky.

DETECTIVE STORIES

That wasn't altogether a surprise: the blood on the floor had prepared me for something of the sort. But when another followed him—facing me, this one, with a dark, distorted face—I dropped the one I had caught and jumped back.

And as I jumped a third man came tumbling out after the others.

From behind me came a scream and a thud as the maid fainted. I wasn't feeling any too steady myself. I'm no sensitive plant, and I've looked at a lot of unlovely sights in my time, but for weeks afterward I could see those three dead men coming out of that clothespress to pile up at my feet: coming out slowly—almost deliberately—in a ghastly game of "'ollow your leader."

Seeing them, you couldn't doubt that they were really dead. Every detail of their falling, every detail of the heap in which they now lay, had a horrible certainty of lifelessness in it.

I turned to Stacey, who, deathly white himself, was keeping on his feet only by clinging to the foot of the brass bed.

"Get the woman out! Get doctors—police!"

I pulled the three dead bodies apart, laying them out in a grim row, faces up. Then I made a hasty examination of the room.

A soft hat, which fitted one of the dead men, lay in the center of the unruffled bed. The room key was in the door, on the inside. There was no blood in the room except what had leaked out of the clothespress, and the room showed no signs of having been the scene of a struggle.

The door to the bathroom was open. In the bottom of the bathtub was a shattered gin bottle, which, from the strength of the odor and the dampness of the tub, had been nearly full when broken. In one corner of the bathroom I found a small whisky glass and another under the tub. Both were dry, clean, and odorless.

The inside of the clothespress door was stained with blood from the height of my shoulder to the floor, and two hats lay in the puddle of blood on the closet floor. Each of the hats fitted one of the dead men.

That was all. Three dead men, a broken gin bottle, blood.

THE BODIES PILED UP

Stacey returned presently with a doctor, and while the doctor was examining the dead men, the police detectives arrived.

The doctor's work was soon done.

"This man," he said, pointing to one of them, "was struck on the back of the head with a small blunt instrument, and then strangled. This one"—pointing to another—"was simply strangled. And the third was stabbed in the back with a blade perhaps five inches long. They have been dead for about two hours—since noon or a little after."

The assistant manager identified two of the bodies. The man who had been stabbed—the first to fall out of the clothespress—had arrived at the hotel three days before, registering as Tudor Ingraham of Washington, D.C., and had occupied room 915, three doors away.

The last man to fall out—the one who had been simply choked—was the occupant of this room. His name was Vincent Develyn. He was an insurance broker and had made the hotel his home since his wife's death, some four years before.

The third man had been seen in Develyn's company frequently, and one of the clerks remembered that they had come into the hotel together at about five minutes after twelve this day. Cards and letters in his pockets told us that he was Homer Ansley, a member of the law firm of Lankershim and Ansley, whose offices were in the Miles Building—next door to Develyn's office.

Develyn's pockets held between $150 and $200; Ansley's wallet contained more than $100; Ingraham's pockets yielded nearly $300, and in a money belt around his waist we found $2,200 and two medium-sized unset diamonds. All three had watches—Develyn's was a valuable one—in their pockets, and Ingraham wore two rings, both of which were expensive ones. Ingraham's room key was in his pocket.

Beyond this money—whose presence would seem to indicate that robbery hadn't been the motive behind the three killings—we found nothing on any of the persons to throw the slightest light on the crime. Nor did the most thorough examination of both Ingraham's and Develyn's rooms teach us anything.

In Ingraham's room we found a dozen or more packs of carefully marked cards, some crooked dice, and an immense amount of data on race-horses. Also we found that he had a wife who lived on East Delavan Avenue in Buffalo, and a brother on Crutcher Street in Dallas; as well as a list of names and addresses that we carried off to investigate later. But nothing in either room pointed, even indirectly, at murder.

Phels, the Police Department Bertillon man, found a number of fingerprints in Develyn's room, but we couldn't tell whether they would be of any value or not until he had worked them up. Though Develyn and Ansley had apparently been strangled by hands, Phels was unable to get prints from either their necks or their collars.

The maid who had discovered the blood said that she had straightened up Develyn's room between ten and eleven that morning, but had not put fresh towels in the bathroom. It was for this purpose that she had gone to the room in the afternoon. She had gone there earlier—between 10:20 and 10:45—for that purpose, but Ingraham had not then left it.

The elevator man who had carried Ansley and Develyn up from the lobby at a few minutes after twelve remembered that they had been laughingly discussing their golf scores of the previous day during the ride. No one had seen anything suspicious in the hotel around the time at which the doctor had placed the murders. But that was to be expected.

The murderer could have left the room, closing the door behind him, and walked away secure in the knowledge that at noon a man in the corridors of the Montgomery would attract little attention. If he was staying at the hotel he would simply have gone to his room; if not, he would have either walked all the way down to the street, or down a floor or two and then caught an elevator.

None of the hotel employees had ever seen Ingraham and De-

THE BODIES PILED UP

velyn together. There was nothing to show that they had even the slightest acquaintance. Ingraham habitually stayed in his room until noon, and did not return to it until late at night. Nothing was known of his affairs.

At the Miles Building we—that is, Marty O'Hara and George Dean of the Police Department Homicide Detail, and I—questioned Ansley's partner and Develyn's employees. Both Develyn and Ansley, it seemed, were ordinary men who led ordinary lives: lives that held neither dark spots nor queer kinks. Ansley was married and had two children; he lived on Lake Street. Both men had a sprinkling of relatives and friends scattered here and there through the country; and, so far as we could learn, their affairs were in perfect order.

They had left their offices this day to go to luncheon together, intending to visit Develyn's room first for a drink apiece from a bottle of gin someone coming from Australia had smuggled in to him.

"Well," O'Hara said, when we were on the street again, "this much is clear. If they went up to Develyn's room for a drink, it's a cinch that they were killed almost as soon as they got in the room. Those whisky glasses you found were dry and clean. Whoever turned the trick must have been waiting for them. I wonder about this fellow Ingraham."

"I'm wondering, too," I said. "Figuring it out from the positions I found them in when I opened the closet door, Ingraham sizes up as the key to the whole thing. Develyn was back against the wall, with Ansley in front of him, both facing the door. Ingraham was facing them, with his back to the door. The clothespress was just large enough for them to be packed in it—too small for them to slip down while the door was closed.

"Then there was no blood in the room except what had come from the clothespress. Ingraham, with that gaping slit in his back, couldn't have been stabbed until he was inside the closet, or he'd have bled elsewhere. He was standing close to the other men when he was knifed, and whoever knifed him closed the door quickly afterward.

"Now, why should he have been standing in such a position? Do you dope it out that he and another killed the two friends, and that while he was stowing their bodies in the closet his accomplice finished him off?"

"Maybe," Dean said.

And that "maybe" was still as far as we had gone three days later.

We had sent and received bales of telegrams, having relatives and acquaintances of the dead men interviewed; and we had found nothing that seemed to have any bearing upon their deaths. Nor had we found the slightest connecting link between Ingraham and the other two. We had traced those other two back step by step almost to their cradles. We had accounted for every minute of their time since Ingraham had arrived in San Francisco—thoroughly enough to convince us that neither of them had met Ingraham.

Ingraham, we had learned, was a bookmaker and all around crooked gambler. His wife and he had separated, but were on good terms. Some fifteen years before, he had been convicted of "assault with intent to kill" in Newark, N.J., and had served two years in the state prison. But the man he had assaulted had died of pneumonia in Omaha in 1914.

Ingraham had come to San Francisco for the purpose of opening a gambling club, and all our investigations had tended to show that his activities while in the city had been toward that end alone.

The fingerprints Phels had secured had all turned out to belong to Stacey, the maid, the police detectives, or myself. In short, we had found nothing!

So much for our attempts to learn the motive behind the three murders.

We now dropped that angle and settled down to the detail-studying, patience-taxing grind of picking up the murderer's trail. From any crime to its author there is a trail. It may be—as in this case—obscure; but, since matter cannot move without disturbing other matter along its path, there always is—there must be—a trail of some sort. And finding and following such trails is what a detective is paid to do.

In the case of a murder it is possible sometimes to take a short-cut to the end of the trail, by first finding the motive. A knowledge of the motive often reduces the field of possibilities; sometimes points directly to the guilty one.

So far, all we knew about the motive in the particular case we were dealing with was that it hadn't been robbery; unless something we didn't know about had been stolen—something of sufficient value to make the murderer scorn the money in his victims' pockets.

We hadn't altogether neglected the search for the murderer's trail, of course, but—being human—we had devoted most of our attention to trying to find a short-cut. Now we set out to find our man, or men, regardless of what had urged him or them to commit the crimes.

Of the people who had been registered at the hotel on the day of the killing there were nine men of whose innocence we hadn't found a reasonable amount of proof. Four of these were still at the hotel, and only one of that four interested us very strongly. That one—a big raw-boned man of forty-five or fifty, who had registered as J. J. Cooper of Anaconda, Montana—wasn't, we had definitely established, really a mining man, as he pretended to be. And our telegraphic communications with Anaconda failed to show that he was known there. Therefore we were having him shadowed—with few results.

Five men of the nine had departed since the murders; three of them leaving forwarding addresses with the mail clerk. Gilbert Jacquemart had occupied room 946 and had ordered his mail forwarded to him at a Los Angeles hotel. W. F. Salway, who had occupied room 1022, had given instructions that his mail be readdressed to a number on Clark Street in Chicago. Ross Orrett, room 609, had asked to have his mail sent to him care of General Delivery at the local post office.

Jacquemart had arrived at the hotel two days before, and had left on the afternoon of the murders. Salway had arrived the day before the murders and had left the day after them. Orrett had arrived the day of the murders and had left the following day.

Sending telegrams to have the first two found and investigated, I went after Orrett myself. A musical comedy named *What For?* was being widely advertised just then with gaily printed plum-colored handbills. I got one of them and, at a stationery store, an envelope to match, and mailed it to Orrett at the Montgomery Hotel. There are concerns that make a practice of securing the names of arrivals at the principal hotels and mailing them advertisements. I trusted that Orrett, knowing this, wouldn't be suspicious when my gaudy envelope, forwarded from the hotel, reached him through the General Delivery window.

Dick Foley—the Agency's shadow specialist—planted himself in the post office, to loiter around with an eye on the 'O' window until he saw my plum-colored enveloped passed out, and then to shadow the receiver.

I spent the next day trying to solve the mysterious J. J. Cooper's game, but he was still a puzzle when I knocked off that night.

At a little before five the following morning Dick Foley dropped into my room on his way home to wake me up and tell me what he had done.

"This Orrett baby is our meat!" he said. "Picked him up when he got his mail yesterday afternoon. Got another letter besides yours. Got an apartment on Van Ness Avenue. Took it the day after the killing, under the name of B. T. Quinn. Packing a gun under his left arm-- there's that sort of a bulge there. Just went home to bed. Been visiting all the dives in North Beach. Who do you think he's hunting for?"

"Who?"

"Guy Cudner."

That was news! This Guy Cudner, alias "The Darkman," was

THE BODIES PILED UP

the most dangerous bird on the Coast, if not in the country. He had only been nailed once, but if he had been convicted of all the crimes that everybody knew he had committed he'd have needed half a dozen lives to crowd his sentences into, besides another half-dozen to carry to the gallows. However, he had decidedly the right sort of backing—enough to buy him everything he needed—in the way of witnesses, alibis, even juries and an occasional judge.

I don't know what went wrong with his support that one time he was convicted up North and sent over for a one-to-fourteen-year hitch; but it adjusted itself promptly, for the ink was hardly dry on the press notices of his conviction before he was loose again on parole.

"Is Cudner in town?"

"Don't know," Dick said, "but this Orrett, or Quinn, or whatever his name is, is surely hunting for him. In Rick's place, at "Wop" Healey's, and at Pigatti's. "Porky" Grout tipped me off. Says Orrett doesn't know Cudner by sight, but is trying to find him. Porky didn't know what he wants with him."

This Porky Grout was a dirty little rat who would sell out his family—if he ever had one—for the price of a flop. But with these lads who play both sides of the game it's always a question of which side they're playing when you think they're playing yours.

"Think Porky was coming clean?" I asked.

"Chances are—but you can't gamble on him."

"Is Orrett acquainted here?"

"Doesn't seem to be. Knows where he wants to go but has to ask how to get there. Hasn't spoken to anybody that seemed to know him."

"What's he like?"

"Not the kind of egg you'd want to tangle with offhand, if you ask me. He and Cudner would make a good pair. They don't look alike. This egg is tall and slim, but he's built right—those fast, smooth muscles. Face is sharp without being thin, if you get me. I mean all the lines in it are straight. No curves. Chin, nose, mouth, eyes—all straight, sharp lines and angles. Looks like the kind of egg we know Cudner is. Make a good pair. Dresses well and doesn't look like a rowdy—but harder than hell! A big-game hunter! Our meat, I bet you!"

"It doesn't look bad," I agreed. "He came to the hotel the morning of the day the men were killed, and checked out the next morning. He packs a rod, and changed his name after he left. And now he's paired off with The Darkman. It doesn't look bad at all!"

"I'm telling you," Dick said, "this fellow looks like three killings wouldn't disturb his rest any. I wonder where Cudner fits in."

"I can't guess. But, if he and Orrett haven't connected yet, then Cudner, wasn't in on the murders; but he may give us the answer."

Then I jumped out of bed. "I'm going to gamble on Porky's dope being on the level! How would you describe Cudner?"

"You know him better than I do."

"Yes, but how would you describe him to me if I didn't know him?"

"A little fat guy with a red forked scar on his left cheek. What's the idea?"

"It's a good one," I admitted. "That scar makes all the difference in the world. If he didn't have it and you were to describe him you'd go into all the details of his appearance. But he has it, so you simply say, 'A little fat guy with a red forked scar on his left cheek.' It's a ten to one that that's just how he has been described to Orrett. I don't look like Cudner, but I'm his size and build, and with a scar on my face Orrett will fall for me."

"What then?"

"There's no telling; but I ought to be able to learn a lot if I can get Orrett talking to me as Cudner. It's worth a try anyway."

"You can't get away with it—not in San Francisco. Cudner is too well-known."

"What difference does that make, Dick? Orrett is the only one I want to fool. If he takes me for Cudner, well and good. If he doesn't, still well and good. I won't force myself on him."

"How are you going to fake the scar?"

"Easy! We have pictures of Cudner, showing the scar, in the criminal gallery. I'll get some collodion—it's sold in drug stores under several trade names for putting on cuts and scratches—color it, and imitate Cudner's scar on my cheek. It dries with a shiny surface and, put on thick, will stand out enough to look like an old scar."

It was a little after eleven the following night when Dick telephoned me that Orrett was in Pigatti's place, on Pacific Street, and apparently settled there for some little while. My scar already painted on, I jumped into a taxi and within a few minutes was talking to Dick, around the corner from Pigatti's.

"He's sitting at the last table back on the left side. And he was alone when I came out. You can't miss him. He's the only egg in the joint with a clean collar."

"You better stick outside—half a block or so away—with the taxi," I told Dick. "Maybe brother Orrett and I will leave together and I'd just as leave have you standing by in case things break wrong."

Pigatti's place is a long, narrow, low-ceilinged cellar, always dim with smoke. Down the middle runs a narrow strip of bare floor for dancing. The rest of the floor is covered with closely packed tables, whose cloths are always soiled.

Most of the tables were occupied when I came in, and half a dozen couples were dancing. Few of the faces to be seen were strangers to the morning "line-up" at police headquarters.

Peering through the smoke, I saw Orrett at once, seated alone in a far corner, looking at the dancers with the set blank face of one who masks an all-seeing watchfulness. I walked down the other side of the room and crossed the strip of dance-floor directly under a light, so that the scar might be clearly visible to him. Then I selected a vacant table not far from his, and sat down facing him.

Ten minutes passed while he pretended an interest in the dancers and I affected a thoughtful stare at the dirty cloth on my table; but neither of us missed so much as a flicker of the other's lids.

His eyes—gray eyes that were pale without being shallow, with black needle-point pupils—met mine after a while in a cold, steady, inscrutable stare; and, very slowly, he got to his feet. One hand—his right—in a side pocket of his dark coat, he walked straight across to my table and sat down.

"Cudner?"

"Looking for me, I hear," I replied, trying to match the icy smoothness of his voice, as I was matching the steadiness of his gaze.

He had sat down with his left side turned slightly toward me, which put his right arm in not too cramped a position for straight shooting from the pocket that still held his hand.

"You were looking for me, too."

I didn't know what the correct answer to that would be, so I just grinned. But the grin didn't come from my heart. I had, I realized, made a mistake—one that might cost me something before we were done. This bird wasn't hunting for Cudner as a friend, as I had carelessly assumed, but was on the war path.

I saw those three dead men falling out of the closet in room 906!

My gun was inside the waist-band of my trousers, where I could get it quickly, but his was in his hand. So I was careful to keep my own hands motionless on the edge of the table, while I widened my grin.

His eyes were changing now, and the more I looked at them the less I liked them. The gray in them had darkened and grown duller, and the pupils were larger, and white crescents were showing beneath the gray. Twice before I had looked into eyes such as these—and I hadn't forgotten what they meant—the eyes of the congenital killer!

"Suppose you speak your piece," I suggested after a while.

But he wasn't to be beguiled into conversation. He shook his head a mere fraction of an inch and the corners of his compressed mouth dropped down a trifle. The white crescents of eyeballs were growing broader, pushing the gray circles up under the upper lids.

THE BODIES PILED UP

It was coming! And there was no use waiting for it!

I drove a foot at his shins under the table, and at the same time pushed the table into his lap and threw myself across it. The bullet from his gun went off to one side. Another bullet—not from his gun—thudded into the table that was upended between us.

I had him by the shoulders when the second shot from behind took him in the left arm, just below my hand. I let go then and fell away, rolling over against the wall and twisting around to face the direction from which the bullets were coming.

I twisted around just in time to see—jerking out of sight behind a corner of the passage that gave to a small dining-room—Guy Cudner's scarred face. And as it disappeared a bullet from Orrett's gun splattered the plaster from the wall where it had been.

I grinned at the thought of what must be going on in Orrett's head as he lay sprawled out on the floor confronted by two Cudners. But he took a shot at me just then and I stopped grinning. Luckily, he had to twist around to fire at me, putting his weight on his wounded arm, and the pain made him wince, spoiling his aim.

Before he had adjusted himself more comfortably I had scrambled on hands and knees to Pigatti's kitchen door—only a few feet away—and had myself safely tucked out of range around an angle in the wall; all but my eyes and the top of my head, which I risked so that I might see what went on.

Orrett was now ten or twelve feet from me, lying flat on the floor, facing Cudner, with a gun in his hand and another on the floor beside him.

Across the room, perhaps thirty feet away, Cudner was showing himself around his protecting corner at brief intervals to exchange shots with the man on the floor, occasionally sending one my way. We had the place to ourselves. There were four exits, and the rest of Pigatti's customers had used them all.

I had my gun out, but I was playing a waiting game. Cudner, I figured, had been tipped off to Orrett's search for him and had arrived on the scene with no mistaken idea of the other's attitude. Just what there was between them and what bearing it had on the Montgomery murders was a mystery to me, but I didn't try to solve it now.

They were firing in unison. Cudner would show around his corner, both men's weapons would spit, and he would duck out of sight again. Orrett was bleeding about the head now and one of his legs sprawled crookedly behind him. I couldn't determine whether Cudner had been hit or not.

Each had fired eight, or perhaps nine, shots when Cudner suddenly jumped out into full view, pumping the gun in his left hand as fast as its mechanism would go, the gun in his right hand hanging at his side. Orrett had changed guns, and was on his knees now, his fresh weapon keeping pace with his enemy's.

That couldn't last!

Cudner dropped his left-hand gun, and, as he raised the other, he sagged forward and went down on one knee. Orrett stopped firing abruptly and fell over on his back—spread out full-length. Cudner fired once more—wildly, into the ceiling—and pitched down on his face.

I sprang to Orrett's side and kicked both of his guns away. He was lying still but his eyes were open.

"Are you Cudner, or was he?"

"He."

"Good!" he said, and closed his eyes.

I crossed to where Cudner lay and turned him over on his back. His chest was literally shot to pieces.

His thick lips worked, and I put my ear down to them. "I get him?"

"Yes," I lied, "he's already cold."

His dying face twisted into a grin.

"Sorry . . . three in hotel . . . ," he gasped hoarsely. "Mistake . . . wrong room . . . got one . . . had to . . . other two . . . protect myself . . . I . . ." He shuddered and died.

A week later the hospital people let me talk to Orrett. I told him what Cudner had said before he died.

THE BODIES PILED UP

"That's the way I doped it out," Orrett said from out of the depths of the bandages in which he was swathed. "That's why I moved and changed my name the next day.

"I suppose you've got it nearly figured out by now," he said after a while.

"No," I confessed, "I haven't. I've an idea what it was all about but I could stand having a few details cleared up."

"I'm sorry I can't clear them up for you, but I've got to cover myself up. I'll tell you a story, though, and it may help you. Once upon a time there was a high-class crook—what the newspapers call a master-mind. Came a day when he found he had accumulated enough money to give up the game and settle down as an honest man.

"But he had two lieutenants—one in New York and one in San Francisco—and they were the only men in the world who knew he was a crook. And, besides that, he was afraid of both of them. So he thought he'd rest easier if they were out of the way. And it happened that neither of these lieutenants had ever seen the other.

"So this master-mind convinced each of them that the other was double-crossing him and would have to be bumped off for the safety of all concerned. And both of them fell for it. The New Yorker went to San Francisco to get the other, and the San Franciscan was told that the New Yorker would arrive on such-and-such a day and would stay at such-and-such a hotel.

"The master-mind figured that there was an even chance of both men passing out when they met—and he was nearly right at that. But he was sure that one would die, and then, even if the other missed hanging, there would only be one man left for him to dispose of later."

There weren't as many details in the story as I would have liked to have, but it explained a lot.

"How do you figure out Cudner's getting the wrong room?" I asked.

"That was funny! Maybe it happened like this: My room was

609 and the killing was done in 906. Suppose Cudner went to the hotel on the day he knew I was due and took a quick slant at the register. He wouldn't want to be seen looking at it if he could avoid it, so he didn't turn it around, but flashed a look at it as it lay—facing the desk.

"When you read numbers of three figures upside-down you have to transpose them in your head to get them straight. Like 123. You'd get that 321, and then turn them around in your head. That's what Cudner did with mine. He was keyed up, of course, thinking of the job ahead of him, and he overlooked the fact that 609 upside-down still reads 609 just the same. So he turned it around and made it 906—Develyn's room."

"That's how I doped it," I said, "and I reckon it's about right. And then he looked at the key-rack and saw that 906 wasn't there. So he thought he might just as well get his job done right then, when he could roam the hotel corridors without attracting attention. Of course, he may have gone up to the room before Ansley and Develyn came in and waited for them, but I doubt it.

"I think it more likely that he simply happened to arrive at the hotel a few minutes after they had come in. Ansley was probably alone in the room when Cudner opened the unlocked door and came in—Develyn being in the bathroom getting the glasses.

"Ansley was about your size and age, and close enough in appearance to fit a rough description of you. Cudner went for him, and then Develyn, hearing the scuffle, dropped the bottle and glasses, rushed out, and got his.

"Cudner, being the sort he was, would figure that two murders were not worse than one, and he wouldn't want to leave any witnesses around.

"And that is probably how Ingraham got into it. He was passing on his way from his room to the elevator and perhaps heard the racket and investigated. And Cudner put a gun in his face and made him stow the two bodies in the clothespress. And then he stuck his knife in Ingraham's back and slammed the door on him.

That's about the—"

An indignant nurse descended on me from behind and ordered me out of the room, accusing me of getting her patient excited.

Orrett stopped me as I turned to go.

"Keep your eye on the New York dispatches," he said, "and maybe you'll get the rest of the story. It's not over yet. Nobody has anything on me out here. That shooting in Pigatti's was self-defence so far as I'm concerned. And as soon as I'm on my feet again and can get back East there's going to be a master-mind holding a lot of lead. That's a promise!"

I believed him.

THE ROAD HOME

"You're a fool to pass it up! You'll get just as much credit and reward for taking back proof of my death as you will for taking me back. And I got papers and stuff buried back near the Yunnan border that you can have to back up your story; and you needn't be afraid that I'll ever show up to spoil your play."

The gaunt man in faded khaki frowned with patient annoyance and looked away from the bloodshot brown eyes in front of him, over the teak side of the jahaz to where the wrinkled snout of a muggar broke the surface of the river. When the small crocodile submerged again, Hagedom's gray eyes came back to the pleading ones before him, and he spoke wearily, as one who has been answering the same arguments again and again.

"I can't do it, Barnes. I left New York two years ago to get you, and for two years I've been in this damned country—here and in Yunnan—hunting you. I promised my people I'd stay until I found you, and I kept my word. Lord! man," with a touch of exasperation, "after all I've gone through you don't expect me to throw them down now—now that the job's as good as done!"

The dark man in the garb of a native smiled an oily, ingratiating smile and brushed away his captor's words with a wave of his hand.

"I ain't offering you a dinky coupla thousand dollars; I'm offer-

THE ROAD HOME

ing you your pick out of one of the richest gem beds in Asia—a bed that was hidden by the Mran-ma when the British jumped the country. Come back up there with me and I'll show you rubies and sapphires and topazes that'll knock your eye out. All I'm asking you is to go back up there with me and take a look at 'em. If you don't like 'em you'll still have me to take back to New York."

Hagedorn shook his head slowly.

"You're going back to New York with me. Maybe man-hunting isn't the nicest trade in the world but it's all the trade I've got, and this jewel bed of yours sounds phoney to me. I can't blame you for not wanting to go back—but just the same I'm taking you."

Barnes glared at the detective disgustedly.

"You're a fine chump! And it's costing me and you thousands of dollars! Hell!"

He spat over the side insultingly—native-like—and settled himself back on his corner of the split-bamboo mat

Hagedorn was looking past the lateen sail, down the river—the beginning of the route to New York—along which a miasmal breeze was carrying the fifty-foot boat with surprising speed. Four more days and they would be aboard a steamer for Rangoon; then another steamer to Calcutta, and in the end, one to New York—home, after two years!

Two years through unknown country, pursuing what until the very day of the capture had never been more than a vague shadow. Through Yunnan and Burma, combing wilderness with microscopic thoroughness—a game of hide-and-seek up the rivers, over the hills and through the jungles—sometimes a year, sometimes two months and then six behind his quarry. And now successfully home! Betty would be fifteen—quite a lady.

Barnes edged forward and resumed his pleading, with a whine creeping into his voice.

"Say, Hagedorn, why don't you listen to reason? There ain't no sense in us losing all that money just for something that happened over two years ago. I didn't mean to kill that guy, anyway.

You know how it is; I was a kid and wild and foolish—but I wasn't mean—and I got in with a bunch. Why, I thought of that hold-up as a lark when we planned it! And then that messenger yelled and I guess I was excited, and my gun went off the first thing I knew. I didn't go to kill him; and it won't do him no good to take me back and hang me for it. The express company didn't lose no money. What do they want to hound me like this for? I been trying to live it down."

The gaunt detective answered quietly enough but what kindness there had been in his dry voice before was gone now.

"I know—the old story! And the bruises on the Burmese woman you were living with sure show that there's nothing mean about you. Cut it, Barnes, and make up your mind to face it—you and I are going back to New York."

"The hell we are!"

Barnes got slowly to his feet and backed away a step.

"I'd just as leave—"

Hagedorn's automatic came out a split second too late; his prisoner was over the side and swimming toward the bank. The detective caught up his rifle from the deck behind him and sprang to the rail. Barnes' head showed for a moment and then went down again, to appear again twenty feet nearer shore. Upstream the man in the boat saw the blunt, wrinkled noses of three muggars, moving toward the shore at a tangent that would intercept the fugitive. He leaned against the teak rail and summed up the situation.

"Looks like I'm not going to take him back alive after all—but my job's done. I can shoot him when he shows again, or I can let him alone and the muggars will get him."

Then the sudden but logical instinct to side with the member of his own species against enemies from another wiped out all other considerations, and sent his rifle to his shoulder to throw a shower of bullets into the muggars.

Barnes clambered up the bank of the river, waved his hand over his head without looking back, and plunged into the jungle.

THE ROAD HOME

Hagedorn turned to the bearded owner of the jahaz, who had come to his side, and addressed him in his broke Burmese.

"Put me ashore—yu nga apau mye—and wait—thaing—until I bring him back—thu yughe."

The captain wagged his black beard protestingly.

"Mahok! In the jungle here, sahib, a man is as a lei Twenty men might find him in a week, or a month, it may take five years. I cannot wait that long."

The gaunt white man gnawed at his lower lip and looked down the river—the road to New York.

"Two years," he said aloud to himself, "it took to find him when he didn't know I was hunting for him. Now—Oh, hell! It may take five years. I wonder about them jewels of his."

He turned to the boatman.

"I go after him. You wait three hours," pointing over head, "until noon—ne apomha. If I am not back then do not wait—malotu thaing, thwa. Thi?"

The captain nodded.

"Hokhe!"

For five hours the captain kept the jahaz at anchor, and then, when the shadows of the trees on the west bank were creeping out into the river, he ordered the latten sail hoisted, and the teak craft vanished around a bend in the river.

RUFFIAN'S WIFE

Margaret Tharp habitually passed from slumber to clear-eyed liveliness without intermediate languor. This morning nothing was unusual in her awakening save the absence of the eight o'clock San Francisco boat's sad hooting. Across the room the clock's hands pointed like one long hand to a few minutes past seven. Margaret rolled over beneath the covers, putting her back to the sunpainted west wall, and closed her eyes again.

But drowsiness would not come. She was definitely awake to the morning excitement of the next-door chickens, the hum of an automobile going toward the ferry, the unfamiliar fragrance of magnolia in the breeze tickling her cheek with loose hair-ends. She got up, slid feet into soft slippers, shoulders into bathrobe, and went downstairs to start toast and coffee before dressing.

A fat man in black was on the point of leaving the kitchen.

Margaret cried out, catching the robe to her throat with both hands.

Red and crystal glinted on the hand with which the fat man took off his black derby. Holding the doorknob, he turned to face Margaret. He turned slowly, with the smooth precision of a globe revolving on a fixed axis, and he managed his head with care, as if it balanced an invisible burden.

"You—are—Mrs.—Tharp."

RUFFIAN'S WIFE

Sighing puffs of breath spaced his words, cushioned them, gave them the semblance of gems nested separately in raw cotton. He was a man past forty, with opaquely glistening eyes whose blackness was repeated with variety of finish in mustache and hair, freshly ironed suit, and enamelled shoes. The dark skin of his face—ball-round over a tight stiff collar—was peculiarly coarse, firm-grained, as if it had been baked. Against this background his tie was half a foot of scarlet flame.

"Your—husband—is—not—home."

It was no more a question than his naming her had been, but he paused expectantly. Margaret, standing where she had stopped in the passageway between stairs and kitchen, was still too startled not to say "No."

"You're—expecting—him."

There was nothing immediately threatening in the attitude of this man who should not have been in her kitchen but who seemed nowise disconcerted by her finding him there. Margaret's words came almost easily. "Not just—I expect him, yes, but I don't know exactly when he will come."

Black hat and black shoulders, moving together, achieved every appearance of a bow without disturbing round head's poise.

"You—will—so—kindly—tell—him—when—he—comes—I—am—waiting. I—await—him—at—the—hotel." The spacing puffs prolonged his sentences interminably, made of his phrases thin-spread word-groups whose meanings were elusive. "You—will—tell—him—Leonidas—Doucas—is—waiting. He—will—know. We—are—friends—very—good—friends. You—will—not—forget—the—name—Leonidas—Doucas."

"Certainly I shall tell him. But I really do not know when he will come."

The man who called himself Leonidas Doucas nodded frugally beneath the unseen something his head supported. Darkness of mustache and skin exaggerated whiteness of teeth. His smile went away as stiffly as it came, with as little elasticity.

"You—may—expect—him. He—comes—now."

He revolved slowly away from her and went out of the kitchen, shutting the door behind him.

Margaret ran tiptoe across the room to twist the key in the door. The lock's inner mechanism rattled loosely, the bolt would not click home. The warmly sweet fragrance of magnolia enveloped her. She gave up the struggle with the broken lock and dropped down on a chair beside the door. Points of dampness were on her back. Under gown and robe her legs were cold. Doucas, not the breeze, had brought the breath of magnolia to her in bed. His unguessed presence in the bedroom had wakened her. He had been up there looking with his surface-shining eyes for Guy. If Guy had been home, asleep beside her? A picture came of Doucas bending over the bed, his head still stiffly upright, a bright blade in his jeweled fist. She shivered.

Then she laughed. Little silly! How conceivably could Guy—her hard-bodied, hard-nerved Guy, to whom violence was no more than addition to a bookkeeper—be harmed by a perfumed, asthmatic fat man? Whether Guy slept or Guy woke, if Doucas came as an enemy, then so much the worse for Doucas—a fleshbound house dog growling at her red wolf of a husband!

She jumped up from her chair and began to bustle with toaster and coffeepot. Leonidas Doucas was put out of her mind by the news he had brought. Guy was coming home. The fat man in black had said so, speaking with assurance. Guy was coming home to fill the house with boisterous laughter, shouted blasphemies, tales of lawlessness in strangely named places; with the odors of tobacco and liquor; with odds and ends of rover's equipment that never could be confined to closet or room, but overflowed to litter the house from roof to cellar. Cartridges would roll underfoot; boots and belts would turn up in unexpected places; cigars, cigar ends, cigar ashes would be everywhere; empty bottles, likely as not, would get to the front porch to scandalize the neighbors.

Guy was coming home and there were so many things to be done in so small a house; windows and pictures and woodwork to be washed, furniture and floors to be polished, curtains to be hung, rugs to be cleaned. If only he did not come for two days, or even three.

The rubber gloves she had put aside as nuisances—had she put them in the hall closet or upstairs? She must find them. So much scrubbing to do, and her hands must not be rough for Guy. She frowned at the small hand raising toast to her mouth, accused it of roughness. She would have to get another bottle of lotion. If there was time after she finished her work, she might run over to the city for an afternoon. But first the house must be made bright and tidy, so Guy could tweak a stiff curtain and laugh, "A damned dainty nest for a bull like me to be stabled in!"

And perhaps tell of the month he had shared a Rat Island hut with two vermin-live Siwashes, sleeping three abed because their blankets were too few for division.

The two days Margaret had desired went by without Guy, another, others. Her habit of sleeping until the eight o'clock boat whistled up the hill was broken. She was dressed and moving around the house by seven, six, five-thirty one morning, repolishing already glowing fixtures, laundering some thing slightly soiled by yesterday's use, fussing through her rooms ceaselessly, meticulously, happily.

Whenever she passed the hotel on her way to the stores in lower Water Street she saw Doucas. Usually he was in the glass-fronted lobby, upright in the largest chair, facing the street, round, black-clothed, motionless.

Once he came out of the hotel as she passed.

He looked neither at her nor away from her, neither claimed recognition nor avoided it. Margaret smiled pleasantly, nodded pleasantly, and went on down the street away from his hat raised in a jewelled hand, her small head high. The fragrance of magnolia, going a dozen steps with her, deepened her feeling of somewhat amused, though lenient, graciousness.

The same high-held kindliness went with her through the streets, into the shops, to call on Dora Milner, to her own street door to welcome Agnes Peppier and Helen Chase. She made proud sentences for herself while she spoke other sentences, or listened to them. *Guy moves among continents as easily as Tom Milner from drug counter to soda fountain,* she thought while Dora talked of guest-room linen. *He carries his life as carelessly in his hands as Ned Peppier his briefcase,* she boasted to the tea she poured for Agnes and Helen, *and sells his daring as Paul Chase sells high-grade corner lots.*

These people, friends and neighbors, talked among themselves of "poor Margaret, poor little Mrs. Tharp," whose husband was notoriously a ruffian, always off some distant where, up to any imaginable sort of scoundrelism. They pitied her, or pretended to pity her, these owners of docile pets, because her man was a ranging beast who could not be penned, because he did not wear the dull uniform of respectability, did not walk along smooth, safe ways. Poor little Mrs. Tharp! She put her cup to her mouth to check the giggle that threatened to break in rudely on Helen's interpretation of a disputed bridge point.

"It really doesn't matter, so long as everyone knows what rule is to be followed before the game starts," she said into a pause that asked words of her, and went on with her secret thinking.

What, she wondered with smug assurance that it never could have happened to her, would it be like to have for husband a tame, housebroken male who came regularly to meals and bed, whose wildest flying could attain no giddier height than an occasional game of cards, a suburbanite's holiday in San Francisco, or, at very most, a dreary adventure with some stray stenographer, manicurist, milliner?

Late on the sixth day that Margaret expected him, Guy came.

Preparing her evening meal in the kitchen, she heard the creaking halt of an automobile in front of the house. She ran to the door and peeped through the curtained glass. Guy stood on the sidewalk, his broad back to her, taking leather traveling bags out of the car that had brought him up from the ferry. She smoothed her hair with cold hands, smoothed her apron, and opened the door.

RUFFIAN'S WIFE

Guy turned from the machine, a bag in each hand, one under his arm. He grinned through a two-day stubble of florid beard and waved a bag as you would wave a handkerchief.

A torn cap was crooked on his tangled red hair, his chest bulged a corduroy jacket of dilapidated age, grimy khaki trousers were tight around knotted thighs and calves, once-white canvas shoes tried to enclose feet meant for larger shoes, and failed to the extent of a brown-stockinged big toe. A ruddy viking in beggar's misfits. There would be other clothes in his bags. Rags were his homecoming affectation, a laborer-home-from-the-fields gesture. He strode up the walk, careless bags brushing geraniums and nasturtiums back.

Margaret's throat had some swollen thing in it. Fog blurred everything but the charging red face. An unvoiced whimper shook her breast. She wanted to run to him as to a lover. She wanted to run from him as from a ravisher. She stood very still in her doorway, smiling demurely with dry, hot mouth.

His feet padded on steps, on porch. Bags fell away from him. Thick arms reached for her.

The odors of alcohol, sweat, brine, tobacco cut her nostrils. Bearded flesh scrubbed her cheek. She lost foothold, breath, was folded into him, crushed, bruised, bludgeoned by hard lips. Eyes clenched against the pain in them, she clung hard to him who alone was firmly planted in a whirling universe. Foul endearments, profane love names rumbled in her ear. Another sound was even nearer—a throaty cooing. She was laughing.

Guy was home.

The Evening was old before Margaret remembered Leonidas Doucas.

She was sitting on her husband's knees, leaning forward to look at the trinkets, Ceylonese spoils, heaped on the table before her. Cockleshell earrings half hid her ears, heavy gold incongruities above the starched primness of her housedress.

Guy—bathed, shaved, and all in fresh white—tugged beneath his shirt with his one free hand. A moneybelt came sluggishly away from his body, thudded on the table, and lay there thick and apathetic as an overfed snake.

Guy's freckled fingers worked at the belt's pockets. Green banknotes slid out, coins rolled out to be bogged by the paper, green notes rustled out to bury the coins.

"Oh, Guy!" she gasped. "All that?"

He chuckled, jiggling her on his knees, and fluttered the green notes up from the table like a child playing with fallen leaves.

"All that. And every one of 'em cost a pint of somebody's pink blood. Maybe they look cool and green to you, but I'm telling you every last one of 'em is as hot a red as the streets of Colombo, if you could only see it."

She refused to shudder under the laugh in his red-veined eyes, laughed, and stretched a tentative finger to the nearest note.

"How much is there, Guy?"

"I don't know. I took 'em moving," he boasted. "No time for bookkeeping. It was bing, bang, get clear and step in again. We dyed the Yoda-ela red that one night. Mud under, darkness over, rain everywhere, with a brown devil for every raindrop. A pith helmet hunting for us with a flashlight that never found anything but a stiff-necked Buddha up on a rock before we put it out of business."

The "stiff-necked Buddha" brought Doucas's face to Margaret.

"Oh! There was a man here to see you last week. He's waiting to see you at the hotel. His name is Doucas, a very stout man with—"

"The Greek!"

Guy Tharp put his wife off his knees. He put her off neither hastily nor roughly, but with that deliberate withdrawal of attention which is the toy's lot when serious work is at hand.

"What else did he have to say?"

"That was all, except that he was a friend of yours. It was early in the morning, and I found him in the kitchen, and I know he had been upstairs. Who is he, Guy?"

"A fellow," her husband said vaguely around the knuckle he bit. He seemed to attach no importance to, not even be interested by, the news that Doucas had come furtively into his house. "Seen him since then?"

"Not to talk to, but I see him every time I pass the hotel."

Guy took the knuckle from between his teeth, rubbed his chin with a thumb, hunched his thick shoulders, let them fall lax, and reached for Margaret. Slumped comfortably in his chair, holding her tight to him with hard arms, he fell to laughing, teasing, boasting again, his voice a mellow, deep-bodied rumble under her head. But his eyes did not pale to their normal sapphire. Behind jest and chuckle an aloof thoughtfulness seemed to stand.

Asleep that night, he slept with the soundness of child or animal, but she knew he had been long going to sleep.

Just before daylight she crept out of bed and carried the money into another room to count it. Twelve thousand dollars were there.

In the morning Guy was merry, full of laughter and words that had no alien seriousness behind them. He had stories to tell of a brawl in a Madras street, or another in a gaming house in Saigon; of a Finn, met in the Queen's Hotel in Kandy, who was having a giant raft towed to a spot in mid-Pacific where he thought he could live with least annoyance from the noise of the earth's spinning.

Guy talked, laughed, and ate breakfast with the heartiness of one who does not ordinarily know when he will eat again. The meal done, he lit a black cigar and stood up. "Reckon I'll trot down the hill for a visit with your friend Leonidas, and see what's on his mind."

When he mauled her to his chest to kiss her, she felt the bulk of a revolver bolstered under his coat. She went to a front window to watch him go away from the house. He swaggered carelessly down the hill, shoulders swinging, whistling, "Bang Away, My Lulu."

Back in the kitchen, Margaret made a great to-do with the breakfast dishes, setting about cleaning them as if it were a difficult task attempted for the first time. Water splashed on her apron, twice the soap slipped from her hand to the floor, a cup's handle came away in her fingers. Then dishwashing became accustomed work, no longer an occupation to banish unwanted thoughts. The thoughts came, of Guy's uneasiness last night, of his laughter that had lacked honesty.

She fashioned a song that compared a fleshbound house dog with a red wolf; a man to whom violence was no more than addition to a bookkeeper, with a perfumed, asthmatic fat man. Repetition gave the unspoken chant rhythm, rhythm soothed her, took her mind from what might be happening in the hotel down the hill.

She had finished the dishes and was scouring the sink when Guy came back. She looked a brief smile up at him and bent her face to her work again, to hide the questions she knew her eyes held.

He stood in the doorway watching her.

"Changed my mind," he said presently. "I'll let him write his own ticket. If he wants to see me, he knows the way. It's up to him."

He moved away from the door. She heard him going upstairs.

Her hands rested on idle palms in the sink. The white porcelain of the sink was white ice. Its chill went through her arms into her body.

An hour later, when Margaret went upstairs, Guy was sitting on the side of the bed running a cloth through the barrel of his black revolver. She fidgeted around the room, pretending to be busy with this and that, hoping he would answer the questions she could not ask. But he talked of unrelated things. He cleaned and greased the revolver with the slow, fondling thoroughness of a chronic whittler sharpening his knife, and talked of matters that had no bearing on Leonidas Doucas.

The rest of the day he spent indoors, smoking and drinking the afternoon through in the living-room. When he leaned back, the revolver made a lump under his left armpit. He was merry and profane and boastful. For the first time Margaret saw his thirty-five years in his eyes, and in the individual clearness of each thick facial muscle.

After dinner they sat in the dining-room with no illumination but the light of fading day. When that was gone neither of them got up to press the electric button beside the portiered hall door. He was as garrulous as ever. She found speech difficult, but he did not seem to notice that. She was never especially articulate with him.

They were sitting in complete darkness when the doorbell rang.

"If that's Doucas, show him in," Guy said. "And then you'd better get upstairs out of the way."

Margaret turned on the lights before she left the room, and looked back at her husband. He was putting down the cold cigar stub he had been chewing. He grinned mockingly at her.

"And if you hear a racket," he suggested, "you'd better stick your head under the covers and think up the best way to get blood out of rugs."

She held herself very erect going to the door and opening it.

Doucas's round black hat came off to move with his shoulders in a counterfeit bow that swept the odor of magnolia to her.

"Your—husband—is—in."

"Yes." Her chin was uptilted so she could seem to smile on him, though he stood a head taller than she, and she tried to make her smile very sweetly gentle. "Come in. He is expecting you."

Guy, sitting where she had left him, fresh cigar alight, did not get up to greet Doucas. He took the cigar from his mouth and let smoke leak between his teeth to garnish the good-natured insolence of his smile.

"Welcome to our side of the world," he said.

The Greek said nothing, standing just inside the portiere.

Margaret left them thus, going through the room and up the back stairs. Her husband's voice came up the steps behind her in a rumble of which she could pick no words. If Doucas spoke she did not hear him.

She stood in her dark bedroom, clutching the foot of the bed with both hands, the trembling of her body making the bed tremble. Out of the night questions came to torment her, shadowy questions, tangling, knotting, raveling in too swiftly shifting a profusion for any to be clearly seen, but all having something to do with a pride that in eight years had become a very dear thing.

They had to do with a pride in a man's courage and hardihood, courage and hardihood that could make of thefts, of murder, of crimes dimly guessed, wrongs no more reprehensible than a boy's apple-stealing. They had to do with the existence or nonexistence of this gilding courage, without which a rover might be no more than a shoplifter on a geographically larger scale, a sneak thief who crept into strangers' lands instead of houses, a furtive, skulking figure with an aptitude for glamorous autobiography. Then pride would be silliness.

Out of the floor came a murmur, all that distance and intervening carpentry left of words that were being said down in her tan-papered dining-room. The murmur drew her toward the dining-room, drew her physically, as the questions drove her.

She left her slippers on the bedroom floor. Very softly, stockinged feet carried her down the dark front stairs, tread by tread. Skirts held high and tight against rustling, she crept down the black stairs toward the room where two men—equally strangers for the time—sat trafficking.

Beneath the portiere, and from either side, yellow light came to lay a pale, crooked "U" on the hall floor. Guy's voice came through.

"... not there. We turned the island upside down from Dambulla all the way to the Kala-wewa, and got nothing. I told you it was a bust. Catch those limeys leaving that much sugar lay round under their noses!"

"Dahl—said—it—was—there."

Doucas's voice was soft with the infinitely patient softness of one whose patience is nearly at end.

Creeping to the doorway, Margaret peeped around the curtain. The two men and the table between them came into the opening. Doucas's over-coated shoulder was to her. He sat straight up, hands inert on fat thighs, cocked profile inert. Guy's white-sleeved forearms were on the table. He leaned over them, veins showing in forehead and throat, smaller and more vivid around the blue-black of his eyes. The glass in front of him was empty; the one before Doucas still brimmed with dark liquor.

"I don't give a damn what Dahl says." Guy's voice was blunt, but somehow missed finality. "I'm telling you the stuff wasn't there."

Doucas smiled. His lips bared white teeth and covered them again in a cumbersome grimace that held as little of humor as of spontaneity.

"But—you—came—from—Ceylon—no—poorer—than—you—went."

Guy's tongue-tip showed flat between his lips, vanished. He looked at his freckled hands on the table. He looked up at Doucas.

"I didn't. I brought fifteen thousand hard roundmen away with me, if it's any of your business," he said, and then robbed his statement of sincerity, made a weak blustering of it, with an explanation. "I did a thing a man needed done. It had nothing to do with our game. It was after that blew up."

"Yes. I—choose—to—doubt—it."

Soft, sigh-cushioned, the words had a concussive violence no shouted *You lie!* could have matched.

Guy's shoulders bunched up, teeth clicked, blood pulsed in the veins that welted his face. His eyes flared purplishly at the dark baked mask before him, flared until the held breath in Margaret's chest became an agony.

The flare went down in the purple eyes. The eyes went down. Guy scowled at his hands, at his knuckles that were round white knobs.

"Suit yourself, brother," he said, not distinctly.

Margaret swayed behind her shielding curtain, reason barely checking the instinctive hand with which she clutched for steadiness at it. Her body was a cold damp shell around a vacancy that had been until today—until, despite awakening doubts, this very instant—eight years' accumulation of pride. Tears wet her face, tears for the high-held pride that was now a ridiculous thing. She saw herself as a child going among adults, flaunting a Manila-paper bandeau, crying shrilly, "See my gold crown!"

"We—waste—time. Dahl—said—half—a—million—rupees. Doubtless—it—was—less. But—most—surely—half—that—amount—would—be—there." The pad of breath before and after each word became by never-varying repetition an altogether unnatural thing. Each word lost association with each other word, became a threatening symbol hung up in the room. "Not—regarding—odd—amounts—my—portion—would—be—say—seventy-five—thousand—dollars. I—will—take—that."

Guy did not look up from his hard white knuckles. His voice was sullen.

"Where do you expect to find it?"

The Greek's shoulders moved the least fraction of an inch. Because he had for so long not moved at all that slight motion became a pronounced shrug.

"You—will—give—it—to—me. You—would—not—have—a—word—dropped—to—the—British—consul—of—one—who—was—Tom—Berkey—in—Cairo—not—many—yesterdays—back."

Guy's chair spun back from him. He lunged across the table.

Margaret clapped a palm to her mouth to stop the cry her throat had no strength to voice.

The Greek's right hand danced jewels in Guy's face. The Greek's left hand materialized a compact pistol out of nothing.

"Sit—down—my—friend."

Hanging over the table, Guy seemed to become abruptly smaller, as oncoming bodies do when stopped. For a moment he hung there. Then he grunted, regained his balance, picked up his chair, and sat down. His chest swelled and shrank slowly.

"Listen, Doucas," he said with great earnestness, "you're all wrong. I've got maybe ten thousand dollars left. I got it myself, but if you think you've got a kick coming, I'll do what's right. You can have half of the ten thousand."

Margaret's tears were gone. Pity for self had turned to hatred of the two men who sat in her dining-room making a foolish thing of her pride. She still trembled, but with anger now, and contempt for her boasted red wolf of a husband, trying to buy off the fat man who threatened him. The contempt she felt for her husband was great enough to include Doucas. She had a desire to step through the doorway, to show them that contempt. But nothing came of the impulse. She would not have known what to do, what to say to them. She was not of their world.

Only her pride had been in her husband's place in that world.

"Five—thousand—dollars—is—nothing. Twenty—thousand—rupees—I—spent—preparing—Ceylon—for—you."

Margaret's helplessness turned contempt in on herself. The very bitterness of that contempt drove her to attempt to justify, recapture some fragment of, her pride in Guy. After all, what knowledge had she of his world? What standards had she with which to compute its values? Could any man win every encounter? What else could Guy do under Doucas's pistol?

The futility of the self-posed questions angered her. The plain truth was she had never seen Guy as a man, but always as a half-fabulous being. The weakness of any defence she could contrive for him lay in his needing a defence. Not to be ashamed of him was a sorry substitute for her exultance in him. To convince herself that he was not a coward still would leave vacant the place lately occupied by her joy in his daring.

Beyond the curtain the two men bargained on across the table.

"... every—cent. Men—do—not—profitably—betray—me."

She glared through the gap between portiere and frame, at fat Doucas with his pistol level on tabletop, at red Guy pretending to ignore the pistol. Rage filled her weaponless, impotent rage. Or was it weaponless? The light-button was beside the door. Doucas and Guy were occupied with one another—

Her hand moved before the motive impulse was full-formed inside her. The situation was intolerable; darkness would change the situation, however slightly, therefore darkness was desirable. Her hand moved between portiere and doorframe, bent to the side as if gifted with sight, drove her finger into the button.

Roaring blackness was streaked by a thin bronze flame. Guy bellowed out, an animal noise without meaning. A chair slammed to the floor. Feet shuffled, stamped, scuffled. Grunts punctuated snarls.

Concealed by night, the two men and what they did became for the first time real to Margaret, physically actual. They were no longer figures whose substance was in what they did to her pride. One was her husband, a man who could be maimed, killed. Doucas was a man who could be killed. They could die, either or both, because of a woman's vanity. A woman, she had flung them toward death rather than confess she could be less than a giant's wife.

Sobbing, she pushed past the portiere and with both hands hunted for the switch that had come so readily to her finger a moment ago. Her hands fumbled across a wall that shuddered when bodies crashed into it. Behind her, fleshed bone smacked on fleshed bone. Feet shuffled in time with hoarse breathing. Guy cursed. Her fingers fluttered back and forth, to and fro across wallpaper that was unbroken by electric fixture.

The scuffling of feet stopped. Guy's cursing stopped in mid-syllable. A purring gurgle had come into the room, swallowing every other sound, giving density, smothering weight to the darkness, driving Margaret's frenzied fingers faster across the wall.

Her right hand found the doorframe. She held it there, pressed it there until the edge of the wood cut into her hand, holding it from frantic search while she made herself form a picture of the wall. The light-switch was a little below her shoulder, she decided.

"Just below my shoulder," she whispered harshly, trying to make herself hear the words above the purring gurgle. Her shoulder against the frame, she flattened both hands on the wall, moved them across it.

The purring gurgle died, leaving a more oppressive silence, the silence of wide emptiness.

Cold metal came under sliding palm. A finger found the button, fumbled too eagerly atop it, slid off. She clutched at the button with both hands. Light came. She whirled her back to the wall.

Across the room Guy straddled Doucas, holding his head up from the floor with thick hands that hid the Greek's white collar. Doucas's tongue was a bluish pendant from a bluish mouth. His eyes stood out, dull. The end of a red silk garter hung from one trouser-leg, across his shoe.

Guy turned his head toward Margaret, blinking in the light.

"Good girl," he commended her. "This Greek was no baby to jump at in daylight."

One side of Guy's face was wet red under a red furrow. She sought escape in his wound from the implication of *was*.

"You're hurt!"

He took his hands away from the Greek's neck and rubbed one of them across the cheek. It came away dyed red. Doucas's head hit the floor hollowly and did not quiver.

"Only nicked me," Guy said. "I need it to show self-defence."

The reiterated implication drove Margaret's gaze to the man on the floor, and quickly away.

"He is—?"

"Deader than hell," Guy assured her.

His voice was light, tinged faintly with satisfaction.

She stared at him in horror, her back pressed against the wall, sick with her own part in this death, sick with Guy's callous brutality of voice and mien. Guy did not see these things. He was looking thoughtfully at the dead man.

"I told you I'd give him a bellyful if he wanted it," he boasted. "I told him the same thing five years ago, in Malta."

He stirred the dead Doucas gently with one foot. Margaret cringed against the wall, feeling as if she were going to vomit.

Guy's foot nudged the dead man slowly, reflectively. Guy's eyes were dull with distant things, things that might have happened five years ago in a place that to her was only a name on a map, vaguely associated with Crusades and kittens. Blood trickled down his cheek, hung momentarily in fattening drops, dripped down on the dead man's coat.

The poking foot stopped its ghoulish play. Guy's eyes grew wide and bright, his face lean with eagerness. He snapped fist into palm and jerked around to Margaret.

"By God! This fellow has got a pearl concession down in La Paz! If I can get down there ahead of the news of the killing, I can— Why, what's the matter?"

He stared at her, puzzlement wiping animation from his face.

Margaret's gaze faltered away from him. She looked at the overturned table, across the room, at the floor. She could not hold up her eyes for him to see what was in them. If understanding had come to him at once—but she could not stand there and look at him and wait for the thing in her eyes to burn into his consciousness.

She tried to keep that thing out of her voice.

"I'll bandage your cheek before we phone the police," she said.

THE SECOND-STORY ANGEL

Carter Brigham—Carter Webright Brigham in the tables of contents of various popular magazines—woke with a start, passing from unconsciousness into full awareness too suddenly to doubt that his sleep had been disturbed by something external.

The moon was not up and his apartment was on the opposite side of the building from the streetlights; the blackness about him was complete—he could not see so far as the foot of his bed.

Holding his breath, not moving after that first awakening start, he lay with straining eyes and ears. Almost at once a sound—perhaps a repetition of the one that had aroused him—came from the adjoining room: the furtive shuffling of feet across the wooden floor. A moment of silence, and a chair grated on the floor, as if dislodged by a careless shin. Then silence again, and a faint rustling as of a body scraping against the rough paper of the wall.

Now Carter Brigham was neither a hero nor a coward, and he was not armed. There was nothing in his rooms more deadly than a pair of candlesticks, and they—not despicable weapons in an emergency—were on the far side of the room from which the sounds came.

If he had been awakened to hear very faint and not often repeated noises in the other room—such rustlings as even the most adept burglar might not avoid—the probabilities are that Carter would have been content to remain in his bed and try to frighten the burglar away by yelling at him. He would not have disregarded the fact that in an encounter at close quarters under these conditions every advantage would lie on the side of the prowler.

But this particular prowler had made quite a lot of noise, had even stumbled against a chair, had shown himself a poor hand at stealthiness. That an inexpert burglar might easily be as dangerous as an adept did not occur to the man in the bed.

Perhaps it was that in the many crook stories he had written, deadliness had always been wedded to skill and the bunglers had always been comparatively harmless and easily overcome, and that he had come to accept this theory as a truth. After all, if a man says a thing often enough, he is very likely to acquire some sort of faith in it sooner or later.

Anyhow, Carter Brigham slid his not unmuscular body gently out from between the sheets and crept on silent bare feet toward the open doorway of the room from which the sounds had come. He passed from his bed to a position inside the next room, his back against the wall beside the door during an interlude of silence on the intruder's part.

The room in which Carter now stood was every bit as black as the one he had left; so he stood motionless, waiting for the prowler to betray his position.

His patience was not taxed. Very soon the burglar moved again, audibly; and then against the rectangle of a window—scarcely lighter than the rest of the room—Carter discerned a man-shaped shadow just a shade darker coming toward him. The shadow passed the window and was lost in the enveloping darkness.

Carter, his body tensed, did not move until he thought the burglar had had time to reach a spot where no furniture intervened. Then, with clutching hands thrown out on wide-spread arms, Carter hurled himself forward.

His shoulder struck the intruder and they both crashed to the floor. A forearm came up across Carter's throat, pressing into it. He tore it away and felt a blow on his cheek. He wound one arm around the burglar's body, and with the other fist struck back. They rolled over and over across the floor until they were stopped by the legs of a massive table, the burglar uppermost.

With savage exultance in his own strength, which the struggle thus far had shown to be easily superior to the other's, Carter twisted his body, smashing his adversary into the heavy table. Then he drove a fist into the body he had just shaken off and scrambled to his knees, feeling for a grip on the burglar's throat. When he had secured it he found that the prowler was lying motionless, unresisting. Laughing triumphantly, Carter got to his feet and switched on the lights.

The girl on the floor did not move.

Half lying, half hunched against the table where he had hurled her, she was inanimate. A still, twisted figure in an austerely tailored black suit—one sleeve of which had been torn from the shoulder—with an unended confusion of short chestnut hair above a face that was linen-white except where blows had reddened it. Her eyes were closed. One arm was outflung across the floor, the other lay limply at her side; one silken leg was extended, the other folded under her.

Into a corner of the room her hat, a small black toque, had rolled; not far from the hat lay a very small pinch-bar, the jimmy with which she had forced an entrance.

The window over the fire escape—always locked at night—was wide-open. Its catch hung crookedly.

Mechanically, methodically—because he had been until recently a reporter on a morning paper, and the lessons of years are not unlearned in a few weeks—Carter's eyes picked up these details and communicated them to his brain while he strove to conquer his bewilderment.

After a while his wits resumed their functions and he went over to kneel beside the girl. Her pulse was regular, but she gave no other indications of life. He lifted her from the floor and carried her to the leather couch on the other side of the room. Then he brought cold water from the bathroom and brandy from the bookcase. Generous applications of the former to her temples and face and of the latter between her lips finally brought a tremor to her mouth and a quiver to her eyelids.

Presently she opened her eyes, looked confusedly around the room, and endeavored to sit up. He pressed her head gently down on the couch.

"Lie still a moment longer—until you feel all right."

She seemed to see him then for the first time, and to remember where she was. She shook her head clear of his restraining hand and sat up, swinging her feet down to the floor.

"So I lose again," she said, with an attempt at nonchalance that was only faintly tinged with bitterness, her eyes meeting his.

They were green eyes and very long, and they illuminated her face which, without their soft light, had seemed of too sullen a cast for beauty, despite the smooth regularity of the features.

Carter's glance dropped to her discolored cheek, where his knuckles had left livid marks.

"I'm sorry I struck you," he apologized. "In the dark I naturally thought you were a man. I wouldn't have—"

"Forget it," she commanded coolly. "It's all in the game."

"But I—"

"Aw, stop it!" Impatiently. "It doesn't amount to anything. I'm all right."

"I'm glad of that."

His bare toes came into the range of his vision, and he went into his bedroom for slippers and a robe. The girl watched him silently when he returned to her, her face calmly defiant.

"Now," he suggested, drawing up a chair, "suppose you tell me all about it."

She laughed briefly. "It's a long story, and the bulls ought to be here any minute now. There wouldn't be time to tell it."

THE SECOND-STORY ANGEL

"The police?"

"Uh-huh."

"But I didn't send for them! Why should I?"

"God knows!" She looked around the room and then abruptly straight into his eyes. "If you think I'm going to buy my liberty, brother"—her voice was icy insolent—"you're way off!"

He denied the thought. Then: "Suppose you tell me about it."

"All primed to listen to a sob story?" she mocked. "Well, here goes: I got some bad breaks on the last couple of jobs I pulled and had to lay low—so low that I didn't even get anything to eat for a day or two. I figured I'd have to pull another job for getaway money—so I could blow town for a while. And this was it! I was sort of giddy from not eating and I made too much noise; but even at that"—with a scornful laugh—"you'd never have nailed me if I'd had a gun on me!"

Carter was on his feet.

"There's food of some sort in the icebox. We'll eat before we do any more talking."

A grunt came from the open window by which the girl had entered. Both of them wheeled toward it. Framed in it was a burly, red-faced man who wore a shiny blue serge suit and a black derby hat. He threw one thick leg over the sill and came into the room with heavy, bearlike agility.

"Well, well"—the words came complacently from his thick-lipped mouth, under a close-clipped gray mustache—"if it ain't my old friend Angel Grace!"

"Cassidy!" the girl exclaimed weakly, and then relapsed into sullen stoicism.

Carter took a step forward.

"What—"

" 'S all right!" the newcomer assured him, displaying a bright badge. "Detective-Sergeant Cassidy. I was passin' and sported somebody makin' your fire escape. Decided to wait until they left and nab 'em with the goods. Got tired of waitin' and came up for a look-see."

He turned jovially to the girl.

"And here it turns out to be the Angel herself! Come on, kid, let's take a ride."

Carter put out a detaining hand as she started submissively toward the detective.

"Wait a minute! Can't we fix this thing up? I don't want to prosecute the lady."

Cassidy leered from the girl to Carter and back, and then shook his head.

"Can't be done! The Angel is wanted for half a dozen jobs. Don't make no difference whether you make charges against her or not—she'll go over for plenty anyways."

The girl nodded concurrence.

"Thanks, old dear," she told Carter, with an only partially successful attempt at nonchalance, "but they want me pretty bad."

But Carter would not submit without a struggle. The gods do not send a real flesh-and-blood feminine crook into a writer's rooms every evening in the week. The retention of such a gift was worth contending for. The girl must have within her, he thought, material for thousands, tens of thousands, of words of fiction. Was that a boon to be lightly surrendered? And then her attractiveness was in itself something; and a still more potent claim on his assistance—though not perhaps so clearly explainable—was the mottled area his fists had left on the smooth flesh of her cheek.

"Can't we arrange it somehow?" he asked. "Couldn't we fix it so that the charges might be—er—unofficially disregarded for the present?"

Cassidy's heavy brows came down and the red of his face darkened.

"Are you tryin' to—"

He stopped, and his small blue eyes narrowed almost to the point of vanishing completely.

"Go ahead! You're doin' the talkin'."

Bribery, Carter knew, was a serious matter, and especially so when directed toward an officer of the law. The law is not to be lightly set aside, perverted, by an individual. To fling to this gigantic utensil a few bits of green-engraved paper, expecting thus to turn it from its course, was, to say the least, a foolhardy proceeding.

Yet the law as represented by this fat Cassidy in baggy, not too immaculate garments, while indubitably the very same law, seemed certainly less awe-inspiring, less unapproachable. Almost it took on a human aspect—the aspect of a man who was not entirely without his faults. The law just now, in fact, looked out through little blue eyes that were manifestly greedy, for all their setting in a poker face.

Carter hesitated, trying to find the words in which his offer would be most attractively dressed; but the detective relieved him of the necessity of broaching the subject.

"Listen, mister," he said candidly. "I get you all right! But on the level, I don't think it'd be worth what it'd cost you."

"What would it cost?"

"Well, there's four hundred in rewards offered for her that I know of—maybe more."

Four hundred dollars! That was considerably more than Carter had expected to pay. Still, he could get several times four hundred dollars' worth of material from her.

"Done!" he said. "Four hundred it is!"

"Woah!" Cassidy rumbled. "That don't get me nothin'! What kind of chump do you think I am? If I turn her in I get that much, besides credits for promotion. Then what the hell's the sense of me turnin' her loose for that same figure and runnin' the risk of bein' sent over myself if it leaks out?" Carter recognized the justice of the detective's stand.

"Five hundred," he bid.

Cassidy shook his head emphatically.

"On the level, I wouldn't touch it for less'n a thousan'—and you'd be a sucker to pay that much! She's a keen kid all right, but the world's full of just as keen ones that'll come a lot cheaper."

"I can't pay a thousand," Carter said slowly; he had only a few dollars more than that in his bank.

His common sense warned him not to impoverish himself for the girl's sake, warned him that the payment of even five hundred dollars for her liberty would be a step beyond the limits of rational conduct. He raised his head to acknowledge his defeat, and to tell Cassidy that he might take the girl away; then his eyes focused on the girl. Though she still struggled to maintain her attitude of ironic indifference to her fate, and did attain a reckless smile, her chin quivered and her shoulders were no longer jauntily squared.

The dictates of reason went for nothing in the face of these signs of distress.

Without conscious volition, Carter found himself saying, "The best I can do is seven hundred and fifty."

Cassidy shook his head briskly, but he caught one corner of his lower lip between his teeth, robbing the rejecting gesture of its finality.

The girl, stirred into action by the detective-sergeant's indecision, put an impulsive hand on his arm and added the weight of her personality to the temptation of the money.

"Come on, Cassidy," she pleaded. "Be a good guy—give me a break! Take the seven fifty! You got rep enough without turning me in!"

Cassidy turned abruptly to Carter. "I'm makin' a sap o' myself, but give me the dough!"

At the sight of the check book that Carter took from a desk drawer, Cassidy balked again, demanding cash. Finally they persuaded him to accept a check made payable to "Cash."

At the door he turned and wagged a fat finger at Carter.

"Now remember," he threatened, "if you try any funny business on this check I'm going to nail you if I have to frame you to do it!"

"There'll be no funny business," Carter assured him.

THE SECOND-STORY ANGEL

There was no doubt of the girl's hunger; she ate ravenously of the cold beef, salad, rolls, pastry, and coffee that Carter put before her. Neither of them talked much while she ate. The food held her undivided attention, while Carter's mind was busy planning how his opportunity might be utilized to the utmost.

Over their cigarettes the girl mellowed somewhat, and he persuaded her to talk of herself. But clearly she had not accepted him without many reservations, and she made no pretence of lowering her guard.

She told him her story briefly, without going into any details.

"My old man was named John Cardigan, but he was a lot better known as 'Paper-Box John,' from his trick of carrying his tools around in an unsuspicious-looking shoebox. If I do say it myself, he was as slick a burglar as there was in the grift! I don't remember Ma very well. She died or left or something when I was a little kid and the old man didn't like to talk about her.

"But I had as good a bringing up, criminally speaking, as you ever heard of. There was the old man, a wizard in his line; and my older brother Frank—he's doing a one-to-fourteen-year stretch in Deer Lodge now—who wasn't a dub by any means with a can opener—safe-ripping, you know. Between them and the mobs they ran with, I got a pretty good education along certain lines.

"Everything went along fine, with me keeping house for the old man and Frank, and them giving me everything I wanted, until the old man got wiped out by a night watchman in Philly one night. Then, a couple weeks later, Frank got picked up in some burg out in Montana—Great Falls. That put me up against it. We hadn't saved much money—easy come, easy go—and what we had I sent out to Frank's mouthpiece—a lawyer—to try to spring him. But it was no go—they had him cold, and they sent him over.

"After that I had to shift for myself. It was a case of either cashing in on what the old man and Frank had taught me or going on the streets. Of course, I wouldn't have had to go on the streets actually—there were plenty of guys who were willing to take me in—it's just that it's a rotten way of making a living. I don't want to be owned!

"Maybe you think I could have got a job somewhere in a store or factory or something. But in the first place, a girl with no experience has a hard time knocking down enough jack to live on; and then again, half the dicks in town know me as the old man's daughter, and they wouldn't keep it a secret if they found me working any place—they'd think I was getting a job lined up for some mob.

"So, after thinking it all over, I decided to try the old man's racket. It went easy from the first. I knew all the tricks and it wasn't hard to put them into practice. Being a girl helped, too. A couple times, when I was caught cold, people took my word for it that I had got into the wrong place by mistake.

"But being a girl had its drawbacks, too. As the only she-burglar in action, my work was sort of conspicuous, and it wasn't long before the bulls had a line on me. I was picked up a couple times, but I had a good lawyer, and they couldn't make anything stick, so they turned me loose; but they didn't forget me.

"Then I got some bad breaks, and pulled some jobs that they knew they could tie on me; and they started looking for me proper. To make things worse, I had hurt the feelings of quite a few guys who had tried to get mushy with me at one time or another, and they had been knocking me—saying I was up-stage and so on—to everybody, and that hadn't helped me any with the people who might have helped me when I was up against it.

"So besides hiding from the dicks I had to dodge half the guns in the burg for fear they'd put the finger on me—turn me up to the bulls. This honor among thieves stuff doesn't go very big in New York!

"Finally it got so bad that I couldn't even get to my room, where my clothes and what money I had were. I was cooped up in a hangout I had across town, peeping out at dicks who were watching the joint, and knowing that if I showed myself I was a goner.

"I couldn't keep that up, especially as I had no food there and couldn't get hold of anybody I could trust; so I took a chance tonight and went over the roof, intending to knock over the first likely-looking dump I came to for the price of some food and a ducat out of town.

"And this was the place I picked, and that brings my tale up to date."

They were silent for a moment, she watching Carter out of the corners of her eyes, as if trying to read what was going on in his mind, and he turning her story around in his head, admiring its literary potentialities.

She was speaking again, and now her voice held the slightly metallic quality that it had before she had forgotten some of her wariness in her preoccupation with her story.

"Now, old top, I don't know what your game is; but I warned you right off the reel that I wasn't buying anything."

Carter laughed. "Angel Grace, your name suits you—heaven must have sent you here," he said, and then added, a little self-consciously, "My name is Brigham—Carter Webright Brigham."

He paused, half expectantly, and not in vain.

"Not the writer?"

Her instantaneous recognition caused him to beam on her—he had not reached the stage of success when he might expect everyone to be familiar with his name.

"You've read some of my stuff?" he asked.

"Oh, yes! 'Poison for One' and 'The Settlement' in *Warner's Magazine*, 'Nemesis, Incorporated' in the *National,* and all your stories in *Cody's!*"

Her voice, even without the added testimony of the admiration that had replaced the calculation in her eyes, left no doubt in his mind that she had indeed liked his stories.

"Well, that's the answer," he told her. "That money I gave Cassidy was an investment in a gold mine. The things you can tell me will fairly write themselves and the magazines will eat 'em up!"

Oddly enough, the information that his interest had been purely professional did not seem to bring her pleasure; on the contrary, little shadows appeared in the clear green field of her eyes.

Seeing them, Carter, out of some intuitive apprehension, hastened to add: "But I suppose I'd have done the same even if you hadn't promised stories—I couldn't very well let him carry you off to jail."

She gave him a sceptical smile at that, but her eyes cleared.

"That's all very fine," she observed, "as far as it goes. But you mustn't forget that Cassidy isn't the only sleuth in the city that's hunting for me. And don't forget that you're likely to get yourself in a fine hole by helping me."

Carter came back to earth.

"That's right! We'll have to figure out what is the best thing to do."

Then the girl spoke: "It's a cinch I'll have to get out of town! Too many of them are looking for me, and I'm too well-known. Another thing: you can trust Cassidy as long as he hasn't spent that money, but that won't be long. Most likely he's letting it go over a card table right now. As soon as he's flat he'll be back to see you again. You'll be safe enough so far as he's concerned—he can't prove anything on you without giving himself away—but if I'm where he can find me he'll pinch me unless you put up more coin; and he'll try to find me through you. There's nothing to it but for me to blow town."

"That's just what we'll do," Carter cried. "We'll pick out some safe place not far away, where you can go today. Then I'll meet you there tomorrow and we can make some permanent arrangements."

It was late in the morning before their plans were completed.

Carter went to his bank as soon as it was open and withdrew all but sufficient money to cover the checks he had out, including the one he had given the detective-sergeant. The girl would need money for food and fare, and even clothing, for her room, she was confident, was still watched by the police.

She left Carter's apartment in a taxicab, and was to buy clothes of a different color and style from those she was wearing and

THE SECOND-STORY ANGEL

whose description the police had. Then she was to dismiss the taxicab and engage another to drive her to a railroad station some distance from the city—they were afraid that the detectives on duty at the railroad stations in the city, and at the ferries, would recognize her in spite of the new clothes. At the distant station she would board a train for the upstate town they had selected for their rendezvous.

Carter was to join her there the following day.

He did not go down to the street door with her when she left, but said goodbye in his rooms. At the leave-taking she shed her coating of worldly Cynicism and tried to express her gratitude.

But he cut her short with an embarrassed mockery of her own earlier admonition: "Aw, stop it!"

Carter Brigham did not work that day. The story on which he had been engaged now seemed stiff and lifeless and altogether without relation to actuality. The day and the night dragged along, but no matter how slowly, they did pass in the end, and he was stepping down from a dirty local train in the town where she was to wait for him.

Registering at the hotel they had selected, he scanned the page of the book given over to the previous day's business. "Mrs. H. H. Moore," the name she was to have used, did not appear thereon. Discreet inquiries revealed that she had not arrived.

Sending his baggage up to his room, Carter went out and called at the two other hotels in the town. She was at neither. At a newsstand he bought an armful of New York papers. Nothing about her arrest was in them. She had not been picked up before leaving the city, or the newspapers would have made much news of her.

For three days he clung obstinately to the belief that she had not run away from him. He spent the three days in his New York rooms, his ears alert for the ringing of the telephone bell, examining his mail frantically, constantly expecting the messenger, who didn't come. Occasionally he sent telegrams to the hotel in the upstate town—futile telegrams.

DETECTIVE STORIES

Then he accepted the inescapable truth: she had decided—perhaps had so intended all along—not to run the risk incidental to a meeting with him, but had picked out a hiding place of her own; she did not mean to fulfil her obligations to him, but had taken his assistance and gone.

Another day passed in idleness while he accustomed himself to the bitterness of this knowledge. Then he set to work to salvage what he could. Fortunately, it seemed to be much. The bare story that the girl had told him over the remains of her meal could with little effort be woven into a novelette that should be easily marketed. Crook stories were always in demand, especially one with an authentic girl-burglar drawn from life.

As he bent over his typewriter, concentrating on his craft, his disappointment began to fade. The girl was gone. She had treated him shabbily, but perhaps it was better that way. The money she had cost him would come back with interest from the sale of the serial rights of this story. As for the personal equation: she had been beautiful, fascinating enough—and friendly—but still she *was* a crook....

For days he hardly left his desk except to eat and sleep, neither of which did he do excessively.

Finally the manuscript was completed and sent out in the mail. For the next two days he rested as fully as he had toiled, lying abed to all hours, idling through his waking hours, replacing the nervous energy his work always cost him.

On the third day a note came from the editor of the magazine to which he had sent the story, asking if it would be convenient for him to call at two-thirty the next afternoon.

Four men were with the editor when Carter was ushered into his office. Two of them he knew: Gerald Gulton and Harry Mack, writers like himself. He was introduced to the others: John Deitch and Walton Dohlman. He was familiar with their work, though he had not met them before; they contributed to some of the same magazines that bought his stories.

THE SECOND-STORY ANGEL

When the group had been comfortably seated and cigars and cigarettes were burning, the editor smiled into the frankly curious faces turned toward him.

"Now we'll get down to business," he said. "You'll think it a queer business at first, but I'll try to mystify you no longer than necessary."

He turned to Carter. "You wouldn't mind telling us, Mr. Brigham, just how you got hold of the idea for your story 'The Second-Story Angel,' would you?"

"Of course not," Carter said. "It was rather peculiar. I was roused one night by the sound of a burglar in my rooms and got up to investigate. I tackled him and we fought in the dark for a while. Then I turned on the lights and—"

"And it was a woman—a girl!" Gerald Fulton prompted hoarsely.

Carter jumped.

"How did you know?" he demanded.

Then he saw that Fulton, Mack, Deitch, and Dohlman were all sitting stiffly in their chairs and that their dissimilar faces held for the time identical expressions of bewilderment.

"And after a while a detective came in?"

It was Mack's voice, but husky and muffled.

"His name was Cassidy!"

"And for a price things could be fixed," Deitch took up the thread.

After that there was a long silence, while the editor pretended to be intrigued by the contours of a hemispherical glass paperweight on his desk, and the four professional writers, their faces beet-red and sheepish, all stared intently at nothing.

The editor opened a drawer and took out a stack of manuscripts.

"Here they are," he said. "I knew there was something wrong when within ten days I got five stories that were, in spite of the differences in treatment, unmistakably all about the same girl!"

"Chuck mine in the wastebasket," Mack instructed softly, and the others nodded their endorsement of that disposition. All but Dohlman, who seemed to be struggling with an idea. Finally he addressed the editor.

"It's a pretty good story, at that, isn't it, all five versions?"

The editor nodded.

"Yes, I'd have bought one, but five—"

"Why not buy one? We'll match coins—"

"Sure, that's fair enough," said the editor.

It was done. Mack won.

Gerald Fulton's round blue eyes were wider than ever with a look of astonishment. At last he found words.

"My God! I wonder how many other men are writing that same story right now!"

But in Garter's mind an entirely different problem was buzzing around.

Lord! I wonder if she kissed this whole bunch, too!

AFRAID OF A GUN

Owen Sack turned from the stove as the door of his cabin opened to admit "Rip" Yust, and with the hand that did not hold the coffeepot Owen Sack motioned hospitably toward the table, where food steamed before a ready chair.

"Hullo, Rip! Set down and go to it while it's hot. 'Twon't take me but a minute to throw some more together for myself."

That was Owen Sack, a short man of compact wiriness, with round china-blue eyes and round ruddy cheeks, and only the thinness of his straw-colored hair to tell of his fifty-odd years, a quiet little man whose too-eager friendliness at times suggested timidity.

Rip Yust crossed to the table, but he paid no attention to its burden of food. Instead, he placed two big fists on the tabletop, leaned his weight on them, and scowled at Owen Sack. He was big, this Rip Yust, barrel-bodied, slope-shouldered, thick-limbed, and his usual manner was a phlegmatic sort of sullenness. But now his heavy features were twisted into a scowl.

"They got 'Lucky' this morning," he said after a moment, and his voice wasn't the voice of one who brings news. It was accusing.

"Who got him?"

But Owen Sack's eyes swerved from the other's as he put the question, and he moistened his lips nervously. He knew who had got Rip's brother.

"Who do you guess?" with heavy derision. "The Prohis! You know it!"

The little man winced.

"Aw, Rip! How would I know it? I ain't been to town for a week, and nobody never comes past here any more."

"Yeah, I wonder how you would know it."

Yust walked around the table, to where Owen Sack—with little globules of moisture glistening on his round face—stood, caught him by the slack of his blue shirt bosom and lifted him clear of the floor. Twice Yust shook the little man—shook him with a lack of vehemence that was more forcible than any violence could have been—and set him down on his feet again.

"You knowed where our cache was at," he accused, still holding the looseness of the shirt bosom in one muscular hand, "and nobody else that ain't in with us did. The Prohis showed up there this morning and grabbed Lucky. Who told 'em where it was? You did, you rat!"

"I didn't, Rip! I didn't! I swear to—"

Yust cut off the little man's whimpering by placing a broad palm across his mouth.

"Maybe you didn't. To tell the truth, I ain't exactly positive yet that you done it—or I wouldn't be talking to you." He flicked his coat aside, baring for a suggestive half-second the brown butt of a revolver that peeped out of a shoulder holster. "But it looks like it couldn't of been nobody else. But I ain't aiming to hurt nobody that don't hurt me, so I'm looking around a while to make sure. But if I find out that you done it for sure—"

He snapped his big jaws together. His right hand made as if to dart under his coat near the left armpit. He nodded with slow emphasis, and left the cabin.

For a while Owen Sack did not move. He stood stiffly still, staring with barren blue eyes at the door through which his caller had vanished; and Owen Sack looked old now. His face held lines that had not been there before; and his body, for all its rigidity, seemed frailer.

Presently he shook his shoulders briskly, and turned back to the stove with an appearance of having put the episode out of his mind; but immediately afterward his body drooped spiritlessly. He crossed to the chair, dropped down on it, and pushed the cooling meal back a way, to pillow his head upon his forearms.

He shuddered now and his knees trembled, just as he had shuddered and his knees had trembled when he had helped carry Cardwell home. Cardwell, so gossip said, had talked too much about certain traffic on the Kootenai River. Cardwell had been found one morning in a thicket below Dime, with a hole in the back of his neck where a bullet had gone in and another and larger hole in front where the bullet had come out. No one could say who had fired the bullet, but gossip in Dime had made guesses, and had taken pains to keep those guesses from the ears of the Yust brothers.

If it hadn't been for Cardwell, Owen knew that he could have convinced Rip Yust of his own innocence. But he saw the dead man again whenever he saw one of the Yusts; and this afternoon, when Rip had come into his cabin and hurled that accusing "They got Lucky this morning" across the table, Cardwell had filled Owen Sack's mind to the exclusion of all else—filled it with a fear that had made him talk and act as if he had in fact guided the Prohibition enforcement officers to the Yusts' cache. And so Yust had gone away more than half convinced that his suspicions were correct.

Rip Yust was, Owen Sack knew, a fair man according to his lights. He would do nothing until he was certain that he had the right man. Then he would strike with neither warning nor mercy.

An eye for an eye was the code of the Rip Yusts of the world, and an enemy was one to be removed without scruple. And that Yust would not strike until he had satisfied himself that he had the right man was small comfort to Owen Sack.

Yust was not possessed of the clearest of minds; he was not fitted, for all his patience and deliberation, to unerringly sift the false from the true. Many things that properly were meaningless might, to him, seem irrefragable evidence of Owen Sack's guilt—now that Owen Sack's fears had made him act the part of a witness against himself.

And some morning Owen Sack's body would be found as Cardwell's had been found. Perhaps Cardwell had been unjustly suspected too.

Owen Sack sat up straight now, squaring his shoulders and tightening his mouth in another half-hearted attempt to pull himself together. He ground his fists into his temples, and for a moment pretended to himself that he was trying to arrive at a decision, to map out a course of action. But in his heart he knew all the time that he was lying to himself. He was going to run away again. He always did. The time for making a stand was gone.

Thirty years ago he might have done it.

That time in a Marsh Market Space dive in Baltimore, when a dispute over a reading of the dice had left him facing a bull-dog pistol in the hands of a cockney sailor. The cockney's hand had shaken; they had stood close together; the cockney was as frightened as he. A snatch, a blow—it would have been no trick at all. But he had, after a moment's hesitancy, submitted; he had let the cockney not only run him out of the game but out of the city.

His fear of bullets had been too strong for him. He wasn't a coward (not then); a knife, which most men dread, hadn't seemed especially fearful in those days. It traveled at a calculable and discernible rate of speed; you could see it coming; judge its speed; parry, elude it; or twist about so that its wound was shallow. And even if it struck, went deep, it was sharp and slid easily through the flesh, a clean, neat separation of the tissues.

But a bullet, a ball of metal, hot from the gases that propelled it, hurtling invisibly toward you—nobody could say how fast—not to make a path for itself with a fine keen edge, but to hammer out a road with a dull blunt nose, driving through whatever stood in its way. A lump of hot lead battering its irresistible tunnel through flesh and sinew, splintering bones! That he could not face.

AFRAID OF A GUN

So he had fled from the Maryland city to avoid the possibility of another meeting with the cockney sailor and his bull-dog pistol.

And that was only the first time.

No matter where he had gone, he had sooner or later found himself looking into the muzzle of a threatening gun. It was as if his very fear attracted the thing he feared. A dog, he had been told as a boy, would bite you if he thought you were afraid of him. It had been that way with guns.

Each repetition had left him in worse case than before; until now the sight of a menacing firearm paralyzed him, and even the thought of one blurred his mind with terror.

In those earlier days he hadn't been a coward, except where guns were concerned; but he had run too often; and that fear, growing, had spread like the seepage from some cancerous growth, until, little by little, he had changed from a man of reasonable courage with one morbid fear to a man of no courage at all with fears that included most forms of physical violence.

But, in the beginning, his fear hadn't been too great to have been outfaced. He could have overcome it that time in Baltimore. It would have required an enormous effort, but he could have overcome it. He could have overcome it the next time, in New South Wales, when, instead, he had gone riding madly to Bourke, across a hundred-mile paddock, away from a gun in the hands of a quarrelsome boundary rider—a desperate flight along a road whose ruts stood perversely up out of the ground like railway tracks, with frightened rabbits and paddy-mellons darting out of the infrequent patches of white-bearded spear grass along his way.

Nor would it have been too late three months after that, in north Queensland. But he had run away again. Hurrying down to Cairns and the Cooktown boat, this time, away from the menace of a rusty revolver in the giant black hand of a Negro beside whom he had toiled thigh-deep in the lime-white river of the Muldiva silver fields.

After that, however, he was beyond recovery. He could not then by any effort have conquered his fear. He was beaten and he knew it. Henceforth, he had run without even decent shame in his cowardice, and he had begun to flee from other things than guns.

He had, for instance, let a jealous half-caste *garimpeiro* drive him out of Morro Velho, drive him away from his job with the British São João del Rey Mining Company and Tita. Tita's red mouth had gone from smiling allure to derision, but neither the one nor the other was strong enough to keep Owen Sack from retreating before the flourish of a knife in the hand of a man he could have tied in knots, knife and all. Out of the Bakersfield oil fields he had been driven by the bare fists of an undersized rigger. And now from here. . . .

The other times hadn't, in a way, been so bad as this. He was younger then, and there was always some other place to attract him—one place was as good as another. But now it was different.

He was no longer young, and here in the Cabinet Mountains he had meant to stop for good. He had come to look upon his cabin as his home. He wanted but two things now: a living and tranquillity, and until now he had found them here. In the year 1923 it was still possible to wash out of the Kootenai enough dust to make wages—good wages. Not wealth, certainly, but he didn't want wealth; he wanted a quiet home, and for six months he had had it here.

And then he had stumbled upon the Yusts' cache. He had known, as all Dime knew, that the Kootenai River—winding down from British Columbia to spend most of its four hundred miles in Montana and Idaho before returning to the province of its birth to join the great Columbia—was the moving road along which came much liquor, to be relayed to Spokane, not far away. That was a matter of common knowledge, and Owen Sack of all men had no desire for more particular knowledge of the river traffic.

Why, then, had his luck sent him blundering upon the place where that liquor was concealed until ready for its overland journey? And at a time when the Yusts were there to witness his discovery? And then, as if that were not enough in itself, the Prohibition enforcement officers had swooped down on that hiding-place within a week.

Now the Yusts suspected him of having informed; it was but a matter of time before their stupid brains would be convinced of that fact; then they would strike—with a gun. A pellet of metal would drive through Owen Sack's tissues as one had driven through Cardwell's....

He got up from the chair and set about packing such of his belongings as he intended taking with him—to where? It didn't matter. One place was like another—a little of peace and comfort, and then the threat of another gun, to send him elsewhere. Baltimore, New South Wales, north Queensland, Brazil, California, here—thirty years of it! He was old now and his legs were stiff for flight, but running had become an integral part of him.

He packed a little breathlessly, his fingers fumbling clumsily in their haste.

Dusk was thickening in the valley of the Kootenai when Owen Sack, bent beneath the blanketed pack across his shoulders, tramped over the bridge into Dime. He had remained in his cabin until the last minute, so that he might catch the stage which would carry him to the railroad just before it left, avoiding farewells or embarrassing meetings. He hurried now.

But, again, luck ran against him.

As he turned the corner of the New Dime Hotel toward the stage terminus—two doors beyond Henny Upshaw's soft-drink parlor and poolroom—he spied Rip Yust coming down the street toward him. Yust's face, he could see, was red and swollen, and Yust's walk was a swagger. Yust was drunk.

Owen Sack halted in the middle of the sidewalk, and realized immediately that that was precisely the wrong thing to do. Safety lay—if safety lay anywhere now—in going on as if nothing out of the ordinary were happening.

DETECTIVE STORIES

He crossed the street to the opposite sidewalk, cursing himself for this open display of his desire to avoid the other, but nevertheless unable to keep his legs from hurrying him across the dusty roadway. Perhaps, he thought, Rip Yust's whisky-clouded eyes would not see him hurrying toward the stage depot with a pack on his back. But even while the hope rose in him he knew it for a futile, childish one.

Rip Yust did see him, and came to the curb on his own side of the street, to bellow:

"Hey, you! Where you going?"

Owen Sack became motionless, a frightened statue. Fear froze his mind—fear and thoughts of Cardwell.

Yust grinned stupidly across the street, and repeated:

"Where you going?"

Owen Sack tried to answer, to say something—safety seemed to lie in words—but, though he did achieve a sound, it was inarticulate, and would have told the other nothing, even if it had traveled more than ten feet from the little man's throat.

Yust laughed boomingly. He was apparently in high good humor.

"Now, you mind what I told you this afternoon," he roared, wagging a thick forefinger at Owen Sack. "If I find that you done it—"

The thick forefinger flashed back to tap the left breast of his coat.

Owen Sack screamed at the suddenness of the gesture—a thin, shrill scream of terror, which struck amusingly upon the big man's drunken fancy.

Laughter boomed out of his throat again, and his gun came into his hand. His brother's arrest and Owen Sack's supposed part in that arrest were, for the time, forgotten in his enjoyment of the little man's ridiculous fright.

With the sight of the gun, Owen Sack's last shred of sanity departed. Terror had him fast. He tried to plead, but his mouth could not frame the words. He tried to raise both his hands high above his head in the universal posture of submission, a posture that had saved him many times before. But the strap holding his pack hampered him. He tried to loosen the strap, to fling it off.

To the alcohol-muddled eyes and brain of the man across the street Owen Sack's right hand was trying to get beneath his coat on the left side. Rip Yust could read but one meaning into that motion—the little man was going for his gun.

The weapon in Yust's hand spat flame!

Owen Sack sobbed. Something struck him heavily on one side. He fell, sat down on the sidewalk, his eyes wide and questioning and fixed upon the smoking gun across the street.

Somebody, he found, was bending over him. It was Henny Upshaw, in front of whose establishment he had fallen. Owen Sack's eyes went back to the man on the opposite curb, who, cold sober now, his face granite, stood awaiting developments, the gun still in his hand.

Owen Sack didn't know whether to get up, to remain still, or to lie down. Upshaw had struck him aside in time to save him from the first bullet; but suppose the big man fired again?

"Where'd he get you?" Upshaw was asking.

"What's that?"

"Now take it easy," Upshaw advised. "You'll be all right! I'll get one of the boys to help me with you."

Owen Sack's fingers wound into one of Upshaw's sleeves.

"Wh—what happened?" he asked.

"Rip shot you, but you'll be all right. Just lay—"

Owen Sack released Upshaw's sleeve, and his hands went feeling about his body, exploring. One of them came away red and sticky from his right side, and that side—where he had felt the blow that had taken him off his feet—was warm and numb.

"Did he shoot me?" he demanded in an excited screech.

"Sure, but you're all right," Upshaw soothed him, and beckoned to the men who were coming slowly into the street, drawn forward by their curiosity, but retarded in their approach by the sight of Yust, who still stood, gun in hand, waiting to see what happened next.

"My God!" Owen Sack gasped in utter bewilderment. "And it ain't no worse than that!"

He bounded to his feet—his pack sliding off—eluded the hands that grasped at him, and ran for the door of Upshaw's place. On a shelf beneath the cash register he found Upshaw's black automatic, and, holding it stiffly in front of him at arm's length, turned back to the street.

His china-blue eyes were wide with wonder, and from out of his grinning mouth issued a sort of chant:

> *"All these years I been running,*
> *And it ain't no worse than that!*
> *All these years I been running,*
> *And it ain't no worse than that!"*

Rip Yust, crossing the roadway now, was in the middle when Owen Sack popped out of Upshaw's door.

The onlookers scattered. Rip's revolver swung up, and roared. A spray of Owen Sack's straw-colored hair whisked back.

He giggled, and fired three times, rapidly. None of the bullets hit the big man. Owen Sack felt something burn his left arm. He fired again, and missed.

"I got to get closer," he told himself aloud.

He walked across the sidewalk—the automatic held stiffly before him—stepped down into the roadway, and began to stride toward where pencils of fire sprang to meet him from Yust's gun.

And as the little man strode he chanted his silly chant, and fired, fired, fired.... Once something tugged at one of his shoulders, and once at his arm—above where he had felt the burn—but he did not even wonder what it was.

When he was within ten feet of Rip Yust, that man turned as if to walk away, took a step, his big body curved suddenly in a grotesque arc, and he slid down into the sand of the roadway.

Owen Sack found that the weapon in his own hand was empty, had been empty for some time. He turned around. Dimly he made out the broad doorway of Upshaw's place. The ground clung to his feet, trying to pull him down, to hold him back, but he gained the doorway, gained the cash register, found the shelf, and returned the automatic to it.

Voices were speaking to him, arms were around him. He ignored the voices, shook off the arms, reached the street again. More hands to be shaken off. But the air lent him strength. He was indoors again, leaning over the firearm showcase in Jeff Hamline's store.

"I want the two biggest handguns you got, Jeff, and a mess of cartridges. Fix 'em up for me and I'll be back to get 'em in a little while."

He knew that Jeff answered him, but he could not separate Jeff's words from the roaring in his head.

The warmer air of the street once more. The ankle-deep dust of the roadway pulling at his feet. The opposite sidewalk. Doc Johnstone's door. Somebody helping him up the narrow stairs. A couch or table under him; he could see and hear better now that he was lying down.

"Fix me up in a hurry, Doc! I got a lot of things to tend to."

The doctor's smooth professional voice:

"You've nothing to attend to for a while except taking care of yourself."

"I got to travel a lot, Doc. Hurry!"

"You're all right, Sack. There's no need of your going away. I saw Yust down you first from my window, and half a dozen others saw it. Self-defense if there ever was a case of it!"

" 'Tain't that!" A nice man was Doc, but there was a lot he didn't understand. "I got a lot of places to go to, a lot of men I got to see."

"Certainly. Certainly. Just as soon as you like."

"You don't understand, Doc!" The doc was talking to him like he was a child to be humored, or a drunk. "My God, Doc! I got to back-track my whole life, and I ain't young no more. There's men I got to find in Baltimore, and Australia, and Brazil, and California, and God knows where—all. And some of 'em will take a heap of finding. I got to do a lot of shootin'. I ain't young no more, and it's a mighty big job. I got to get going! You got to hurry me up, Doc! You got to ..."

Owen Sack's voice thickened to a mumble, to a murmur, and subsided.